EVER FALLEN

SHADOW GUARDIANS BOOK 2

ELLE SCOTT

BOOKS BY ELLE SCOTT

THE INCANDESCENT SERIES
Ray of Light
Harbour of Light
Symphony of Light

SHADOW GUARDIANS
Ever Marked
Ever Fallen
… plus more to come

SHADOW GUARDIANS ACADEMY
The Shadow Society
… plus more to come

BEHIND GLASS SERIES
Behind Glass
… plus more to come

For my cousin, my confidant, my best friend, Alicia.
For being my safe place to fall.

THURSDAY

noon

Leila

Hunger. Blood-lust. Revenge.

Repeat.

Leila watched her best friend, Gabby, stare at a sheet of paper she was holding. Her brown eyes narrowed, and her nostrils flared in and out, synchronized with her hastened breath. It seemed, to Leila, as though anger boiled through the marrow of Gabby's bones.

"Breathe deeper," Leila said, calmly raising her hands. "You can't exactly shift into a wolf right here at school."

Gabby peered over the paper and shot Leila a piercing glare. She took a long breath and dropped her hands, holding the paper loosely in her grasp. Leila glanced at the bold red lettering on the top right corner of the page.

"B plus, Leila. How can I get a B plus? I can't keep my scholarship on grades like that," Gabby wailed, scrunching the edges of the paper. "There has to be some mistake. I'm gonna kill that teacher."

Leila darted her eyes around the busy locker hall, hoping no one heard Gabby's impulsive threat. She knew Gabby didn't mean it, but who knew who was listening and how they'd react?

The corridor was abuzz with hungry teens. They slammed their lockers shut and rushed towards the cafeteria like vultures. Leila sighed with relief. She'd felt a little self-conscious lately, as though all eyes were on her, waiting for her to slip up and show her true self. A lion, as it were. She tried to be careful. Riley had rules he expected them to obey—rules she wasn't sure she could obey, considering she'd just broken one without even thinking.

No talking about their Guardians in public... especially at school. *Oops.* That one always seemed to slip her up.

No shifting in public... especially at school. That rule was Leila's favorite. She laughed when Riley said it. As if any of them would do that.

No—what was the third one—oh yeah, *just act normal... especially at school.* She imagined Riley saying that last one with a wave of his hand, as though it was the easiest thing in the world to pretend they weren't shape-shifters. He'd be looking over the black-rim of his glasses with a glint in his eyes. *Those* eyes—those light-brown, like autumn leaves hit by the setting sun, eyes.

"I think..." Leila said, turning back to Gabby who was on the edge of breaking all three rules. "In this instance, a simple maiming could suffice. Save the killing for when you get a B minus."

Gabby looked at Leila sideways, then burst out laughing. The French braid resting on her shoulder, bounced up and down with the movement. The lime green ends that offset Gabby's jet black hair caught the lights, sending them fluorescent.

"By the way, I like your hair," Leila said.

Gabby pinched the end of her braid and glanced down. "Don't mind it. Think I prefer the red."

Leila used the distraction to tuck her own paper into her

locker. But as she did, Gabby caught a glimpse. "You got an A? What the heck, Leila?"

Shrugging, Leila tried not to make a big deal out of it. The thing was, it kinda *was* a big deal. Since Leila became a Guardian three months earlier, she'd excelled in all things academic. What once was Gabby and Riley's thing, belonged to her too. She'd even joined Advanced Math.

Leila swung her locker door wide. It was a complete mess. Rolls of film, Polaroids tacked to the inside of the door, hair ties, a library book she hadn't read, the schedule for school events stuck to the back of locker.

She hoped Gabby would be relieved to see it. At least that part of Leila hadn't changed. She was still a hoarder of eclectic goods.

Gabby sighed, looking at the bold B plus that taunted her. Leila knew that she'd changed, too. But whether it was for the better or worse was another thing entirely. She seemed distracted a lot — less interested in studies and more invested in perfecting her broody stare.

Grief did different things to different people.

"Leila! Gabby!" Sadie called from across the hall. She sprung towards them, smiling brightly at people as she passed. Sadie was the smallest of the three. Leila often wondered if that was why she tried so hard for everyone to like her.

Today, Sadie's golden locks were swept up in a messy bun. Leila smiled to herself. It looked effortless but knowing Sadie it probably took a few minutes to get it looking that way. Her uniform was impeccable bar one side of her collar rolled up against her neck. She made a conscious — sometimes too conscious — effort to be her best self at school in front of everyone. Leila and Gabby were the only ones she allowed to see the real version of her. Which, truth be told, wasn't much different. A little more self-conscious than she let on, with a touch of judgment and a splash of whimsy.

She folded her arms around the two, and even though they weren't quite long enough to reach the whole way, she made it seem like they were being embraced by a loving grandmother.

She let go, and as she sighed, the weight of her mask fell. "Mr Robertson is the best, isn't he?"

Gabby rolled her eyes. "You're pathetic."

Leila smiled. She knew Sadie better than that. Sadie crushed hard on people, but when it came down to it, she was after a connection and held out for something deeper. Something meaningful. And she wasn't giving herself up for anything less. Even if Mr. Robertson made a creepy move, Sadie wouldn't have a bar of it.

"You wouldn't understand." Sadie cocked her chin up in faux defense. "If you liked boys, you'd know. Right, Leila?"

Leila shrugged and took her lunch bag from her locker. "I have to admit, he is kind of a hottie now."

"I'm telling Riley." Gabby glared.

Leila feigned shock. "You wouldn't!"

"What's this?" Sadie's petite fingers grabbed a hold of Gabby's paper. As she scanned the mark, she gaped. "B plus? Is this yours?"

Clenching her teeth, Gabby snatched it back. She hissed, "Yessss, it's mine."

Sadie's wide eyes glanced at Leila then back to Gabby. "Oooh, okay. It's good." She winced as if waiting for Gabby's rebuttal.

Leila melted. The air in Sadie's voice always made it hard to be mad at her. Even Gabby, who could keep a grudge for eternity, still couldn't stay mad at Sadie.

Gabby scrunched the paper up and pushed it deep into her pocket "Just peachy. Only my livelihood rests on good grades. You know what this school is like, they'll drop my scholarship like a bag of rotten potatoes. Before you know it, I'll be sitting on the bus heading to public school."

Sadie shuddered theatrically.

Leila closed her locker and began walking for the cafeteria. "I love you Gabby, but you've got nothing to stress about. A B plus *is* good, okay?"

"That's how it starts. A B, then a C, and before you know it... well, you know the rest."

Sadie and Leila shared a glance. Gabby wasn't usually that dramatic. She was the rock of the friends—level-headed and controlled. She'd always been a little punchy, but these days, her moods had been unpredictable. Ever since Riley found her crouched over her stepfather's lifeless body.

Sadie swung an arm around Gabby, stretching further than what looked naturally possible. "We'll get through it, together."

As they ascended the wide staircase, a familiar jock in a gray and blue letterman jacket bounded down as if he owned the whole school. Sebastian Weir used to be nice. Then, he was a grade A jerk. Now, well, Leila couldn't quite figure him out. There were moments of goodness, wrapped up in the bad.

Sebastian slowed, and a mischievous twinkle hit his eyes. "Well, if isn't my favorite trio of juniors."

Sadie grinned immediately. She tilted her head into what Leila liked to call her flirty, cute look. "Have you heard how Morgan is at her new school?"

Ignoring her, Sebastian declared, "I've got nicknames for all of you now." He winked at Sadie. "You're Itsy—'cause you're a tiny piece." His gaze drifted to Leila. "You're Bitsy —'cause, well, you're bits of everything, remember?" His eyes rested on Gabby. "And ... Gab, dark souled, lesbian Gab, you're Spider. Together, you're..." He moved his hands as though conducting an orchestra. "Come on, say it with me, Itsy Bitsy Spider."

Gabby rolled her shoulders back, clenching her jaw. Her eyes flashed green as she half-shifted. Leila was quick to hold her back.

Sebastian tutted, wagging his finger. "Careful Spider, you're wolf is showing."

"Bite me," Gabby hissed, fighting against Leila's grip.

"I would," Sebastian replied. He sighed and took a few steps down. "But I've got better people to waste my time with. Later."

He ruffled Sadie's hair as he passed them. Her gaze followed him as he leapt the last three steps and greeted his friends. Leila tried not to laugh as Sadie rubbed her bottom lip over her upturned collar.

"I don't know how you girls can like him." Gabby huffed, crossing her arms. "Did you hear what he said? Or are you just looking at his well-shaped face?"

Leila scrunched her nose. Yes, she heard what he said. It wasn't cool, but she couldn't help but look past his facade. "I don't necessarily *like* him, not what he shows us anyway. But I still have hope for who he is on the inside."

Sadie composed herself and straightened her collar, patting it against her blazer. "He did save my life."

"Yeah?" Gabby shook her head. "And everyone loved Cap—but that didn't stop him from killing a bunch of innocents. We have to draw the line somewhere, and being a racist bigot is my line. Fair warning, if he does it again, I'll rip his throat out."

"You asked about Morgan before," Leila said, taking a seat at a spare table.

Gabby slid into the chair next to Leila and dropped her tray onto the table. A few tater tots jumped from their spot on the plate and rolled onto the steel table. "Dammit," Gaby muttered scooping them up and throwing them in her mouth.

Sadie took a spot opposite Leila and leaned closer. "How is she?"

"Settling into her new school. She said it's much nicer to sit in class and not be reminded of Cap every day. She sent me a photo of her scar." Leila flicked through her phone and placed it on the table.

The screen showed a photo of Morgan in her new cheer uniform. She held one side of her top up, baring the skin from her hips to her under boob. Purple marks formed the shape of a mouth where Cap's teeth punctured her skin.

"She was lucky to survive the bite." Sadie shuddered. Leila knew it was because that could've been her.

Damien — eagle Guardian, muscles-rippling, over-confident — Damien, sat down next to Sadie, his eyes only on her.

"Seriously girls." Riley placed his tray at the end of the table and leaned over it. With a loud whisper, he scolded, "How many times do I have to tell you about the rules? Stop talking about it in public."

"Especially in school," the three girls harmonized together.

"Okay." Riley straightened. "That is *not* what I sound like."

Leila reached across the table and dragged Riley's tray to the spot next to her. She grinned at him and teased, "It kinda is."

Riley shook his head and moved behind Leila. He wrapped his arms around her, hands sweeping across her middle, tugging her in close. He nuzzled his face into her neck. "How was last period?"

Gabby shoved her hand into her pocket and retrieved the wrinkled paper. She held it a few inches in front of his face, flaring her nostrils.

Giving her a dubious glance, Riley took the paper and unravelled it. "Wow, that's unusual," he said. "Do you think it's because of —"

"Shhh," Leila hushed with a smirk. "You know the rules."

Riley looked over the rim of his glasses and sat down. He held the graded paper out for Gabby, still staring at Leila. "Touché."

"No, I think you should say it. Because of what?" Gabby

took the paper, not as amused as Leila. She crossed her arms, scrunching the paper under her pit. "Go on, say it."

Riley frowned and turned to his food. Picking at pieces of lettuce, he muttered, "Can we practice this afternoon, after school? There's no football training yet, we'll have lots of space."

"We've tried already, a million times," Gabby moaned. "Besides you should celebrate, Leila got an A."

Riley's light-brown eyes lit up. "You did?"

Leila tucked her curly hair behind her ear and nodded. She wanted to smile but kept glancing at Gabby so as not to rain on her already miserable result. She stole a tot from Riley, "No big deal."

Riley swatted her hand away. "I don't think I'll ever get used to seeing you put fried food in your mouth. Do I need to make rules about eating from my plate?"

Maybe he did. Leila ate healthy. Well, until she was Marked and turned. Every now and then, she got the taste for something sweet, or salty, or deep fried. Sometimes she didn't even know what she ate until it was already in her mouth.

"Stop!" Sadie cried.

Leila glanced across the table. She chewed on the delicious potato and watched her best-friend flirt. Which would have been normal, except she was flirting with Damien. And that would have been normal, too, because just look at him, except there was touching involved, and Sadie never took her flirting that far.

Damien sat close, so close their shoulders kept bumping into each other. His newfound confidence and posture was never not surprising. He curved his hand around her ear and whispered. Sadie glanced at him side-ways, eyes oozing hunger. She bit her lip and swatted his hand away.

His gaze drifted over her head and locked onto her high bun. With a cheeky grin, he pressed a finger on the mound and squished. "It looks like a bunny tail."

A muffled laugh filled Leila's ear. She shot a glance at Riley, who was staring at the scene with his hand covering his mouth. Noticing Leila, he dropped his hand and peered around to Gabby. "Anyway," he said, all joviality gone in a snap. "About practice."

Gabby ignored him. She kept her eyes on Sadie and Damien, clearly bemused, and ate her lunch.

Leila sat back and smiled to herself. There they were, the Guardians of Cedar Falls. Plus Sadie, who wasn't a Guardian at all, but their honorary member.

It was a makeshift clan of Riley's doing. He was the Alpha but hardly ever pulled rank. Except when it came to Gabby and the possibility of her being a Fallen.

A raucous a few tables down caught Leila's attention. Sebastian was laughing loud with his jock friends. He leaned back on his chair, throwing chicken pieces at the table of goths. His gaze fell on Leila and his smile disappeared. Two chair legs clunked to the ground as he turned back to his lunch.

Sebastian was, by all accounts, a Fallen. But somehow his humanity overshadowed his darker impulses. He took down one of his own to protect Sadie. Leila considered that he was neither Fallen nor True… he was rogue, a lone wolf.

If he asked to join the group she would let him. But Riley wouldn't have it. He could barely stand the thought of Gabby being a Fallen. Even though Leila was certain her best-friend who loved country music and could eat a box of donuts on her own in one sitting, couldn't possibly be a Fallen.

Leila floated between loving her boyfriend and siding with her friends. It was a trapeze act she was becoming quite skillful at. Lucky for both Gabby and Riley, this particular debate benefited both of them.

"Come on Gab, please," Leila urged. "If it works, your grades might improve again."

Gabby tore her eyes from Sadie. She sighed. "Fine."

THURSDAY

afternoon

Leila

The air was fresh—not warm, but not freezing either. It smelled of wet grass and newborn leaves, the kind of smell that promised warmer tomorrows. Almost Spring.

Just like the season, Leila and Riley were on the verge of something. They weren't sure what, but it had to do with their Imprint powers, and Gabby was the only one semi-willing to participate.

They stood in the middle of the school oval, shoes caked in mud from the melting of the morning's snowfall.

"Okay, stand there." Leila held Gabby's shoulders and nudged her to the left a little. She let go, still hovering her hands at Gabby's sides. "Don't move."

Gabby sighed as she picked at the dirt beneath her nails. "Just hurry up, I'm hungry."

Riley moved beside Leila, narrowing his eyes. "What for?"

"Human heart." Gabby said with a straight face. Then she shook her head. "Seriously, Riley."

The blazer Leila was wearing suddenly felt restrictive around her. She hated the way Riley treated Gabby. As though she were a criminal. Sure, she'd killed her own stepfather, but he'd killed her brother first *and* hurt her mother. Murder was never right, but if it was, that would be the time. Leila rolled up her sleeves and grabbed one of Riley's hands with both of hers. Tugging him backwards, she kept her eyes on Gabby, giving an apologetic tilt of the head.

Gabby rolled her eyes.

Riley turned to Leila. "You ready?"

"Same as always," Leila replied.

They'd tried this before. To rid Gabby of her Guardian. Riley had this notion that because she'd killed a civilian, it automatically turned her into a Fallen. Shadow Guardians were meant to protect; apparently now, she wanted to harm. Leila didn't believe in that though.

Of course, she believed some Guardians were bad. But just like people, it was a sliding scale. Gabby had an attitude, and she was in pain from her brother's death — but she wasn't a Fallen. She couldn't be.

Leila glanced at her best friend. Gabby shoved a fingernail into her mouth then spat it out before going for the next one. There was no harm in trying anyway.

She turned to Riley and with a deep breath, stared into his soulful eyes. Leila lunged for him, wrapping her arms around his body. His hands found her back and he pulled her in close. She squeezed her eyes shut and hugged him as tight as she could, as though together they could save the world. Or at least Gabby.

A chuckle echoed through the air and Leila peeled her eyes open.

"Sorry guys. But you look ridiculous."

Riley let his hands escape Leila. He snapped, "Well,

maybe it's not us that's doing something wrong here."

"Riley!" Leila hushed, loud enough for Gabby to hear. "Maybe it's not her, maybe she's fine."

Gabby threw her arm in the air and shouted. "Thank you, sister. I do. I feel fine."

Riley looked at Gabby sideways. "For now."

Leila sighed. Gabby had the patience of a saint with Riley. She knew the story of his sister, how traumatic it was for him to see his flesh and blood turn from a normal shy teen into a cold-blooded Fallen, who destroyed his and his mother's lives. Patience though, could only last so long.

"It's been three months. I get it, you're scared for me. But if I were to turn into a big bad monster wouldn't it have happened by now?"

"Maybe," Riley said, rubbing at the base of his skull. "I'm sorry. But can we try just once more?"

Gabby's shoulders dropped. "Fine."

As much as Leila wanted to do this, for Riley and Gabby, something wasn't right. They were missing an important step. Remembering the first and only time they were able to remove a Guardian, Leila thought of Crystal and Thomas as they hunted for Riley's blood. Somehow, they'd combined their auras to create a ripple effect.

A light bulb switched on. They'd only tried in backyards and open spaces. But what if they tried something different? Actually go deep in the forest a few miles from the border of town. Maybe it wasn't the Imprint thing, maybe it was a location thing.

Leila blurted, "What if we go to the spot?"

"The spot?" Riley frowned.

Nodding, Leila became more excited as if maybe she'd just solved all their problems. "Where it happened before, with Crystal and Thomas."

Gabby let out a moan. "I can't believe this is my life now. B plusses and being a third wheel to you two crazies."

Riley pointed at Leila, realization sinking in. He jumped

a few steps and grabbed Gabby's wrist. As he dragged her past Leila, he said, "Just humor us."

As her eager boyfriend stormed toward his car, Leila mouthed "Sorry." She didn't want to be controlling or make Gabby feel like there was something wrong with her. But if Leila was honest, she feared for Gabby as much as Riley did.

Riley pulled his car over at the end of the straight where their fight against the Fallen occurred. As she got out of the car, Leila glanced up the hill on the other side of the road. Between trunks and low branches she spotted *the* tree. It was almost identical to those that surrounded it, but she knew the one. The spot where Riley turned her.

"It was up here," Riley said, charging ahead to the bend in the road.

Gabby walked along the side of the road, not quite as fast as Riley, scuffing her heels along the bitumen. Leila took one last look at the tree and caught up with Gabby. Together, they followed Riley.

"Will this be the last time?" Gabby whispered.

Leila hooked her arm around Gabby's elbow. "I'll have a talk to him."

"Yes, but what do you think of all this? Do you think I'm dangerous?" She didn't look at Leila as she asked it and there was a vulnerable tone in her voice. Gabby didn't usually care what anyone thought of her and would tell that to peoples' faces.

Leila knew why she asked it though. Because her opinion mattered to Gabby. There was too much heaviness in that, enough to render her speechless.

The tops of the trees danced in the wind and white fluffy clouds covered the sky overhead. At the floor of the forest, a movement caught Leila's attention. Scurrying away and zigzagging between trees was a small animal. Pale gray with black stripes. "Was that a cat?"

"What?" Gabby asked, looking around.

They stopped, and side-by-side they stared into the forest. Everything was silent bar Riley's shoes as they hit fallen branches and twigs. And then Riley's voice:

"Come on, you two, it's down here."

With their arms still entwined, the two girls followed him. Leila pondered Gabby's question again, wanting to find the right words. "I think you mean too much to me to risk not trying this."

Gabby was quiet for a while as they trudged through wet soil and weaved through the forest. As they stepped into a small clearing where Riley stood, Gabby let go of Leila's arm. She leaned over and with a hushed voice, said, "Good."

Leila stopped in her tracks as Gabby pushed forward to Riley. It was one word. Small and often overused. But the depth behind it caught her off guard. Did Gabby want to be rid of her Guardian? Was there something she wasn't telling them?

Renewed with the desire to make this work, Leila glanced around the clearing. Riley was standing in a spot close to where it happened. Memories of him at near death came flooding to the surface.

Leila pointed beside him. "A little to the left."

He side-stepped and looked at her. "Here?"

Leila took Gabby's hand and led her a few yards to the right. She looked back at Riley, then turned to Gabby and pushed her back a few steps. "There. This is where Crystal ran from."

"And what exactly am I doing?" Gabby asked. She furrowed her brow as she looked beyond Leila.

Riley had made himself comfortable on the ground, first by sitting, then by laying. He tilted his head up. "Is this how I was? I can't remember."

Standing back away from them, Leila took the whole scene in. Right before it happened, Crystal had dragged her away from Riley. Then she had to pull Thomas away. As she was fighting with Thomas, Crystal lined Riley up for the kill.

"No!" Leila blurted, storming back to Gabby. She dragged her to Riley. "You're here. Now, you lift your foot. Fully shifted, pretend you're a wildebeest."

Gabby raised one eyebrow. "A wildebeest?"

"Mmmhm. I'm starting from over there." Leila pointed to where she first placed Gabby. "I want you to raise your paw and aim for Riley's head."

Gabby looked down at Riley, laying on the damp forest floor. "You want me to stamp his pretty face?"

"Yes!" Leila threw her hands up, all too aware at how maniacal she sounded. "I need to feel the fear, so you have to sell it, okay? Make me believe you want to hurt him."

Gabby shrugged and tilted her head at Leila. With a smirk on her lips, she said, "I can do that."

"Am I right? Was I like this?" Riley asked again.

He looked adorably cute in such a vulnerable position. Gabby towered over him, as he pretended to be unconscious. Leila bit her lip and smiled. "You're perfect, as always."

Assuming position a few meters away, Leila got down to her knees. Summoning her Guardian, she called her lion to align. With growing fangs, she said, "Okay, Gabby. Let's get that Guardian away from you."

Riley laid back and closed his eyes. Gabby—now her wolf—raised her paw. And Leila scrambled to them. She threw herself onto Riley, arms wrapping around his body, and peered up. Leila could see Gabby through the green outline of her wolf. Together, their foot hovered a few inches from Leila's face and then, gently moved to the ground.

"Gabby!" Leila moaned, climbing off Riley. "Ya gotta mean it. Come at us like you want to squish our brains."

Gabby gave her look and blinked slowly with fake disdain. "And you think *I'm* the one who needs help."

"Just one more time," Leila said, shuffling back to her

spot. "And, action."

Stifling a laugh, Gabby raised her foot once more. Riley kept one eye open as Leila dived for him. They swung their arms around each other, and Riley half-shifted, his eyes shining neon blue. For a moment, Leila saw the reflection of her own golden irises in his eyes. When this worked the last time, it was almost like they shared their Guardians. Each of them sporting one golden eye and one blue. She clutched him tighter, waiting for their auras to combine and cascade like an explosion from their bodies. But instead, Gabby's foot clocked the back of Leila's head.

"Oww," Leila scrambled off Riley, rubbing her head.

"Crap!" In a flash, Gabby returned back to her human form. "I'm so sorry, Leila. You told me to."

Leila sat back with a forlorn expression, her shoulders slumped. Not because of the pain. But because it didn't work. She was sure she found the solution.

Gabby plonked herself on the ground and picking up a small twig, she dug it through the dirt. "What now?"

Leila looked at Riley as he sat up properly. He lifted his leg, bending it at the knee, and rested an arm over the top of it. His fingertips just reached Leila's shoulder. He gave her a sad smile before turning to Gabby. "What do you want?"

The twig in Gabby's grasp snapped. "I want…" her voice hitched as she placed her hand on her heart. "I want this monumental black hole in my heart to be gone."

THURSDAY

early evening

Sadie

Sadie stood in the middle of her room with the entire contents of her wardrobe strewn on the floor around her feet. If her clothes were an altar, she was the sacrifice. Wearing nothing but a set of pink, lacy underwear, she glanced over the items, mentally imagining herself in a multitude of ensembles. What did one wear on a date? She'd never been on one before, she wouldn't have known.

Damien asked her to dinner during lunch. Not that anyone else noticed, they were too occupied by Gabby and her Fallen conundrum. Sadie didn't tell them either. From the way she saw Gabby teasing Leila over Riley, those kinds of things were best kept a secret.

But Damien. With his muscles and square-jaw, his epic shoulder-length hair and gray eyes lined by thick lashes — how could she say no? It was more than that, though. She wasn't completely superficial. He also had a sincere way about him. He was smart and thoughtful. Sometimes, she'd

22

catch him tuck his impossibly ratty yet smooth hair behind his ears, and hunch out of the spotlight, as though apologizing for being in the same room as, well, anyone. He was funny too, when he wasn't being obnoxious. That was the other side to him, one that complicated things. Cocky and demanding, like he didn't know he was fine just the way he was before he became a Guardian. That's how she could have said no.

But she didn't. She said yes. And as she looked over her clothing options, she wished she could talk to Leila or Gabby about it. Clarity often came with more minds than her own which went in circles. Sadie sighed and looked over at her white dresser with wooden handles on its drawers. Resting on its top was a photo of Sadie and her two best friends, their faces squished together to fit inside the frame. It was a Polaroid, one of many Leila had given her. Sadie's own thoughts would have to do this time, considering the date was a secret and all.

Sadie returned her gaze to the floor, and her bottom lip rolled out as she contemplated. On one side of the floor were her normal everyday choices: blue jeans, camel chinos, one-toned shirts with scooped necklines. And on the other side, was a much smaller pile of her untouched favorites: an array of pastels and light colors intercepted by a splattering of tans, browns, and grays. A style that was opposite to Leila's —it was more bohemian than edgy. Leila could get away with edgy. Her personality stretched beyond her body. Somehow, she managed to encompass everyone she came in contact with, all without realizing she was doing it. It was the same for Gabby, who's style was understated. She loved grungy dark colors like maroon, navy blue, and mustard yellow, and was never without her trusty Doc Martin boots. Even in flannelette shirts, Gabby didn't have to try to make an impression either. It was harder for Sadie. She felt small and mousey and easily forgettable. It was as though she had to make the effort of both Leila and Gabby combined just to be noticed. Being extra approachable, extra friendly, extra normal. Being something not quite like herself.

She knew exactly where her fake self ended and her real self began. Her true self was in the little things. In a geometric painting of a tiger, hanging on the wall above the dresser. It was in an octagon lampshade made of rose-gold metal that sat on her bedside table. And beside the lamp, it was in a tarot deck, the favorite of five she owned. Every book had its rightful place on her shelf, organized by the way the story made her feel. She categorized everything. Even now, with her wardrobe exploded across the room, there was a pile that made her feel normal and unobtrusive, and another pile that made her feel like dancing. It wasn't hard for her to make the distinction between which clothes she adored and which ones she owned because they seemed safe.

That's how it was for Sadie, her real self hidden behind the walls of her room. She sighed and picked up a white long-sleeve top. Probably not the right item to wear to an Italian restaurant. She threw it back onto the pile, all at once dismayed at her collection of boring blue jeans and emotionless tops. They were simple and judgment free, something she craved but also despised. She let her eyes drift over to her treasures of obscurity. Pieces of herself that to an outside eye would seem out of place—things she loved but could never bring herself to wear. There were skirts that flowed and shirts that hugged. Floral and lace. An earthy femininity that matched her bedroom.

Torn between two versions of herself, Sadie wondered which version she would give to Damien on their date. Or the more honest question, which version would he like better?

Sadie pulled on a pair of tan jeans with white lace at the seams. She paired it with a lilac, long-sleeve top that showed her midriff and accentuated her modest curves. Something she'd only dare wearing on her bravest of days.

She'd be herself.

"Sadie!" Summer, Sadie's fifteen-year-old sister,

screeched from behind the closed door. "I need to borrow your jacket. The denim one."

With only a two-year age gap between them, Summer was already taller than Sadie—she also bloomed in the areas where Sadie was lacking. Still, they wore the same sized clothes. Sadie scoured the floor until her eyes landed on her pile of boring yet safe items. She picked up the faded blue jacket and stepped over the pile to her door. Opening the door just a crack, Sadie squeezed the jacket through.

Summer thwacked her palm on the door, swinging it wide open. Behind Summer, hovered her best friend, Imogen. They were like two peas-in-a-pod, joined at the hip, bringing terror to all they came in contact with. It didn't surprise Sadie when she found out Imogen was Sebastian Weir's little sister.

A wry smile cracked Summer's pretty face as her eyes ran the length of Sadie. But that didn't mean much, Summer was often smirking at her for some reason or another.

"I like your outfit," Imogen said in a way that could have been genuine, but Sadie wasn't so sure.

Summer threaded her arms through the denim jacket, her gaze on Sadie's missing floor. "Where are you going?"

"Not that it's your business," Sadie said, grabbing a long beaded necklace with an amethyst at the end and hanging it around her neck. "But I'm going on a date."

Summer laughed, trading a quick glance with Imogen. "You? No, really? Where are you going?"

Sadie rolled her eyes. And noticing both the girls were now both wearing jackets, she returned the question, "Where are *you* going? Are you sure you want to push your luck?"

With a tendency to sneak out, Summer had only just come off her grounding from going to an unsupervised waterfall party and drinking four beers. Fifteen. Sadie couldn't imagine doing that two years ago at that age. But then, she still didn't do it now. So, how can she blame her sister for laughing when she really was the boring one?

"Okay, Mom. We're going to hers." Summer threw a thumb in Imogen's direction, who smiled with her lips hidden inside her mouth.

Sadie didn't know if Summer was lying. It was hard to tell these days with the amount of fib-telling practice she'd had. But honestly, Sadie didn't care to press the matter. She was done playing her sister's keeper. And she was done pretending to be something she wasn't.

"Just don't drink anything alcoholic. The last thing I need is to babysit your grounded ass for another three months." Sadie slammed the door on her shocked sister's face.

Turning around and seeing the mess on her floor, Sadie sighed. It pained her to ignore it, but the cleanup would have to wait. Something was missing from her outfit.

Standing in front of her mirror, Sadie tugged at the hair-tie that held the top-knot on her head. Her long blond tendrils—wavy from the bun—fell over her shoulders and half-way down her back. Sadie smiled, knowing exactly what she needed.

She lunged across her room and pulled her drapes open. The windowsill was adorned with a random collection of trinkets. From pretty rocks to painted feathers to handwritten notes. Sadie crouched, running her fingers along a few feathers until she found the one she was after. It was white and brown, the ends tipped in rose gold. Perfect. Blindly, she pulled thin strands of hair from above her ears and tied them at the back, tucking the feather in.

As she stood, she grabbed her tarot cards from her bedside table. Damien wasn't just going to get the real her, he was going to get all of her. The quirky and the kind.

THURSDAY

evening

Sadie

Jimmy's Italian Restaurant wasn't busy. But it seemed to be the night of high school dates. A few couples sat in booths, hands gripping, eyes swooning, lips locking. Sadie let Damien lead the way to the counter and was surprised to see Sebastian standing at the till. Why, of all people, would Sebastian Weir, grandson of the mayor, need a job?

He stood there, palm pressed against the bench as though it held his whole body weight. He didn't bother to look at them as he asked what they wanted to order. His tone and expression oozed boredom, like he'd rather be anywhere else but there.

With his head hanging low, Sadie realized how much his hair had grown recently. Actually, she couldn't remember the last time he'd caked his hair in gel to slick it back. A signature look — all but forgotten. She noted to herself that this new tousled look suited him.

Sebastian tapped at the screen. "Any drinks? Milk?"

"Milk?" Damien balked.

"Isn't that what boring people drink?" Sebastian reached for a table number and placed it in front of him, eyes still anywhere but on them.

Sadie gawked at Damien, waiting for him to react to Sebastian's taunt. His face was more confused than annoyed though and it was the most endearing thing to see.

"Water's fine," she said.

Sebastian sniffed with indifference and tapped the screen. "Dutch or Chivalry?"

"Beg pardon?"

Sebastian looked up then, speaking slowly as if Damien was hard of hearing. "Will. You. Be. Paying. For. Her?"

"Oh no." Sadie whipped out her dad's credit card. "Dutch please."

Sebastian's eyes floated casually to Sadie and his lips twitched slightly into something that resembled a smirk.

After they paid and Sebastian jabbed a finger at their table's direction, they sat down.

Damien scowled in a hushed tone, "What a dick."

Sadie looked over at Sebastian as he served the next customer. His eyes stared at the screen, and he spoke with a sharp tone and bored face. She shrugged. "He's harmless. All bark, no bite."

She tried not to laugh at the pun, considering he was a wolf and all.

"You're only saying that because he saved your life," Damien said it like it was an accusation.

Sadie swung her head back to Damien. "And that's a bad thing?"

"No!" Damien said quickly, reaching his arm out and hovering his hand just above hers. "I didn't mean that. It's a great thing, a more than great thing. Having you alive is definitely a great thing."

His stuttering made her smile. There he was, the Damien she knew.

Sadie flung her hair over shoulder and run her teeth over her bottom lip. A sensual look flitted to her eyes. She caught herself then, being the thing she'd promised herself she wouldn't be—someone that wasn't herself. She took a quick breath.

No need to flirt, Sadie Sloan. Just be yourself.

"Do you want a tarot reading?" She dug her hand into her bag and pulled out her cards.

Damien stared at her hands as she began shuffling. The backs of the cards were swirls of pastel pink and blue with the tree of life embossed in gold foil. She loved those cards.

When Sadie realized he was staring, she stopped. "Orrr not?"

Damien smiled and looked down at his hands. His hair fell forward, covering his face like a mask. He peered at her through dark tendrils. The vision caught Sadie off guard. What a pair they were. She knew this side to Damien well, it was all he'd shown anyone—until he became a Guardian. It was a weird feeling. Knowing that she could render him vulnerable, revert him to the person he was before he had the confidence that came with being a Guardian. But also, it made her realize, she wasn't the only one who was afraid of being their true self. Where he hid behind his hair, she hid behind her overly friendly smile.

"I mean." He squeezed his hands together, kneading his fingers anxiously. "I don't believe in that sort of thing, but sure. If you want."

Sadie smiled. Not a fake smile either. It was wide and genuine. "Okay then." She pushed the cards to him. "You're supposed to shuffle them."

A brightness lit his eyes. He took the cards happily and began to shuffle. His long slender fingers flicked the cards with ease, fanning them fast. Wide arms, then close hands. It all looked so effortless. Sadie wondered what his hands would feel like running through her hair.

"I play canasta a lot. I've been in a tournament a few times. In Seattle," He said, passing them back. As an afterthought, he added, "You just looked surprised at my shuffling. So, that's why. Practice."

Sadie bit her lip to stop herself from laughing and placed the deck on the table. As she turned three cards over in a row, she said, "Under all that muscle, you're still a nerd."

"A nerd?" He snapped his shoulders back and sat upright, brows pressing down to his eyes.

"It's okay," Sadie said softly. "I never said it was a bad thing."

Damien nodded once and jutted his chin out defensively. Sadie kept her face even as she watched his gentle side slip away. He slid his jacket off and hung it over the back of his chair, his eyes darting to his bulging bicep as he moved. His dark spiral tattoo peeked out from under the sleeve.

He leaned across the table, and with a glint in his eyes, he said, "I can be whatever you want me to be."

Sadie recoiled. She didn't want to flirt. Didn't he know that? Didn't he want the same thing as her? To get to know each other.

"Drinks," Sebastian announced at the side of the table.

Sadie sat back, surprised by his sudden appearance. Sebastian slammed the bottle of water onto the table and drops of liquid spilled out over the top and ran down the side of the glass. His eyes drifted to the tarot cards, then up to Sadie's disenchanted expression. He looked back to the cards once more and picked up one from the top of the pile. Sadie watched his eyes dart over the card—his mouth twitched slightly, as though teasing a smile. Without saying a word, he placed it back where he found it and headed back to the cafe counter.

Sadie turned back to Damien. "Just be yourself."

She peered down to the cards and changed the subject. "So, I've done a three-card spread. One for your past, one for your present, and one for your future."

"Tell me, oh wise mage, what does it say?"

Sadie didn't like the mocking tone to his voice, but she

didn't show it. The first card, for his past, showed a person sitting alone in a field of dandelions. "This card is The Hermit. It shows you in solitude. Someone who gains strength from being alone. There's always a time for isolation, so it's not a bad card at all." She didn't look up as she moved onto the next card. "The card for you as you are right now is the six of wands. It means you've just come off a victory. You're reaping the rewards."

"I like the sound of that."

Sadie glanced up to see his chest rise. He raised his eyebrows. "You know this whole thing is baloney, but I'll take it."

A sharp smile flew quickly across Sadie's face. If he wasn't careful, Damien would see the snark she reserved for her sister. Turning back to the cards, her fingers slid over the last card. Another lone figure, but this time its head was bowed and its arms were open wide, welcoming its fate. The Death card.

"And I rest my case. Death?" Damien jeered. "Am I going to die?"

"The death card doesn't mean literal death," Sadie said a little too defensively for the *nice girl* image she tried so hard to uphold. "It means change. A new path. Releasing something important to you and starting afresh completely."

Smooth fingernails grazed across Sadie's hand. Damien placed his palm down and leaned forward. "Sadie Sloan, I gotta say it. You're gorgeous when you're cranky."

A crash came from across the room, followed by a "shit!" Sebastian poked his head up from behind the counter, eyes straight on Sadie. He winced and stood back up, holding a broken mug, and scrambled into the back kitchen.

Sadie slid her hand from beneath Damien's and gathered her cards from the table, placing his spread on the bottom of the deck. As she moved them back to her bag, curiosity got the better of her. She lifted the card from the top, the one Sebastian had taken.

In front of a sunrise, colored orange and pink, two people

embraced. The Lovers card.

The kitchen door swung open and Sadie glanced up. Sebastian walked through, holding two bowls of spaghetti bolognaise.

As he placed their meals in front of them, he glanced at her hands and his mouth jerked open — not a gasp, not a smile, just slightly open like he'd been caught with his hand deep in the cookie jar. She was still holding the tarot card.

"Enjoy your meal, Itsy," he said before rushing away.

For some unforeseen reason, her heart skipped a beat.

After dinner, they stood on the sidewalk of the well-lit main street of Cedar Falls. The sun had set in the time it took them to eat. Sadie shivered at the chilled air and gazed at the night sky half covered in clouds. A part of the sky, right above the mountain ledge that over-looked the town, was clear. Twinkling stars shone above as though an invitation.

"You wanna go for a walk to the lake?" Damien asked, threading his arms through his jacket.

"Don't know if we should…"

"I'll protect you, besides there's been no attacks since Leila and Riley became Imprints." He took her hand, a gentle smile beaming down at her.

She didn't mean they shouldn't because of the attacks. Those were Cap and his minions and they were all gone now. The town had lifted its caution and life went back to normal, as though all those people didn't just die.

What she meant was, she wasn't sure if they should continue their date… if they were compatible.

"Come on," he said, tugging at her arm. "You'll be safe, I promise."

There was something kind in his eyes that made her step with him. He wasn't a bad person, far from it. Maybe she just needed to see how things went a little more. Maybe she just needed to dig a little bit deeper and wait for his real self to re-appear.

They walked down the path, hand-in-hand, until they reached the turn-off for the lake. The dim light from the street lamps casted a yellow tint over Damien's face. He stood a whole foot above her and as he looked down at her, shadows deepened his features.

"Oh," he said, peering over her head. "You got something..." He whipped the feather from her hair and tossed it away.

Sadie opened her mouth say that it was hers —

"You know, I've had a few dates in the last three months. And I have to say, this is one of my favorites."

"Um, thanks?" Sadie wriggled her hand free. She looked back to the path behind them, but in the darkness, the feather had disappeared.

Damien peered at her sideways, and when he realized what he'd said, he swung an arm around her shoulders. "No, no. Don't get all defensive again. It's a compliment. It means I like you."

She stared at his hand as it hung over her shoulder, precariously close to her breast. He danced too quickly between personalities, she was having a hard time keeping up. As their feet hit to the dewy grass that surrounded the lake, Sadie ducked out from under his hold and ran to the edge.

Damien stepped beside her and pointed to the right side, where the path led up to the mountain ledge. "Check out the ice, it's melting."

Sure enough, water laid upon the solid ice, long cracks zigzagging through.

"The swallows will come back soon," Sadie mused, a smile rising. She loved the sound of a swallow's song. It reminded her of picnics and friendship and spring.

"You like swallows?" Damien nodded to himself, his hands clasped in front of him. Sadie didn't know whether his nod was for storing the information away for future need, or if he was teasing her.

"What's your favorite animal?" she asked, hoping to bring out his nerdy side again.

A crease formed between his eyes and he looked down at her with a grin. "Do you even have to ask?"

His eyes flashed yellow for a second before returning to their normal gray-blue.

"Eagle," Sadie stated, trying not to freak out at his almost half-shift. "Of course."

She loved being the only human in their clan, like she was privy to a secret she didn't have to live. But she tried to stay away from their shifts. The whole thing brought her back to Cap's devilish eyes as he ran for her, intent to kill. Luckily, Damien's Guardian wasn't a land predator with fangs or claws. She could deal with talons.

"Can I be truthful?" Damien said, snapping Sadie out of her memory.

"Mmm?" she replied, glancing up.

He was smiling, the edges of his eyes wrinkled yet soft. He lifted a hand and gently ran his fingers along her cheek bone. "I want to kiss you."

Sadie coughed, almost choking on her own saliva. Kiss? She hadn't even thought about kissing. She made a few noises in the back of her throat that, if a few octaves higher, would sound like a frog's mating call. Then, she laughed.

Frowning, Damien stepped back. "It wasn't meant to be a joke. I didn't think I repulsed you."

He turned around and shoving his hands in his pockets, he began walking back towards the street.

Guilt gripped Sadie. She hated when people felt bad, she particularly hated it when they felt bad because of something she'd said. It was why she was so nice and polite all the time. Conflict made her feel sick. She ran to catch up with him and clutched at his elbow. "Wait. I don't think you're repulsive."

He stopped, standing tall as his neck arched back. Looking up at the sky, he said, "I thought you were different from the other girls. But not in the complete opposite way."

"The other girls?" As soon as she said the words, she regretted them. She didn't want to hear about his conquests. About his other dates. She just wanted to hear about him and who he was. She wanted to connect on a real level.

Damien slowly turned around. His eyes darted around Sadie's face and he licked his lips before saying. "They're superficial. They just want to date me because I'm a Guardian. Not that they know I'm a Guardian, but they see the effects of it. In my stature, in my attitude. I'm not who they want. They just want what they *think* I am." He took a quick breath before continuing. "Sadie, I like you. Really. A lot. I thought..." His words drifted into the cooling air and he rolled his eyes.

What he said was fair enough, but the words annoyed Sadie. He expected her to accept the real him, but he didn't want to show her the real him. How was that supposed to work? She'd given total honesty the whole night and he gave her nothing. If she were to go on anything he'd been that night, she'd dump him in a heartbeat.

She bit her bottom lip, but there was no flirt in her eyes. She was simply trying to concoct a meaningful sentence that told him what she was thinking without hurting his feelings.

Finally, she said, "Can't you just be yourself?"

His hands splayed from his neck to his feet. "This is me, a better me."

"Yes." She didn't waste any time trying to think of a nicer way to say it. "But before, you were humble. Isn't that better?"

Damien chortled, rolling his shoulders back. "Sades, confidence is everything."

Straight-faced, she quipped, "So is humility."

That word seemed to affect him. His face shifted from arrogant to defeated. "You're right, sorry. I get carried away sometimes, it's just a nice feeling being like this. I was scared before. Lame. I hated myself." He absent-mindedly tugged at the ends of his shoulder-length hair, as though physically placing the mask over his face. "Why would I want to be something I hate?"

"You've always been nice. A little shy but…" Sadie grabbed his fist and gently guided it away from his hair — the black locks hung limply over his hanging head. "I mean, you're hot now. Super hot, like I've had to force myself not to flirt like a mad woman." She sighed and stepped closer, tucking his hair behind his ears so she could see his whole face. "But I want to be myself with you, and I want you to be yourself with me."

As she was about to move her hands from behind his ears, he placed his own on top of them. He clasped them and brought her palms to his cheeks. Then, he moved his own to her face, cupping her petite jaw in his hands, stroking her cheek bone with his long slender fingers.

He's going to kiss me.

But Sadie wasn't sure whether she was ready to be kissed, yet. The thought had crossed her mind — as Cap was homing in on her, before Sebastian saved her life — that she was stupid for not having kissed anyone yet. But now, with Damien looming over her with wanting eyes and parted lips, she truly wasn't sure.

She'd never had a real relationship before, flirting was as far as she'd gotten. Did she know him well enough? Should there be a second date? Were they better off as friends? It would be awkward to the others in their clan, if they didn't work out.

Maybe we should wait, she thought. *Just to make sure they we're on the same page before committing.*

She opened her mouth to suggest they slow things down —

Her movement became an invitation and Damien closed the gap, pressing his lips over hers. He kissed her in the moonlight, with tender strokes and gliding tongue. Sadie stared at his shut eyelids, too close to see properly, and followed his direction—closing her lips when he closed his, opening when he did, too. She didn't do the tongue thing, though, but let his inside her mouth whenever he deemed appropriate. By the way his fingers clutched through her hair, and the way his chest pressed harder against hers the longer they kissed, it was obvious he'd had much practice. It was nice, she guessed, compared to nothing else.

When he pulled away, he let his hands rest on her waist. She gave a small smile in appeasement.

Dammit.

It was too late to say anything, now. They weren't just on different pages, they were reading completely different books.

FRIDAY

morning

Leila

Leila clutched her back-pack strap as her feet hurled along the pavement. She couldn't imagine a time where she didn't love running—it made her feel free, fierce, in charge. Every now and then, she could sense her lion Guardian close to her, begging her to shift so it too could feel the freedom. That wasn't an option here in suburbia, but sometimes on a weekend, she would make her way to the forest edge and let her inner Guardian out among the trees and nature.

From her house, Riley's place was almost the same distance as the school—in the opposite direction. But as it often did, love defeated logic. It was their morning ritual. She'd run across town to his house, his mom would serve them hot pancakes for breakfast, then he'd drive her to school.

Leila knocked on the front door, moving her legs on the spot to warm down. A flash of movement to the side caught her eye. As she searched for what made the noise, Riley's mom opened the door.

"Well, good morning!" Gail beamed, as though Leila's appearance was a surprise. The sides of Gail's dark-blond hair were pinned up and she wore an apron with a dusting on flour on the front.

"Good morning," Leila puffed, catching her breath.

"Did you have a nice run?" Gail asked, before quickly adding, "Hang on."

She ran inside. A few moments later she returned holding a broom. Bypassing Leila, Riley's mom charged off the front step, waving the broom. A small gray cat with tabby stripes scurried over the fence and into the neighbor's yard. Gail turned around, fixing a loose strand of hair, and returned to the porch.

"That darn cat won't take the hint. It's been hanging out all week like our lawn is a resort for felines..." Gail's eyes widened as she realized her gaff. "Uh, no offense to you and your Guardian, sweetheart. You're always welcome." She cleared her throat. "Are you hungry? Come in."

Leila smiled at Gail's slip-of-the-tongue and stepped inside. The waft of maple syrup and sugar filled the living room. She watched Gail rush across the open space to the kitchen bench, and with a cheeky smile, Leila said, "I'm so famished I could eat a whole gazelle."

"Ha!" Gail snorted. She picked up a batter-coated wooden spoon and waved it in Leila's direction. "I see what you did there. Riley's in his room."

Leila's heart skipped at the sound of his name. Sure, she'd seen him the day before, and they spoke on the phone before bed, but that was almost ten hours ago. Leila took the few steps to his room and swung herself around the door frame. "Hello, handsome."

Riley looked up. His arms criss-crossed in front of him as he held two ends of a tie around his neck. A smile lit his face, brightening his cedar-brown eyes. "Hey, you."

Beside Riley, sitting on the end of his bed, Leila was

shocked to see Ren.

"Oh, hi." She straightened, slightly embarrassed about her dramatic entrance. "I didn't know you were in town."

Ren didn't smile at Leila's arrival. Though, she didn't let it bother her, he rarely smiled. Leaning forward, Ren rested his elbows onto his knees and ran his fingers through his gravity defying mohawk. There were other things that defied universal laws with Ren. Things like the fact that his face looked young and could pass for a seventeen-year-old, yet there was a wisdom behind those eyes that only came with age. He was old, Leila guessed, but how old? His real age had never been discussed. Ren tended to only speak when absolutely necessary. He'd seen things, experienced things. But what exactly, remained unspoken.

"I called him. I thought he might be able to help with Gabby. He thinks we should…" Riley turned to Ren. "Well, you explain it."

Ren cleared his throat and sat up straight. "I think you should visit the Elders of the Veil."

Leila looked between Riley and Ren, trying not to laugh. "The what now?"

A wince shot across Ren's face. Riley glared at Leila—an almost unnoticeable shake of his head told her that she'd over-stepped the line. Ren had turned Riley and it was known that he was very selective about who he turned. How many? Again, no one knew. The only thing Leila knew, is that it was a privilege to be a part of his sire line and that demanded respect.

But had her almost laugh offended him? Leila couldn't quite tell what each of his expressions meant. Was he annoyed she seemed to mock the Veil or was he amused that she had no idea what he was talking about?

Ren tucked his hands inside the pockets of his leather jacket and pulled it across his torso. Looking at Riley, he said, "You didn't tell her where her Guardian comes from?"

"She's a terrible listener," Riley offered. He spun on his heels and opened his closet to retrieve his blazer.

"I listen!" Leila protested, placing her fists onto her hips. Turning to Ren, she proudly recalled the lesson. "The Veil. It's where our Guardians live, like an alternate dimension."

Ren flashed a grin and just as quickly snapped his mouth shut. "I wouldn't call it a dimension. More like a hidden part of our world that only we can see and… gain access to."

"You're saying we can go there?" Leila clasped her hand around the bag still on her back, as if she was readying herself.

"Yes." Ren stood. He was slightly shorter than Riley, a little less muscular, too. But he was svelte and stood in such a way to indicate he knew ancient martial arts. With a glint in his dark eyes, he explained. "Just like we can bring our Guardians over, we can also use them to move through the Veil."

"Don't forget to tell her about the Elders," Riley enthused, sifting through his sock drawer.

"The Elders are who created the first Guardians. They live in the Veil, watching, ordering, shit like that."

Leila balked at the unexpected curse word as it flew effortlessly out of Ren's mouth. He really was an enigma to her. And, judging by the hint of a smirk, he reveled in her shock.

He continued, "The Elders used to have more of an impact on Guardians. That guidance ceased when the Fallen rose…" He stared past her, eyes clouding over as though recalling a memory. A short moment passed, and catching himself, he blinked and shook his head. "Anyway, they know things. They might be able to tell you how you were able to clear those kids of their Guardians."

"And then we can replicate it for Gabby?" Leila straightened her arms and let her backpack slide to the floor. "I'm in. How do we do it?"

"What about school?" Riley hopped across his bedroom, struggling to put his shoe on.

"I'll talk you through it," Ren said. He glanced at Riley,

bemused. "But you should go to school. I haven't visited the Veil in eons, there's something I'll have to organize first."

"Breakfast!" Gail called from the kitchen. "Ren, I've made enough for you, too."

Ren nodded at Leila with his best poker face and brushed past her. "You're amazing, Gail," he cooed. Leila could definitely hear the smile in his voice. "How did you know pancakes were my favorite?"

"He's so weird," Leila whispered to Riley as he stood beside her.

They hovered in his doorway, watching Ren greet Gail with a hug. He sat at the table, piled five pancakes onto a plate, and drizzled copious amounts of maple syrup over the stack. Such. An. Enigma.

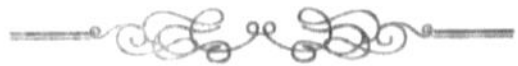

Sadie

Sadie rushed to her locker. She needed to be quick. Three tasks: Grab her things; get to class; avoid Damien. There'd be no waiting for Leila or Gabby like usual. She couldn't risk running into Damien and any awkward conversation he'd start about their date. Or worse yet, he'd try to kiss her again.

She grabbed her history book out and clutched the side of her locker. Her gaze drifted down, seeing two legs right beside her. The body and face were hidden by her locker door, but she had an inkling of who they belonged to, and she cursed herself for not even being about to get one task done. Sighing, she closed her locker and who she came face-to-face with surprised her.

"S...S... Sebastian?" she stuttered.

Immediately, she felt stupid. There he was, the boy who saved her life, the most popular guy at school, leaning against the locker beside hers, looking at her with his dark blue eyes. And she was… what? Nervous?

Sadie shook herself out of it, urging herself to just be cool. "Do you need something?"

"Is Summer here today?"

Sadie shrugged, eyes darting to Damien's unoccupied locker. "Who knows with that kid."

"You don't know if your own sister is at school?" Sebastian scoffed, brows lowering.

Meeting his gaze, Sadie frowned. "Well, they stayed at your place and I literally just got here, so, no I don't know."

"Wait! Backtrack." With one hand still pressed against the locker at the side of her head, his free hand tapped his chest. The scent of dirt and soap wafted between them. "They didn't stay at my house. Imogen told me they were staying at your house."

Sadie internally moaned. Summer was up to her old tricks again—lying and skipping school. "Guarantee they didn't."

"Dammit." Sebastian dropped his hand from her locker and ran it through his hair. He took a few steps backwards and pointed at Sadie. "If you see either of them let me know, yeah?"

Sadie watched him rush off down the hall, scanning his eyes along the locker walls. His concern surprised her. She knew he was capable of caring, obviously, but the way he stormed away, head jerking from side-to-side showed a warmth to him.

A gentle hand cupped her shoulder, followed by a quiet; "Hello, there."

Sadie closed her eyes. *Oh, nuts.* Thanks to Sebastian holding her up, she'd now have to face Damien. She opened her eyes and turned around slowly, smiling. "Oh, hi."

"How did you sleep?" Damien leaned his shoulder onto a locker and looked down at her with dreamy eyes.

Sadie cringed inwardly. He really was a nice guy. Letting him down was going to be hard. Placing her best cheery expression in place, she said, "Good. And you?"

"Perfect." He lifted his hand to her cheek and stroked her skin with his knuckles. Then, he leaned down, eyes on her lips.

Heart rate rising, Sadie watched him go in for the kiss. As he pushed forward, she pulled back. "I, uh, it's good to see you but I'm late for class."

She shuffled out of his grasp and turned. Running down the hall, she heard his voice echo through the corridor, "The bell doesn't go for another ten minutes!"

FRIDAY

mid-morning

Leila

School didn't much feel like it used to for Leila. Everything became easier, as though a secret compartment in her brain had opened up for her to store as much information as needed. Some classes took more time to retrieve the information though; the harder ones—like calculus. But Mr. Robertson said if she kept it up, she'll move into Riley, Damien and Gabby's advanced math before the end of semester. The way he'd said it sounded like a threat, but that didn't mean much when most things he said sounded like a threat.

Mr. Robertson sat with his feet crossed on top of his desk, intently picking at his fingernails with an apple slicer. Leila wondered if he realized what class he was teaching. Math, or earth science, or history. Leila darted her eyes to the textbook in front of her… math, it was math. She'd completed it so long ago, even she'd forgotten. When Leila glanced back up, she found her teacher watching her. He lifted the slicer to his forehead and saluted.

Leila gave a grim smile. She wasn't sure whether the work was easier or if he didn't care for teaching as much. Maybe a bit of both. If she was different as a student, so was he as a teacher. Becoming a Guardian had opened his eyes to a whole new world, and teaching wasn't exactly what he wanted to do with his life anymore. But he also seemed lost, like he didn't know what to do with all the extra ions zinging through his veins.

Leila understood that. That's why she ran. What she couldn't understand was, why couldn't he focus all of the extra energy into being a good teacher instead of staring into space wishing he was anywhere but there. Better yet, why didn't he just leave, go and explore the world, find what it is he was really craving?

Beside her, Sadie tapped her pen against their shared desk. Gazing down, Leila balked at Sadie's empty worksheet.

"Are you okay?" Leila whispered.

Sadie dropped her pen along with a sigh, as if she'd been waiting for Leila to ask. "Can you keep a secret?"

Leila tried not to guffaw in the middle of class. She curled her hand in a crescent around her face, leering at Sadie. "You're kidding, right? You know I can."

"Yes, but even from Riley… and…" Sadie winced, biting the inside of her mouth. "And Gabby?"

"What's happened?" Leila asked, immediately worried.

Sadie took a long deep breath. She grabbed her pen and began scrawling spirals on her paper. "I went out with Damien last night."

"Are you serious?" Leila said a little too loud. Then quieter, "I've been waiting for you two to get your act together."

Sadie dropped the pen again, and along with it, her head. She slipped her hands under her forehead and moaned.

Leila lowered her face, resting her cheek on the desk. She

urged, "Tell me."

"We kissed," Sadie whispered. The way her eyes hooded down at their edges told Leila all she needed to know.

"No good?"

Sadie sighed again and pushed herself up. "The kiss was okay. But the whole thing, just… I don't think it's going to work, and I don't know how to tell him."

"Oh." Leila looked over to see Mr Robertson glaring at them. He lifted a blank piece of paper and waved it around. "Pretend to do your work."

"He leaned into me this morning. I think he thinks he can kiss me whenever he wants." Sadie began scribbling wildly on the page. She slid it across to Leila.

Can you distract him for a while, until I figure out how I feel?

Leila put her pen to the paper and tapped at her answer with the ballpoint.

Yes.

When the bell rang to signal the end of class, Sadie gathered her belongings at lightning speed. She stood up and leaned across the desk. "I'll be hiding in the library for lunch, just so you know where not to be."

Sadie scurried to the door, stopping to peer into the corridor. It must have been clear because next moment she was gone, the sound of her footsteps sending echoing thumps into the classroom. Leila piled her things into her arms and smiled to herself. The things she did for her friends.

Okay, Leila said to herself. *Project keep-Damien-from-Sadie is now in force.*

She pressed her completed worksheet to her chest, waiting for a few students to pass in front of her. She looked at Mr Robertson, who remained sitting at his desk with his feet crossed. He still had the apple slicer in his hand and flipped it between his fingers, absent-mindedly staring out the window. He seemed so bored.

A crazy thought popped into Leila's mind. *Maybe it wasn't his choice to stay there?* She weaved through the hoard of students all gunning for the door and stopped by his desk.

"Did Kiko order you to stay here in Cedar Falls?" Leila asked.

She knew Ren wasn't the order giving type, he'd mostly give advice and help Riley when he deemed fit. And even though in Ren's absence, Riley stepped up as their leader, he certainly would never tell them what they could or couldn't do. But maybe Kiko was a different Alpha.

Mr. Robertson swung his legs down and peered around Leila. He waited for the last trickle of students to leave the room, and hissed, "Has she said something?"

Leila shook her head. "No. I haven't seen her in a while. Not since her and Kale moved to Seattle together. I just... well, you don't seem to enjoy it here. What's keeping you from spreading your wings?"

"You wouldn't understand," Mr. Robertson scowled. He planted the tip of the apple slicer into the wooden desk and stood up. "Don't worry your pretty head about it. I'm here and that's all there is to it."

"Okay," Leila nodded, unconvinced. "But I can look after myself, you know? If she has ordered you to watch over me, you can tell her I'm more than capable of getting by."

"Leave," he said, slumping onto his chair and spinning around to his bookshelf. With hunched shoulders he leaned forward and shoved papers into his messenger bag.

Leila stood there, stomach sinking. She studied the feeling as it sent warning signals to her brain. Something was wrong. "Sir, if you need—"

Mr. Robertson looked up, still facing the wall. He groaned, "Are you still here?"

A light tap on the door took Leila's attention. She glanced over her shoulder to see Riley waiting at the door. She turned back to Mr, Robertson. "I'm going. But if you wanna talk about it, Riley and I are available."

Mr Robertson huffed and swung around in his chair. As he stood, he placed a hand on Leila's shoulder. He opened his mouth to say something, then closed it again, shaking his head. He squeezed her shoulder and pushed off, passing Riley to leave the room.

When the room was clear, Riley held out his hand. As Leila took it, he threaded his fingers through hers and pulled her in close to his side. "Is everything okay?"

"Who knows." Leila shrugged and sighed. Then, remembering Sadie's request, she asked, "Where's Damien?"

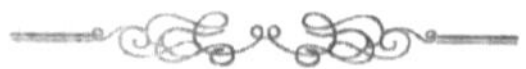

"Where's Sadie?" Damien asked, placing his tray on the table. He slid next to Riley, scanning the cafeteria.

"Uh, I think she had to stay behind in class. She needed to finish an essay or something..." Leila lied. She wasn't so great at lying, though. She tended to trip on her words, say too much or not enough. Before Damien could pick up on it, she leaned forward and changed the subject. "I think Kiko ordered Mr Robertson to keep an eye on us."

Damien frowned and pointed his spoon to the back corner. "Is that why he's staring at us?"

Leila swiveled around. Sure, enough. There was Mr Robertson, leaning against the wall, crunching into an apple. When he noticed the three of them staring, he shifted his gaze.

"Well, that's annoying," Riley said, stabbing a tater tot. "We don't need a babysitter."

"That's what I told him." Leila turned back around and pulled out a sandwich her mom made. Tomato, swiss cheese, premium ham, and mayonnaise.

Damien stared into his soup, swirling the spoon around in circles. He rested his elbow on the table and curved his palm around his chin. Eyes downward, he mumbled, "And Sadie has to stay in class for all lunch?"

"What's your fascination with Sadie?" Riley thumped his palm against Damien's shoulder-blade. "Gabby's not here either, but I don't hear you asking about her."

Looking up, Damien glared at Riley. "Dude. Don't be lame."

Riley guffawed. "Me? Lame? I think you've got the wrong person."

Leila chuckled. How quickly Damien had forgotten where he came from. She watched him turn back to his soup, hair falling around his face. Then, she realized maybe he hadn't forgotten, maybe he was still trying so desperately hard to forget.

The table vibrated as Riley's phone buzzed once. He picked it up and tapped the screen. Leila took a large bite of her sandwich as she watched Riley's eyes dart over the message.

His brows raised and his mouth twisted down. A small "heh" resonated from his throat. Finally, he looked up. "It's from Ren. You wanna go visit the Veil?"

"Now?" Leila said with a mouthful. She dropped half her sandwich back into its bag and sprung to her feet.

"Have fun, you two," Damien said, tapping the spoon in and out of his bowl. "I'll stay here with all my friends."

"Come on," Leila said, grabbing her lunch bag. She couldn't exactly promise Sadie she'd distract him and then not follow through. Plus, there wasn't any reason why she couldn't help both Gabby and Sadie at the same time. "You've gotta come, too."

"Yeah, man. You're coming." Riley wiggled his phone in between two fingers. "From what Ren says, we're going to need the back-up."

FRIDAY

noon

Sadie

"Why are we eating in the library instead of the cafeteria?" Gabby asked, balancing her tray on her lap.

"Just for something different," Sadie said, wistfully. She wasn't ready to tell Gabby about Damien, not yet anyway.

At the back of the double-floored library, the two of them sat opposite each other on matching maroon, suede sofas. Sadie propped up on her knees and leaned over the back of the sofa, pressing her head against the wall-sized window. The second-floor view overlooked the oval, where students hung out in cliques.

"I don't buy it," Gabby said, placing her tray onto the sofa. "Are you distracting me from something? Have Riley and Leila finally given up on my redemption?"

"What?" Sadie turned around, confused. "No. Why would they do that?"

Gabby shoved a piece of roast chicken in her mouth and

waved her fork in the air. "No matter. So, what is this about then?"

Behind Gabby, the library doors swung open. Sadie's eyes widened and she folded herself over, chest to thighs. With her head in a cushion, she asked, "Who is it?"

"The varsity team. What the heck are you doing, weirdo?"

Sadie relaxed and sat up. She shrugged and turned back to the window. "You know, Bianca from twelfth grade is gay. You should date her."

"Now I really think you are distracting me. Anyway, I'll bite. What's your point? Thomas is heterosexual, you should date him."

Sadie swung her head at the sound of the doors creaking open. A bunch of giggling freshmen made their way out. At their absence, the room fell silent. She noticed the basketball-come-water polo team huddled by the sports section, flicking through strategy books. Sebastian pointed Thomas to the clean romance section and laughed. His laugh was a booming staccato, loud enough to incur a warning from the librarian, but also warm enough to make Sadie's mouth twitch.

Almost smiling, Sadie returned her attention back to Gabby and leaned forward. "No, I shouldn't date Thomas just because he's hetero… ew."

Gabby raised her brow. "Exactly."

"I know, but…" Sadie's eyes flitted to Sebastian and back. "You don't think Bianca is nice?"

"Of course," Gabby smirked. "And she's hot, too."

Sadie threw her arms in the air. "So date her."

"Quiet!" The librarian demanded, causing the whole team to look their way. As Sebastian's gaze fell on Sadie, his eyes turned to slits.

"You're kidding? Like this?" Gabby half-shifted, silver flashing across her irises. "I don't think so. She's human."

Sadie winced. She really hated when they shifted in front

of her. She understood what Gabby was getting at though, it really wasn't ideal. But she'd already begun her defense and there was no turning back. "Well, I'm human."

"And you're not going to date a Guardian..." Gabby placed her tray onto the seat beside her. She studied Sadie's expression, and dubiously said, "Right?"

"Maybe I already have." Sadie retorted, slumping back into the sofa. As soon as her back hit, she sat up again, eyes glued to Sebastian as he approached them.

"What?" Gabby burst, her voice echoing up around the lofted ceiling. "Who? When? Where—"

"Itsy. Spider." Sebastian greeted them, placing his hands on the back of Gabby's sofa. "It just doesn't have the same ring to it without Bitsy."

Gabby scowled at the interruption. "What do you want?"

"I need to talk to Shorty," Sebastian said, meeting Sadie's gaping stare.

Gabby didn't bother checking with Sadie before vocalizing her thoughts on his random request. "No. Go away."

Clenching his teeth, Sebastian glowered at Gabby. "I wasn't asking you, bleacher girl. Can you give us a moment, please?"

Gabby turned to Sadie and gave an apologetic glare. It was all Sadie needed to know that Gabby was about to do something reckless.

"Sorry Sades," Gabby said, pupils dilating. Silver burst from her eyes.

"No! Gabby!" Sadie whispered as loud as she could.

But it was too late. Gabby rose, chin jutting forward as fangs began to grow. She spun around to face him. "I said no, *Sebastian*. Now, for the last time. Go away."

Sebastian cracked his neck and took a deep breath. Behind a curling lip, his canine teeth lengthened. Claws popped from his nails, puncturing holes into the top of the sofa. "You really wanna have a brawl right here in the library, with all these innocents around?"

Oh god, here they go, Sadie thought, watching Sebastian's sky-blue eyes brighten. She leaped from the sofa and clutched at Gabby's wrist. "Stop, Gabby. It's fine."

Turning to Sebastian, Sadie hitched a thumb to the history section, and stormed into the aisle. She moved along the row, until she could no longer see Gabby. As soon as Sebastian appeared, she hissed, "Are you crazy?"

"Probably." Sebastian smirked. The rims of his irises became a deep blue, like the sky right before night fall.

"Please, put your wolf away," she demanded, cowering back.

Noticing her discomfort, Sebastian blinked rapidly until his eyes returned to normal. He grimaced as his fangs and claws retracted.

Sadie took a rushed breath. She'd never seen Leila do that. "Does it hurt?"

Sebastian shrugged as if it were no big deal. But from that moment, she decided it *was* a big deal. She never considered shifting was painful. No wonder Gabby was cranky all the time.

Sebastian lifted his hand to a book and tilted it from the spine. Letting the book fall back into its place, he sighed. "Why are fifteen-year-olds such jerks?"

"Huh?" It took Sadie a few beats to realize what he was talking about. "Oh. I take it you haven't seen them yet?"

"No. Have you?" A hint of vulnerability laced his voice as he looked at her sideways, hopeful.

Leila always claimed that Sebastian Weir possessed a soft side. And it seemed, Sadie Sloan had just discovered that it came in the shape of his little sister. Imogen.

Sadie shook her head. "Sorry. I've been… pre-occupied."

Turning to her fully, Sebastian raised both his hands to his head, threading his fingers through his disheveled locks. His blazer wrinkled over his biceps.

Sadie blinked, forcing her gaze back to his face.

"I wouldn't be so worried if there weren't such things as Guardians." Sebastian let his hands drop to his sides. "And it's weird 'cause she's a sweet kid. I mean, she tries to be cool — your sister doesn't help. But we are close, she would have told me if she wasn't coming home."

The look on his face worried Sadie. If the immovable Sebastian Weir was worried, maybe she should be, too.

He sighed and a bored expression fell across his face. "Call me if they show up."

As he spun on his heels, Sadie dug her phone out from her blazer pocket. "I don't have your number."

Sebastian turned with a lop-sided grin. He snatched the phone out of her fingers and punched at the screen. He placed it back in her hand, and with the smile still planted on his face he turned and walked away.

Curious, Sadie looked at what he'd just entered.

His number was listed under: *"your crush"*.

Sadie rushed to the end of the history section and gawked as Sebastian walked past a scowling Gabby. She called out to the back of him. "I... I don't have a crush on you!"

Without looking back, Sebastian waved at her over his head.

FRIDAY

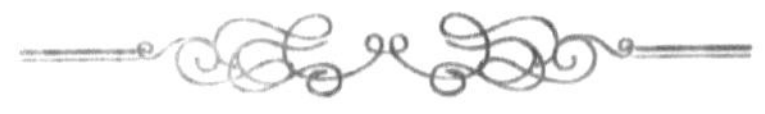

afternoon

Leila

Leila stood in her garage beside Riley, Ren, and Damien. She stared at the odd sight in front of her. Two heavy chains curled in a pile, both ends attached to a neck brace.

She remained speechless as Ren picked up a chain and opened the neck brace. "I'll take you, Riley."

Leila and Riley shared a hesitant glance. It was obvious he wanted to chain them up. But why?

"Dammit." Ren dropped the chain. "You seriously don't know how it all works?"

Riley gave a nervous smile and rubbed the nape of his neck. "All I know is what you've told me. Please don't take offense, but you haven't told me much."

The fluorescent light on the garage ceiling flickered off Ren's dark irises. He rolled his eyes. "I'm not an Alpha. This is why I don't turn many people. The responsibility is too heavy."

"Ren?" Leila spoke up, finding her voice. "Why do we need chains?"

Ren sighed, frustrated. He ran both his palms up his mohawk. "Okay. Let's make this simple. We, as Guardians, are the door to the Veil. The animals we've connected with are very real, we just can't see them as real because we are acting as the conduit in that moment. It's why when half-aligned we can see the Veil, waiting for our doors to open."

"And the chains?" Leila asked, still not sure why the hell they were needed.

A small moan rumbled in the back of Ren's throat. He glared at Leila, as if annoyance itself would make her understand.

Riley said, "Because when we step into the Veil, our Guardians anchor us here."

"Bingo!" Ren's shoulders dropped with relief. He wagged a finger at Riley. "I knew I chose you for a reason. Yes. Your wolf and lion stay here, while you shift through the other side. Without you to control them, they are nothing but a wild animal."

Leila balked, eyes wandering to the neck brace. She squeaked out an "Oh," followed by, "You could have started with that."

"Damien," Ren ordered. "You hold Leila."

Damien secured the neck brace on Leila. It was loose, balancing on the top of her shoulders. She was somewhat relieved, but still on edge.

After Ren did the same for Riley, he moved in front of them, clasping the end of the chain. "All right, ready?"

Leila felt Riley's hand slip into hers. She nodded her reply, even though she didn't think she was. Or if she'd ever be.

"I want you to align with your Guardian, meet them in the middle in half-shift." Ren's voice was gentle, decidedly less sharp than his frustration earlier.

If she didn't have a heavy piece of steel lumped on her,

she may have found his tone soothing. Nevertheless, she pushed through the discomfort and aligned with her lion. Her aura shone golden, and she felt the power of its energy rippling through her.

"That's it," Ren continued, taking the chain with both hands. "Now, instead of letting your Guardian move forward, I want you to move back into the Veil. Your destination is the sanctuary. You'll know it when you see it. And for the love of all good things, don't stay long."

The softness of Ren's voice broke on the last sentence. For a split second, she wondered whether it was a good idea at all. Leaving a wolf and a lion inside her garage. But then she thought of Gabby and the promise she made to help her. Swallowing any hesitation, Leila tightened her grasp on Riley's hand and took a step back.

A shimmer crossed in front of her eyes. The world around them dulled, as though she was looking at her garage through a sepia-stained mirror. She saw Ren, his muscles bulging as he half-shifted to increase his strength. Damien did the same, his eyes widening as he looked in Leila's direction.

"I think it's this way," Riley said, snapping her attention away. He pointed to a bright light, shining just beyond the driveway.

They moved towards it together. As they got closer, Leila glanced over shoulder. A large white wolf and majestic lion bucked wildly against the chains that held them—Damien and Ren using all their strength to keep them contained.

"I think we should hurry," Riley said, tugging on her hand.

Leila nodded and they rushed toward the light.

As they stepped through, the sight took Leila's breath away. An array of colors, bolder and brighter than anything their world possessed, surrounded them.

"Is this real?" Leila gasped. "It's like a painting."

She peered back to the garage, but the density had all but

disappeared. In its place was a ghostly, transparent shimmer in the shape of her house, as though hidden by magic.

"Yeah," Riley agreed, pulling on her hand to follow him.

Leila turned back, and as if her memory had a momentary lapse, the deeper hues of the Veil stunned her once more. She blinked slowly. As her eyes adjusted, a pathway appeared in front of them.

They walked down a cobblestone path that hugged a winding creek. They followed the slow trickle of water, until the stones led them to a clearing. A building, similar to a church with steeples and stained-glass windows, sat at the bottom of a small hill.

To the right, rows of cherry blossoms stretched out as far as the eye could see. A few animals wandered in between the blossoms close to the clearing, eyes glued to the intruders. Leila noticed a wildebeest identical to Crystal's staring at her.

An ominous forest loomed next to the orchard. Its evergreens reached for the sky, and olive-green leaves created a canopy that turned the forest floor into darkness. Silhouettes of animals lurked in the shadows.

"Do we knock?" Riley asked.

Leila jerked her head to him. She was about to ask what the heck he meant when she realized they'd walked right up to the temple. Spiral glyphs decorated two floor-to-ceiling doors.

Leila stepped forward and lifted her hand, as her knuckles were about to hit against the wooden door, it opened. Someone in a dark-blue robe stepped out, hood covering their face.

They spoke with a deep and warm voice, "Ahh, William. It's nice to finally meet you."

Riley swallowed hard. "Actually, it's Riley now."

"Ah, different name, same you. Interesting."

A growl grabbed Leila's attention. At the edge of the dark forest, a cougar leaned onto its hind legs, ready to

pounce. Leila would have recognized it anywhere. "Is that
—"

"Mmm," the person said. "Daniel. Or as you called him,
Cap. Don't fret, he cannot pass the Exile limits. In a little
while, once his Fallen parts have healed, we hope to allow
him into the Sanctuary." A long, brown-skinned finger
poked through the sleeve of the robe and pointed to the
cherry blossoms. "The place where Guardians go to rest…
Or wait for a new host."

Leila darted her eyes to the orchard, spotting the
wildebeest. It must have been Crystal's. A kind of comfort
warmed her heart. The Guardian now had the chance to be
with a True host, instead of a Fallen.

As Leila turned around, she spotted Riley hunching his
shoulders and stretching his neck, as if trying to see inside
the elder's hood.

"Forgive me," they said, raising their hands and
removing the hood.

It was a man with wide brown eyes and a strong jaw. To
Leila he looked thirty-ish, but in the game of Guardians, she
knew age-guessing wasn't the easiest to play.

"I'm an Elder of the Veil. You may call me Samuel."

"Pleased to meet you," Leila replied. She didn't know
whether to bow or curtsy, if only Ren was more giving with
his information. She tucked a foot behind the other and
began to lower her head.

Samuel cupped his hand around her shoulder. "No need,
child."

Leila glanced at Riley and smiled bashfully. He covered
his mouth trying not to laugh.

"Let us walk, Imprints." Samuel dropped his hand and
swiveled around.

Riley's amusement faded. "You know about that?"

"Oh yes, we know," Samuel said, walking around the
temple. "What is it *you* would like to know?"

Leila and Riley hurried to catch up. Riley explained, "A

few months ago something happened between us, a collision of sorts. We combined our Guardians and created an explosion of light that expelled two Guardians from their humans."

Samuel was silent as they ascended the rolling hill.

"Did he hear you?" Leila whispered.

Samuel chuckled and his shoulders danced with delight. "I heard you. What is it you would like to know?"

Frowning, Leila glanced at Riley. "We ahh… We'd like to know how to recreate it."

"Mm-hmm." Samuel nodded and strode to the crest of the hill. When he reached the top, he raised his face to the sky and inhaled.

Leila and Riley soon joined him. The hill rolled down to a beach, and beyond it lay an expansive ocean.

On exhale, Samuel faced them and spoke, "The first Guardians were chosen by us almost a hundred years ago. Three siblings were tasked to care for the humans, one assignment at a time. We allowed them to create their own bloodlines, turning those who they saw fit to join them on their quest. The middle child was always vexing." He glanced at Leila before turning his gaze back to the ocean. "When the middle child fell in love, the first Imprints were created. Their strength was beyond anything we could imagine. But the stronger they became, the hungrier they got. They ignored our assignments and sought their own without our guidance. It was no harm at first, so we let it continue, until one of them killed an innocent in a moment of weakness. A deep darkness evolved inside them. The first Imprints became the first Fallen. They turned countless people, setting countless Fallen onto your world. And every person who was turned by them became a darker version of the one before them. The other two siblings took it upon themselves to separate the Imprints, thinking their love spawned the madness. But it only fueled it. In fits of rage and jealousy, the middle child can't bear to see any other Imprints in existence, mostly killing them before they can be turned."

Leila felt her mouth go dry. She'd heard parts of it before from Ren but hearing it from the mouth of an Elder sent shivers soaring down her spine. "That middle child, are they still out there?"

Samuel looked at her for a long time before replying, "Yes."

She didn't want to ask her next question, afraid of the truth. But she'd gotten this far, so why the hell stop now. "Do they know we are Imprints?"

Samuel turned back to the view. He asked, "When you combined your power, it removed Guardians from their human host. It's called the surge and it's something only Imprints can do. It sends Guardians to either Exile or Sanctuary, depending on the depth of their nature.

"Tell me, young ones." Samuel spun around to face them. "When you created the surge for the first time, what were you feeling?"

Remembering the moment, Leila answered, "I was scared. Like I would rather die with him that live without him."

Samuel's face remained expressionless as he asked, "Why?"

Leila replied without thinking, "Because I love him."

A hint of pride washed over Samuel's face. He raised his brow, glancing between Leila and Riley. "So, you were fueled by love not fear?"

Leila looked at Riley. His brown eyes twinkled as she said, "Yes."

"Interesting." Samuel clasped his hands behind his back and began walking down the hill as if his work was done.

"Was that it?" Leila scrunched her nose. "Was that his answer?"

Riley snatched Leila's hand and ran to keep up with Samuel. "Is that how the surge works? With love."

Samuel smiled to himself and took another knowing

glance at each of them. "Better hurry back. Wild animals don't like to be contained."

With that, he walked around the corner toward the temple doors. When he reached the entrance, he spun on his heels. "Oh, and you should know there's a Fallen in your midst."

"We know," Riley sighed. "Gabby."

"Shh," Leila hissed, hurt by his comment.

Was being a Fallen really so black and white? Sebastian had proved to her that he wasn't all bad. He may have killed Mrs. Little, but he saved Sadie's life. Didn't that count for something?

"One more thing," Samuel said, opening the door. "Be careful. Together you are powerful, separate you are at risk."

The temple doors slammed shut and Leila tried to grasp what had just happened. As they ran along the cobblestone path, she moaned, "Well, that was a bust."

Riley gave her a side eye and shook his head. "You weren't listening… as always."

Leila frowned as they made it back to the door of the Veil. "I was listening. We do the surge with love. Somehow."

Chuckling, Riley clasped her hand. "We'll try again with Gabby tomorrow."

Leila nodded and together, they stepped through the shimmering gateway between worlds. In an instant, air rushed over her palm where Riley's hand had been. She spun around in a circle.

Riley was gone.

As she searched the Veil, she caught a glimpse of Damien standing with his hands on his head. The chain fell beside him in a crumpled steel pile, and next to it was her lion, unconscious.

FRIDAY

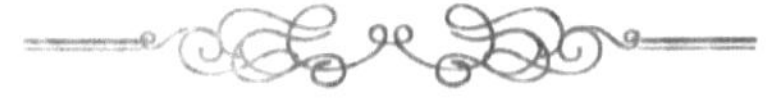

late afternoon

Sadie

Sadie laid on her stomach on her unmade bed, staring out the window. Her eyes drifted to the sill and she frowned at the space her favorite feather had once occupied. Damien threw it away like it was a piece of garbage. But it wasn't garbage, it was a reflection of her essence and he tossed it away as though that part of her was worthless.

She sighed and smashed her face onto the mattress, turning her cheek to her closet. Half her wardrobe was still out on the floor—a boring, safe mound of plain tees and denim jeans and other understated items. She had considered giving them away to charity, but couldn't bear the thought of giving up that part of her. Not yet.

Sadie's mom, Natalie, tapped on her door. She knew it was her mom because of the three gentle knocks. Her dad normally hit the door with the side of his fist, shaking the hinges with every beat. And Summer rarely bothered knocking at all.

"Yeah?" Sadie called, her face still squishing against the wrinkles of her quilt.

Sadie's mom pushed the door open. "There's a boy here."

"A boy?" Sadie sat up and almost broke her neck as she spun around.

"Mm-hm. He's very—" Natalie raised her brows—"Good looking."

Sadie felt herself recoil. Damien was persistent. "Can you tell him I'm not here?"

"Don't be silly." Natalie left the door open as she ran to the stairwell. Leaning over the banister, she called, "She's coming!"

"Mooom!" Sadie whisper-moaned.

Natalie turned around, brimming with excitement. Sadie didn't bring boys home. Ever. It must have been a great surprise for her mom. Not so much for Sadie.

"Aww come on, Sades. He seems super lovely. If I was younger…"

"All right, all right." Sadie bounded off her bed, anything to stop her mother swooning about a teenage boy. "I don't need to hear what you'd do if you were younger."

Natalie nodded once, smile beaming. She pointed at the stairs, finger stretching as far as it would go. She didn't say anything, but she didn't need to. Sadie knew that her mother was eager to see how it would turn out.

Sadie took a big breath and moped down the stairs, taking her time with each step. Her mom meant well, but she didn't know what Sadie was dealing with. And even if she told her, she'd probably say she was being silly.

Why couldn't he have just waited to see me at school on Monday? Sadie thought. *But no, he had to come to my house… make it awkward.*

Sadie tried to think of what she could say to let him down, but her thoughts got caught behind the fact that she'd upset him. And she hated the thought of it.

As she scaled the last step and headed for the foyer, she

heard her dad, Martin, chatting away in the kitchen. "And, if you use cinnamon, oh boy, does she love it!"

Sadie tip-toed down the hall and stopped behind the kitchen door. Was her dad giving Damien lessons on how to make her egg nog? *Oh my god, this is the worst day ever.*

She'd often laugh at how her dad would take Summer's boyfriends under his wing and welcome them into their home. But Sadie had never brought a boy home and the actions were decidedly less endearing.

"Oh yeah?" A voice replied. "I'll have to remember that."

Sadie straightened. It wasn't Damien. It was…

"Sebastian?" she balked, bursting into the kitchen.

Sebastian glanced over his shoulder. He was still in his school uniform—blue and gray letterman jacket buttoned up to his collar. Spotting Sadie, he gave a smirk.

"Ahh, here's the girl of the moment, " Sadie's traitor father said, holding a stick of raw cinnamon. "I was just teaching your boyfriend how to—"

"He's not my boyfriend," Sadie snapped. She marched across the room, grabbed Sebastian by the wrist, and dragged him into the dining room. She let him go and hissed, "What are you doing here?"

The smirk dropped from Sebastian's face. "Any sign of them?"

"Them?" Sadie asked.

Sebastian winced. "Uh, our sisters. You really don't give a shit, do you?"

Sadie's heart sunk at the accusation. She did care but the truth was she hadn't thought about Summer since he last asked. Did that make her a bad sister? Sadie shrugged the thought off as quick as it came. She wasn't a bad sister — Summer did this sort of thing all the time. There had to come a time in her life when she just had to let the rotten child learn from her own mistakes.

"I've been preoccupied," Sadie tried to defend herself but the unimpressed look on Sebastian's face made her realize it wasn't good enough. She sighed and called out, "Dad, is Summer home?"

"Not yet," Martin called back. "But I tell you what, she's grounded again."

Wincing, Sebastian said, "We should go look for them."

There it was again, a vulnerable hint in his eyes.

Sadie swallowed. Ignoring the sinking feeling in her gut, she waved her hand dismissively. "They're probably just doing rebellious things that bratty fifteen-year-olds do."

"For two days?" Sebastian gave his iconic scowl. "Screw this. I'm not hanging around waiting to hear the news that they've been slaughtered. Are you coming or what?"

A chill ran down her spine. He was right. She didn't want to admit it, but Sebastian Weir was goddamn right. "Fine, wait here," she sighed, heading to the stairs. As she took the first step, she glanced over her shoulder. "Don't talk to my dad."

Sadie ran upstairs and into her room. She leapt over the pile of boring clothes and burst her closet open. She grabbed a pastel purple knitted sweater that she'd never worn before and held it out in front of her. Now wasn't the time to be indecisive about her style. It was this or nothing.

As she closed her closet and spun around, she caught sight of Sebastian, leaning on her door frame. His eyes were wide as he scanned her room. Sadie kicked the pile of clothes and marched toward him. She pushed him back into the hallway and peeled her sweater on. "Are we going or not?"

Taking one last peek at her room, a smile grew across Sebastian's face. He jerked his head to the stairwell. "Come on then. You get to meet my girlfriend."

He had a girlfriend? Sadie's face involuntarily dropped as she watched him descend the stairs two steps at a time. Of course he had a girlfriend, this was Sebastian, not a choir boy. She shook her head and followed him.

As she walked through the hall toward the foyer, both

her parents hovered in the living room archway. Two proud faces beamed at Sebastian and then at Sadie as she passed.

"Have fun!" Natalie cooed, clutching onto Martin's elbow with both hands.

"Home by ten," Martin ordered, trying to hide his excitement. "Don't wanna ground you, too."

"It's not a date or anything," Sadie moaned, rolling her eyes.

Secretly though, she loved their enthusiasm. She was the golden child. The easy and unassuming one. The one who'd never been grounded. And, her own parents thought *she* had a boyfriend. The most popular boy in school no less. How highly they must have thought of her. The truth was less exciting.

Smiling to herself, Sadie stepped onto the porch and closed the door. As she turned around, her eyes landed on a motorcycle. Sebastian walked up to it and ran his palm along the leather seat.

"Is this yours?" Sadie asked, scanning the street for his blue Nissan.

"Sadie, meet Precious. Precious, this is Shorty." Sebastian opened a compartment behind the seat and pulled out a helmet.

"Precious?" Suddenly, it clicked. "*This* is your girlfriend?"

Smirking, Sebastian passed her the helmet and grabbed his own from the front. He tapped the seat behind him. "Let's go."

As he started the engine, Sadie stared at the small space behind him. She'd never been on a bike before. She pushed the helmet over her face and slid her leg over. The seat arched up a little at the back, forcing her pelvis to press against him. She shuffled back a little, resting her hands on her thighs.

Sebastian glanced over his shoulder, and even through his visor Sadie could see his eyes roll. He grabbed her hands and wrapped her arms around him, securing them at his waist.

"Make sure you move with the bike," he said.

As Sadie was about to ask what he meant, he twisted the throttle and the bike took off. The force jolted her back and she clutched the pockets of his jacket for balance. As they drove down the street, she swore she could feel him laughing.

They sped through the main street, veering around a car turning off at the lake. They drove past the street that led to Leila's house and veered to the edge of town. As the houses became further apart and the flat streets turned into hills, Sebastian wound out the throttle.

The speed increased, sending her sweater rippling in the wind. Sadie tightened her grip on Sebastian, not caring that her chest was now pressed right up to his back. Her heart raced as she held on for dear life. A bubble rose in her belly and she fought the urge to laugh. It surprised her. Because it wasn't very Sadie-like to love motorcycles.

Sebastian slowed and pulled into a long driveway that wound up a hill. Lining the driveway were evergreen trees hugged by lush green grass—the kind Sadie had only seen at country clubs and resorts. At the crest of the hill a large three-floor house came into view. It was surrounded by sweeping paddocks and immaculate garden beds.

They pulled up alongside Sebastian's Nissan, which was parked in front of a newly renovated barn with high windows showcasing a loft inside.

Sebastian jumped off the bike and waited for Sadie to dismount and take the helmet off before saying, "I figured it might be better if we take my junk car. Night will fall soon."

He motioned to the Nissan. "Jump in, I'm just gonna make sure she's not here one more time."

As he marched to the entrance of his mansion, Sadie yanked on the passenger door. It was locked. She leaned against the car and let her eyes wander to the house. Sebastian had left the front door open and she could hear him calling for his sister. The house was so big it could take him ten minutes to find her.

She wandered around the water feature and headed for the open door. "Sebastian?" she called, peering in. "Are they here?"

The inside of the house was darker than she anticipated. All the drapes were drawn, and a dim light shone from the top of the winding stairwell. Sadie slowly walked across the foyer, waiting for her eyes to adjust.

"You must be special." A voice said. "He never brings girls home."

A woman in her forties leaned in a doorway, she had a bottle in her hand and wore a tattered cardigan. She twirled the ends of her unbrushed hair, looking Sadie up and down.

Sadie recognized her. It was Sebastian's mom. Except, not quite like the campaign leader she used to be. In the press photos Sadie had seen of Sebastian's grandfather's mayor run, her hair was pristine and smile bright. Now, she was a shadow of that.

Sebastian tore down the stairs, wild eyes swinging between Sadie and his mom. He strode to Sadie and hissed, "I told you to stay in the car."

"It was locked," Sadie replied, not being able to take her eyes off the woman his mother had become.

"It's never locked, it's just a piece of shit door that jams." Sebastian clutched her elbow and ushered her to front door.

"Yeah that's it, be like your father," his mom said, taking a swig from the bottle.

Sebastian's grip loosened, hesitating for a moment. His breath rushed across Sadie's neck as he spun around. "What is that supposed to mean?"

She tucked her cardigan across her chest, bottom lip rolling out. "You're leaving me like this."

Sebastian stormed towards her, swiped the bottle, and emptied its contents into a nearby pot plant. He let his fingertips graze the top leaf and returned to his mom. "I told you that your daughter is missing. Do you even care?"

His mom chewed on her lip, tears forming in her sunken eyes. She lifted her hand and reached for him. He grimaced as she stroked his face. "I'm sorry, my sweet boy. I'm so lucky to have you. You'll never leave me, will you?"

Sebastian gave a quick glance at Sadie before peeling his mom's hands from his face. "Get some rest, momma. I'm going to find Imogen and bring her home."

FRIDAY

early evening

Sadie

Tension seemed to fill every inch of the car. Sadie felt as though she'd witnessed a part of Sebastian's life that no-one else had. A part he'd hidden well. She wondered whether his mother's drinking habit began the same time his personality changed. Long before they knew Guardians existed, something happened in the Weir household.

As they drove down Sebastian's perfect driveway, Sadie kept her eyes on the window, too nervous to look at him. "Sorry about going into your home."

"Whatever." Sebastian huffed. "Just open the glove box."

She looked at him then, letting out an apprehensive, "Why?"

Sebastian's eyes darted to her and back to the road. He sighed, shaking his head. "Just do it."

Opening a glove box would generally be a normal thing. But it was Sebastian, and the more time she spent with him, the less she realized she knew him. She stared at the latch, hands clasped in her lap.

"What do you think is in there?" Sebastian asked, amusement in his tone.

Sadie shrugged. "I don't know. Beef jerky, drugs, a severed hand?"

Sebastian guffawed. He rested his elbow on the car door and ran his thumbnail over his lips. "Fine. Don't open it then."

Curiosity got the better of her. Sadie clicked the latch and the glove box fell open. A feather, brown and white with a rose-gold painted tip, sat on top of a first-aid kit. She plucked it out—amazed and thankful at first, then disturbed. It was the feather she wore on her date, the one she lost when Damien flicked it out of her hair… right before he kissed her.

Sadie whipped her head around. "You were spying on me?"

"Don't be vain," Sebastian scoffed. "I was taking the trash out at work and saw Damien throw something. You looked upset so I searched for what it was."

Sadie glided her fingertips along the feather. "Is that all you saw?"

Sebastian didn't reply. He kept his eyes on the road as a small smirk lit his face.

"Oh my god, you saw us, didn't you?" Sadie slumped in the seat, wishing the world to swallow her whole.

Sebastian sniffed. His smirk dropped as he shot her a glance. He re-gripped the steering wheel and took a left into the main street of Cedar Falls.

"Tell me what you saw, please," Sadie begged. God help her if the rumor mill started up. It was hard enough avoiding Damien as it was. If Sebastian blabbed, the whole school knowing would make it ten times harder to tell him the truth.

"I won't tell anyone, if that's what you're worried

about." Sebastian slowed the car, eyes scanning the sidewalks.

Sadie swallowed, relieved yet surprised. "You wouldn't?"

Stopping at a red light, Sebastian tore his eyes from the sidewalks and met her gaze. "Don't be so shocked, Shorty. I can be a nice person…" He pressed his lips together, hiding a smile. "How was it anyway? You like him?"

Sadie frowned and repositioned herself in the seat. She couldn't believe this was happening. How on earth did she get stuck in a conversation with Sebastian about kissing. She pointed at the front of the car. "The light's green."

The edges of Sebastian's mouth twitched. Composing himself he put his foot back on the gas. But it wasn't over. It was far from over.

"Come on," he urged. "Give me a rating. One to ten."

"I don't know… There's not much to compare it to."

Sebastian pulled into the curb and slammed on the breaks.

"You've seen them?" Sadie asked.

She sat up straight, looking into the boutique they'd parked next to.

"Sadie Sloan," Sebastian declared. She shifted her gaze to find him facing her. "That was your first kiss?"

Sadie slammed her palm across her mouth. Had she just told him that? Where was that hole to swallow her when she needed it? "I uh… "

Sebastian waited for her answer, staring at her as though she hadn't showered in fifty days.

The conversation seemed to be happening whether she liked it or not. Resigning, she threw her hands in the air. "Yeah, sure. All right. It was my first kiss. My first ever kiss was with Damien. There, happy?"

"Happy for you? No. He's a douche nozzle."

"He's not that bad." Sadie found herself defending him.

Sebastian raised his brows. "Be honest."

How they got to this point, Sadie didn't know. But they'd come that far already, so she answered. "Okay, I'll be honest. I rate it a three out of ten. I'd rather kiss underneath the filthy bleachers than kiss him ever again. Happy now?"

Sebastian grinned and nodded once. He twisted back around, and after a long sigh he slumped onto his seat. "I really have no idea where to look for these little runaways."

Sadie wasn't like Summer. She'd never leave home without asking. She didn't know what it was like to have a rebellious bone in her body... but she did know what it was like to be a female who wanted to escape for a while.

"What's Imogen's sanctuary?" she asked.

"Huh?" Sebastian looked like she'd asked him on a date.

"Her sanctuary from the world?" Sadie explained. "Everyone has somewhere they go to get away. Mine's my bedroom."

Sebastian thought for a while. "Mine's the garden."

"The garden?" Surely he was joking.

"Don't mock it," Sebastian snarled. "You have no idea who I am."

"Okay," Sadie said, raising her hands in surrender. "Do you know where Imogen's might be?"

Sebastian thought for a moment longer. "When Dad left, she didn't take it well. So, I made a thing of brother-sister days. Every now and then, we go to the forest, along the river just up from the falls. We have picnic lunch and just chill. She told me she goes there alone sometimes, when she's feeling down."

A glimpse of the old Sebastian, the one from freshman year, shone through. Sadie didn't know how to respond. But she didn't have to. Sebastian started the ignition and swung the car around, steaming down the road to the falls.

Ten minutes later, the bitumen turned to gravel and they ascended the mountain in silence. Sadie kept her eyes out the window, searching for any teen that may be living it up in the forest. As they veered around a hair pin turn, Sadie's gaze dropped to the forest floor.

"Stop!" she screamed, already unbuckling her seat belt.

"What is it?" Sebastian asked, pulling over.

Sadie jumped out of the car and slid down the bank. Underneath the first line of trees, a blue jacket sat on top of a shrub. Sadie picked it up and turned around. As Sebastian scuttled around the car toward her, she said, "This is mine. Summer took it last night."

All color bled from his face. His expression reminded her of the look he gave, right before he saved her from Cap. She saw the neon blue glint hit his eyes. Seeing his eyes shine in the twilight made her heart pound.

Then, it hit her. Sebastian was a Guardian. A wolf Guardian.

"Can you sniff?" she blurted, holding out the jacket.

He took the jacket slowly, frowning. "I've never tried."

He cracked his neck and fully shifted into his wolf. She placed her hand on a tree, and slowly stepped behind it, bringing space between them. The wolf sniffed the jacket and a moment later, Sebastian half-shifted back. He stood up straight, glowing eyes boring into Sadie.

Noticing her hiding behind the tree, he winced. "You don't have to be afraid of me."

Summoning all her bravery, Sadie took a few steps forward and shrugged. "Oh no, I'm not."

"You're a shitty liar." As he said the last word, his fangs popped out between his lips.

Seeing Sebastian half-shifted sent Sadie's brain into overdrive. There she was on the edge of a road in the forest, just like the time when he saved her. When Cap had his eyes on her. When she thought she was going to die.

"It's just memories." Desperate to move on from that topic, she asked, "Did you pick up a scent?"

Clutching the jacket, Sebastian faced the sky and closed his eyes. His nostrils flared and within a second, his eyes burst open. He spun around to the right, and charging across the road, he called, "This way."

Sadie ran to keep up with him as he weaved through the trees, running deeper into the forest. In less than a minute, he stopped, resting his hand against the wet bark of a tree. Sebastian closed his eyes, lifting his chin up. Again, his eyes burst open and he took off to the left.

Sadie trailed behind him, sometimes losing sight. Every now and then, he'd glance back to see if she was still following. After a while, he called, "Hurry up, Shorty. Your legs will take us twice as long to find them."

As she struggled to see in the dimming light, she returned fire, "It's all right for you and your night vision."

Sebastian stopped and waited. As she approached, he stared at her and lifted the jacket back to his nose. He closed his eyes and dropped his hands, nostrils flaring as he tried to find the scent.

When he opened his eyes again, neon blues seemed to bore through her soul. Sadie flinched. She hated how on edge she was.

Sebastian tilted his head thoughtfully. "Do they know?"

"Does who know what?" Sadie frowned.

"Your friends." He began walking again, pace slow enough for her to keep up. "Do they know you're afraid of them?"

Sadie looked over at him. His eyes remained forward as he waited for her answer. It was weird that he managed to bring them to conversations that she was uncomfortable with. But that wasn't the weirdest part. The weirdest part was that he seemed genuinely interested in her answers, or that at least, she felt as though he wouldn't judge her.

She thought for a moment. No, her friends didn't know that she was afraid of them. She liked being with them and knowing their secrets, but she'd never tell them that their glowing eyes and growing fangs gave her nightmares. It would hurt them too much. And she didn't do that. She didn't hurt people. She'd hidden her true self so she didn't have to do that, amongst other things.

"There's a lot of things they don't know about me," she mused.

Sebastian glanced at her sideways and a soft smile lit his face. "Then, I guess we have something in common."

Snap.

The sound of a twig breaking in the distance caused them to halt. Sebastian swung his arm protectively in front of Sadie and he scanned the area.

"Summer?" Sadie called.

"Shh," Sebastian hushed. He dropped his arm and curled his fingers slowly around her wrist. "We gotta go."

Sadie looked down at his hand and the claws that he strategically pointed away from her skin. "What's wrong."

"Now!" he yelled, galloping back from where they came. He dragged her along behind him, dodging trees and broken branches.

Behind them, the sound of more footsteps followed. Sebastian let go of Sadie and propelled her on as he turned around to face their stalker. "Go back to the car."

Sadie peered over her shoulder. The space between the forest and the road was a good hundred yards away. Shadows of tree trunks made the path obscure. She turned back, hesitating, "But I…"

Sebastian boomed, "Sadie, seriously. You need to—"

"I don't want to be alone," she blurted.

Sebastian's face dropped. "Man. Cap really messed you up, hey?"

Sadie didn't want to cry. Not in front of the biggest jock of the school. She blinked rapidly, averting her gaze.

A few trees down, two bright pink eyes shone in the darkness. As the last light trickled through the leaves, Sadie made out the shape of a wolf. Growling, Sebastian took a hold of her hand.

Together, they ran back toward the car with the sounds of paws thumping along the ground behind them.

FRIDAY

evening

Leila

Leila burst through the Veil door. In an instant, she blinked her eyes open. The sky was dark and street lamps lit up parts of the street. In particular, two sneakers standing on the wet sidewalk before her. Craning her neck, she looked up at Damien. "We weren't there that long, were we?"

Damien jolted on the spot as though zapped by an invisible current. "Holy crap. When did you shift back?"

"Just then." Leila sat up, rubbing her head. "What happened? Where's Riley and Ren?"

Damien plonked himself onto the curb, resting his elbows onto his knees. "You were getting too strong for us. Ren said it was because you're Imprints and more powerful together. So, we separated you."

"Right. Well, that explains why Riley disappeared as soon as we got to the Veil."

Damien nodded politely as though he knew what she meant. Then, he chuckled. "I gotta tell you, seeing Ren walk a massive wolf like a dog down the street was one of the weirdest moments of my life."

Leila peered down the street, imagining the scene. She smiled. Her eyes drifted to the ground and a tiny pool of blood at her side. "Why was I on the ground?"

A grimace replaced Damien's grin. "I knocked you out. Sorry, okay? I didn't want your lion to get away on me." He stood up and reached his hand down. "Forgive me?"

Leila grabbed his hand, looking up to his sorrowful eyes. How could she be mad? His expression almost broke her heart. "Of course."

Damien gave a soft smile and shook his head, flicking the hair off his face. He hauled her upright. As she bounced to her feet, he stared at her, pupils dilating.

"I… uh…" Leila said, feeling slightly unnerved at his gaze. She casually dusted herself off. "I guess I'll see you tomorrow."

"Mmm," he mumbled, eyes bearing down on her. "Can I ask you a question?"

Leila glanced over her shoulder. She really needed to see Riley and unpack what they'd just experienced. But something seemed to be weighing on Damien and she'd feel guilty all night if she left him hanging. Turning around, she said, "Yeah?"

"Has Sadie said anything?" Damien's head dropped.

Crap! Leila had completely forgotten about Sadie's request to keep him away. At least she unintentionally helped. Trying to seem oblivious she replied, "About?"

Damien sniffed and roll shoulders back. "Aw nothin'. It doesn't matter." He cleared his throat. "Will you be at the game tomorrow?"

"Yeah, I have to photograph it."

Damien pressed his lips together in a sad smile. He began walking backward, "Okay, I'll see you there."

Remembering their newfound knowledge on how the Imprint surge works, she said, "Maybe before that. I have a mission for us."

As she turned to run for Riley's house, she swore she heard Damien mutter sarcastically, "A Leila mission. Yippee".

Leila tapped on Riley's half-open door and slid through the gap into his room. He was laying on his bed, one arm propped behind his head and the other stroking a tabby cat that had curled up on his chest. The very same cat that his mom had shooed away earlier that morning.

"That is not what I thought I'd be walking in on," Leila said, grabbing the edge of the door to close it. Remembering his mother's rule, she kept it open a sliver. She turned around and asked, "Where's Ren?"

"He went for a walk to cool off. Apparently, my wolf got outta hand." Riley propped up onto his elbows and the cat rolled to his lap. "How are you?"

Leila moved to the side of his bed and sat down. She picked up a thick book from his bedside table. As she absentmindedly flipped through pages, she wondered if she should tell him that Damien knocked her out. "I'm good."

"Are you ready for tomorrow?" Riley stopped patting the cat, his hand hovering above its back. As a revolt, the cat stood and turned, smooching its head into Riley's hand.

"Absolutely." Leila gave a curious frown. Keeping her eyes on the cat, she dropped the book onto his mattress. Shaking her head, she turned her attention to Riley and smiled. "I think this time it's really going to work."

Riley's lips lifted into a smirk. "So, you were listening to Samuel?"

Leila playfully backhanded his shoulder. "I listen!" she argued.

She leaned across the bed, eyes on his mouth, and caught him smiling before their lips connected. Almost immediately, Riley tensed.

"Oww," he cried, pushing her away. He lifted the cat, prying its claws from his thigh.

As soon as the cat was free, it darted to the window. Riley rolled off his bed and opened the window a crack. The cat slid through the opening and ran across the lawn.

Riley walked back, rubbing his legs. "It got me good."

"Is it yours now or what?" Leila asked. "Your mom was shooing it away this morning."

"Leilani Belmonte, are you jealous?" Riley teased. He plonked himself next to her and swept an arm over shoulders, pulling her into him. She rested her head on his chest, feeling the deep rumble of his voice as he said, "Don't worry, you're my favorite feline."

Leila pulled herself away and glared at him in bemusement. He gave a wide grin and pulled her back to him again, planting his lips to her forehead. "The Veil was really something, huh?"

"Mhmm," Leila agreed, letting herself snuggle into his embrace.

"You know, I've been thinking. If it works... if we can save Gabby from being a Fallen then maybe—" he paused.

Leila peered up catching Riley running his teeth over his bottom lip. "Are you thinking about your sister?"

"Yeah." Riley gently removed his arm from Leila and leaned forward. Hair fell onto his glasses as he peered over them. "Is that stupid?"

"Of course not." Leila scuttled forward and rested her hand on his back. "I mean, if it works on Gabby... Who knows, right?"

Riley nodded. He reached behind Leila and opened his bedside drawer, pulling out a photo. Moving back to his spot, he tilted it so Leila could see. The photo was of Riley and his sister, standing at a lookout. The vast space stretched behind them, the sea and the sky. Their cheeks were almost touching, and they wore identical smiles—wide and toothy. Riley didn't look much younger, he had the same hair but no glasses. Tessa's hair looked freshly dyed — a flaming red hue that curled on her shoulders. She was beautiful and a certain sparkle glistened in her eyes.

"This was on one of our trips to visit Dad. Right before she left us."

Riley didn't talk about his dad much. A few throw away comments here and there, nothing substantial enough for Leila to grab a clear idea. All she knew was that his mom had raised the two of them alone.

Testing her luck, she asked, "Is that where he lives?"

"Yeah. It's on the Pacific coastline in Oregon, near Astoria. Great place, but we only get to see him once or twice a year. I haven't seen him for a while..." his voice petered out. He rested his thumb right against Tessa's temple as though if he kept it there he'd really be touching her.

Riley inhaled sharply and dropped the photo onto the bedside table. "I have to remember what she did to us... what she is now."

He was hurting, Leila knew it from the pained expression. But even if his emotions weren't written all over his face, she'd still know. She clutched his fingers into her grasp. "We can save her," Leila said, urging Riley to meet her gaze. "We can save her, Riley."

SATURDAY

early morning

Sadie

Sadie sprung up in bed. She clutched her quilt, heart racing and lungs working overtime.

As she regained her senses and realized she was in her own room, she calmed. Sebastian had dropped her off after their ordeal in the forest. They'd been chased by someone… something. As soon as he pulled up to her curbside, she'd run inside and crawled into bed terrified.

Somehow, she'd fallen asleep from exhaustion. Or maybe it was the need to escape. It didn't really matter how she'd managed to fall asleep, because now she was wide awake.

Cedar Falls had at least one new Guardian.

And Summer was still missing.

No longer in denial, Sadie threw her quilt off and ran out of her room. She pushed her sister's door open—once a move that would have gotten her chastised. Worrying about that sort of thing seemed trivial now. It'd been two days since she'd seen her.

Summer's room was empty. Her bed still perfectly made. Heart racing, Sadie bolted down the stairs and into the living room.

Her mom was sitting on the sofa with her head buried in her hands.

While Martin paced the room yelling at the ceiling. "What did I do to deserve this? Where did I go wrong as a father? Should I have had more daddy-daughter dates? Taken her to the park more when she was little?" His gaze shifted from the ceiling to Sadie. "Am I a terrible father?"

Sadie frowned. "You're an amazing dad… apart from trying to make best friends with the boys we bring home."

Martin's bushy brows fell over his wide blue eyes. He pointed at Sadie and turned to her mom. "Why are they so different?"

"Be quiet, Marty," Natalie snapped. "It's just who she is. I don't think there's anything we could've done to change that."

Sadie slowly made her way into the middle of the room. "What are you talking about?"

Her dad pulled his phone from his back pocket, unlocked it and turned it to Sadie. The screen showed a message from Summer:

I know you don't care about me, but I'm not coming home. I thought you should know that I'm safe. Imogin and I are on the road together.

Sadie took the phone from her father and forwarded the message to her phone before passing it back. "Are you calling the police?"

Natalie sniffed. "We already have. They've got an APB out on her, so if they see her they can bring her home but considering she left of her own free will there's not much else they can do."

"She's fifteen!" Sadie declared, horrified.

Martin threw his arms in the air and began pacing in front of the sofa. He muttered, "Fifteen and a runaway. I'm the worst father in the world. Did I hug her wrong when she was a baby? Did I not feed her enough brussel sprouts." He jerked his head up. "You ate your sprouts didn't you, Sades?"

Sadie shook her head. It was no use, her parents had given up. Resigning to the fact that their rebel daughter had finally flown the coop.

Sadie ran back up the stairs. She knew better. There wouldn't be any giving up on her side.

Retrieving her phone, she found two messages displayed on the screen. The one from Summer that she forwarded from her dad's phone and one from Sebastian.

I'll be at yours in ten. Meet me out front.

Checking the time, he'd sent the message eight minutes ago. She threw on the same clothes she wore the night before and quickly brushed her hair. Her legs stretched as far as they could go as she whipped down the stairs and swung through the dining room. She grabbed an apple from the fruit bowl and burst past her parents.

"I'm going out. I'll be back later."

Sadie sat on the curb and crunched into the apple, her leg bouncing nervously as she waited. The air was as crisp as the apple, winter still holding on. She tucked her spare hand into her jeans pocket and felt something soft inside. Pulling it out, she twirled a feather between her fingertips. The golden tip shimmered as it spun.

Sadie smiled. Her heart warmed at the reminder of Sebastian's thoughtfulness to retrieve it for her. As she stared at the feather, Sebastian's car turned into her street.

She put the feather back into her pocket, dropped the half-eaten apple, and bounced to her feet.

The car stopped right in front of her and Sebastian leaned

across the passenger seat to open the door. As soon as she sat down he shoved his phone in her face. A message from Imogen:

I'm safe. Summer and I are on the road. Don't look for us.

The thrum of Sebastian's motor vibrated against Sadie's back as she read. She shook her head and unlocked her own phone. As she held it out for him to read over Summer's message, Sadie said, "I don't believe it. The grammar is too good. Summer uses text speak, even with Dad. She didn't write that."

"Imogen's name is spelled wrong." Sebastian nodded and twisted to face her. "Listen, you don't have to come if you don't want... if it's too much for you. But I'm going back to the forest where we were last night. I need to find that Guardian. She's got them, I know it."

Sadie frowned. "She?"

Sebastian squinted, one brow rising. It was a look that seemed to ask her if she was stupid. A moment later, realization hit his face. "Oh, yeah. I forget you can't see the person behind the Guardian. When I'm shifted, half or full I can see the human part of them."

"Oh." Sadie turned her gaze to her phone. She pressed her fingertips along the edges then took a shaky breath. "I'll come."

Sebastian put his hands on the wheel. "Are you sure?"

"Yes," Sadie hissed. "Just go, before I change my mind."

A smile flashed across his face and he pressed his foot to the gas. Rubber burned as he spun the car around and sped off. Sadie clutched the edges of the seat, their speed making her stomach drop.

As Sebastian slowed down, Sadie mused, "Do you think that girl is the Fallen that turned Cap?" She glanced at him, and seeing him frown, she added, "I mean, we'd known him since middle school, he wasn't always a Guardian. Someone had to have turned him."

"Haven't thought about it," Sebastian muttered, peering into the rear-view mirror.

"Maybe they were passing through town? What if they're back? And our sisters are their first victims?"

Sebastian's eyes narrowed and he leaned closer to the wheel. His eyes flitted between the mirror and the road. "We're being followed."

Sadie twisted in her seat and peered out the back window. A white hatchback with scratches on the hood sat close behind them. A woman with flaming red hair, stared back at her.

Sebastian took one hand off the wheel and tugged on Sadie's seatbelt, making sure it was fastened. He pressed his foot down and sped through the main street. Sadie held onto the ceiling, the door, the dash, anything she could grasp. He veered the car to the outskirts of town and careened down his road. The car drifted slightly as he turned into his driveway, kicking up clouds of gravel behind them.

He brought the car to a halt outside the renovated barn. Sadie's heart pounded as she stared back through the plumes of dust, waiting for the white car to appear. Sebastian leaned across her, hand reaching for the door. She could hear his breath, fast and shaking as he pushed it open.

"Get out," he commanded.

Sadie had no problems in complying. She jumped out of the car and followed him toward the barn. He slid the door open and pushed her inside.

As he closed the door behind them, Sadie glanced around. His motorcycle was parked along the wall with a sheet covering it. Lined beside the bike were gardening tools and small plants in pots. On the other side of the large room, a ladder led up to a loft-style bedroom.

Sebastian pointed to the back of the barn under the loft. "Bathroom's there. Make yourself at home."

As he headed back for the door, Sadie exclaimed, "Wait!

Where are you going?"

He faced her with his hand up against the sliding door ready to push it open. "I'm going to meet with this Guardian, find out where our sisters are. I can't bring you, Shorty. I can't risk it."

Sadie's heart dropped. He was leaving her?

He waited for a moment, softening at the look on her face. "I know you don't want to be alone. But it's the only way. Stay. Please."

Mouth dry, she just nodded her reply.

Taking it as a yes, Sebastian slid the door open and stepped outside. He closed it and peered in for a moment before racing back to the car. As he tore down the driveway, Sadie flicked the lock on the door.

Turning around, Sadie gazed up at the loft. It was a small space, enough for a double bed — unmade, she noted — that pressed up against the triangle-shaped window. Her heart reached her throat. She was in Sebastian's private room. She wondered how many girls he'd brought there. Her eyes drifted to the gardening tools and soil scattered on the floor. Maybe not that many. Maybe this was the Sebastian he never showed anyone. His mom did say he'd never brought a girl over.

Noticing a sofa behind the ladder, Sadie sauntered over and plonked herself onto it. She pulled out her phone and re-read the message from Summer-not Summer. Someone had gone to a lot of trouble to make sure she wouldn't be found.

Tears formed in her eyes. If Sebastian wasn't so close to his sister, god knows how long it would've taken her to notice something was wrong. Maybe she would have believed the message, too.

The sound of tires traveling along gravel caught her attention. She dabbed the wetness from her eyes and smiled to herself. Sebastian must have changed his mind about her company. He could protect her and find their sisters at the same time.

Sadie craned her neck to see a white hatchback pulling up around the water feature. Her heart double-timed. She dropped her phone and leapt off the sofa, crouching behind the ladder. As the woman stepped out of the car, Sadie turned her back to the ladder and squeezed her eyes shut. Her chest felt like it was going to explode.

As footsteps crunched along the gravel, closer and closer, Sadie's fight or flight response kicked in. She darted her eyes open, staring straight out towards the back of the barn. A door.

Without looking back, she leapt over the sofa and bolted for the door. Turning the handle, she was relieved to find it unlocked. She wasn't brave like Leila or Gabby. She was a weak scaredy cat, destined to be the easy prey. Just like with Cap.

Hoping against all hope that the person didn't see her, Sadie ran out into a paddock and headed for the forest boundary. It wasn't until she reached the tree-line when she took a quick moment to glance over her shoulder. The white car was still parked in the driveway, but no sign of the woman… or an animal.

The sound of more tires barreling down the driveway echoed across the hill. Sebastian's car came screaming up to the barn and he let it stall as he jumped out.

Even from fifty yards away, she could see his eyes as they flashed neon-blue. He stared at something, slowing moving closer to the barn. Then, he shifted into his wolf. It was enough to jolt Sadie back into a full-pelt run. She moved into the forest, letting the branches and leaves block the sunlight and cast shadows into the lingering morning fog.

She decided if she kept running straight, eventually she'd hit the road. Someone was sure to see her and stop. A crack behind her made her heart skip a beat. With legs that felt like jelly, she picked up her pace. She wasn't sure how much longer she could run at that speed; she definitely didn't have the athleticism for it. She looked over her shoulder and saw a shadow dart between two trees. *Quicker, Sadie Sloan, quicker.* As she looked forward again, her foot caught a fallen branch and she fell forward, crashing onto soil and dead leaves.

"Sadie?" She heard Sebastian call for her. His voice sounded so far away.

"Sebastian!" She screamed, rolling over to assess the damage. Her knee stung and blood seeped through her already ripped jeans. Her breath rolled out in front of her face, the chill of the day finding her lungs. Between a small gap in the trees, she saw the road.

Would she wait for Sebastian or find help for herself? A wolf's howl lifted into the air around her. Making her decision, she scrambled to her feet and propelled herself toward the road. As she broke through the forest and her shoes hit the bitumen the sound of an approaching car made her gasp a sigh.

She began waving her arms in preparation.

"Sadie?" Sebastian's voice sounded closer.

She glanced over her shoulder, straining her eyes to see him. But the forest was dark and shadowy and full of fearful possibilities. The car rolled along the road and Sadie turned back, eager for safe reprieve.

As the car came into view, her face dropped as she recognized the white hatchback with scratches on the hood. The woman with red hair, pulled the car to the side of the road and opened the door. Sadie hurled herself back into the forest.

"Sebastian!"she screamed.

"Sadie?" he replied, his cry echoing through the trees.

Sadie stopped, head jerking in all directions. It was difficult to know where his voice came from. She hesitated, palm resting against a tree. Which way would she run?

The split second was enough to seal her fate.

A growling rumble rose from behind her.

Slowly turning around, Sadie found piercing neon-pink eyes staring at her. The wolf wasn't as large as Sebastian or

Riley or even Gabby, but its fur was light brown, a beautiful cedar color that looked soft to the touch. For a split moment, Sadie was mesmerized by the beauty but then she noticed a drop of blood trickle from a fang to the ground.

The wolf shook its head, transforming into a woman around twenty years of age. Up close, Sadie noticed her wavy hair was dyed. The woman wore a graphic tee with a panda on it and a black choker hugged her neck. Her eyes lowered and she wiped her bloody chin with the back of her hand.

She stepped closer to Sadie. "I've got your sister and now I've got you."

SATURDAY

morning

Leila

Gabby crossed her arms. She stood in the clearing in front of the falls and tapped her maroon Doc Martin boots on the soil. "And this is the last time we'll try this?"

Leila nodded. "Very last, I promise. If it doesn't work, we will stop."

A small wrinkle deepened in between Gabby's brows, almost as if she was afraid of the outcome. She nodded to herself.

"It'll work," Riley said, reassuringly. Then, under his breath, he mumbled, "It has to."

Swallowing, Gabby dropped her arms to her sides. "Where do you want me?"

"There's fine," Leila said, glancing over her shoulder to Ren.

He tugged on the bottom of his leather jacket and sniffed. As hard as he was to read, his presence calmed Leila. It reminded her of the Veil. Like some kind of deep knowledge lived within him.

Ren moved to Gabby and nodded at the ground. "You might want to sit. If their combined power is as strong as it should be, you'll want to be anchored."

Gabby's eyes widened, she peered around him to Leila. "Will it hurt?"

"I…" Leila swallowed. "I don't know."

There was something final about that moment. They'd tried and hoped before but right then in that place and time, Leila felt something significant was about to happen. She'd found the key to ignite their power and maybe Gabby sensed her fear. How strong were they?

Gabby took a quick breath and sat. She brought her knees up to her chest and hugged her arms around them. It was a different Gabby than Leila was used to seeing. Once head strong and defiant, now a puddle of nerves and uncertainty.

Behind them, Damien cleared his throat. "And what do you want me to do?"

"Don't know about you," Ren said, rushing out of the clearing. "But I'm gonna stand back a bit." He passed the forest edge a few trees in and found a trunk to lean against. Sweeping his arm beside him, he motioned for Damien to join him.

"Yeah, just stick around, in case…" Riley darted his eyes to Gabby and back to Damien. "Just… keep watch."

Leila felt her insides tighten. This was it. Everything she'd worried about for the last three months was about to all become better. She wasn't scared. She was excited.

"Are you ready?" Leila asked.

Gabby pulled her legs in closer to her body, clasping her forearms. "Hurry the hell up. Let's get this over with."

Riley moved beside Leila, and as he took her hand, Gabby squeezed her eyes shut.

"Okay," Riley whispered. "You know what you have to

do?"

Leila took one more look at Gabby. After this moment, all her pain will wash away with her Guardian. A sense of peace rushed through Leila. She was about to save her best friend from the darkness that chased her.

Facing Riley, Leila took both his hands in hers. She smiled as she let her eyes dance over his face. He'd lifted his glasses and rested them on his head, and a few blond strands poked through the middle. His brown eyes flitted between hers, and she knew, with his super vision, he could see every hue in her hazel irises. He gave a small tilted smile.

"I know exactly what to do," she replied.

Re-gripping his hands, she pulled them up, resting their clenched fists between them. Riley shuffled closer, his eyes locked on her. Leila nodded and together, they half-shifted, bringing their Guardians in alignment. She felt an aura of strength fill her senses, a golden glow around her as her lion stepped forward.

Riley jerked his head to the side and his wolf arched its neck, howling to the sky. She clutched his hands so tight she could hardly feel anything else but the steady strum of his pulse through his palms. Leila licked her lips and remembered what Samuel had said. The surge was fueled by their love. She allowed herself to revel in it.

She loved him.

He lied to her and yet she loved him.

He marked her and yet she loved him.

He loved her and…

She loved him.

She loved him.

She loved him.

In a split second, she saw her shimmering aura reach for him. His did the same. Their lights came together in the middle, and like glass shattering, specks of gold and blue burst outward. It tumbled around them like a dust storm, gathering up speed and momentum as it went. An almighty crack thundered around them as the cluster of light expanded.

Leila flicked her head to Gabby and watched the surge fly through her. Leila watched as Gabby's silver wolf stood beside her, its paws planted on the ground as though weathering a storm. The propulsion moved through Gabby, tumbling beyond the clearing.

It hit Ren next, pushing his back against a tree. His panther beside him blinked once, then shook its head. The surge of light washed over Damien, and as it moved through him, it took a hold of the yellow eagle, standing stoically by his side. The eagle shrieked as it tumbled backward, its aura breaking apart into a million flickers.

The surge petered out and Leila returned her eyes to Riley, noticing one of them was gold and the other blue. She let his hands go and stepped back to watch his golden eye switch back to normal.

"My eagle!" Damien cried, his jawline suddenly less defined. He patted his shrinking biceps. "What have you done to me?"

Gabby stood, she gazed down to her side, her wolf still in prime place next to her. Ren's eyes flashed obsidian as he pored over Damien, craning his neck to see around.

But there was nothing to see.

There was no eagle beside Damien. He had no Guardian. He was no Guardian.

Just a regular human, like before.

Quiet chatter echoed through the swimming hall. People milled to the stand, taking their seats ahead of the game. Cedar Falls Varsity team were playing against their long-term rivals from Graystone Academy. It was the biggest game of the season so far.

And Leila couldn't care one bit.

She fiddled with her camera settings and lifted the viewfinder to her eye. She tried to focus on something; a net cutting through the water, a cheerleader stretching, the referee's whistle around his neck, but her finger shook too much to press the shutter button.

Riley sat next to her, his leg bouncing underneath him. The movement distracted Leila, with the camera still up to her eye she peered at her anxious boyfriend. He lifted his phone and scrolled through to Damien's name. Riley gave Leila a weak smile as he hit the call button and chewed on his lips as he waited for an answer.

"Why him and not me or Ren?" Gabby said on the other side.

Leila sighed and placed her camera in her lap. "I don't know… I really don't know."

"Damien?" Riley said a little too loudly, garnering a few annoyed glances from the people in front. "Where the hell are you?"

Leila shared a glance with Gabby, whose bottom lip rolled out. "It was meant to be me," Gabby sobbed, tears forming in the corners of her eyes.

The sight made Leila's heart sink. She knew Gabby was struggling but the look on her face was something else. It was almost as though she was in turmoil.

Leila placed her hand on Gabby's knee. "Is it —"

"I'm gonna go be with Damien, he's pretty rattled," Riley interrupted. Leila nodded, watching him as he stood. He bent down and kissed her full on the lips. "I'll text you."

Leila watched him side-step out of the aisle. When he was gone, she turned to Gabby. "Is it that bad?"

Gabby shrugged, wiping her cheek. "It's not terrible, like I don't think I'll kill anyone again… I just have this—" She stopped talking and pressed her palm against her heart and tapped.

That was it. Leila couldn't bear seeing her best friend in

so much inner turmoil. She found Gabby's eyes. "I know I said that was the last time, but we can try again if you wanted?"

Gabby averted her gaze and shook her head. "Maybe it's selective. Maybe I'm too far gone. Maybe it's my punishment for not saving my brother."

A splash. And then another. Leila turned her attention to the pool as the team jumped into the water. Thomas swam to the goals. When he was a Fallen, before Leila and Riley dispelled his and Crystal's Guardians, Crystal had said something about Riley being their first kill. And Damien, in any fight, always made sure his opponent was alive.

"They hadn't killed anyone," Leila mused, wondering if that's how the surge worked.

"Huh?" Gabby asked.

A shoulder bumped up against Leila. "Ugh," Taj said, plonking himself in the spot where Riley had been. He ripped his back-pack open and pulled out a small laptop. "They're stalling the game because they don't have their star player."

Leila squinted, glancing over the team as they swam in circles to warm up. She counted their heads but there was no Sebastian. "Where is he?"

"No one's heard from him since yesterday afternoon." Taj gave an ominous smile. "Isn't it great?"

If there was one person she could count on for being forever the same, it was Taj. She teased, "If you say so, drama llama."

Taj cleared his throat. "That's gossip queen to you, Leilani Bel-Montessori."

Leila smirked. "Always a pleasure, my queen."

Taj reached his hand back into his bag and pulled out a packet of Reece's Peanut Butter Cups. He tore the bag open and held it out, "Want one?"

As she dug her hand in, movement in the row behind caught her eye. Someone shuffled in front of people, disturbing the whole row. Knees lifted and annoyed mutters arose. There were plenty of seats at the end of the rows, but the person settled right behind Leila.

Seeing them up close, Leila raised her eyebrows. It was Sebastian. His hair was unkempt and unwashed tendrils fell over his eyes. For a split second, he reminded her of Riley and the way he'd let his hair fall that way sometimes.

Sebastian clenched his jaw and whispered, "Sadie's been taken."

Leila swiveled around fully. Did she hear him correctly? "I'm sorry, what did you say?"

Sebastian huffed, rolled his shoulders forward and leaned so close that his face was barely two inches from hers. "I said. Sadie has been taken. By a Fallen."

Leila shot up and Sebastian was quick to do the same. She stared at him for a short moment as a thought flickered into her mind—what if he's lying? What if she'd been wrong the whole time? What if he was bad and she's misjudged him? What if it was a trap?

He stared at her with imploring eyes. He looked tired and desperate. The same look he gave her when he asked her for help in the library, right after he killed Miss Carson.

"Is he bothering you?" Gabby asked, rising. Her eyes turned to slits and a flash of silver lit them.

Sebastian remained completely still, glaring at Leila. She decided then to trust him. She had to. Handing her camera bag to Taj, she said, "We gotta go."

"Hey?" Taj called as Leila pushed Gabby down the row. "Leila! Not again! You've got a job to do!"

There wasn't time to explain. No time for sorrys. She'd have to make it up to him… again.

As Leila rushed down the stairs, Gabby puffed behind her. "What's going on?"

Leila pushed the doors open. Sebastian was already halfway across the front lawn, heading for his car. Picking up her speed, she called over her shoulder, "He says Sadie's been captured by a Fallen."

"What?" The sound of following footsteps halted.

Leila glanced over her shoulder and noticing Gabby frozen on the spot, she rushed back to her. "I don't know. Okay. I don't know if we should believe him, but if he's telling the truth and we don't do anything—"

"I'll call her." Gabby whipped her phone from her back pocket and pressed number 2 on her speed dial. The longer it rang the quicker her breathing became.

"Are you coming?" Sebastian called.

Gabby glared at him then looked down at her unanswered phone. "I don't trust him."

Leila licked her lips and grabbed her best friend's shoulders. "Come on, Gabs. This is Sadie."

Gabby looked up, decisively. "Stall him. Say you need to make a plan or something. Take him to your house, call Riley. I'll go to Sadie's to make sure she's not home."

"What happened to the reckless versions?" Sebastian said, right behind them. The girls spun to face him. He scowled, "I came to you because you jump first, you act without thinking. But these sniveling versions? Sadie will die before you make your decision to trust me or not."

Leila's heart bounded to her throat. All doubt left her. She called her lion forward, aligning in half-shift. As her fangs grew, she said, "Of course I believe you, let's go find her."

Sebastian smiled and shook his head. "Good, there's the Leila I need. But—I can't believe I'm saying this—" Sebastian pointed to Gabby. "Spider is right. We need a team. Call your dick boyfriend and let's get this search started."

SATURDAY

late morning

Leila

Leila was pacing in her living room when a knock rattled her door. Before she was able to take a step, the door opened and Riley stepped in. He threw a thumb over his shoulder, and Leila peered around him to see Damien skulking through the gate at end of path.

He said, "Found him."

Watching Damien slowly drag his feet down the path, hair hanging limply over his face, she whispered, "How is he?"

Riley opened his mouth to say something but shrugged instead. He walked in and Leila left the door open for Damien. She felt bad for him, she didn't mean to do what they did. But in that moment in time, it was the least of their problems.

She turned to Riley. "We've got a prob—"

"Mark me," Damien demanded. He stood in the

doorway, holding his T-shirt down at the collar.

"Damien," Riley said softly, "I don't know if it will—"

"Just do it."

Riley gave Leila an exasperated glance and moved to Damien. He placed his hand over the curve of Damien's shoulder. For a second, Riley's eyes flashed blue and his fangs popped between his teeth.

When Riley was done, Damien flipped his shirt back up and dragged his sorry body to the sofa. Falling onto the cushions, he covered his face with his hands. "I need this. It has to work, I'm nothing if I'm not a Guardian."

With a sinking heart, Leila forced herself to ignore his pain. She returned her attention to Riley. "We've got a bigger problem."

As he closed the door, he asked. "What's wrong?"

Leila hesitated for a moment, wondering how on earth she could say it. But there was no other way than the truth. "Sadie's missing."

Riley's face dropped. Sheer terror hit his eyes.

"What?" Damien sat up at the same time Gabby and Sebastian entered the room.

The terror on Riley's face morphed into anger. Pointing at Sebastian, he hissed, "What's he doing here?"

Sebastian curled his lip and scowled. "Apparently everyone has been too busy with their little side quests they forgot about the precious human they should've been protecting."

"Just tell them about what happened," Gabby moaned.

Sebastian ran his tongue between his teeth, letting a hissing noise come out. He sighed, and a softer side broke through the cracks in his tough exterior. "It's my fault. Our sisters have been missing since Thursday night. I enlisted Sadie's help to find them, but…" He paused, brows falling to his eyes. "She got caught."

"This is just typical of a Fallen," Riley chided. "Doesn't think about the bigger picture, doesn't care about anyone but their own agenda. Doesn't matter who gets hurt in the process."

"I'm here now aren't I? Doesn't that mean I give a crap?" Sebastian retorted.

Riley tensed, hands balling into fists. "Yeah, what's in it for you? You're working for whoever took her and want us too?"

Before Riley did something he'd regret, Leila stepped in front of him and placed her hands on his chest. "Just hear him out."

Sebastian glanced to Leila as though thankful for back-up, he quickly rolled his shoulders back. "Listen, I get it, this isn't ideal. You think I want to be here in your pissy little clan? No. I just… " He clenched his jaw. "I just want my sister back. And I thought you might like your sidekick back, too."

Leila heard a rush of air expel from Riley's nostrils. He whispered, "I knew he didn't care about her."

From his seat on the sofa, Damien twisted around. "Anyway, what were you doing with Sadie? She's human. She's small. How could she help you find your sister?"

Sebastian chortled to himself. "I thought her friends of all people would know that she hates to be alone." Damien's face dropped and Sebastian seemed to revel in it. He grinned. "Oh, the things I know about her that you don't. Makes you jealous doesn't it? She's tougher than you lot give her credit for."

That statement hurt Leila. She knew Sadie well. Enough to tell her the secret of her mark. Enough to trust her. So, why didn't Sadie tell her about Sebastian and their sisters?

"As if she'd be remotely interested in you," Damien said, standing.

Sebastian's eyes widened. "Whoa, man, you look sick. What the hell is wrong with you?" Half-shifting, his eyes traced Damien's body. "Holy shit, you've lost your Guardian. How'd that happen?"

Behind Sebastian, Gabby's eyes flashed silver, giving a hateful stare to the back of his head. Leila shook her head, urging her friend to calm down. She said, "It doesn't matter. Arguing won't get us anywhere. We need to focus. We need to find Sadie and your sisters."

Leila felt Riley's hand clasp her shoulder and squeeze. He stepped to the middle of the room, chest puffing up. "She's right. What's important is we find them. We need more eyes. I'll call Ren. Leila? Call Kiko."

An hour later, they were all sitting in Leila's living room. Except Gabby, who had gone to Sadie's in case they returned. Bar a few icy glances and grimaces, it was deathly silent.

"Are we really gonna sit here and twiddle our fingers?" Sebastian scowled.

Riley glared at him. "And I suppose you want to run out there and search for her, getting more of us in danger?" He turned to Leila. "He's the Fallen, we were warned about this."

"Stop it." Leila tried to say it without emotion, but a sliver of frustration slipped through. "Kale and Kiko should be here soon. She's been a Guardian longer than any of us. She'll help us."

"I'm just saying," Sebastian said, foot tapping against the coffee table. "We're wasting precious time here."

He was right. Leila itched to get out there, to search for her friend. "Maybe we can get out there and tell them where we are."

Riley frowned as if she'd asked him to bungee jump without a cord. "We're not equipped for this. We need some guidance. We need to be smart about it." He glanced at his phone and dialed Ren's number again. As he waited for an answer, his eyes darted to Sebastian's thumping foot. "Can you stop that?"

Sebastian dropped his foot to the ground and leaned forward in his chair. His eyes turned to slits as he glared at Riley, then Leila, then Damien. Taking in Damien's new form, his lip curled into a smirk. "You should probably go home. You're not a Guardian anymore, it's probably not safe for you."

"No one asked you," Damien hissed.

"That's it, I'm done." Sebastian pushed himself off the chair and headed for the door. "You losers can wait but I'm out. I'll take the action to save their lives."

"Sebastian!" Leila sprung up. He stopped at the door and glanced over his shoulder. "Call me if you find them."

He nodded and left.

As soon as the door shut, Damien stood. He looked between Leila and Riley through darkened tendrils. "He's right, you know. I'm no use."

"You've got brains," Leila offered. "We need brains."

Damien gave a sad smile. "I'll be at home if you need me."

Leila watched him skulk away. She threaded her hands through her hair and walked the length of the living room and back again. "I don't know what to do. I don't know where to start. Why have they taken her? What do they want?"

"It's a game," Riley replied with a somber voice. "The Fallen mark people and let them out into the wild and hunt them. It's all just a heartless thrill."

The thought made her want to hurl. Sadie wasn't a toy. "Is there any way to track other Guardians? I mean, you said when I was marked it was like a beacon, what's that like?"

"It's exactly that. You saw the light that streamed from your mark when Kiko activated the Imprint… it's sort of like that, but we can only see it while in half or full-shift. Like a bright neon sign telling us there's someone waiting to be transitioned."

"Why couldn't you see all the Fallen being marked… from Cap?"

"I didn't go around with my wolf eyes all the time," Riley said, his tone a little defensive.

Leila stopped pacing. "I didn't mean it as an accusation."

"I know," he said, softer. "I just wish I had done that… you know."

Leila moved to the window and aligned with her lion. She stared above roof tops to see any beam of light that may show a newly marked human. Seeing nothing but gray clouds, she returned to human form. She turned around and leaned against the window. "Is there any other way of tracking someone who's already a Guardian?"

Riley leaned his elbows to his knees, dropping his eyes to his feet. "That's what I want to ask Ren. But he won't answer his god-damned phone."

A scratch at the window made Leila jump. She leapt and spun at the same time. As she landed, her eyes fell on a cat. The same one from Riley's house.

"What is with this cat?" Leila tapped on the glass. "Go away."

A light chuckle hit her ears. Riley gently placed a hand on Leila's back and leaned around her to unlatch the window. "It's harmless."

The cat bounded through the gap. It landed at Riley's feet, smooching an infinity symbol around his legs. Seeing the small animal attracted to her boyfriend, softened Leila.

"Look at that," she teased, kneeling down. "You've got a new girlfriend."

Leila hovered her hand above the cat's head, but as she went to stroke it the cat swung its paw at her. Claws dug into her skin and Leila jolted back from the scratch. The cat scuttled under the sofa in fright.

"Hey!" Leila said, offended. She half-shifted. "Don't pick a fight with a lion, Kitty."

"Whoa!" Riley grabbed her by the shoulder, stopping her

from peering under the sofa. "You can't shift in front of a domestic animal. You'll traumatize it."

He bent down and the cat scurried into his arms. He placed it on the windowsill. "You'd better go, pretty one."

"I bet that's what you say to all the felines," Leila teased, rubbing her arm. The scratch had already healed but the rejection was fresh.

"Ha!" Riley guffawed, closing the window. He looked across the lawn and froze. "Oh, my god."

Leila's heart bounced at his sudden change in demeanor. She rushed to his side. "What? Is it Sadie?"

Sure enough, three blond girls ran up the pathway.

"Yeah… and…" Riley spun on his heels and swung the door open.

Leila looked down the path, behind Sadie and Summer and Imogen, was one more person. One with red hair. They looked familiar and Leila couldn't quite get a grasp on how she knew her. Whoever it was, set Riley on edge again.

SATURDAY

Sadie

There was a time in Sadie's life where the worst thing she could imagine happening was showing up to school accidentally naked. Then she learned about Guardians and suddenly bare skin didn't equate to the fear of being hunted. But the worst thing about them wasn't their fangs or their eyes or the way their face contorted when they half-shifted; the worst thing was not knowing who was good and who was bad.

The Guardian with red hair clutched Sadie by the elbow and dragged her into the white hatchback. She didn't say a word as they tore down the road away from Sebastian's property. Sadie had glanced out the rear window, hoping to see a glimpse of him, but they'd driven around the bend too quickly.

"I'm Tessa," the Guardian said, glancing in the rear-view mirror. She smiled but it seemed forced. "And you don't seem surprised that I'm a werewolf. Scared but not surprised."

Sadie looked around the floor of the back seat, wondering if there was a jack or some kind of weapon she could use to knock this Tessa girl out.

"Your friend," Tessa continued. "You know he's a werewolf, too, don't you?"

"He's not a werewolf." Sadie shocked herself with the venom in her normally friendly-to-all-people voice. "He's a Guardian."

Tessa's eyebrows shot up. "Humans aren't supposed to know about Guardians."

"Well, I do." Sadie looked at her hands and her bony wrists. Tessa was small too, but she knew how deceivingly strong Guardians were. There's no way she could attack her and get out of it alive. So, she settled back in the seat and stared at her kidnapper with a scowl. "Where's Summer?"

Hesitating, Tessa swallowed. "She's safe. Now."

Sadie frowned. "What do you mean, now?"

Tessa took a breath and looked at Sadie again as though trying to decide whether or not to answer. She must have decided to tell the truth because the next thing she said was: "Summer and Imogen were taken by a Fallen. The two of them, and you, were on my list."

"And what are you going to do with us?" Sadie asked, stomach sinking.

"What do you mean?" Tessa asked. Through the rear-vision mirror Sadie saw Tessa's eyes squint. "I thought you knew what Guardians were?"

"They're meant to protect humans," Sadie said with spite.

"Right, so you're my charge. I'm protecting you."

Sadie was confused. "I thought you said I was on your hit list?"

"It's not a *hit* list. I'm not a Fallen." Tessa cracked, laughing full and loud. Within a few seconds, her mouth snapped shut and her gaze darted to the mirror again. "Oh my god, are you okay? You must have been so afraid. I didn't mean to…" She pulled up to the curb on the edge of the main street and turned in her seat to look at Sadie face on. "I'm so sorry if I scared you."

Sadie glanced at the unlocked door. She considered bursting out of the car and running inside to the Burger Lounge. But Tessa said she had Summer and Imogen. Plus, Sebastian would never forgive her if she bailed now.

In order to get to the girls, Sadie needed to be brave. They depended on her. She looked Tessa square in the eyes and asked, "Where's my sister and her friend?"

Tessa's mouth grew into a wide grin. She bit her bottom lip to contain it and tapped the window. "They're in here."

Tessa whipped around and threw her door open quickly. She ran to Sadie's door and held it open. As Sadie stepped onto the footpath, Tessa whispered, "They don't know I'm a Guardian, I normally don't mention that kind of thing. Can you keep it a secret?"

Sadie nodded and followed Tessa into the Burger Lounge. At the end booth, two blond haired girls were sitting opposite a guy with denim-blue dreadlocks. Tessa slid in next to him and smiled at the girls, pointing behind them to Sadie.

"Summer?" Sadie rested her hand on the back of the seat and peered into the booth. "Imogen?"

Summer glanced up, dark circles shadowing her eyes. Beside her, Imogen's own eyes glistened with tears. Their hair was unbrushed and ratty—something neither of them would have been comfortable with. They wore the same clothes as the night of Sadie's date; the last time she saw them.

Sadie's heart broke, what kind of trauma had they endured?

Her little sister, once abrasive and vague, lurched off her seat and fell into Sadie's arms. It was the first hug they'd shared in a while. In fact, Sadie couldn't quite remember the last time. Summer held on tight, sobbing into Sadie's hair.

Imogen stood. She crossed her arms across her chest, her eyes scouring the space behind Sadie. "Have you seen Seb?"

"Yes," Sadie replied. She reached for Imogen and dragged her into the huddle. "Your brother has been terrified. He'll be so happy to see you."

Tessa cleared her throat. She glanced at her dread-locked friend and back. "Sit down, girls. I'm just going to talk to Sadie for a bit."

"No," Sadie declared, letting her hands find Summer's and Imogen's hands. "What? Why? I'm not leaving them."

She stood her ground, staring at the boy. She didn't know him. For all she knew he was the Fallen who kidnapped them in the first place, and this was all some sick joke to dangle them in her face before whisking them away again.

"It's not something I wish to say in front of them," Tessa said through her teeth.

Sadie hesitated. She glanced at Imogen's tear-stained cheeks, then to Summer.

"It's okay," Summer urged, slipping her hand from Sadie's grasp. She plonked down into the booth. "They saved us. We can trust them."

The boy with dreadlocks winked at Summer, and Tessa said, "See? Please?"

"Two minutes." Sadie conceded. She pointed out the window. "Outside. I want to see them the whole time."

They moved to the footpath right outside the booth's window. Summer sipped on a milkshake and gave Sadie a gleeful wave. She looked so happy and it was the first real genuine smile she'd gotten from her in years. Maybe Tessa was a good Guardian after all.

Still, Sadie knew she needed to be careful. Cap was the nicest guy in school and look at how that turned out. She tore her eyes from Summer and glared at Tessa. "What is it?"

"Okay," Tessa started, "So, Jamal and I got the charge for

Imogen, and… you."

Sadie felt her hard gaze waver. "What does that mean? Charge?"

Sighing, Tessa explained, "Guardians… True Guardians report to the Veil. We are given jobs, people to watch over. Sometimes that means we hide in the shadows and keep an eye on things. Sometimes that means we intervene, like…" She waved her hand to the girls. "And we stay until we know they are safe from that which threatened them."

"And… what's threatening them." Sadie wasn't too sure she wanted to know, but it was too late, she'd already asked.

"That's the thing. Our charge was for Imogen and you, not Summer. Somehow, we've ended up being caught in two threats."

Sadie couldn't comprehend what Tessa meant. "Two threats?"

Tessa clutched Sadie's shoulder. "Listen, your sister and Imogen were captured by a Fallen, they've been targeted. Either someone thinks they'd make good warriors or they're being used as bait. That wasn't my assignment, something else is going on in this town. My assignment was to protect you and Imogen."

Sadie took a step back, away from Tessa's touch. "Against what?"

A sad look shot across Tessa's face, almost as if she was sorry to say it. "Her brother. Sebastian Weir. He's what threatens her. He's what threatens you."

Shaking her head, Sadie fought the urge to laugh. "That's ridiculous. Sebastian loves her, he'd never do anything to harm her. Not a single hair on her head."

Tessa's eyes turned to slits. "He's a Fallen… you don't know that?"

"Of course I know that," Sadie hissed. "But he's not bad."

"Ha!" Tessa guffawed. "All Fallen are bad."

"He saved my life once, you know? I would have been killed if it wasn't for him. He killed his Alpha just to keep me alive. And, he was trying to protect me from you."

Sadie wanted to add: *"and he's protective. And thoughtful. And caring. And… gorgeous."* She bit her lip, embarrassed at the last thought.

"He killed a Fallen Alpha?" Tessa's brows dropped. She shook her head. "Regardless, that was the assignment. And I'm sorry but Imogen can't return to her brother. We can't risk it."

Sadie's mind whirred. Sebastian won't allow that. He'd tear through everyone to get her back. And that would only prove their point of his Fallen nature. She had to think of something.

"Listen, I appreciate you looking after us. But there are True Imprints here in town. One of them is my best-friend. They can take it from here."

"Imprints? I've heard about them," Tessa said. A wave of concern washed over her face. "Are you sure they're True Guardians? I don't want to go near them if they're Fallen—"

"They're True," Sadie interrupted. "The Truest of True. So True you'll want to puke."

Tessa jerked her head to Jamal and tapped on the glass. Emotionless, she commanded, "Take me to them."

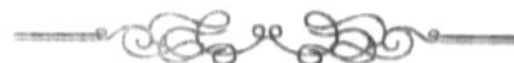

Sitting in the back seat of the car, Sadie stretched her hand over Tessa's shoulder and pointed to Leila's house. As Jamal pulled up to the curb, it took all of her inner strength not to leap out of the car and run for the door. The day had seen her frightened for Summer, frightened for herself, relieved for Summer, and then… unsure of everything. She didn't know if she was doing the right thing by brushing off Tessa's concerns about Sebastian. But there was one thing she did know, Leila's clarity could defuse any situation.

Tessa stepped out first, heading quickly through the front gate. Sadie waited for Summer and Imogen to get out of the car and climbed out. As the three girls followed, a tabby cat bounced across the front lawn.

"You've got to be kidding me!" Tessa chided, stopping in her tracks. She swung her head around and glared at Jamal.

Inside the car, Jamal reached across the car and clicked the passenger door open. The cat leapt inside. Sadie stared for a moment, watching as the cat transformed into a girl.

The front door swung open and footsteps echoed on Leila's porch. Sadie spun around to see Riley. He stared at Tessa, fists clenching and mouth agape.

The tiniest peep flew through Tessa's lips.

Leila peered around Riley's shoulder and Sadie's instincts took over. She couldn't help herself. She tore past Summer and Imogen, muddy shoes thumping awkwardly along the path. Riley stepped to one side as she ran up the steps and burst inside. Clutching Leila's wrist, Sadie glanced back to make sure her sister and Imogen were close behind her.

"Oh my god, Sadie!" Leila said, pulling her in close. "We've been so worried. Are you okay?"

After a short hug, Leila lurched back. She pulled Sadie's sleeve up and inspected her arms. Next, she tugged at her collar, peeking at her neck and shoulder. Leila pressed the back of her hand onto Sadie's forehead as she asked, "Are you itchy? Do you have a fever?"

Trying not to laugh, Sadie grabbed Leila's hands and lowered them. "I'm fine. Not marked."

At the same time Leila visibly relaxed, Riley croaked, "Tessa?"

Leila tensed again, her head whipping to the door. She squawked, "Tessa?"

"Wait?" Sadie said, leaning around to get a better view of Riley. "You know her?"

Tessa stopped on the porch, eyes low and piercing. "Hello, brother."

SATURDAY

noon

Riley

Seeing Tessa sent Riley's heart into overdrive. It was hard for him to look at his sister and not see the one who had comforted him in times of sadness… to not see the one who had teased him endlessly for his love of science fiction… the one who knew his fears and his hopes.

The Tessa Riley grew up with was kind and thoughtful. Even though she had two years on him, she'd never make him feel like he was her annoying kid brother. She'd go out of her way to make him feel wanted, especially the times their dad canceled visits. Growing up, everything she did seemed to be made of pure gold.

But that Tessa disappeared the moment she became a Guardian. She'd almost killed their mother, she'd destroyed their home, she'd run them out of town. The girl he once knew and loved had changed.

He reminded himself of that as he stared at her, standing barely a yard away. His sister was gone. And a monster was living in her body.

With all the girls inside, he placed his hands on either side of the doorway, blocking Tessa out. "What did you do with them?"

"Me? I saved them, Will—"

"It's Riley," he scowled. "My name is Riley now."

"Okay," Tessa said, unimpressed. She took a long breath and smiled to herself. "So, you're the famed Imprint. You can't say fate doesn't have a sense of humor."

"What's that supposed to mean?" None of it seemed funny to Riley. A cruel Fallen was hiding behind his sweet sister's face, taunting him with every sound of her voice.

Tessa's head dropped. Her hands clenched together in front of her. When she looked back up, her eyes glassy with tears.

The sadness in her eyes gave him pause. But only for a moment. His biceps contracted, forcing himself to clutch the door frame harder. Half-shifting, he curled his lips to display his fangs. He couldn't let her deceive him.

Tessa's lips trembled as she asked, "Why did you do this to yourself?"

Riley felt Leila's gentle hand press between his shoulder blades. She seemed to know the answer before he even said it. "To protect our family... from you."

"But them?" Tessa's tear-filled eyes rose to the sky, her nose flaring. "You chose *them* to turn you?"

Riley frowned. "If by them, you mean the good guys, then yes. I chose *them*. Better than becoming someone who would almost kill their own mother."

Tessa snapped her gaze to Riley. "What? You're really gonna play that game?"

How ironic, Riley thought, that she was accusing him of playing a game. He rolled his shoulders and spat, "You started it."

A single tear rolled down her cheek. It damn near broke his heart. Part of him wanted to wrap her in his arms and tell her that he loved her, that he forgave her. But he knew the tears were fake. The Fallen were great at deception. And loyalty was a dangerous game when someone he used to trust was after blood.

He wondered if he and Leila did the surge right then and there, if she'd return to human form. There was only one way to find out. He threw his arm back and Leila's hand fell onto his palm.

He hoped against all hope that Leila knew what he was thinking. Feeling Leila squeeze his hand, he took a deep breath and tried to focus. Doing the surge in suburbia was risky, but what other choice did he have?

"Sadie? Girls?" Tessa called. "I think it's best if you come with me now."

Her statement threw Riley off. He slammed his hand back to the door frame. "That's not gonna happen."

Tessa looked genuinely upset. She muttered to herself, "I can't believe I'm trying to negotiate with a Fallen."

Riley guffawed. She was really messing with him now. "That's a joke. You're the Fallen, Tessa. You're the one they need protecting from."

Brows furrowing, Tessa shook her head. She gave a sympathetic glance between Leila and Riley. "You really believe you're a True, don't you? Tell me, have you been to the Veil? Have you been given any assignments?"

"We've been to the Veil…" Riley hesitated, not knowing what she meant about assignments. Was it a trick to catch him off guard? He snarled, letting his claws dig into the wood his hands rested on.

Tessa covered her mouth with both hands. The tears fell in quick succession. "Oh Will, you've been lied to. You're not a True Guardian."

The accusation sent him over the edge. He wasn't the Fallen here. Swinging around, Riley faced Leila. She nodded and grabbed both his hands. If they were going to save Tessa, it was now or never.

"I'm out," Tessa said, backing down the front steps.

"No, wait!" Leila urged, squeezing Riley's hands.

"I'm not staying here to see how this plays out," Tessa called, dabbing her wet face.

Halfway down the path, Tessa stopped. She glanced over her shoulder, her eyes finding Sadie. She pulled a card out of her back pocket and wiggled it between her fingers, before placing it on the concrete. "I'm sorry I failed you. Call if you need me."

Heart sinking, Riley pulled Leila across her porch. "Tessa! Wait!"

Tessa stared at the path in between them, brow deepening over her eyes. Her breath quivered as she spun around and ran for the car.

Riley let Leila go and watched the car drive off. He stared at his sister's red wavy hair through the window, watching her until the car turned the corner.

Sadie slipped past him and stopped at the small card Tessa left. She picked it up and tucked it into her pocket. Looking back to Riley, she asked, "Are you sure she's Fallen?"

Riley thought back to the last time he'd seen Tessa. Her wild eyes as she stood above his mother, their whole house turned upside down. She had blood on her knuckles and a heaving chest. He watched her run away with shame that day, just as she did then.

"I'm sure," he replied.

SATURDAY

afternoon

Sadie

"Can you tell us what happened?" Riley asked.

He sat on the edge of Leila's coffee table, looking between Imogen and Summer. He clutched his hands together, kneading his knuckles, pressing hard as if digging into clay. Sadie had never seen him so anxious before, seeing his sister must have truly rattled him.

The two girls shuffled closer to each other on the sofa, elbows knocking as Summer played with the cuffs of her sleeves. Imogen asked, "Which part? The part where we were locked up for a day, or the part where Tessa saved us?"

Riley frowned and shared a glance with Leila. He returned his attention to the girls and shook his head. As he opened his mouth, Leila rushed to his side and said, "We want to hear your perspective. Tell it all."

Sadie knew what they were thinking. Telling the girls that it was their perspective insinuated that they could be wrong… That there was another side to the story. Maybe the girls had been tricked by Tessa and Jamal. Maybe they'd staged the kidnapping and saved them to make them look like the good guys.

But Sadie wasn't quite sure.

She took a seat next to Summer and placed her hand over Summer's fidgety fingers. "Start from the beginning. What happened after you took my jacket and left home?"

Summer sniffed, and without making eye contact, she jerked her head toward Sadie. After a few seconds, she sighed and said, "We were going to visit some friends."

"What—" Sadie pressed her lips together, fighting the urge to ask what friends. Boys? Drug dealers? The house ten minutes out of town with five pit bulls? She swallowed her questions and nodded for Summer to continue.

"We were meant to meet them at the lookout—"

A rumble vibrated in the back of Sadie's throat. The lookout? At night? How stupid were these kids? Forget Guardians, what about real cougars and bears?

Summer gave Sadie a glare. "Do you want me to talk or not?"

"Yes," Riley urged. "So, you went to the lookout?"

Imogen shook her head. "We never got there. As we walked around the lake, we sensed someone following us. We kinda freaked out."

Summer lifted her knees and wrapped her arms around her legs. "Then, we ran."

"Toward the falls, right?" Sadie mused, remembering where her and Sebastian had found the denim jacket.

"How did you know?"

Sadie smiled and shrugged. "I found my jacket on the way there. *We* found it... Sebastian and I," Sadie glanced at Imogen. "He thought you might go there, if you were scared."

Imogen's eyes glazed over. "I should call him."

"I already have, he's on his way," Leila said.

A moan spilled from Riley's mouth. It was swiftly

followed by a nudge from Leila. She said, "So, then what?"

"We didn't get far," Summer sighed. "Someone grabbed us."

"Who?" Riley leaned forward. "Did they have pink eyes?"

Imogen furrowed her brow. "Pink eyes? You mean like the crazy blue yours just were?"

Riley sat back. "I… uhh…"

"Yes," Leila replied softly. "Like that."

Summer shook her head. "We didn't see anything. They put bags over our heads and next thing, we're sitting on cold cement, locked in a dark room. No one came in or out for a day."

"And then, Tessa and Jamal came." Imogen took a long breath. "Thankfully."

"Ergh," Riley grumbled. "Sounds suspicious."

"You think we're lying?" Summer scowled.

"No!" Riley held his hands up in surrender. "No, not at all. I think someone *else* is lying."

Summer semi-relaxed. "Oh."

Riley rubbed at his eyes with his palms. He stood and turned around, raking his tense hands through his hair. Leila quickly rushed to him, she tugged at his elbows, bringing his arms back down, and whispered something to him.

Sadie could just hear Riley mutter, "This is so messed up, for her to target innocent people just to get to me."

Leila whispered something else.

Sadie shuffled to the edge of the sofa, ears turning toward the couple. It wasn't that she was a snoop. No, not at all. She just needed to know her sister was safe. Yes, that was it, she was being a caring big sister.

Riley nodded. "I should go home. Make sure Tessa hasn't gone to mom."

Sadie reached forward, lifting her butt off the seat so she could peer around Riley to catch a glimpse of Leila's response.

"Want me to come?" Leila asked.

"No," Riley said. And, as if sensing Sadie's eyes, he glanced over his shoulder.

Sadie snapped her spine straight, sliding her bottom along the sofa.

Riley continued, "Stay here with them, if Tessa comes back they'll need protecting."

As Riley headed for the door, Imogen leaned in and whispered, "My brother will protect me."

When Riley was gone, Leila wandered back and took his place on the coffee table in front of the two girls. She leaned back on her hands and carved her face to the ceiling. Sighing, she said, "What a messed up day."

Sadie noticed Summer staring at Leila with wide eyes. She knew what that look meant, she'd seen it many a time when Summer was lying about something or other to their parents. There was something she was holding in.

"Go on," Sadie said, flinging her hand up. "Spill."

Imogen turned to Sadie, mouth agape. Her eyes flickered to Summer and back, nothing but a squeak coming from her voice box.

Summer leaned forward. "Okay, so. What the hell is happening? What is a Guardian? What is a Fallen? Why did Riley's eye glow blue before? Like, what the actual?"

Sadie pressed her lips together in a tight smile. She scratched her head and looked at Leila. "This one's all you."

Sadie remembered the time when Leila told her about Guardians. She was shocked but couldn't process the information until much later. She'd jumped right in to help Leila without so much of a second thought. It was her fight or flight response—she still didn't know which one she'd used.

Summer and Imogen showed their emotions a lot quicker than Sadie had. They were gobsmacked. After Leila had finished explaining everything, leaving the part about Cap out, they never looked more innocent. Eyes wide, like children waking from a nightmare, Summer and Imogen sat silently, staring into space.

As Sadie wondered what she could say to convince them everything would be okay, a succession of knocks rattled the front door. Summer's whole body jolted at the noise, and she reached across to clutch Imogen's hand. Leila half-shifted, eyes on the door. She stood slowly, her arms splayed out.

"Who is it?" she asked.

"Sebastian!" A voice boomed in reply.

Imogen leapt to her feet and ran for the door. She flung the door open and before Sebastian had even registered who was standing in front of him, she fell into his arms. His shock soon turned to relief as he wrapped her in his embrace.

Sadie stood, nervously playing with the hem of her shirt. Still holding his sister, Sebastian's eyes lifted. He stared at Sadie, and as his hands smoothed the back of Imogen's hair, he gave her a small smile.

Sadie wanted to do what Imogen did—run to him and fall in his arms. She'd never been so scared as when she was running through the forest, not knowing who was chasing her. She'd wanted him to save her, protect her, keep her safe.

And even though he wasn't able to, she knew he'd wished the same.

He mouthed "Hi" to her and let Imogen go. Sadie lifted her hand in a shy wave. "Hi," she mouthed back.

Sebastian took a quick breath and rolled his shoulders back. The softness that had graced his face, suddenly gone. "You, ah, need a lift home?"

"Oh, umm, I think we're gonna stay here," Sadie said. She smiled at Summer. "We're probably going to need some time to think of a great excuse to get back into Dad's good books anyway."

Summer chuckled and retorted, "Yeah. Something that doesn't involve telling our parents of the existence of werewolves."

Sebastian's eyes widened. He whipped his head to Imogen, shaking it ever so slightly.

She took his hand. "It's okay. I know what you are."

Creases deepened between his brow and he turned his face away. He tugged Imogen's arm and led her to the door. Without looking back, he said, "See ya round, Shorty."

As the door shut, Summer said, "Shorty? Is he calling you that?"

Sadie winced. She wasn't used to talking boys with her sister. She mumbled, "I guess."

"Huh!" Summer shrugged. "I mean he's hot and all, but man, he's so hard to read."

Sadie swallowed. *Not so much,* she thought. *Not when we're alone.*

"You okay?" Leila asked.

Sadie blinked out of her daze. "Yeah. Fine. It's been a big day."

"I'll set you up in the guest room," Leila said, waving her hand to the hallway beside the stairs. "You don't mind sharing a bed?"

"That's fine," Summer said quickly.

Sadie smiled. It'd been a while since Summer could bear to even be in the same room as her, let alone in close sleeping vicinity.

"She's not at home!" Gabby's voice called from outside. The door burst open, almost breaking off its hinges, and she stormed in. Her eyes landed on Sadie, and she instantly screamed, "Ah! You're okay?"

"I'm fine," Sadie replied, running to Gabby and giving her a hug.

Gabby pulled away, holding Sadie at arm's length. "You're really okay?" She turned her attention to Leila, "You could have told me!"

"Sorry," Leila grimaced. "It's been hectic."

Gabby slid one arm around Sadie's shoulders, holding her close. She huffed, "Well, it better be a good story for not letting me know that our human bestie was safe."

"Hectic," Leila repeated, bowing her head.

"Riley's sister is here," Sadie offered.

Gabby balked, darting her eyes between Leila and Sadie. "For real? The Fallen sister?"

Peering up, Leila nodded. "For real."

Nodding in approval, Gabby held her arm out for Leila. "You're forgiven. Come here."

Leila sighed and shimmied herself under Gabby's shoulder. "You wanna stay for dinner? I'm thinking pizza. We'll order in. Watch a movie…"

"Sounds good to me," Summer peeped, squeezed herself into the huddle.

SATURDAY

late evening

Leila

A rush of air tickled Leila's cheek and she woke with a startle. A lone figure stood in her doorway, silhouetted by the hallway light. She assumed it was a man, going by the height and round shoulders. It wasn't Riley's shape — he wasn't that tall. And her dad, well he was more rounded. Heart thumping, instinct took over. She threw her quilt off and leapt to her feet, calling her lion forward. As she half-shifted, the sight before her changed. The man in the doorway wasn't alone, he had a Guardian with him. A bronze bear, looming as an aura beside him.

"Kale!" Leila exclaimed, running.

As she reached him, Kale let his arms envelop her. He held her tight and replied, "Hey sis. It's good to see you."

Leila pulled away and thwacked him with the back of her hand. "What took you so long? We had a crisis!"

"Sorry." Kale grimaced, raising his hands in surrender. "We had some things to take care of. But we're here now. Is

Sadie okay?"

Leila raised her brows, unimpressed by the vague reason. She scoffed, "No thanks to you."

With a crooked smile Kale rubbed her head. "Man, I've missed you."

Tired and even more cranky, Leila ducked her head away from his touch. "Seriously Kale, she was kidnapped, you had things to take care of?"

Kale's smile faded, lips turning inside his mouth. He sighed and nodded. "I know. We weren't just in Seattle though… we had to catch a plane."

"From where?"

"We were in Vegas," he mused, leaning casually onto her chest of drawers. He lifted his hands, twisting a ring around a finger.

Leila's eyes drifted to the ring. Solid gold. Around his fourth finger. Her mouth fell open.

Kale grinned.

"You got married?" Leila whispered, unable to keep her eyes off his wedding ring.

Shrugging, Kale replied, "We're already Imprints, so I figured why not make it official."

"Ha!" Leila tore her eyes from Kale's hand and found his face beaming with pride. Her heart burst. She threw her arms around his neck. "Congratulations."

After a moment, she released him and pushed him back. "I can't believe you got married without me there."

Kale rolled his eyes and smiled. "Don't worry. We're having a celebration here in Cedar Falls. We've booked out a lodge and will make a whole day of it."

Leila's annoyance disappeared. She grabbed his wrists. "Do we get to dress up?"

"Yes," Kale said in a teasing tone. "We'll all dress up." He slipped his hands from hers and squeezed her shoulder. "Anyway, get some rest. Kiko thinks there are Fallen lurking around the town again, so we'll need to make a plan on how to deal with them. We don't want it to get as bad as last time."

"Oh, I don't know—" Leila half-shifted for a split second, flashing her eyes golden. "Last time wasn't so bad."

"Don't get cocky. Last time we got lucky." Kale rubbed her head with his knuckles and backed out of her room. "Text all your friends who were involved. Kiko wants to talk with everyone at 8am."

Leila skipped back to her bed, already reaching for her phone on the bedside table. "Okay."

SUNDAY

early morning

Leila

Leila gave her mirror a glance as she left her room, half-caring about her appearance yet not quite invested to fully take her reflection in. There may have been a few strands of hair out of place. She nonchalantly pushed them off her face as she checked her phone for the time. It was seven fifty-two.

An unread message from Riley lit up on her screen.

On my way!

Even just imagining the sound of his voice made her heart skip a beat. Man, she loved that boy.

As Leila bounced down the stairs, she heard chatter rising from the kitchen. Sadie's voice trilled sweetly about how stunning the back garden looked.

"Thank you, lovely one," Leila's mom, Aileen, replied with all the gooey warmth she possessed.

Leila smiled and rolled her eyes in amusement. With her

mom, it was either an aloof *"Mm? What was that?"* or an all encompassing smother of maternal care.

"What's with all the vervain anyway?" Gabby's voice was quieter than the other two, Leila assumed it was muffled by food.

Leila knew what was with all the vervain. Her mom had found out it had more qualities than just a cure ingredient. It had protective qualities, too, like a deterrent of sorts. Whenever the woody, grassy smell hit her nostrils, Leila felt like she was coming down with a cold. Aileen, of course, was sympathetic, but mostly excited about the discovery.

Leila leapt over the bottom step and landed gracefully into the space between the living and dining areas. She threw her body through the open doorway, peering into the kitchen.

Sadie, Gabby, and Aileen were hovering around the island bench staring at clippings of lavender, roses, and other flowery stems. Aileen had lined up three vases and Sadie was helping her fill them with off cuts from the garden, while Gabby munched on a pop tart.

"I think it's wise to have a good supply... just in case," Aileen cooed. She looked up over her glasses and spotted Leila. Her eyes lit up and she spun around to the coffee machine. "Good morning, sweetheart! Want a coffee?"

"Morning!" Leila beamed at the same time a knock rattled the front door. She swiveled on her heels and called over her shoulder, "It's Riley."

As she hurried to the door, she heard Gabby mutter, "it's always Riley."

Before Leila reached the door, it opened. Riley appeared sheepish, as he often did, hoping that his presence was welcome. Leila ran to greet him, because that boy was always welcome.

"Good morning, Riley," Aileen said, walking into the living room. She lifted a mug and blew the steam away, sending the stray curls of her auburn fringe flying. "Would you like a drink?"

Riley smiled politely and his eyes drifted to Leila's lips then quickly flitted back to Aileen. "I'm fine thanks, Mrs. Belmonte, I had some juice before I left home."

"Oh, Riley," Aileen teased, swiping her hand through the air. "Call me by my name, honestly. And kiss your girl, I won't watch."

Leila giggled, and grabbed both sides of Riley's face, planting her lips on his for a peck.

"So sweet," Aileen said, wandering back to the kitchen.

"My mom loves you more than I do, I think," Leila said, squeezing his cheeks playfully.

Riley raised his brow and with a wry smile, replied, "I hope not."

"So do I," a deep voice vibrated behind them.

Leila spun around to see her dad, Tate, standing at the bottom of the stairwell. His eyes were glistening with amusement. Taking a step toward them, the levity in his demeanor suddenly vanished. "Did you know your brother was married?"

Grimacing, Leila nodded. She opened her mouth to say something, but her dad sighed loudly causing her to lose her train of thought. He curved his hands around the back of the sofa and hunched over, his large frame reminding Leila of Kale's bear.

Tate sighed again and twisted his gaze to Leila and Riley. "Leila or, well both of you really, Riley you're here more than I am... part of the family—" His eyes drifted around the living room, resting on nothing in particular. He snapped his eyes back to the couple. "I know you're almost adults and all you important Guardians have business to discuss, but would you mind telling me your plans? I'd still like to pretend I have adequate knowledge of my daughter's life."

Leila's heart nearly broke in two. She loved her dad. He was all things protective and warm but since she'd turned, he'd also become a little lost. It seemed he didn't quite know how to deal with the change.

Leila thought showing her parents the shift would reassure them that it wasn't all that terrible.

Her mom lost it, in the best way. She loved every moment and often asked Leila to shift just to watch. She researched Guardians as much as she could but there was only one folklore scholar in her circles who had an inkling about any of it... and his information was sparse at best.

But her dad? He took it a little different, almost as if she'd taken something away—his little girl all but gone. He didn't quite know how to treat her. Sometimes staying well away, and sometimes looming in the background, as though hoping to get a better grasp on what she had become.

Leila lurched herself forward and stood in front of Tate. "Of course, Dad. I'll tell you whatever you want me to. You're still my dad, you always will be. No matter how strong I am."

Tate nodded in appeasement, but the sadness in his eyes didn't convince Leila that he believed her. He glanced at Riley, then pushed himself up straight. Turning to Leila, a slight smile lifted his tanned cheeks. He reached for Leila's face and pinched a stray hair between his fingers. Tucking it behind her ear, he said, "You'll always be my little girl."

Maybe this transition was inevitable. At some stage, she'd stop being a child and become an adult. It just happened a little earlier than they both expected and she felt a little guilty for it. Because the truth was, she didn't need his strong arms to help her feel safe anymore. Leila nodded and softly said, "I know. But just because I don't need your protection doesn't mean I don't need your love."

Tate dropped his hand on her shoulder and gave it a quick squeeze. There was something final about the way he did it, like ripping a Band-aid off a not-quite-healed wound. As if right then and there he knew he had to allow their relationship to change. Leila tried not to cry as he took a step back.

Tate pressed his lips together, nodded, and said, "Mom

and I will be in the garden. She wants to plant more vervain." Then, he turned on his heels and left.

Riley cleared his throat, moving close behind Leila. She turned around and gazed into his sympathetic eyes. As she let herself fall into his arms, he said, "That must have been hard for him."

"Okay!" Kiko boomed, startling Leila out of Riley's hold. When Kiko noticed the practically empty room, she glanced at the clock. The time read seven fifty-seven. "You told them eight, didn't you?"

Kale leapt off the stairwell and rushed to his new wife's side. "Don't worry, they'll be here."

Riley peered around Leila at Kiko. "Have you heard from Ren?"

Kiko's top lip rolled into itself and her eyes shot to the ceiling. "Don't worry about my little brother. He tends to disappear when things get complicated and there are actual lives at stake." With her eyes on the clock again, she asked, "What time did you tell everyone to arrive?"

"Relax, baby." Kale tugged on her arm as he dragged her toward the sofa. Kiko gave a curt smile but allowed herself to fall onto his lap.

Leila wanted to say congratulations on getting married, but Kiko seemed on edge. Which made her on edge. So instead of saying anything, she plonked herself onto the other end of the sofa, leaving a space for Riley in the middle.

"So," Kale said, stretching out the word. "Can you do that surge thing on call yet?"

Kiko moved to her feet faster than a cheetah hunting a gazelle. She gave Leila a piercing glare before marching to the window. She rested her hand on the frame and peered outside.

"Sure can." Riley answered proudly, slipping his hand into Leila's. He either didn't notice Kiko's mood, or really didn't care.

Kale sighed and threw his hand in Kiko's direction.

"We've tried, just can't get it."

Was that it? Leila wondered. Was that what Kiko was upset about? Leila looked at her new sister-in-law with anticipation. "Oh, we could help you both! We've got some tips from—"

"Finally!" Kiko declared. She jogged to the door, throwing it wide open.

Imogen and Sebastian stood on the front porch, Imogen nervously eying Kiko and Sebastian glancing around the room with a scowl.

Leila felt Riley tense beside her. He leaned over and whispered, "What's *he* doing here?"

"Shh," Leila hushed. "He's fine, okay."

Riley simply replied with an, "Mmm."

Kiko stepped aside and Imogen sauntered in, giving Leila a shy smile. As soon as Imogen had passed, Kiko stepped back, blocking Sebastian between the door and the living room. She tilted her head, frozen, staring at him.

"Uhh, hello?" Sebastian sounded annoyed.

"Sorry," Kiko said, holding her hand out. "It's not very often you get to meet an Alpha killer."

Sebastian frowned, dropping his gaze to her hand and back. Ignoring her hand-shake offer, he pushed past and muttered, "It's not a badge I wear with pride."

Kiko watched him as he found himself a seat on the recliner, Imogen quickly finding a spot on the arm rest beside him. Kiko shrugged and took the door handle in her grasp. Before she could close it completely, a hand slammed against the door.

Mr. Robertson pushed through, his dark hair slicked back perfectly, hooded eyes locked on Kiko. They nodded in silence to each other. Then, he shuffled to the back wall and leaned against it, looking around the room without smiling.

Sadie's melodic voice resonated from the dining room. Leila swung around in her spot to see Sadie and Gabby wandering through the archway—Sadie completely oblivious to her surroundings.

"And, oh my god," she sang. "You should have seen his face when he realized it was his sist—" Sadie snapped her mouth shut, darting her gaze from one person to the next. All eyes were on the gossip queen.

From the recliner, Sebastian stifled a laugh. Which was followed quickly by Imogen ramming her elbow into his ribs.

Gabby stood beside Sadie, protectively glaring at anyone who might dare tease her friend. Sadie's fingers clutched at the hem of her shirt, scrunching the material nervously in her grasp. She hesitated a quick glance in Riley's direction.

Leila looked at Riley, too, waiting for his reaction. He blinked rapidly, turning his attention to Leila. A smile, quick and small, graced his face.

Leila had always admired that side of Riley. The side that didn't bite back. Even when Sadie was talking about him… and, even when Sebastian was laughing about it.

Sadie remained in the archway, mouth agape. Leila imagined she would be freaking the heck out about her social error. Not just about the possibility of upsetting Riley but what others might be thinking of her. Leila threw her arm in a circle, waving her friends over. *All is well*, Leila tried to say telepathically.

"We've been waiting for you guys!" Riley cooed gently as though the whole room wasn't waiting for him to snarl. He added, "Where's Summer?"

"Here!" Summer appeared from behind Sadie. She weaved around her sister, bumping her as she passed, and made a bee-line for Imogen.

Gabby used the distraction to guide Sadie into the living room. She grabbed her hand and dragged her around the sofa. Avoiding eye-contact with Riley, they both plonked themselves on the floor in front of Leila.

With elbows casually resting on his knees, Sebastian leaned forward, piercing eyes on Sadie. "Hi," he said softly.

"Is that everyone?" Kiko asked, closing the door. "Is your friend Damien coming?"

Riley glanced over his shoulder and shook his head. "I doubt it."

"Why not?" Kale's brow deepened. "He's a Guardian, too. We'll need all the hands we can get."

Sebastian chortled. "He's not much of a Guardian."

Leila grimaced. That retort wasn't far off the truth. No thanks to her.

"He's not a Guardian at all," Gabby said, monotone.

"What?" Sadie jerked her head around, staring at Gabby as though she'd declared her hate for donuts.

Gabby let her gaze drift to Sadie. Raising one brow, she shrugged and repeated, "He's not a Guardian anymore."

Riley rubbed nape of neck, sheepishly looking around the room. "Yeah, we kinda practiced our surge and... " he brought his hand out, pressing his fingertips together. As his fingers sprang open, he continued, "Poof. I tried to mark him again, so we'll see how he feels in the next day or two."

Kiko stared at Riley, nostrils flaring. She spat, "Well done, rookies. Honestly, I don't know why you have the special power if you can't even use it properly."

The words stung. Leila shifted in her spot, looking to her brother for back up. He gazed her at for a moment, before starting, "Kiko, I don't think—"

"Sorry," Kiko blurted, color draining from her face. She rushed behind the sofa and placed her hand over Leila's shoulder. "I'm really sorry. I didn't mean it. I'm just..." She clenched her fists at her sides, then released them. "I'm just scared for you, that's all."

Leila nodded. Her living room was crammed with ten people. They were all waiting on Kiko for answers. Before, when Leila had been marked, Kiko was a tower of strength. She held command and control with grace. But now, Leila realized, Kiko was shaken to her core.

"No, I'm sorry," Leila hurried. "You're right, we are

rookies. That's why we asked you here. We need your help."

Kiko inhaled, taking a moment to regain composure. She gave a sad smile, brushed the front of her blouse, and turned to the only humans in the room, Sadie, Summer, and Imogen. "Girls, for some reason you're targeted by the Fallen. And I'm really sorry about it, because you're human… but it's our job to protect you, so you'll need to follow my every order. Is that okay?"

With arms linked together, Imogen and Summer nodded in unison. Sadie swiveled around, her eyes finding Leila's as though asking a silent question. Leila nodded, and then, so did Sadie.

"Good," Kiko sighed the word, visibly relaxing. "The main thing we all need to do is lay low, until we figure out exactly who we're dealing with."

"We know who it is," Riley mumbled, sliding his hand into Leila's. "It's Tessa."

"Tessa? Your sister?" Kiko brought finger to her lips and tapped her nails against her teeth. "It's worse than I thought."

"No," Summer protested. "It wasn't her that kidnapped us. It was her that saved us."

Kiko shook her head and gave Summer a sympathetic smile, as if poor Summer, the human teen, didn't know what she was talking about. "This is how the Fallen work, see? They hurt you, then act like they're the ones who've saved you. We can't trust them. If Tessa's Alpha is with them, we need to…" She stopped talking for a moment, frown deepening. Voice shaking, she finished her sentence, "He's evil. The kind of person who'd give an ice-cream to a child and lace the insides with poison."

Goosebumps rushed over Leila's arms. She clutched Riley's hand tight.

"You think he's here in Cedar Falls?" Gabby asked, shuffling closer to Sadie.

Kiko threw her hand in Leila and Riley's direction, then

to Kale. "There are four Imprints here. It was only a matter of time before the reckoning came."

"The reckoning?" Sadie asked, eyes as wide as saucers. She was sitting on the floor in front of Leila, legs crossed like an innocent child. Leila noted how small she seemed. How human she was. A chill ran down her spine.

"I don't mean to be dramatic," Kiko said, pulling her long hair off her face. She held it there for a moment, showing her ear-rings lined from lobe to tragus. "But Imprints don't usually even last this long. The Fallen hate them because they threaten their existence. We need to... leave."

"Leave?" Sebastian asked, half guffawing. "Cedar Falls?"

"Yes," Kiko replied, straight faced. "We need to get away from here. At the moment, we are sitting ducks. We'll be picked off one-by-one. It's better if we get somewhere secluded, regroup ourselves and plan for an attack."

Gabby gasped. Leila placed her hand on Gabby's shoulder. She wanted to comfort her, she wanted to comfort everyone. But the reason they were all in danger was because of her and Riley being Imprints. They put a massive target on Cedar Falls. The fact they had to leave sent guilt waves through her.

"Where will we go?" Riley asked.

Sebastian cleared his throat and said, "My dad has a cabin near the coast. I'm sure he won't mind us crashing—"

"No offense," Kale pushed himself off the sofa. "But you're a Fallen, so I'm not even sure I'm comfortable with you going."

Sadie's back straightened. She burst, "Gabby might be, too!" Immediately cringing, she gave Gabby an apologetic frown.

"Wow," Gabby mouthed.

Kiko whipped her head from Gabby to Leila. "What's going on? You have Fallen in your clan?"

Leila swallowed. She bent her knees under her and

glanced at Sebastian. Sure, he was arrogant and had a chip on his shoulder the size of Texas, but still, there was something good lurking beneath the facade. "Yeah, so Sebastian was turned by a Fallen, but since Cap died… since he saved us from Cap, he's been trustworthy. And Gabby," Leila clutched Gabby's shoulder. "She killed an innocent, who I don't think was truly innocent, not really. But ever since, she's been feeling a little off. I just think that maybe it's not as clear as someone having bad intentions if they're Fallen. Like, everyone has some good in them. Right?"

Kiko gave a soft smile. "You're very sweet, Leila. I hope you're right. But from my experience with these types of Fallen, it's clear that they have bad intentions. But…" Her shoulders dropped a little and the tension that had seemed to exude from her disappeared. "If you trust your friends, then they should come, too."

"I do," Leila urged, nudging Riley with her elbow. "We do."

Riley shuffled in his seat. He cleared his throat and muttered, "We do."

"Okay," Kiko said, clapping her hands. "Pack lightly, we leave in half an hour."

SUNDAY

afternoon

Sadie

A convoy of three cars zoomed along route 82. Mr. Robertson drove alone at the front, leading two more carloads alongside the Cascades. Sadie sat in the back of Sebastian's car with her sister next to her. Imogen had been quick to claim the front. Sadie leaned over and craned her neck to see through the rear vision mirror. Riley's car trailed behind them. Leila, Gabby, Kale and Kiko were with him.

She regretted blurting out Gabby's possible Fallen status. But something had stirred within her when Kale had pointed Sebastian out as being a Fallen. The thought of people seeing him as a bad person made her involuntarily stand up for him. She wanted everyone to see the Sebastian she did. If they could trust Gabby, they could trust him, too.

As she stared through the rear-view mirror trying to telepathically tell Gabby she was sorry, Sebastian tilted his head and caught her gaze. He winked and Sadie felt her insides melt into a puddle of goo. She stared back immobile, feeling the warmth of blood as it filled her cheeks.

With a lopsided smirk, he asked, "You okay back there, Shorty?"

"Fine," Sadie replied. He looked so cocky with that arrogant grin plastered on his face. She remembered what Tessa had said about him being dangerous. Scared by the thought, she quickly turned to Summer, "You okay?"

A dark expression fell over Summer. She glared at Sadie and said, "Oh, yeah. Totally fine. I've been kidnapped, kept in a dank beaten down cabin, and then saved by someone who I've been told wants us dead. Totes peachy."

Sadie tried not to smile. There was the Summer she knew, with a bite in her voice and scowl on her face.

Noticing the look on Sadie's face, Summer softened. Her hand reached for Sadie's. "But thanks for looking out for me."

Sadie squeezed Summer's hand, and as she settled back in her seat, she noticed Sebastian's gaze quickly shift from her to the road in front of them. He cleared his throat and reached across the front of the car to ruffle Imogen's hair. She pushed his hand away in defiance and returned the teasing gesture by shoving his shoulder playfully.

Sebastian's laugh echoed through the car. "Easy, sister. I'm driving."

An explosion of warmth spread across Sadie's chest. There was no way Sebastian was even a little bit Fallen. He couldn't possibly be dangerous. The way he treated his sister proved that. Sadie ran her teeth over her bottom lip and decided right then and there that Tessa was unequivocally wrong about him.

The drive took six hours. Mostly silent, apart from Imogen and Summer's impromptu karaoke sing along. Trees reached up around them as Sebastian parked his car next to Mr. Robertson's. Sadie had no idea where they were. They'd passed through Yakima and somewhere after that they'd crossed the border into Oregon. Towns were few and far between. Deep in woodland, that's all she knew.

Everyone began climbing out of their cars, except for Sebastian, who turned in his seat. He glanced at Imogen, then Summer, and then kept his eyes on Sadie as he said, "Better stay in the car, until we know the area is safe."

Sadie nodded and watched him get out of the car to meet the others. As they all branched off, retrieving tents and goods from their cars, Sebastian leaned in through his open door. "Ugh, tents," he moaned, "We should have gone to dad's cabin."

Imogen frowned. "I'd rather stay in tents."

Clenching his jaw, Sebastian pushed off the car. "I'll be back."

Curiosity taking hold, Sadie shuffled to the edge of her seat. "Why would you rather stay in tents than go to your dad's cabin?"

Imogen gave Sadie a side-eye, then sprung her door open. Without saying a word, she stepped out and slammed the door. It was almost uncanny, Sadie thought, how alike those Weir siblings were.

"Don't worry," Summer said, opening her door. "She always gets like that when I bring up her dad, too. She's only seen him a couple times in the last two years."

Sadie's door swung open and Leila peered in. "Mom and Dad made a quick trip to the store before we left, they got us a few tents to share." As Sadie climbed out of the car, Leila added, "Pretty sure they were hoping I wouldn't share one with Riley."

"Will you?" Sadie asked as they wandered toward the cluster of sticks Kale and Riley had accumulated.

"I don't know. Maybe." Leila hooked her arm through Sadie's and whispered, "Most definitely."

Gabby approached, looking at the soon-to-be campfire. "This is not something I thought I'd be doing this weekend."

"Better than being kidnapped," Sadie offered.

Still staring at Riley pile sticks upon sticks, Gabby teased, "Wow, Sades, way to bring the mood down."

"Sorry," Sadie said, guilt rising in her throat. "And sorry about before, too. I didn't mean to throw you into the fire."

"Mmm?" Gabby faced her, eyes slitted. In a matter of seconds, a smile tugged at her lips. "I know. You were just trying to take the spotlight off Sebastian... for some reason I will never understand. But one I will accept." She glanced back at Riley as he dumped a heap of sticks and ran off again. Gabby rolled her eyes and said, "I think these boys need some help." She knelt at the campfire and began creating a pyramid with the sticks.

Leila nudged Sadie with her elbow. Pointing in the distance, she said, "This will be funny."

Sadie turned around to see Riley sauntering across the clearing, carrying even more sticks. He spotted Gabby hunched over the pile he'd created and frowned. "What are you doing?"

"If you want to light a fire, it needs air," Gabby said, raising one brow at the collection in his arms. "I think we're good for sticks. Once this thing gets going we'll need bigger logs."

"He's a city boy," Leila defended.

"Actually—" Riley half-shifted and his eyes beamed bright neon-blue. Fangs poked through his mouth as he grinned and said, "I'm also part wild."

The sight of him like that made Sadie lift her face to the sky. She took a long breath, trying to center herself. Forget the fire, *she* needed air.

No matter how often she saw them shift, it still unnerved her. And that was just her friends, those whom she trusted with her life. What about the others, the Fallen, those who wanted to hurt her? Fear taking hold, she turned to Leila. "Do you think we'll be safe here?"

Leila's face fell in the way it often did when Sadie was upset—eyes hooded and pained, head tilting slightly. "I won't let anything happen to you, I swear it."

Leila's words came with a heartfelt promise that Sadie

almost believed. But still, she knew Leila couldn't truly understand what it felt like to be in her place. She couldn't know how intimidating it was to be surrounded by so much power.

Trying to find the right words was going to be hard. She'd put her foot in it enough times in one day. So, instead of speaking she just smiled and nodded.

On the other side of Leila, Sebastian walked past holding an orange tent under his arm, Imogen close on his tail. He glanced at Sadie, and as if noticing her fear, his eyes drifted straight to Riley.

"Check yourself, bro," Sebastian scowled. "There are humans here, who believe it or not, may be afraid to see your ugly half-shifted phase."

By the time night had come, the fire was roaring and its sparks darted up into the darkness. Tents had been set up in a circle a safe distance from the fire, with logs placed between them. Sadie sat on one beside the tent she'd claimed, scraping her nails along bark.

Gabby plonked herself beside Sadie, narrowly missing her fingers. She held a flask out. "Want some vodka?"

Sadie gawked at the silver bottle in Gabby's grasp. "You brought alcohol?"

"Duh," Gabby said, unscrewing the lid.

"I'm good, thanks."

"Suit yourself." Gabby lifted the flask to her lips and took a large swig. As she swallowed, Riley stepped out of his tent. Gabby leapt to her feet and ran toward him. "Riley! Have you asked Odette to join us?"

Somewhere on the other side of the fire, Sadie heard Leila laugh. She was sitting with Kale and Kiko, and Sadie figured they were probably talking about all deeper things Guardian. A conversation she didn't need to be a part of.

On her other side, she could hear Summer and Imogen chatting quietly inside their shared tent. And Sebastian, silent and somewhat moody, lurked at the clearing's tree-line, swiveling his head at every minuscule noise in the forest.

A twig snapped behind her, sending her heart into overdrive. Sadie jerked her head around and squinted into the shadows of trees. A brown wolf with glowing green eyes moved toward her. She had the urge to scream but it got lodged in her throat, floating out as barely a gasp.

The wolf returned to human form and Mr. Robertson moved in beside her. His hand clasped the groove of her shoulder and he gave a comforting squeeze. "I hope I didn't scare you. I just went for a run around the perimeter."

At school, before Guardians or the dangers of death, she would have reveled in the moment her teacher crush gave her attention. But things were different now. She shrugged his hand off and glanced across the clearing to Sebastian. Lying she said, "I'm used to it."

"Jay?" Kiko called from the other side of the fire. She stepped into view, high flames licking in front of half her body. "Anything?"

"All clear," Mr. Robertson replied.

"Okay, I'll do a sweep. You can take over from Sebastian." Kiko's eyes flashed as bright as the fire. She noticed Sadie watching her and smiled, letting her fangs poke through her lips. Then, she fully shifted into her red fox and bounced into the forest.

Sadie's stomach flipped. She glanced at her tent but the thought of going to sleep didn't appeal to her. How could she sleep surrounded by shifters?

"Want some?"

Sadie looked up, surprised to see Sebastian standing in front of her. She glanced at a tin mug in his grasp. "What is it?"

"Gabby poured some vodka in my soda." He said it so

nonchalantly, that it didn't seem as big of a deal as it did before.

"Gabby gave you something?" Sadie asked, taking his cup.

Sebastian shrugged. "Hell hath frozen over."

Sadie lifted the cup to her lips and took a sip. The tang hit her throat unexpectedly. She scrunched her nose as she passed the cup back to Sebastian. It wasn't like she hadn't had alcohol before, that was inevitable with a friend like Gabby. But she'd preferred smoothies or hot cocoa or green tea.

Sebastian sculled the rest of the drink and sat down. "You look lonely, Shorty."

Sadie shrugged. "Just a little out of place."

"You should try and squeeze into the tent with the girls. Might be cozy?"

Sadie faced him, studying his expression to see if he was joking. He wasn't. It was eerie how in tune he was with her. That he could tell what she was thinking. It felt like he took the time to see her, the real her.

"I think the tents are a bit too small for three. Besides, yesterday was the first time in years that Summer looked at me like she didn't hate me, I don't want to push it."

Sebastian chuckled and placed his empty cup on the log between them. The cup wobbled for a moment, Sebastian's hand hovering close to catch it if it fell, but soon it balanced in place. Sebastian curved his palms over his knees and let out a long sigh. "So… do you wish he was here?"

"Who?" Sadie asked.

Sebastian gave her a side-eye and raised his brow. "Damien."

Disappointment flooded her. Maybe he didn't see the real her after all. She muttered, "No."

Sebastian smiled then, broad and toothy. He sighed again and slid his elbows to his knees. "You know, I'm not surprised that was your first kiss."

Sadie didn't know whether he meant to offend her. She asked precariously, "Why?"

A glint hit Sebastian's eyes as he looked over his shoulder at her. "C'mon. Flirty Sadie one day, Frosty Sadie the next. That's what they call you."

"I'm sorry what? When? Who?" Sadie swung around so fast her thigh hit Sebastian's cup. It tumbled off the log and fell into a shrub behind them.

Sebastian's gaze followed the cup. He stared at it for a moment, before returning his attention to Sadie. "The boys. You do this cute little giggle and tuck your hair behind your ear, fluttering those eyelashes. And then, when someone wants to take it further, you run away."

Sadie's heart pounded. How on earth did he manage to do that, peel her like an onion? Here they were again, talking about topics that revealed pieces of her she wanted to hide. "That's just..." Sadie hesitated for a moment. But there was no use hiding, not from him. "It's just not the real me."

"I figured," he said, bumping her shoulder with his.

She shrugged. "I don't know why I do that. I'm okay until a certain point of closeness, then this wall goes up. I tried to be myself with Damien on our date. But by the end, I didn't want to kiss him. Not because I'm frosty... but because he wouldn't show me his real self."

"That's understandable. It has to be a two-way street, right?" Sebastian stretched his legs out, crossing the ankles over. "You know, you're not as fake and two-faced as people say."

"Sebastian!" Sadie gaped. She couldn't believe the nerve of him sometimes. "That's so mean."

Sebastian raised his hands. "Hey! Don't shoot the messenger."

A fire rose inside her. She never bit back, always the nice one, but right then and there, she had to let the truth fly. "But you didn't have to tell me. You were the one who decided to tell me what people have said about me. And in turn, that means you're the one who hurt me."

Confusion settled on his face. "You'd rather me lie?"

Sadie shook her head. She didn't know whether to laugh or cry. "Just don't say anything."

It was quiet for a while. Sadie considered running into her tent, just to get away from the feeling that had washed over her. But that would just prove his point. She was scared of her real self to be seen… the vulnerable side included.

So they sat there in silence, Sadie picking at the bark that she sat on, and Sebastian staring into the cloudy sky. Finally, Sebastian lowered his head. He waited for Sadie to meet his gaze before he said, "Sorry."

His voice was low. Not quite a whisper but the power behind it reverberated to her core. He meant the apology. She could tell. She could also see that same softness she discovered a few days earlier. Her own vulnerability mirrored in his eyes.

Staring into his blue irises, she said quietly, "You know, I see glimpses of you. The *real* you."

Sebastian raised a brow. "The real me?"

"Yeah. You used to be…" Sadie cleared her throat, trying to find better words. "At the end of your sophomore year, you changed. You were nice before then. Remember? You introduced Leila to me because I quit the cheer squad and the girls pretended I didn't exist. Don't tell me you've forgotten."

Sebastian breathed out a laugh. "I remember thinking how brave you were for quitting that bitch squad."

"See, you were nice." Sadie nudged his bicep. "Then junior year started and you were different."

Sebastian dropped his head, staring at Sadie's fingers as they pinched a torn piece of bark.

"Why did you change?" Sadie urged.

Turning his head away, Sebastian replied, "To protect myself."

"From what?" Sadie leaned around, trying to catch his eyes. "Surely Cap hadn't turned you way back then."

Sebastian shook his head. "No, he turned me literally a few days before that whole… thing."

"Okay, so then something else happened?" Sadie hovered her hand above his, hesitating for a second before letting their skin touch. His knuckles clenched, then relaxed beneath her palm. She looked at his face, the edges of his eyes creased into a grimace. He looked a little bit like Imogen then, when she'd asked her about their dad. "Something happened to your family?"

Sebastian whipped his hand from under hers at the same time he swung his head back around to face her. His eyes fell to the log again. "I don't really want to talk about it."

He didn't want to talk about it? Sadie couldn't accept that. She was so close. There he was, right in front of her. The old Sebastian. The somewhat kind Sebastian.

A few months ago, it was Leila's mission to find him in there and Sadie was so close she could almost grab him and drag him out of himself. She pushed, "Is it the same reason why your mom is sad?"

"Don't!" Sebastian said a little too loudly. Gabby and Riley glanced their way. Softer, he repeated. "Don't." He rose to his feet and moved in front of her. Eyes blazing a hole through her, he hissed, "You don't get to speak about my mother. Ever. Get that, Itsy?"

SUNDAY

early evening

Leila

Leila felt weird about leaving her parents, but it was probably for the best to keep them out of it all. Her dad thought it was a good idea anyway: "… to save any more smashed windows, holes in walls, and broken roses." Leila knew he was downplaying the depth of it all. And she was a little grateful. The less they wanted to know, the better.

Leila peered around the fire. She watched Sebastian storm off into his tent, leaving Sadie alone, peeling bark between her fingers. She said, "I feel responsible."

A heavy arm draped around her shoulders and Kale pulled her into his embrace. "It's not your fault."

She wished she could believe him.

Kiko moved swiftly through the break in the forest and slid toward them. Smiling, she said, "My two favorite people."

Kale spread his free arm, inviting her to join them. Kiko

nestled into the crook of his shoulder and sighed. Leaning around Kale, she said, "We'll keep doing this on rotation. You want to go next, Leila?"

"Sure," Leila said, sitting up straight. A little run sounded enticing. "How far do you need me to go?"

Kiko threw a thumb over her shoulder. "Just do a loop. Head out about a mile and swing around."

Leila nodded.

"Jay will stand watch overnight," Kiko added.

Leila turned to look at Mr. Robertson. He was leaning against a tree, bored eyes staring into the fire. It was the same numb-like expression he'd held in the classroom for months.

"All night?" Leila asked, feeling sorry for him. "Don't you want everyone to take shifts?"

"Yeah, someone can replace him at dawn," Kiko replied.

Leila balked and turned back around. "Dawn? That's a long time—"

"Leila," Kale warned, bronze shimmering behind his eyes like a threat. "We get that Riley has been lax as your clan leader, but Kiko's been a Guardian for a long time. Trust her."

"I do," Leila said quickly, trying not to think about the insult on Riley. "I'm sorry, I never meant to—"

Kiko reached across Kale and tapped Leila's thigh. "It's fine. I didn't take offense." She rolled her eyes in Kale's direction and whispered, "He's kinda protective. I don't mind it."

Dark clouds moved in front of the moon, and Leila noticed a slight change in the air. It wasn't just the moon covered by the clouds, it was the whole sky. The only light source was now the flickering flames of the fire and a moving torch inside one of the tents. She breathed in the cooling air, it smelled like snow.

The orange glow from the fire danced over Kale's face as he frowned at Kiko. "What did you say?"

Leila grinned. "She said you're an overreacting oaf."

"No! I didn't!" Kiko exclaimed, giving Leila a playful pout. She turned to Kale and placed her hands on his chest. "You know I love it."

"I know," Kale replied, eyes traveling up and down her body. He clutched her waist and dragged her closer to him.

"Aww, you guys," Leila teased, shuffling down the log.

Kiko pulled away from Kale and, grinning as wide as a Cheshire cat, she faced Leila. Her grin softened as she closed her lips and rested her head against her new husband's chest.

Leila smiled back. "Congratulations, too, by the way. I never got the chance to say it before. Kale told me you got married. I guess we're sisters now."

Kiko leapt up. She stood in front of Leila, offered both her hands and said, "I'm sorry we didn't tell you. It was a spur of the moment thing." She motioned to her hands, wiggling the tips of her fingers. "Wanna see something?"

Leila barely had a chance to nod before Kiko grabbed her by the wrist and dragged her to a tent. Kiko burst through the entrance, leaving Leila standing at the entrance. Leila watched Kiko as she ruffled through a duffel bag. She lifted out a big bunch of blue material, sequins and tulle, that seemed to go on for miles. Kiko held it at neck height and it unraveled, displaying a beautiful gown.

Kiko smiled to herself as she held it against her body. Her fingers pinched at the cuff and she held it out, showcasing the delicate sleeve. "We want to hold a reception with family and friends later in the month. I'm going to wear this. What do you think?"

"It's gorgeous!" Leila proclaimed. "Put it on!"

"What?" A mix of shock and embarrassment laced Kiko's voice. "No, I couldn't. We're in the woods."

A rush of hot air warmed Leila's neck as Gabby peered in.

"Sure you can!" Gabby peeped. "Let's see it."

Leila felt excitement bubble through her. Something good on an otherwise stressful day. Kiko glanced her way and Leila nodded enthusiastically. "Why not?"

"Okay," Kiko conceded. "Gimme a sec."

Leila and Gabby stepped out of tent, letting Kiko change in private. "So," Leila said, clutching Gabby's wrist. "Is Odette coming?"

Gabby pressed her lips together as if trying to hide her smile, but she gave it away with her delighted eyes. "Yeah."

Snow began to fall, light and sporadic. It wasn't quite thick or cold enough to settle, the flakes dissipating before they hit the ground. Leila craned her face to the sky, embracing the soft splatter on her cheeks. She had a feeling that it was winter's send off—the last hoorah before spring truly arrived.

The rustling of the tent entrance brought Leila back to earth. Kiko stood in front of her tent wearing the floor-length navy gown. Delicate sequins formed shapes of flowers along the cuff and bodice. She'd let her hair down and it framed her face like silk curtains. The gown hugged her waist tightly and from there, tulle—so much tulle— flowed to the ground. As Kiko spun in a circle, the hem of her dress brushed heavily along thick grass. Her smile was infectious.

"You look amazing," Leila said, stepping closer. She couldn't help but touch the material, rubbing it between her fingertips. "I can't wait until the reception. What should *I* wear?"

Kiko thought for a while. Then, eyes twinkling, she said, "Something bright, like you."

Leila almost burst at the seams. She couldn't contain her face, her cheeks stretching to their limits in the biggest smile she'd had all day. She didn't often allow her emotions to run free, either masking them with sarcasm or diverting attention away. But there was something about that moment, where she felt totally safe to be vulnerable.

She said, earnestly and with gusto, "Thank you... For

making my brother happy."

Kiko reached down and grabbed her tulle skirt, hitching it off the ground. "Help me take it off?"

Leila rushed to follow Kiko into the tent and zipped it shut behind her. Kiko turned around, holding her hair away to show an unlatched clasp at the base of her neck. She reached her hand over her shoulder, not quite able to reach.

"I couldn't do it up the whole way. But could you unzip it for me?"

"Sure." Leila pinched the clasp, slowly unzipping with care as though she was holding a newborn baby. When she was done, she turned to leave.

"Wait!" Kiko said, glancing over her bare shoulder. "I want to talk with you about something private."

Leila kept her back to Kiko until she was sure she was fully dressed. Then, she plonked herself on the thin roll out mattress. "What's up, sista?"

"I like that," Kiko said softly, taking a seat opposite Leila. "And it's kind of why I wanted to talk to you." She took a breath and winced. "It's about who I am. I think, considering we are family now. That you should know about my past."

"Oh." Leila was unsure of what else to say. She could have said, "you got it, sis." Or, "I'm all ears." Or, "tell me all about it, and don't leave out the juicy bits." But no, she didn't say any of that. All that she could manage was an: "oh". She was losing her touch.

Kiko grabbed the ends of her hair and gently placed them behind her shoulders. "I guess I'll just spit it out then." She waited a moment, as if making sure she had Leila's full attention. Then blurted, "I'm the first Guardian. Well, one of them."

"Oh," Leila said again.

The fact didn't truly surprise her. Not with how elegant Kiko was. What surprised her was the memory of what Ren and the Elder of the Veil had said about the first Guardians.

There were three, and one of them was a —

"I know what you're thinking. Yes, there were three first Guardians. I have another brother. He's Tessa's Alpha. The Fallen."

Leila swallowed. She pressed her lips together, trying not say another *Oh*.

Kiko continued, "Ren and I have been in hiding from him for a long time but it seems he's found us again."

The pained expression Kiko gave made Leila's heart sink. She reached for Kiko's hand. "I'm so sorry. You must be so scared."

Tears welled in Kiko's eyes. She shook her head emphatically. "No, silly girl. *I'm* the one who should be sorry. I never wanted to drag you into my family troubles. Or Kale. But my brother, he's jealous of Imprints. I knew it was only a matter of time before the Fallen came for me…" Kiko's eyes dropped. She turned her hand around in Leila's and clasped tight, as if she was holding on for dear life. "And you."

Leila's lion was a protective Guardian. She felt it close to her, the need for justice pulsating from its aura to hers. It wanted to align, to start a war, to fight for her family.

Kiko continued, "You have to know my brother isn't just any Fallen. He's the first. Evil has lived in his heart for almost a century. He took everything I loved away from me. If you ever have the misfortune of coming face-to-face with him, be wary. He's manipulative—great at deception. He will twist things in his favor. Make you think things. He will probably try and turn you against me."

Leila proclaimed, "We'll keep each other safe. Nothing will happen to any of us. I promise!"

"I'm so lucky to have you." Kiko threw herself at Leila, embracing her tightly.

When they were ready, they went outside together. Leila tried hard to grasp her thoughts. She was grateful to have solidified her bond with Kiko, but the shared moment that brought them closer also brought the danger level up a few notches.

Kale wandered over from his spot near the fire. He mouthed, "Did you tell her?"

Kiko only needed to nod for him to envelop her in his arms. Leila heard him whisper, "I'm so proud of you."

As if they were the only people in the world, Kale swept Kiko around the waist and led her to their tent. Leila cringed. She didn't want to think about what her brother was about to do. So she focused on the good part. The part that was happy for him finding someone to love.

"Well, that's gross," Gabby teased.

"Seriously," Leila winced. "I don't wanna think about it."

"Will you though?" Gabby wriggled her brows up and down and gave a dramatic wink. "Later tonight, with Riley?"

"With me what?" Riley asked, joining them.

"Hiiiii," Leila chirped. She threw a glare to Gabby and said, "Oh nothing, I just have to do a perimeter check and Gabby asked if you were coming."

How easy it was to lie. But honestly, the last thing she wanted to do was talk with her best-friend and boyfriend about what they might or might not do in their tent.

"Sure!" Riley replied.

Leila nodded once then turned to Gabby, "If you don't mind?"

"Nah." Gabby winked again. "I'll keep the fire going, lovers."

Riley glanced around the camp site. Most people were in their tents, except for Sadie who sat alone on a log. He furrowed his brow at Gabby, "Are you sure you'll be okay on your own?"

Gabby gave a deadpan expression. "Yeah, I might just sit here and toast some marshmallows, then coat them with the blood of a virgin." She hitched her thumb in the direction of Sadie.

"Ugh," Riley moaned. "You're getting as bad as Leila with your sarcasm."

Gabby grinned.

Eyes turning to slits, Riley added, "That is if you are being sarcastic?"

Gabby's smile vanished. She eyed Leila then Riley then Leila.

"Pfff," Leila burst, tapping her knuckles against his shoulder. "Oh my god, good one, Riley."

"Yeah," Gabby said, uneasily. "Good one."

"Howl if you need anything," Leila said, grabbing Riley's hand. She dragged him toward the tree line, tugging on his arm to bring him closer. "You totally were joking, right?"

Riley cleared his throat and replied, "Mmhm."

SUNDAY

evening

Leila

The snow had stopped falling somewhere around the time that the dim light of the fire became nothing but an orange flicker behind them. Overhead, the moon peered between a break in the clouds. Leila let go of Riley's hand and regrasped him properly, sliding her fingers through his.

Riley squeezed his fingertips against her knuckles. "How are you?"

"It's been a bit hectic," Leila replied, Kiko's confession rolling through her mind.

She wished she'd known sooner. It wasn't just a random Fallen they were dealing with anymore, it was Kiko's blood. There was history behind it.

Leila glanced at Riley. "I can't stop thinking about what that Elder said."

"Samuel? Which part?"

"About the first Imprint being a Fallen, making it their

job to hunt other Imprints. Do you think that's what happening here? That they're playing with us?"

"Back in Seattle, when Tessa—" Riley paused to sigh. He ran his fingers through his hair, and continued, "When she destroyed our home, I got a glimpse of the Fallen and what they could do. I think they're definitely playing with us."

Leila couldn't hold it in any longer. Riley needed to know the truth, whether it will hurt him or not. She blurted, "Kiko's brother is Tessa's Alpha."

"I'm sorry what?" Riley turned to Leila. He let out a nervous laugh. "It sounded like you said Ren is Tessa's Alpha."

"No, not Ren." Leila said it slowly, to help the words sink in. "The first Guardians were Ren, Kiko... and their brother."

Riley froze, he looked out into the darkness, as if searching for answers among the trees.

Leila continued, "I'm assuming Kiko's the eldest of the three, and Ren the youngest. And the middle brother was the Imprint who became Fallen."

Riley's eyes shot to her. Realization hitting him, he said, "The one who's my sister's Alpha?" His voice shook at the last part.

"Yup. Told you. Hectic." Leila grimaced a smile. "It's a little bit day-time soap opera, isn't it?"

A soft smile lifted Riley's cheeks. He reached for Leila's hand, stroking his thumb gently over her palm. "I'd say it's more like an episode of the Twilight Zone."

Leaves rustled close by—too close for comfort. Riley spun around, immediately aligning with his wolf. Their vision was better than perfect even when they were human —Riley's glasses nothing but a ruse—but half-shifted their sight became amplified.

Leila half-shifted, too. She danced her gaze around the forest. She could see all the splinters in tree trunks, all the leaves as they grew from branches, and an owl flitting its wings into the night sky.

Leila gently touched Riley's warm back and threaded her arms around to his chest. Feeling his heart pounding onto her palms, she whispered, "Not everything is out to get us."

"I know," he breathed the words.

"Are you sure?" Leila asked, letting him go. "Because not five minutes ago you literally thought that Gabby wanted to eat marshmallows covered in Sadie's blood."

Shaking his head, Riley turned around to face her. "I just wonder if we made the right choice, you know? Letting me turn you instead of someone else, like Ren. We wouldn't be Imprints. We wouldn't have the Fallen on our backs."

Even in the shadows of the trees, Leila hoped Riley could still see her *"are you kidding me?"* expression. "Yeah, but Kiko and Kale would still be Imprints, so we'd still be in this mess. And, even if they weren't Imprints, maybe her brother would be after her regardless. It's hardly our fault for being who we are. Besides, we're pretty kick-ass right? Remember what that Elder of the Veil said... We are stronger together."

"Samuel," Riley said. "The Elder's name is Samuel. And don't forget what else he said, about a Fallen being in our midst."

Leila let out a long groan. If she was being honest with herself, she was hoping he wouldn't have brought that up. Where she saw hope, Riley always saw doubt. They were never going to agree on it.

She threw her arm to the west and began walking. "We should keep going."

Riley muttered, "Typical. Just when things get too hard."

Leila stopped, spinning back around. She knew exactly what he meant. It was typical that she hid from some of the heavier discussions. Either by making a joke, or deflecting, or walking away, literally.

It didn't matter that it was true. It still hurt.

She didn't need to say anything before Riley's face dropped. He placed both hands on his head, wincing his pained eyes. "I just mean—" He let his hands fall to his sides. "You don't want to talk about the possibility we're being played from the inside?"

Okay, Leila thought. *If he wants to talk about it, let's talk about it.*

"By who? Sebastian?"

Riley shrugged his shoulders. "If the shoe fits."

The topic infuriated her. Yes, technically he was Fallen, but he didn't do Fallen things. "You don't remember what happened with Cap? If Sebastian wasn't there to save Sadie—"

"*You* would have saved her," Riley interrupted.

"Yeah, after she became Cap's dinner. Seriously, Riley, I wouldn't have gotten to her in time. Sebastian literally saved her life. Isn't that what Guardians do?"

Riley rolled his eyes.

This was the side of Riley that confused Leila. In all other areas of his life, he was perfect. The perfect student, the perfect son, the perfect boyfriend. But when it came to Guardians, he was static, rigid, and self-righteous.

Stepping toward him, she warmed her tone and implored, "Why do you hate him so much?"

Riley's bottom lip rolled out into a sad smile and Leila knew she'd reached him. He sighed, then said, "You wanna know the truth? It's because of what he represents. You saw my sister, she acted innocent, she saved the girls, but deep down she's still done horrible things. She's still a monster. That's what Fallen do."

Leila lifted her hand to Riley's face and scooped a wavy tendril off the rim of his glasses. She knew how much his past had hurt him, she just wished he didn't compare it to everything in their present. She whispered, "I love you."

Riley squinted, a teasing glimmer hitting his eyes. "Why do I feel like there's a *but* coming?"

"But you're a bit judgmental sometimes. I mean, you've always been serious, but ever since I became a Guardian, you've been *extra* serious."

Leila huffed out a quick sigh, happy to have let that off her chest.

Riley nodded to himself, unable to maintain eye contact. Looking into the distance, he said, "I have to be. Right? *I'm* the leader of our clan. I have to be on edge. I have to be in control."

"You have to be fair, too, though." Leila tried to make her voice as gentle as possible.

Riley dropped his head. "This isn't just about Sebastian, is it?"

"It's about Gabby."

Nodding, he looked over the top of his glasses. "I know. I'm a dick."

"No!" Leila proclaimed, grabbing both his hands and covering them with hers in a protective embrace. "No one thinks that. We know you care. But... sometimes that care comes across as judgment, as though you think there's something wrong with them. Gabby's had enough of that in her life. And that truth is, she knows something isn't right within her. We don't need to remind her every moment. She knows."

Riley chewed the inside of his mouth. "And you want me to give her some slack?"

"Riley." Leila dropped his hands and moved her touch to his face, curving her palms around his jawline. "I really do love you."

Riley's mouth twitched. "No *buts* this time?"

Shaking her head, Leila moved in. "No buts," she whispered.

The warmth of Riley's breath rushed over her chin before he pushed his fleshy lips upon her. He gave her a smattering of small pecks, that slowed into a long open-mouthed kiss. As Riley slid his tongue into her mouth, Leila leaned in, feeling her body tingle with excitement.

He placed his hands on either side of her face and pulled

away slightly. Resting his forehead onto hers, Riley mumbled, "Am I really that serious?"

As Leila exhaled through her nose in silent laughter, the energy of the kiss awakened her instincts. She bounced between her feet and she took a deep inhale. "I love the smell of the forest."

Riley smiled. "You wanna run?"

"Yes!" she replied with delight.

Riley peered over the rim of his glasses. "Was that a yes to me being super serious or yes to running?"

Leila grinned so wide her cheeks began hurting. She forced herself to reel it in, squeezing her lips shut. Throwing her arm, she said, "We'll circle around."

She called her lion forward, fully shifting, and ran.

"You didn't answer—" Riley called behind her. "Ugh, never mind."

Leila slowed until Riley caught up and they ran side-by-side, wolf and lion, the night air rushing over their fur. It didn't take long for Leila to pull ahead of Riley, she urged forward, desperate for speed. The faster she ran, the better it felt. Leaving him behind, Leila pushed into a full run. She tore through the forest, weaving trees and jumping shrubs. It was bliss in the way that nothing else mattered. The whole world melted away and it was just her, the lion, and the earth at their feet.

"Leila?" Riley called. He sounded puffed.

She slowed again, the weight of the world tumbling back in again. The thump of the white wolf's paws reverberated through the soil. Closer. Closer... really close.

A thunk rang out, fur against bark. An "ow" followed. Leila stopped and spun around in time to see Riley's wolf tumbling along the ground, a white ball of fuzz heading directly for her. His shoulder connected with her torso and ricocheted a few yards away.

Leila felt her ribs crack. Gasping for air, she dropped to her knees. The pain was unbearable. Her lion retreated, taking her back to human form. She fell backward, laying on dirt and small twigs. She took a few shaky breaths, calling upon her Guardian's healing power to aim for the wound. Slowly, the agony subsided.

Riley clambered over, already back to human form. As soon as he reached her, she felt the wound healing faster. She took a gulp of air, relieved for the pain to be gone.

"Are you okay?" Riley asked on all fours above her. "I tripped."

"Mm," Leila nodded. "I'm fine. I healed faster when you got here."

Riley sighed, glasses falling down his nose. "I notice that, too. If I get a scratch or something when I'm near you, I heal quicker than if you're not around."

She looked up at him and felt nothing but love. Leila could do incredible things. She could ace exams, run a marathon twice over, open jars even her dad couldn't. She could hear, see, and taste things on a higher scale than any human. But together, they were something else. They were unstoppable.

As he hovered over her, she took his face in her hands and brought him closer. He collapsed against her unbroken ribs and they kissed. Just once.

Riley lifted, placing his palms on the ground on either side of her head. He gave a tilted smile, then stood up. Half-shifting, he scanned their surrounds, neon-blues shining. "We should finish the perimeter check."

"Okay," Leila said, a cheeky glint in her eyes. "I'll beat you to it."

Then, she jumped to her feet, fully shifted, and ran.

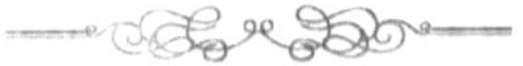

By the time they got back to camp, everyone except Mr. Robertson were in their tents. He sat at the base of a tree on the edge of camp, digging a pocket knife under his nail.

Without looking up, he said, "See you in the morning."

"Good night," Leila replied, taking Riley's hand.

She led him to her tent. As they reached the entrance, Riley tugged on her arm.

"You want me to stay with you?" he whispered, glancing over his shoulder at Kale and Kiko's tent.

Leila nodded and walked in. He followed her and zipped up the tent, closing them in. She kept her eyes on him as she removed her sweatshirt. Riley's eyes widened. He gulped, watching her every move.

She settled herself onto the mattress, flipping the blanket open and tapping on the space beside her. He moved in, crawling into the spot. As soon as she let the blanket fall, he wrapped his arms around her, cradling her in close to him.

The first move was hers. She lunged over him and kissed him, not like before. As their lips glided together, pressing hard and hungry, his hands gripped at her hips. She slipped her tongue around the inside of his top lip, and Riley let out a moan. He twisted under her and slowly sucked her bottom lip. Leila's body ignited. Nothing else mattered in that moment. Leila dug her fingertips around the base of his hairline, urging him to come closer. She felt his chest heaving into her breasts as his hands squeezed her backside.

Then, as quickly as they started, they separated. Panting, Riley pushed her off him. He rolled her around and kissed the nape of her neck.

"We should get some sleep," he whispered.

Leila didn't know why she expected this time would have been any different to all the times she'd tried to make a move before. He always stopped them before things got too heated. She wished sometimes he could stop being so tense and just go with it. He was always the serious one in their relationship. She didn't see why everything was always such a heavy decision to him. She would have let him sleep with her on the floor of the forest for all she cared.

I have to be in control. Riley's words rang through her

mind.

The realization hit her like an avalanche. It was never her burden to bear. It was always on him. The decisions. The rules. The safety of their clan. Every possible thing that could go wrong was on his shoulders. No wonder he was always on edge.

She clutched at his wrist and draped it over her body, nuzzling her back against his chest.

"Comfy?" Riley asked.

"Mm," Leila mumbled, the urge of sleep washing over her.

The last thing she remembered was Riley kissing her shoulder.

MONDAY

morning

Leila

Leila woke to the sound of quiet chatter outside her tent. Imogen and Summer giggled, and one said, "Oh my god, you're so lame, just mix the porridge with a stick."

Riley took a deep breath and Leila rolled over in time to see him throw one arm up over his head. The tent wobbled as his hand connected with the side of it. He took another deep breath, mouth falling slightly agape as he continued to sleep. Leila smiled at how peaceful he looked. The weight of the clan off his shoulders for at least a few hours.

Leila recalled the first time they'd spent the night sleeping next to each other. She'd been marked and felt so safe with him. He was on edge then too, but it was different now, like his worries had multiplied.

She hovered over him and, wishing she could remove some of the heaviness and stress, she ran her thumb around his temple. Riley rustled. In the next moment, his eyes peeled open.

Noticing Leila, a smile crept across his face. He reached for her hair and twisted a loose curl around his finger. "Morning, beautiful."

Then, almost as quickly as his face lit up, it darkened. He sighed. The invisible weight he carried all at once returned.

Leila placed her hand on his chest, spreading her fingers over the grooves of his pecs. "You know we're in this together, right? You don't have to bear the burden all alone?"

Riley gave a sad smile and tucked his hands under his head. "Mm."

"Come on," Leila said, sitting up. "Share it with me."

"How? That sounds easier than it'd actually be." Riley propped himself up onto his elbows.

"Well, say for example you're worried about something or someone… talk to me. And I can tell you whether it's something to be worried about."

Riley chortled. "According to you there is nothing to worry about."

Leila balled her fist and playfully pushed at his shoulder, causing him to fall back onto the pillow. She pouted and said, "Hey, I worry. The fact that Kiko's Fallen brother, the very first Fallen ever, is hunting us… Imprints. *That* worries me."

"Okay then," Riley said, sitting up. The blanket fell to his hips, baring the waist of his black boxer briefs. "And, how do you propose we deal with that?"

Leila thought for a bit, then shrugged. "I dunno. Maybe leave it to Kiko to make a plan?"

A croaking moan vibrated at the back of Riley's throat. "That's kinda my point. Do you think we should leave everything up to Kiko?"

"What do you mean?"

"I mean…" Riley brushed his hand through his messy locks. "What if her plan sucks? What if she can't be trusted?"

Leila felt her mouth drop. Kiko was a little testy lately,

and maybe she was making odd decisions like forcing Mr. Robertson to stay out all night, but to say she couldn't be trusted? Riley had been over-thinking more than she knew.

"Okay, now you're being paranoid," Leila quipped.

"Maybe I am."

Riley reached for his jeans and stood. As he slid them on, Leila's eyes drifted from the mark on his shoulder blade to the dip of his back. He looked over his shoulder, catching Leila's sneaky gaze. Riley cleared his throat and Leila snapped her eyes to his.

"Breakfast?" he asked with a tilted smirk.

"Oh, hell no!" Leila exclaimed. There was no way Riley got out of it that easily. If she had to stop running from conversations, he did, too.

"You're not hungry?" Riley frowned.

"No... well, yes, starving, but you can't just say that about Kiko and leave it at that."

Riley's eyes washed over into a daze, staring at nothing at all. After a few moments, he sniffed and looked at Leila. "It's not about Tsukiko. Not really. So, just don't worry about it."

As he stepped for the tent's entrance, Leila leapt to her feet. She grabbed his wrist and implored, "Riley, please. Talk to me."

Riley inhaled and exhaled quickly, as though psyching himself up. He nodded once, moved back to the mattress, and sat down. "Fine," he said, lifting a knee and resting his elbow over it. "Let's talk."

There was an eerie second of silence. Leila hesitantly sat down. The way he said it sounded grave. As though, he was about to tell her the darkest of secrets.

"So, remember when I told you about that girl I had a thing with while my sister destroyed our lives?"

Leila nodded. He lost his virginity to *that girl*. She didn't mean to, but she muttered her reply with a spiteful tone, "I remember."

Riley picked up the edge of the blanket and squeezed it between his fingers. "I didn't tell you something."

"What?"

Riley shook his head, rolling his eyes to himself. "The girl… the one I slept with… she was a Guardian. I didn't know until later that night when I found my sister hovering over my mom. And this girl, this one who was all over me not half an hour earlier, she rushed in and told Tessa they had to go."

Leila's heart skipped. "She knew Tessa?"

Dropping the blanket, Riley let his gaze fall on her. A tear had formed in the corner of his eye, and when he blinked it stuck to his eyelashes. "It was their plan the whole time. She was meant to distract me so Tessa could do what she needed. Ruin our home. Hurt mom."

"Oh my god, Riley," Leila said, "Why didn't you tell me this?"

"Because I regret every second of it. I don't even remember her name for God's sake." Riley paused for a moment, then added, "I guess I'm just ashamed."

"Ashamed? Of what? Being human? Falling for someone?"

Riley shrugged. "I wasn't thinking with my proper brain."

Leila burst out laughing. "Is that it? Is that why you don't want to sleep with me? Because you're afraid your thinking with your—" she motioned to his crotch. "I'm your girlfriend. We love each other. I love you. This is natural, not a mistake." Leila leaned over, resting her hands on his knees. "Not everything is a cycle, Riley. History doesn't always repeat itself. Gabby isn't turning into Tessa and I'm not some bitch who will sleep with you and use you."

Riley laughed then. "I know you're not. I know. You and I are endgame, Leila. But there's always something looming, some threat. We're always overshadowed by the possibility of bad. What if one minute we're naked and the next Gabby comes tearing through with the blood of innocents on her hands?"

A slight pang hit Leila's chest. "Do you really think that every time things get heated with us?"

"It's not just that. It's not just the sex thing. It's the trust thing." Riley took a shaky breath in. "Like, I had no idea she was playing me. Who else could be, you know? I mean, do we really know that Kiko isn't the Fallen sibling that went crazy being an Imprint?" Riley swallowed and recoiled as if tasting something rotten.

"Riley," Leila muttered his name, almost defeated by his constant negativity.

He gasped for air. "What if they all are? Gabby? Sebastian? Your brother? I can't..."

Riley gasped again. And again. As though he couldn't catch the oxygen fast enough. With labored breath, he continued, "We're Imprints too, you know?"

Inhale, exhale.

"The Fallen."

Inhale.

"Are after us."

Exhale.

"Watching, waiting for us to slip up, to be vulnerable—"

He hunched over, lungs working overtime. He bunched the blanket into fists, chest heaving in and out.

"Stop." Leila clutched his shoulders, dipping her head to catch his eyes. "Breathe Riley, breathe."

He peered up at her, breathing four times to her one. She placed her hand on his chest and underneath her palm she felt his heart racing. It was enough to bring tears to her eyes.

"Breathe slower," she urged.

Leila took a breath in, nodding at him to do the same. He copied her, breath wavering as he did. Out she breathed, making sure he mimicked her. Slow and steady Leila coached him, one long inhale and one long exhale. Over and over she continued until his heart-rate returned to normal.

Once he'd calmed, she said, "There's always a risk of something bad happening or someone double crossing us. It will never end. It could be whether we're attacked by a Fallen or whether we have to listen to Mom rave about vervain for the millionth time. That's the point of having each other. That *we will be the good* even when surrounded by bad."

Riley sat back on his heels. "I know it. It's just hard for me grasp lately."

"You've been focusing too much on what could go wrong, you forget to notice what's right."

Riley reached for her and tucked a stray hair behind her ear. "When did you become the guru?"

"Just comes natural, I guess." Leila shrugged. A teasing smile lit her face as she grabbed her top from the bottom hem and slid it over her head. She felt her own breath shake then, sitting half-naked in front of her boyfriend. "And when I say notice what's right. I also mean, what's right in front of you."

Cedar brown eyes stared back at her. Riley shuffled closer, and reaching for her hips, he whispered, "What if we get caught?"

"The good, Riley," Leila said, tugging at the waist of his jeans. "Look for the good."

He let her undo his jeans and watched her intently as she slid them off. As soon as she was done, his fingers grabbed the grooves of her ribs and he flipped her onto her back. Straddling his legs over her, he lowered himself onto her.

Leila gazed into his eyes and tilted her hips, pushing herself against him. His breath hitched and she watched his chest rise and fall. It was different to before, as though his body was working for him instead of against him.

Of course, Leila waited for him to pull away, as he always did. She waited for him to put a stop to their escapades and tell her now wasn't the time for play. She stared up at him… and waited.

But instead, Riley sunk to his elbows, face now level with hers. The edges of his mouth twitched as he used his index finger to trail her chest and torso. He curved his hand around her waist and let his thumb glide inside the rim of her underwear.

"I love you," he said, eyes dancing over her face. "No buts."

MONDAY

late morning

Sadie

Sadie peeled her eyes open to the glow of the sun beaming through the orange tent wall. The sun was high, which was odd. It really didn't feel like she'd slept that late. Actually, she was surprised she'd slept at all.

As she sat up she felt a twang in her neck. Cursing the thin yoga mat she'd laid on, she pulled her day-old sweater over her head and stepped out of the tent. A few people were milling around, chatting by the fire or washing bowls in a small bucket. Not quite ready for breakfast or small talk, she found herself a patch of dirt in front of her tent and sat cross-legged, wondering what the day would bring.

"Good morning," Leila said, appearing out of nowhere. She shoved a steaming mug in front of Sadie and had an unusual glint in her eyes. "Here. It'll warm you up. No cinnamon, sorry."

Sadie took the mug. She didn't really need to be warmed though, she certainly didn't feel cold. The heat of the fire pulsated against her face, even from five yards away.

"Thank you." Sadie smiled and faced the sky. Closing her eyes, she thanked the heavens for the end of winter. "It feels like spring."

When Leila didn't reply, Sadie opened her eyes. Leila had dashed off, heading for Mr. Robertson with another mug in her grasp. Sadie glanced around the camp and noticed most everyone who was up had a mug in their hands. Trust Leila to make sure everyone was cared for.

She returned her gaze upward and stared at tree tops that silhouetted the sky. There was a rustle beside her, followed by a huff. Sadie swooped her head around to see Sebastian making himself comfortable beside her. He held a bowl in each of his hands.

"It's my peace offering," he said with hooded eyes.

Sadie peered into the bowl. "Porridge? Our ideas of peace offerings are wildly different."

She meant it as a joke but there was no joy in her tone.

Sebastian shrugged and placed the bowl on the ground in front of her. "Hey, if you stayed in my loft, I'd be cooking you waffles or pancakes with berries and jam. But, out here —"

If she stayed in his loft? Why would she ever stay in his loft? A flush of heat fell over her. Sadie took a sip of cocoa to hide the blood that colored her cheeks.

"Anyway," Sebastian interrupted himself. "I'm really sorry for snapping last night. You didn't deserve that. It just... it hurts talking about it."

"I know you didn't mean anything by it." Sadie rested the mug next to her breakfast and took her sweater off. She threw it at her tent and sighed. "That's better."

Sebastian frowned. He looked across to Imogen and Summer, huddled by the fire with their jackets on. "You're not cold?"

Sadie shook her head and picked up the porridge. She sniffed it and the oatmeal smell drifted through her nostrils and instantly made her tummy rumble. Maybe she *was* ready for breakfast. She shoved a spoonful into her mouth.

Sebastian chuckled. "Oh, the things I'm finding out about you, Shorty. You're really something."

As she let the taste savor on her tongue a little, she stared at him. His eyes twinkled and she felt he meant to test her. But she had no inclination to flirt back. She just wanted to learn more about him, too.

She swallowed and said, "When you're ready to tell me, I'm here."

Sebastian clenched his jaw and nodded. He scooped a spoonful porridge and lifted it to his mouth. He held it there for a moment before dropping it back into the bowl. "It's my dad."

"Oh… ah…" Sadie stuttered. She never expected him to actually tell her right then and there.

Sebastian gave a quick sad smile. He placed his bowl on the ground and kept his gaze down, pulling at the laces on his shoes. "In junior year, almost two years ago now, I found out that he was leading a double life."

Sadie immediately spun to face him. As she turned, dots of light crossed her vision as though her brain couldn't quite keep up with the body's movement. She blinked slowly a few times, waiting for the feeling to pass.

When she'd regained her composure, she repeated, "A double life?"

Still tugging on his laces, Sebastian glanced up. "He was a realtor, so frequent trips weren't rare. We were used to it, Mom never questioned him. But those business trips to Seattle were actually visits with a separate family. A whole separate family. Kids and all."

"Wow." Was all Sadie could manage. But she could understand then, why Imogen didn't like his idea to see their dad.

"Apparently, he hadn't been with the other woman since Immy was born. He swore he'd been faithful to mom since then. But the damage had kinda been done and Mom kicked him out. He lives in his cabin, permanently alone."

There it was, the vulnerability she'd seen hints of before, now on full display. Sadie reached to comfort him but stopped short with her hand hovering above his knee. Would he even want her comfort?

Pulling her hand back to her lap, she said, "I'm so sorry. That kind of thing would change anyone."

Sebastian shrugged. He leaned forward, resting his elbows to his knees. "It wasn't so much the secret that broke me. It was mom. She fell apart. She couldn't handle the thought of, well, all of it. She lost all sense of who she was."

"That would've been hard for you to watch. With no other adult to help you make sense of it yourself."

Sebastian looked up and maintained eye contact with Sadie for a good five seconds. It felt like five years. She cringed at herself for saying such platitudes, like she was reading a script direct from psychology 101. She was about to say sorry, that she couldn't possibly understand how he felt, but then he nodded.

"It was hard. I mean, we might see Dad once or twice a year. He doesn't even know she started drinking." Sebastian returned his eyes to his laces, twisting them so tight around his finger the tips went white. "It was a binge session here and there at first, but it didn't take long to become a daily habit. Now, she can't even look at me without alcohol in her system… she says I look too much like him."

Sadie reached for him then, she let her hand cup his knee. He didn't even flinch. "That's rough."

"I try to help her. Cook. Clean. But it's hard being near her. I renovated the barn and made it my own, somewhere to be far enough away from her but close enough to Imogen."

Sadie's heart fled into overdrive. The whole thing made her feel ill. How his family could have been lied to that whole time. That he had siblings out there he'd never met. The responsibility he felt for his mom and Imogen. She wanted to tell him that he was amazing, how well he'd handled everything. Especially becoming a Fallen and not letting his anger and pain control him. But she couldn't find the words.

No, that wasn't it. Not only couldn't she find the words, she also couldn't find oxygen. Her whole throat had zipped shut. She gasped as sweat dripped like rain from her temples. She was hot. So hot.

"Shorty?" Sebastian asked, pressing the back of his hand against her forehead. "You don't look so good."

In front of her, Sebastian's face blurred. His frown deepened under the blobs of sky blue which should have been his eyes.

"I'm tired," she mumbled, patting across the ground as if reaching for a pillow. Her hand brushed up against the mug, tipping it over. Hot cocoa coated the ground.

A chill swooped upon her, like a million cubes of ice tracing her bare skin from her head to her toes. Darkness clouded in around her. And, the last thing she felt was strong arms around her and the vibration of Sebastian's voice as he yelled, "Leila!"

MONDAY

before noon

Leila

Leila had never heard anyone call her name like that before. Sebastian's voice rang through the morning fog and shook the core of her being. She gasped, as though his own hands had gripped her throat.

Sebastian knelt over Sadie, hands cupping the back of her neck as she laid on the ground in front of her tent. His eyes blazed neon as he screamed, "Hurry up!"

The order pushed her into motion. She darted across to them, her lion ready to align. In Sebastian's hold, under the shade of her tent, Sadie was unconscious. Her cheeks were red and her light hair began sticking to her forehead from all the sweat. She was breathing, that was the main thing.

Kiko and Kale rushed to join them.

"I've seen this before," Kale said. "This is what you were like, Leila. When you got sick right before the mark appeared."

"You really think so?" Leila peered down at her best friend who suddenly looked so small and fragile. The thought of Sadie being marked against her will crushed her soul.

"What's going on?" Riley leaned over Leila's shoulder.

"I agree," Kiko said, sadly. "She's definitely in incubation. And considering the timing of her fever, she was marked in the last 12 hours."

Leila put her palm to her heart. If she'd been marked in the last 12 hours, that meant— "Someone here marked her?"

Kiko swiveled on her heels and nearly knocked Leila over as she whizzed past, marching across the camp to her tent.

Riley took no time to point the finger. He clutched Sebastian's collar and dragged him to his feet. Kale was quick to catch Sadie's head as she rolled out of Sebastian's lap.

"Riley!" Leila cried, falling to her knees to check Sadie was all right.

"What's your plan?" Riley demanded, scrunching Sebastian's shirt in his fists.

Sebastian stepped back until Riley lost grip. He raised his hands in surrender, "Not me, bro."

"Don't call me bro," Riley said through gritted teeth. A threatening blue shimmered across his brown eyes.

Before he did something he'd regret, Leila reached for him, clutching at his wrist. "We should move her into the tent."

Riley darted his angry eyes to Leila, and then to Sadie. He blinked a few times, face softening. Nodding, he said, "Okay."

The two of them carried Sadie into the tent, Sebastian was smart enough to walk away. Leila and Riley sat on either side of Sadie's sleepy body. Fighting back tears, Leila brushed Sadie's sticky hair away from her forehead.

"We'll fix this," Riley said.

Leila squeezed her eyes shut. "What's wrong with you?"

"What do you mean?"

As she opened her eyes, a lone tear escaped. "With Sebastian. What the hell was that?"

Riley jerked his head back as though confused by the question. "He marked Sadie."

"I don't think he would—"

"Leila. Please. He's a Fallen."

Turning her attention back to Sadie, Leila gave a frustrated sigh. She didn't have proof that Sebastian wasn't a Fallen and there were only so many times she could talk about him saving Sadie's life. It was just a gut feeling, something inexplicable that told her there was good inside him.

"Get your hands off me."

"Don't think so, buddy."

Leila rushed out of the tent, Riley close behind her. Sebastian had half-shifted, brazen blue eyes wide with terror. Kale had him in a choke hold. He didn't even have to shift at all to be able to keep Sebastian restrained.

"What are you doing?" Imogen screamed. "You're killing him."

Kale's face dropped. He loosened his hold slightly. "I'm sorry but your brother is a Fallen."

"Kale!" Leila cried, rushing over. She stood opposite them, and pleaded, "Let him go."

"Can't do that, Sis. I'm taking orders." Kale clenched his jaw as Sebastian writhed beneath his grasp.

A tent rustled and Kiko appeared holding a duffel bag. She placed the bag on the ground and as her eyes met Leila's, she rolled her bottom lip out in sympathy. "Sorry. He has to go. We shouldn't have allowed a Fallen to be here in the first place."

"No, but..." Leila recalled Sebastian's frightened eyes from the day before, when he told her Sadie was missing. There was no way he marked Sadie. He cared too much.

"Leila," Kiko said softly. "You need to face the truth. We can't be hopeful about things like this. Sadie's been marked."

"What?" Summer broke out of her tent. "What does that mean? She's been marked?"

"It means…" Kiko paused to let all the air out of her lungs. "That someone here is a traitor and a Fallen."

"I think the answer is obvious," Riley said, moving next to Leila. He stared at Sebastian.

Sebastian shook his head, looking at one person only. Imogen. He mouthed the words, "It wasn't me."

Riley scoffed. "He can't even defend himself. Guilty much?"

A wry smile reached Sebastian's mouth as he turned his attention to Riley. "What about Riley's bad sister, who happened to miraculously save the girls? She's a Fallen, right? She touched Sadie."

Kiko walked right up to him, her steely gaze unwavering as she said, "Not within the last twelve hours she didn't. Did you?"

Sebastian flared his nostrils. He thought for a moment, then his eyes fluttered as though caught out in a lie.

"That's what I thought. You have to go." Kiko stepped back and flicked her wrist.

Kale tightened his grasp, letting the crook of his elbow press tighter around Sebastian's neck. He leaned toward Kiko, and whispered, "You want me to…?" He finished the sentence with a tilt of his head.

Kiko glanced over her shoulder at Leila, then to Imogen. She flipped her head back to Kale. "Maybe just a banishment today."

Leila's stomach churned. She knew exactly what Kale had insinuated. Banishment sounded a lot better than the alternative.

"Bye Sebastian," Riley said with ice.

Kale released Sebastian and shoved him toward the cars.

"Time to go, Fallen."

Sebastian spun around and scoffed, "Seriously? After everything I've done to keep her safe? You're just going to kick me out?" He turned to Leila. "You get me, right? I wouldn't hurt Sadie, I promise on my own life."

Leila didn't know how to respond. She was done arguing with Riley about it. And now Kale and Kiko were on the hating Sebastian bandwagon, there wasn't much she could say or do to change their minds.

When Leila didn't answer, Sebastian threw his arm in the direction of Sadie's tent. "Ask her. She'll tell you that I didn't do it."

"Sebastian," Kiko said, gently cupping his elbow and urging him toward his car. "Don't make a scene. You need to go."

A high-pitched cry billowed into the air. "Stop it. He's not a criminal. Stop treating him like a criminal!"

Imogen ran to her brother, clutching at his wrist, trying with all her might to hold him back. With his other hand, Sebastian cupped her jaw. He pulled her into him, one arm wrapping around her shoulders.

From the edge of the camp, hiding behind a low flicker of flame, Gabby chortled. "Seriously girl, wake up. Your brother is a monster."

Imogen peered up into the eyes of her big brother, all color gone from her face. Leila could feel the confusion and heartbreak from where she stood. She thought that was cruel, even for Gabby.

"Like you?" Sebastian hissed in return. As Gabby's cocky grin faded, he continued, "Yeah, I heard Sadie say you were a Fallen. I already knew, though. I could see it in your eyes when you half-shifted in the library. It hurts doesn't it? Shifting is like a thousand needles piercing your soul with poison."

Gabby swallowed and nervously eyed those around the camp.

"Well, she's different," Riley said beside Leila.

"How?" Sebastian re-gripped Imogen, making sure she was tucked well under his arm. "Tell me golden boy, how are her and I different?"

"For starters. She'd never kill her Alpha." Riley's jaw twitched, as though he wasn't quite sure he believed his own words.

Leila knew though. She knew Gabby wouldn't kill anyone. And she knew… well, at least hoped, that Sebastian wouldn't mark anyone without their permission.

She stepped between Riley and Sebastian, hands splayed in surrender. "I just… I think maybe the more we argue the more they win. You know, those who actually want to hurt Sadie. Everyone here wants to keep her safe. Right?"

"Right," Sebastian agreed immediately.

Riley nodded. He gave a hesitant glance at Sebastian. "But—"

"No buts," Leila interrupted. "We're all in this together."

"All right," Kiko huffed. "I've said it before, you're very sweet Leila. But sugar doesn't kill the Fallen." She pointed at Sebastian's car. "You can leave, or we can tie you up."

"We'll go," Sebastian mumbled, leading a crying Imogen to his car. When he reached the driver door, he turned back and pointed at Leila, then to Sadie's tent. "Keep her safe!"

"I will," Leila replied.

As his car rolled down the gravel track, and Summer's sobs echoed around camp, Kiko knelt in front of her duffel bag. She demanded, "I need everyone's blood."

Riley stepped forward. "You think one of us marked her? Shouldn't you have gotten Sebastian's blood first?"

For once Leila agreed with Riley. But she wasn't ready to argue with Kiko about it. She rolled her lips together, pressing them tight and forcing herself to remain silent.

"The Fallen are great at deception, it could be anyone." Kiko pulled out a vial of vervain cream in one hand and a pin in the other. She pricked her finger and dripped blood into the vial. She walked over to Riley and lifted the pin. He held out his hand willingly and Kiko pricked the end of his finger. She moved onto Gabby. "We will all put our blood in the ointment, if it doesn't cure her then we will know it wasn't anyone left here."

Leila let Kiko take her blood. "Will the cure work before the mark appears?"

Kiko nodded, moving onto Kale. She held the vial up and swirled the contents at eye level. "Jay is on a perimeter check, but I turned him, so if it was him who betrayed us, my blood will still make it work. Leila, come with me."

She snapped her fingers around the vial and headed for Sadie's tent. Leila hurried to follow her and the two of them entered Sadie's tent. They each sat down on either side of the sleeping beauty.

"Check for a rash," Kiko said, lifting Sadie's arm.

Leila began with Sadie's wrist, looking for any sign of red or discoloration. She checked her forearm, her elbow, her bicep. Up on Sadie's shoulder, in the groove between bone and neck, Leila noticed a slight inconsistency.

"Here?" she asked, pointing to three faint bumps.

Kiko peered over Sadie and spotting them she returned to the ointment. She dipped her fingers into the vial and coated Sadie's neck in cream. Staring at Sadie's neck, Kiko wiped her fingers on the side of the tent. "She should wake up."

Leila watched and waited. Remembering how the cure worked for Morgan a few months ago, Leila expected Sadie to open her eyes within seconds. But Sadie remained the same, sweaty forehead and labored breath.

Kiko slumped back. "I'm sorry. It must have been Sebastian. He's obviously working with Tessa."

Leila nodded to appease Kiko. Not for one second did she believe he did it. She knew she was stubborn, but there was obviously something they'd missed.

"We've got some more pruning to do," Kiko said, rolling

to her feet. "Come on."

Leila watched Kiko leave the tent. Glancing back at Sadie's neck covered in cream, she whispered, "Wake up, Sades. Tell us who did it."

As she left the tent, Riley stared at her with questioning eyes. She shook her head, eyes falling on Kiko as she marched toward Riley. In one fluid motion, Kiko threw the vial into the dying flames and clutched Riley's wrist.

Riley winced as Kiko tightened her grip, leaning closer to him. She hissed whispers that Leila couldn't quite catch, and Riley's gaze drifted to Gabby. From behind Kiko, Leila could see the look of fear in his eyes.

"Okay," Kiko said, spinning around. "The cure didn't work, which means you're all off the hook." She faced Gabby, her eyes narrowing. "But not you."

Riley quickly stepped in front of Kiko, hands raising in surrender. "This isn't personal Gab, but we're going to have to tie you up."

Leila gasped. Surely she had heard that wrong.

"I'm sorry, what?" Gabby said.

"Listen." Kiko hedged past Riley. "These are your options: you can leave or make friends with a rope."

"Kiko!" Leila exclaimed, unable to contain her silence. "This is madness."

Riley rushed for her. His smooth hands found her shoulders and gave her a tender squeeze. Sad eyes peering down at her, he whispered, "This is for the best."

"You can't be serious?"

"She's a Fallen," he said, and then louder so the whole camp could hear, "She's a Fallen."

Gabby clutched the insides of her maroon flannelette sleeves. As she lifted her chin, the sun hit the tears forming in her eyes. She looked at Kiko and bravely said, "I'll stay. Tie me up."

MONDAY

noon

Leila

Somewhere near the border of Washington and Oregon, the clouds rolled together to become a mass of gray. It covered the sun and half the sky. Mostly though, it covered Leila's heart.

Their clan was dwindling moment by moment. Damien wasn't a Guardian anymore. Ren was M.I.A. Sebastian had been banished. And now Gabby was tied up like an animal.

Leila clutched a big bottle in one hand and a spare T-shirt in the other. She trekked through the forest, following the directions Mr. Robertson had given. There was a fresh-water river nearby. East. The fact that they were out of water was the least of her worries, she just wanted some space.

After she'd walked ten minutes, Leila found the river—which was more like a tiny spring, snaking its way through the forest. She knelt onto the mossy ground and dipped the open bottle into the running water. As the bottle filled, she closed her eyes and listened to the trickle, letting it calm her.

Far from the stench of injustice, she could inhale all the scents of the woodland. Dampness and freshness all at once.

When the bottle was full, she placed it beside her and took the T-shirt, plunging it under the flowing water. The T-shirt bloomed, tie-dyed swirls swimming beneath the surface. The silence soothed Leila's soul. She dipped her hands in next, watching the water as it bobbed around her wrists.

Sebastian marked Sadie. No. It was someone else. Tessa maybe. Kiko said it took around twelve hours for the incubation to begin after being marked, but what if incubation begun earlier, while Sadie slept?

Yes. That was it. Leila decided. It must have been Tessa.

Footsteps resonated behind her and she whipped her head around, dragging the soaking T-shirt with her. As her eyes found Kale, droplets landed onto her jeans, seeping through to her thighs. Leila relaxed and quickly held the T-shirt above the water, away from her body.

Kale waved as he approached. "Hey!"

"Hi," Leila replied, wringing the T-shirt out. "I'm just about done. I wanted to use this to keep Sadie cool."

"Mmm." Kale sighed, air rushing through his nostrils. "Everything has gone a bit too crazy, too fast, hasn't it?"

Leila guffawed. It almost sounded like a joke. "Oh, if only we could go back the days when all I had to worry about was your snoring."

"I don't snore," Kale said, crouching beside her.

Leila raised her brows. She glanced sideways to find a smile on his face. It was the first time she'd seen his infamous cheesy grin since he'd been back.

And then, it vanished. He threw a thumb over his shoulder. "Gabby seems to be taking the whole being tied up thing all right."

"Ha!" Leila shook her head and secured the lid on the bottle. "It's stupid."

"Well, smart really."

Leila snapped her head and glared at him. "How would you feel if I was tied up?"

"That wouldn't happen, you're a True," Kale said, casually reaching for the wet T-shirt. He squeezed and water ran over his fists like heavy rainfall.

"Gimme a break," Leila huffed. "She's innocent and it's stupid. Just like it was stupid to send Sebastian away. Kiko has reduced our forces by a third!"

Kale frowned. "I love you, girl, but you need to be careful with that attitude. Kiko has been a Guardian for a long time, she deserves respect."

Leila pressed her lips together and pushed herself up, balancing in a low squat. She liked Kiko, a lot. But everything was always so black and white with her. She never stopped to think that Guardians, like Sebastian and Gabby, were good. Sure, they'd made mistakes—maybe they had bad thoughts, and maybe it was hard not to act on them, but after all that, they restrained themselves. They always chose the right thing.

"Besides," Kale continued, "Riley is your leader and he agrees."

A bird chirped above them and lurched itself off a branch. Looking up, Leila lost balance and her butt crashed to the ground with a thud. She mumbled, "His judgment is off, too."

Kale snorted. "Lover's quarrel?"

The idea of a lover's tiff was ironic considering she'd lost her virginity to him that morning.

"None of your business," Leila snapped, hauling herself to her feet. She snatched the wet cloth out of his grasp and marched toward camp.

When she got back, everyone was packing up. Mr. Robertson held a rolled up tent under each armpit and threw them into the trunk of his car. Leila watched Kiko throwing items out of her and Kale's tent. One of Riley's car doors was open but he was nowhere to be found.

"He's on patrol," Kiko called, stepping back into her tent.

"Thanks," Leila said. She scuffed her feet against the dirt as she made her way to Sadie's tent.

Summer was sitting out the front, ripping bark off a twig. Leila crouched in front of her and asked, "Do you mind if I go in? Ease her temp a bit?"

Not looking up, Summer shook her head. Leila wanted to say something profound. Like don't worry, everything will be fine. But she didn't know if it would be and she didn't want to lie. So, instead, she gave a sad smile and gently tapped Summer's shoulder as she went inside the tent.

Sadie was half asleep, hooded eyes staring up at nothing in particular. She mumbled, "No, I don't remember who marked me."

Leila placed the damp T-shirt onto Sadie's forehead. "How are you feeling?"

"Leila?" Sadie croaked, blinking slowly. When her eyes finally got a hold of Leila, she said, "When the mark appears, will you be the one to turn me?"

"Let's not think about that right now. It looks like we're packing up to leave, we'll talk about it later, okay?" Leila dragged the cloth from Sadie's forehead down her cheek and rested it on her collarbone.

Sadie threw her hand over Leila's. It seemed as though she was trying to grip but didn't have the strength to curl her fingers. Struggling to sit, she urged, "But, I need to know that you will. I want to be a True, like you."

"We'll get a cure before it even comes to that. Okay? I promise." Leila knew how much Sadie reveled in being the only human in their group. She knew that she hated watching them shift. Becoming a Guardian wasn't what she wanted.

Sadie collapsed back, her hand covering her eyes. "Can you tell Sebastian to come see me?"

"Sebastian?" Leila cleared her throat. "Umm—"

"Leila? You ready? We're almost set!" Kiko called.

Kale's shadow loomed in front of Sadie's tent. "We need to get Sadie into the car so we can pack up this tent."

"Okay," Leila called. She rolled to her feet and looked down into Sadie's hopeful eyes. "I'll go get him," she lied.

Sadie smiled, gave a weak nod, and closed her eyes.

Leila left the tent feeling awful. Not being able to give Sadie anything she wanted sucked. Obviously they just needed Tessa's blood. Then they could cure her and all of this nightmare will be over.

She wandered to Kiko near the dwindling fire. "Kiko?"

"Mmm?" Kiko mumbled, staring into the red coals.

"We need the Fallen's blood. What if we stay here, wait for them to come. What if we fight?"

Kiko tore her eyes from the fire and turned her face to Leila. "That sounds risky. If Sebastian is working for Tessa, and Tessa is working for her Alpha..." Kiko's bottom lip dropped. "He's dangerous, Leila. I think it's best if we steer clear."

"Right, but—" Leila licked her lips, wanting to be as respectful as she could. "But we can't run forever, right? I mean, we'll need to face them eventually. From what you said, it's inevitable. I'd just rather Sadie be cured first. Before everything gets out of control."

A darkness fell over Kiko. She squeezed Leila's bicep. "Honey, everything is already out of control. I just..." Kiko dropped her hand and exhaled loudly. "I'm scared—" Her voice hitched as tears rolled to the corner of her eyes. She sniffed and said, "People I cared about died."

Leila's heart lurched. She'd been so quick to forget. Kiko's brother hadn't just become a Fallen, he'd terrorized the people Kiko loved. Kiko had been on edge, not because she was frustrated but because she was frightened. Memories, excruciating memories, haunted her.

"I'm sorry. I didn't think."

"It's okay. It was a long time ago." Kiko clutched both of Leila's arms and stared right into her eyes. "But I'm not making choices that will put your clan in danger. You know that I care about you?"

Leila nodded. She wrapped her arms around Kiko, squeezing her tight. "Thank you. I care about you, too."

As they pulled away, Kiko peered over Leila's shoulder and jutted her chin. "Riley's back. We should pack up Sadie and leave before Sebastian tells them where we are."

MONDAY

afternoon

Leila

The clan remained on the Washington-Oregon border. They circled back, heading west and stopped somewhere north of Portland. Kiko had said she didn't want to go too far from Cedar Falls, in case they were needed back in town.

The ride was silent. Leila spent the time pretending to be asleep. Riley didn't bother to say anything though, and she was relieved he knew her well enough not to try.

Riley pulled his car up next to Mr Robertson's and turned to Leila. He winked, a nervous smile planted on his face. She gave him nothing in return.

As he climbed out of the car, Leila swiveled in her seat and looked into the back. Sadie was laying across the backseat, her head in Summer's lap. "Are you happy to stay in here with her while we set up?"

Summer gazed down at her big sister and swept sticky hair off Sadie's face. Looking up, she nodded and managed a weak, "Yeah."

Leila hopped out of the car. Her attention immediately landed fifteen yards away, where Kale was holding Gabby against a tree. He aggressively swept a thick rope around her body, attaching her to the trunk. A growl rumbled in Leila's throat as she headed over.

Kale had finished tying Gabby up by the time she reached them. Gabby struggled against the ropes, arms pinned to her sides. As she fought the restraints, rope burns appeared on her skin.

Kale left Gabby, and as he met Leila halfway, she asked, "Why did you have to put her so far away?"

"Probably better she doesn't hear our plans," Kale said, tapping Leila's back as he continued on.

Leila glared at him for a moment, wondering if he'd gone mad. Beyond Kale, Leila caught Riley's eye. He was standing frozen and shell-shocked, as if he'd never seen a member of his own clan tied up before. Rage stormed inside her and a scowl formed on her face. He opened his mouth to say something, sorry maybe, but Leila didn't want a bar of it. She swung around and rushed for Gabby.

"Are you hurting?" Leila asked, following the ropes knot at the back of the tree trunk.

"It's a little tight, I can't move," Gabby said, her voice breaking on the last word.

Leila half-shifted and used her strength to loosen the knot a little. When the ropes were slack enough, Gabby breathed a sigh and slid along the bark until her bottom hit the ground.

Staring at the loosened knot, Leila muttered, "I wonder what they'd do if I let you go."

"Better not," Gabby said, dejected.

Leila didn't bother re-tightening the ropes. She moved around the tree and sat down, resting her head onto Gabby's shoulder. Through the trees she watched the others remaking the camp, as though everything was normal. She watched Riley set up a tent, his eyes darting to them every few moments.

"Kiko seems like a right royal coward," Gabby snarled. "We're all hiding instead of fighting."

Leila lifted her head. "She's just scared."

"Yeah? And what about Sadie?"

Trees rustled from a small gust of wind. Leila stared at Summer helping Sadie from Riley's car to a nearby tent. Shivers ran down Leila's spine—not from the cold. She felt numb as she replied, "She wants me to turn her."

"Oh god!" Gabby rested her head against the tree and closed her eyes. "She hates all of this. You see her mousy little face flinch every time we even look like we'll shift."

"I know."

Gabby wriggled against the ropes. "Ugh, I'm itchy."

"Where?" Leila said, turning to face her.

Gabby nodded to her left arm. "There. Just under the ropes."

Leila slid her fingers under the rope and scratched. Red flaky skin caught underneath Leila's nails. Gabby hissed in pain. A tingling sensation prickled Leila's fingertips.

"They put vervain on the rope!" Leila endured the discomfort as she held the ropes away from Gabby's arm. "Can you heal yourself?"

After Gabby half-shifted, letting her wolf's healing energy wash over her, she said, "I'm okay. Stop stressing."

Both Leila's best friends were out of action. Her heart felt like it was about to shatter. She huffed, "I can't believe Riley agreed to this."

With the movement she could make, Gabby gave a tiny shrug. "He doesn't trust me. Hasn't for a while."

"That's not true." Leila hated that her tone was defensive. "It's more like he doesn't trust himself. He feels responsible for you."

Gabby remained silent. She closed her eyes again, taking long, deep breaths. Leila tried to think of what they'd be doing if the Fallen hadn't returned to Cedar Falls. Maybe they'd be having a sleep over. They'd be sitting on her sofa instead of damp dirt. They'd be eating popcorn and talking about things that didn't matter… and maybe things that did matter.

"We slept together this morning," Leila blurted. She slapped her hand over her mouth, surprised by her own admission.

"What?" Gabby's lids shot open. She studied Leila's face for a while before a twinkle hit her eyes. "About damn time."

Leila wanted to smile but a sigh rushed through her lips instead. A twinge of bitterness pinched at her heart. "He ruined it by agreeing to tie you up."

"Hey now," Gabby scolded. "What goes on between me and him is not a reflection of you and him. Yeah, sure, what a douche for not trusting me… but he does love you. God. The way he gawks at you like a little pup waiting for its owner's next command. It's sickening."

Leila smiled involuntarily at the same time the hoot of an owl echoed above the treetops. Gabby jerked her head to the sky. "Odette?"

A white barn owl with tan feathers around its face made its way to the ground and landed right beside Riley. In a moment, it shifted into a tall modelesque woman. Her hair was platinum blond and touched her shoulders.

Leila could just hear Odette speak. "You guys are hard to find!"

"It's a game of hide and seek," Riley said, trying to make a joke. He flung an arm in Leila and Gabby's direction. "She's over there."

As Odette started running toward them, Gabby tensed beside Leila. "I don't want her to see me like this."

"Oh my god," Odette gasped, covering her mouth. She squatted in front of Gabby, trying to find her hands beneath the ropes to hold. "This shouldn't be happening."

Gabby shrugged. "Probably for the best. My mind gets

ideas sometimes."

Leila felt her heart drop. "What do you mean ideas?"

Gabby glanced at her. "Doesn't matter."

"Right," Leila said, nodding. "Because you don't follow through with them."

"Is that a statement or a question?" Gabby asked.

Leila's throat went dry. She swallowed hard. "A statement, Gab."

After a quick exhale through her nose that sounded like it could be a laugh, Gabby rolled her eyes. She muttered, "Okay, whatever you want to believe."

"I'm gonna stay here with you, all right?" Odette sobbed, letting her tears fall unashamed. "I'll stay right here with you the whole time."

Gabby's chin quivered. And with all the softness of a wispy feather being kissed by the gentle breeze, she whispered, "Okay."

The fire was lit and roaring by the time Leila joined the others at camp. Riley and Kale stood above the flames, looking down on their creation with pride. Riley's eyes flicked up at Leila's approach, and he smiled softly.

Leila resisted returning the gesture and dropped her gaze to the ground. How dare he? He couldn't just smile that sweet, warm, heart-melting smile and expect everything was going to be okay. Leila glanced back at him. His eyes followed her, still smiling, still that inner warmth exuding from him. She felt her cheeks twitch, instincts begging her to surrender and mirror his expression. She pressed her lips together and fought the urge.

It didn't take long for the penny to drop, the pure adoration in his cedar brown irises slowly morphed into sorrow. Creases formed between his brows as he mouthed, "I'm sorry."

"Leila! There you are."

Leila turned to find Kiko rushing toward her. She threw

a pointed finger to a tent behind her. "Sadie is all set."

Nodding, Leila asked, "Is she okay?"

Summer emerged from the tent, holding the T-shirt Leila had dampened earlier. She dropped it on the ground and moved to the fire, rubbing her hands together.

"She's resting," Kiko replied. "We should do the same. God knows when the mark will appear and then we'll have a fight on our hands."

Checking her phone for the time, Leila said, "It's only four o'clock."

"And how much sleep have you gotten in the last three days?" Kiko said. Without waiting for Leila's reply, she gave a sly wink, and added, "That's what I thought."

It sounded a lot like an insinuation. Leila crunched her teeth into her lips, realizing that Kiko knew what her and Riley had done that morning. She leaned close and whispered, "Please don't tell Kale."

"Oh god, no. He'd kill him."

Leila waited for Kiko to laugh, but there was no jest in her tone whatsoever. Leila took a step back and peered around Kiko to where Riley and Kale sat. They seemed happy enough. Brotherly wrath had been averted, for now.

"I think maybe now isn't the best time to be, you know, frolicking in the woods," Kiko said.

Turning back to Kiko, Leila nodded like a jackhammer. "Yeah. I agree. Totally. Not the best time at all."

A smile hit Kiko's eyes. "Because it can be a distraction. And the last thing we need is you two off your game."

"Mhm," Leila mumbled, desperate to not be having that kind of conversation with the wife of her brother. "I get it. For sure." Leila took a few steps back and turned her gaze to the trees. "I'll do a perimeter check, shall I?"

"Sure. And then rest, right?"

"Rest," Leila repeated. She peered over her shoulder, and quickly added, "That's all. Just rest."

MONDAY

late afternoon

Sadie

Barefoot and out of breath, Sadie ran. She didn't know how long she'd been running for, but it felt like a while. Hours, maybe days. Days with no sleep or rest, no time to stop for a moment of peace. Stars were spotted across the darkened sky; the night was clear, well, the parts she could see of it. On either side of her, hedges—at least ten feet tall—enclosed her. She swept through long grass, following the path the hedges laid out for her. Left, right, and right again.

As she approached a T-section she slowed, noticing something she hadn't seen before. A sign. It read:

Choose. Are you an introvert or an extrovert?

Each choice had an arrow pointing in different directions.

Sadie jogged on the spot, feet blistered and aching. *Don't stop moving,* she told herself, worrying that her legs would collapse at any hint of weakness. She gazed down each pathway, both identical. Did she really have to choose? Did it truly matter?

A thumping noise startled her. From the path where she came, footsteps grew louder. From the pattern of the running, four beats and a short break, she knew it wasn't human.

"Extrovert!" she cried, turning right.

It didn't take long to come to the next T-section with another sign slowing her. She read as she approached:

Which do you prefer, winter or spring?

"Duh, spring," she said, following the path to the left.

The further down the path she ran, the longer the grass became. Using her hands to help her push through the knee-height reeds, she urged herself to go faster. At the next T-section, she had to clear the overgrowth away from the sign. As she did, the grass behind her rustled. She jerked her head around, but nothing was there, the grass keeping perfectly still. Heart pounding, she turned back and read the sign.

Where do you want to live, mountains or sea?

That question wasn't so easy.

She grew up in the mountains, but all her visits to the coast gave her a sense of something else... something wonderful. Near the ocean, she felt the expansiveness of the world and herself. But all her friends were in Cedar Falls, they'd for sure answer mountains. So, she went with mountains, veering left again.

The pathway was long; a never-ending wade through long grass. She grazed the hedge with her fingers as she walked. Forever. It felt like forever.

Would there ever be an end?

As she pressed on, the grass turned to dirt. She almost fell as she came out of the reeds, like someone had pushed her from behind. From there she could see flowers blossoming from the hedge walls. Sunflowers on one side and orchids on the other.

A voice boomed, "choose."

Sadie jumped, and then frowned. Choose? She loved both.

"Why?" she said out loud as she picked one of each and placed them behind her ears.

The earth rumbled beneath her. What once seemed like a never-ending pathway, became a crossroad. Another T-section. And along with it, another sign.

Are you True or Fallen?

"True!" Obviously.

Sadie swiveled to the right and took a step. She stopped abruptly. The path was a dead-end. She absent-mindedly lifted her hands to trace the flowers behind her ears as she scanned the area for another path. But the only way to go was with the Fallen choice.

A roar bellowed into the air and down the path, long grass moved to each side. Between the strands, rose gold eyes glowed and a tiger emerged.

Sadie swiveled on her heels. She tore down the Fallen pathway. There was no other choice.

As she ran, night turned to day, sun beaming down. The dirt beneath her feet turned to mud, sticking to her heels as she tried to move faster. An ominous growl from behind teased her.

In front of her, the hedge moved, curving in on itself creating another dead-end. A sign appeared. One that simply said:

Take off your mask.

Sadie reached for her face, feeling the lines of her jaw. "I'm not wearing a mask."

The hedge moved closer, forcing her to step back. She turned around, hoping to find another path. But instead, she saw the tiger creeping toward her.

"I'm not wearing a mask!" she screamed at it.

The tiger leaned back on its hind legs, ready to pounce. Panicking Sadie, felt through the hedge for a gap to slip through, but the branches were too dense. As the tiger lunged for her small body, she screamed.

Sadie sprung upright, arms held out in front of her. A shrill cry that came from her own mouth, pierced her ears. Sweat poured from her forehead as she took in her surroundings.

Summer sat at the end of a tent, looking at her with furrowed brow. She touched Sadie's knee gently and asked, "Are you okay?"

Her brain finally catching up, Sadie fell back to the pillow. She muttered, "It was just a dream."

Summer crawled up beside her and took her hand. "Do you need anything?"

Sadie glanced at her sister's hand. It was weird to have Summer care in that way. Weird, but nice, too.

"I'm sorry to have brought you into this crazy world," she said, wishing that she wasn't in it either.

Summer re-gripped Sadie's hand. Her head shook wildly as she said, "*I'm sorry* you're going through this."

Sadie slipped her hand out of Summer's grasp and wiped her hairline. "I'm not a very good big sister."

"Don't be stupid," Summer spat. She laid down next to Sadie and threw an arm over her. "You're the best."

Sadie didn't want to cry, but the tears fell anyway. The salty liquid coated her eyes, forcing them to close. And as sudden as she had woken, she felt the grip of sleep clutch her again.

Right before she drifted off to sleep, she mumbled, "This is nice."

MONDAY

early evening

Leila

Leila headed out. Riley offered to go with her, but she needed time alone. His judgment was off. She could forgive Kiko for over-reacting about Sebastian and Gabby because her past made her afraid. But Riley was meant to be Gabby's friend—he failed to see that she was still human underneath the Guardian. The pressure of being a clan leader had caused him to have a panic attack earlier and now it had caused him to mistrust those who were only trying to help.

After she'd ran a few miles, Leila veered around to loop back to camp. As she turned, something caught her eye. Right there, a few feet away, standing at the base of a tree was a cat.

Leila blinked a few times, just to make sure she wasn't seeing things.

Because it wasn't just any cat. It was the gray-striped tabby that had been hanging around Cedar Falls. The very cat that had entered *her* house.

Its eyes met hers, two round balls of shimmering aqua. Leila half-shifted in an instant, staring at the cat with her lion's sight. The aqua outline of a human spun on its heels, mid-length ombre hair flinging around.

"Of course," Leila said aloud, throwing her hands in the air. "The damn cat's a spy."

Leila tentatively followed it, all too aware it could lead her into an ambush. By the time she reached where it was, the cat was long gone. Straining her eyes, she gazed into the dying light. A hint of aqua flashed in the distance.

As she took a step, gracefully placing the soles of her shoes without a sound, her name echoed through the forest. She halted, the noise startling her back to human form. Turning, she watched a white wolf stride toward her. When Riley reached her, she mindlessly ran her palm through the silky fur on his head.

"You've been gone a while," he said, returning to human form.

Leila dropped her hand and sighed. "You really need to stop worrying about noth—" she stopped herself and glanced into the depths of the forest, where an aqua glow had been moments earlier. Correcting herself, she said, "… about me."

Riley swallowed. He pressed his lips together and his mouth formed a smile. "Don't think I could ever do that."

The look on his face made her want to scream. How could he gaze at her so lovingly one moment and betray Gabby the next? She pushed her anger down, knowing there were more pressing matters at hand.

Riley's smile turned upside down as he raked a hand through her wind-swept hair. He lifted his eyes to the treetops, shaking his head. "The Fallen are out there Leila… closer than you think. Tessa and her clan are out there. I know what she's capable of. We can't be lax about things."

"You're right." Leila sighed. He didn't even know just how right he was. She *hated* that. Swallowing her pride, she grasped his hand. "Riley. We have to move spots again."

"Why?"

"I saw the cat."

Confused creases appeared between his brows as he asked, "The cat?"

"The one that's been hanging around. I saw it out here." Leila gawked into the darkness. Her eyes widened as she faced Riley. "It was sitting on your freaking lap."

Riley half-shifted, head darting in every direction. "Where is it?"

She knew he meant right at that moment, but Leila stepped back, recalling all the times she had seen the cat. "In the forest, when we were practicing the surge. At your house… twice. At my house when we saw Tessa." She threw her hands in the air. "And there you were saying, *don't shift in front of domestic animals, you'll scare it.* I would have seen who it was, truly. Not a domestic animal."

Riley's face dropped, realization settling in. "It sat on my freaking lap."

"A cat?" Kiko said, eyes dancing between Leila and Riley.

"Where are we gonna go?" Riley asked, visibly tensing. "Into Oregon? Cali? Back home?"

"All right, settle down." Kiko calmly turned to Leila. "Are you sure it was a Guardian?"

"I couldn't get a proper look at them. But they were definitely glowing. Definitely a Guardian." Seeing Summer leave Sadie's tent, Leila whispered, "Do you think that cat works for the Fallen?"

"No doubt," Kiko replied. "Smaller Guardians like cats and owls make great recons."

"What's happening?" Kale asked, stepping into the close huddle.

Leila let out a groan. "There's a Guardian spying on us."

"Just what you thought!" Kale said, looking at Kiko.

"That's not all." Leila swallowed. "We'd seen it before. Around Cedar Falls… at our houses."

Kale swept his hands over his buzz cut. "Jeez, Leila."

"These things happen," Kiko said, reassuring Leila with a sympathetic smile. "It's been following us, I assume. Probably even marked Sadie."

Riley coughed once. "I thought you said it was Sebastian who marked Sadie?"

Kiko inhaled sharply. She placed her hand on Riley's chest and said, "Can you do a quick sweep around the perimeter, we don't want to be ambushed? We'll start packing up here."

Riley paused for a moment, eyes dropping to Kiko's hand. As his head rose, a stoicism washed over his face. He nodded, shifted into his wolf, and ran. Leila watched him until she couldn't see him anymore.

"Let's be quick!" Kale snapped, already stomping on the smoldering fire.

Kiko spun on her heels and marched for her tent. Leila peered into the forest, trying to catch a glimpse of Riley, thinking maybe she should have gone with him.

"Leila?" Odette called, running over.

Leila let her eyes drift to Gabby, sitting against the tree with ropes wrapped around her body. Gabby leaned as far forward as she could go, worry written all over her face. Leila met Odette away from the others.

"Has something happened?" Odette asked.

Nodding Leila said, "There's a Guardian out there. One we don't know. We're moving again."

Odette clasped two hands around the back of her neck. She shook her head and turned around without saying another word. She ran to Gabby, quickly untying the ropes that bound her to the tree.

"Watch out!" Kale hollered, helping Mr. Robertson lug a massive cooler.

Leila jumped out of the way. She glanced into the forest

again, lifting her palm to her heart. She and Riley were Imprints, surely she'd know if something was wrong?

The click of two fingers barely inches from her face brought Leila back to earth. Kale's smirk came into view. He mocked, "Daydreamer. We should leave now, not in five years."

Leila poked her tongue out and instantly felt like she was ten-years-old. She snapped her lips shut, with tongue inside, and glanced around the camp. Summer peeped through the smallest gap in a tent's opening.

"What's going on?" she asked. "What were they saying about someone marking Sadie?"

Leila headed over. "We're moving again. I'm sorry."

"You were talking about someone marking Sadie. Was it a cat?" Summer's wide eyes, almost identical to Sadie's, told more than she spoke.

"Yes?" Leila said the word, urging for more information.

"A stripy one. Mostly gray?" Summer asked.

"Yes! Where? When?"

"When Tessa brought us home. I saw a cat run across your lawn and into Tessa's car. That's kind of odd, right?"

Leila felt her heart double time. That confirmed it. Tessa did mark Sadie and the cat Guardian was going to report back to where she was.

"Kiko!" Leila cried, leaving Summer and rushing to the other side of camp.

Kiko stood on top of half a dismantled tent. She turned to Leila, puffing. "What a cruel joke, huh? Putting things up just to tear—"

"The cat's in Tessa's clan!" Leila interrupted.

"Well, duh," Kiko said unsurprised. She looked behind Leila and lifted her chin. "Riley's back."

Riley walked toward them, raking his hands through dirty hair. Eyes wide and panicked he stumbled toward Leila. She felt his shaking hand as he grabbed her wrist and brought her closer to him.

"What is it?" Kiko asked, already searching the forest around them.

"The cat," he said, wincing.

"You saw it. It's a Guardian, right?" Leila urged.

"Mmm." Riley dropped her wrist, averting his gaze to the ground. "I know who it is."

"Who?" Kiko asked, panic in her voice. "It's someone from your sister's clan isn't it?"

"I don't know her name." Riley forced his eyes onto Leila's. "I just know her face."

Leila knew then, exactly who he was talking about. It was the girl he slept with.

MONDAY

evening

Leila

Leila couldn't say anything, she couldn't even look at Riley. His unbrushed hair and mournful eyes were too much for her to bear. Her insides ached like he'd grabbed her heart and crushed it. She knew it wasn't his fault, not really. But that didn't make it better.

That cat better not show her face here, Leila thought, marching toward Riley's car with a scrunched-up tent in her arms. *Or I'll tear her in two.*

She wished she'd shifted when she first saw it in the woods, or even in Riley's room when it made itself comfy on his lap. The tiny excuse for a cat had hissed at her, too.

"Bitch," Leila muttered to herself.

"What's that?" Riley asked, opening his trunk.

"Nothing," she muttered.

"Leila, listen," Riley said, taking the tent from Leila's hands. He placed the tent into his trunk and turned to face her. "I know you're not happy with me right now. You think I'm awful for agreeing to send Sebastian away and for tying Gabby up… and maybe for knowing who that cat is but—"

"Are you ready?" Kiko said, walking around Riley's car.

Riley winced as though annoyed at the interruption. He placed a fake smile on his face and nodded at Kiko. "Yeah. Can you just give us a few minutes?"

"Don't be long," she replied. She spun on her heels and called out, "Jay? Carry Sadie to Riley's car!"

Riley eyed Kiko until she was out of earshot. He took Leila's hands in his and looked down at them, prodding her knuckles with his fingertips. "Leila, please trust me. I know it seems like I'm making all the wrong choices, it's not easy for me to agree to things that hurt you. I hope you know that."

Leila didn't reply. She wanted to believe him, but every damn choice he took made it difficult to believe anything.

Riley dug his hand into his back pocket. His retrieved his keys and dangled them in front of her. "You want to drive my car and I'll go with Kiko and Kale in Mr. Robertson's car?"

Leila stared at the keys, one for his house and one for his car attached to a gilded book pendant. What he offered was more than to drive his car, he offered her space—he offered her a chance to process everything that had happened without him around.

Leila held her hand out and he dropped them into her palm. She said, "Samuel said we shouldn't be apart."

Riley took a breath—deep and shaky—confidence faltering. He sniffed and waved a dismissive hand. "I'll be a car length away."

"Okay, thank you," Leila replied, reaching to close the trunk.

Odette walked beside Gabby, untying the ropes so they hung loose around her body. As they approached, Riley placed his hand on his cousin's shoulder and leaned in, whispering something. Odette glanced at Leila, then nodded. She led Gabby to the front passenger seat, taking the back seat for herself.

Mr. Robertson led Sadie, her legs like jelly beneath her. As they passed Riley, Sadie lifted her finger and croaked, "Tessa's not bad. She saved me."

"You're delirious, Sadie," Riley replied, hurrying to relieve Mr. Robertson. He slid his arm around her waist and added, "But I'm sorry, would a good person mark you without your consent?"

As he helped Sadie in the backseat next to Odette, she flung her head around to face him. Her words slurred as she said, "Well... I thought she nice. Her hair s'very priddy."

Riley grimaced, like Sadie herself plunged a knife deep into his chest. When he noticed Leila watching him, his eyes turned down at their edges. He still cared about Tessa. Even after all the times he'd said she ruined his life, Leila knew he cared.

Summer rushed between Riley and Leila and climbed over Sadie to sit into the middle seat. As Summer settled herself, Sadie immediately rested her head onto Summer's shoulder.

Leila closed the door, and squeezing the keys in her hand, she hopped into the driver's seat. She hitched the seat forward so her feet could touch the gas. And, taking a breath, she plunged the key into the ignition.

With the door still open, Riley leaned in. He glanced over his shoulder to the others. Looking back, his voice was low as he rasped, "Head to Cedar Falls."

"What?"

He moved closer, letting his lips land softly onto her cheek. His breath rushed over her ear as he whispered, "Go home."

Leila inched back. She felt like she needed to whisper as she asked, "Just us or you, too?"

Ignoring her question, he leaned across her and looked at

Odette in the back, saying, "You know what to do."

There was something she didn't know. His eyes gave it away. They fluttered, shifting away from Leila's stares, but in the small moments of recognition, when he glanced at her long enough for her to catch a glimpse, she saw it. A plan whirring in his brain. And fear, she also saw fear.

"Got it, Cap'n," Odette said, tapping her forehead in a salute.

"Ugh, Cap," Sadie moaned, her cheek pressed against the window.

"Yeah," Gabby growled. "Best not use that nickname."

Riley planted another kiss on Leila's cheek and closed the door. She started the car and stared at him a while. He just stood there chewing on the inside of his mouth, waiting. For a brief moment, she felt like it was all a terrible idea.

"Let's go," Gabby urged. "If the Fallen are close, we don't want Sadie or Summer anywhere near them."

"Yeah!" Sadie said, tapping on the back of Leila's headrest. "Lessss go. Rip it off like a Band-Aid."

Leila reversed the car. After one last look at Riley, she planted her foot on the gas. She drove slowly, waiting for them to catch up. But no matter how many glances she looked in the rear-vision mirror, Mr. Robertson's car was yet to creep into view.

After five minutes, she put her foot on the brakes. "Should we wait for them?"

"Keep going," Odette demanded.

"Yep," Gabby agreed. "Don't stop."

Leila curled her fingers around the steering wheel and pressed her foot on the gas. She didn't like feeling like everyone knew what Riley was up to but her. "What did he say? What is he doing?"

"I don't know," Odette said, wistfully looking out the window. "All he told me was to make sure you kept going, if they're with us or not."

"They were never meant to follow," Leila said to herself,

finally figuring it out. "For some godforsaken reason he wanted us to separate. Why?"

Gabby scoffed. "Lord knows what that boy thinks at the best of times."

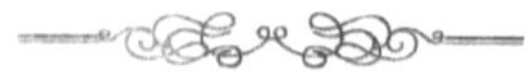

It took around three hours until they reached the familiar roads of Cedar Falls. Weary-eyed, they clambered out of Riley's car and headed inside Leila's house. Her parents were still awake, happy to welcome the girls into the comfort of their home. Aileen even told them she'd sprinkle vervain around the windowsills and doorways, in an attempt to stop any unwanted visitors. As she rushed around sneezing while dropping the crushed plant across the place, Leila made a joke about how she'd perpetually be on the verge of sickness if her mother kept throwing it around like fairy dust.

They set Sadie and Summer up in the downstairs guest room and rolled out the mattress from Kale's room into Leila's for Gabby to sleep on. Leila sat on the edge of her bed and scrolled through her phone to Riley's name. She'd already tried to call him; once, when they stopped for gas, and again, as soon as she pulled the car to a stop in her driveway. He didn't answer both times. As she watched Odette wrap her arms around Gabby, she listened to the unavailable signal beep yet again.

Hanging up, she said, "What do you think he's doing?"

Odette pulled away from Gabby. "I can go check?"

"That's a long flight," Gabby said, frowning.

Odette pressed Gabby's cheeks with her palms. "I'll be back by morning."

Gabby nodded, cheeks squeezed so tight, her lips puckered. Her eyes darted to Leila.

"I'll give you two a minute," Leila said, leaving them alone.

She bounced down the stairs and poked her head into the guest room. Both Summer and Sadie were asleep, their bodies turned into each other. Smiling, Leila gently closed the door and headed out the front door.

The fresh air felt needed. Which was a little bit odd, considering she'd just spent the last two days in nothing else. But there was nothing better than the air around home. She felt safe. Maybe that's what Riley wanted for her.

As Leila took a seat on the top step of the porch, Odette came out of her house. Gabby was close behind her, she closed the door and crossed her arms.

Odette peered over her shoulder. "Are you sure you'll be okay? I don't really want to leave you."

Rolling her eyes, Gabby playfully swiped a dismissive hand toward Odette. "Just go, you big baby. I'm fine now." She glanced at Leila and smiled. "There's no judgmental eyes on me here."

"I'll see you both in the morning," Odette said, shifting into her owl. She flapped her wings for a few beats, staring her wide eyes back at them. Then, with a swift decision, she flitted off into the night.

Gabby plonked herself down onto the step next to Leila and sighed. She stared at the sky, even though Odette was already out of sight. Almost a whisper, she said, "Shut-up."

"I didn't say anything."

Shaking her head, Gabby said, "I know what you're thinking. I don't want a relationship."

"But you do like her. I can tell." Leila leaned over, bumping Gabby's shoulder with hers.

Gabby scuffed her foot along the next step as though she was kicking dirt. "I do."

"And you seriously don't want a relationship?"

"Just because two people are gay doesn't mean they're meant to be together."

Leila was taken aback at the spite in Gabby's tone. She retorted sharply, "I know that."

A rush of air expelled through Gabby's nostrils as she leaned her elbows onto her knees. "Actually, I think I love her."

"Oh?" Leila shuffled to the edge of the step.

Gabby faced Leila, revealing a tear forming in the corner of her eye. "I've become a sap."

Warmth filled Leila. She threw an arm around Gabby. "It's both the best and the worst feeling in the world. The best, because how could you have ever lived without them before? And the worst, because what if you had to?"

Shrugging Leila off, Gabby wiped her cheek and sniffed. "I can't tell her. Don't tell her."

"I won't," Leila promised.

As she settled back in her seat she noticed Gabby rub at her wrists. Red rope marks curved up her arms. Leila sat forward again. "You haven't healed yet?"

Gabby pulled her sleeves down over her hands. "I'm prolonging it."

"What do you mean?"

"Sometimes, when I'm hurt, I prolong the healing process."

"How?" Leila asked, shocked and terrified. "But mostly, why?"

Gabby shrugged, gazing to her feet. "My Guardian and I have a deal. It knows I'm changing. It tries to keep me good, but we both have a rush of… I don't know how to explain it." She turned her head to Leila, eyes remaining low. "Desire, maybe? Just thoughts." She looked up then, eyes square on Leila's. "We don't act on it. But just in case, we made a deal to keep scars, as a reminder to stay True."

A chill ran down Leila's spine. She threw her arms around Gabby and dragged her in close. There was so much to fix. Sadie's mark. The Fallen in town. Gabby's turmoil.

It was a big thing to say, Leila knew it. But she said it anyway. "I'll set this right. I promise!"

TUESDAY

Riley

It was small at first. A sudden fear that he'd left the house unlocked, or a passing thought that he'd slept in on exam day. Then, without warning, it grew to deeper things. Like he'd wake up one morning to all of Cedar Falls covered in blood and it would have been all his fault.

Those kinds of thoughts were hard to shake. And even harder to make sense of. Soon, he was questioning everything. Every single action he made. Every single word he said. Every. Single. Thing.

It wasn't that he thought they'd come true. Though, sometimes he truly thought they would. No, it was more the constant battle inside his mind whether it *was* something to worry about. Was the fleeting fear a premonition or simply his imagination? He could never decipher.

Leila had called him out for being a brat about it all while still being her adorable caring self. She helped him forget the endless haunting thoughts for a moment. A good moment.

But the barrage of bad thoughts still came back. They were like clouds covering the sun, dimming everything around him.

"I bet it was Gabby," Kale huffed, stoking the fire with a long branch.

Riley looked across the camp to the moonlit silhouette of Mr. Robertson's car. All four tires sat limp on the ground. They'd been slashed, that much was obvious.

"She was tied up," Kiko reasoned. "My guess is that Sebastian came back to make a point."

Riley chortled. That actually sounded right. "Most likely."

It had been hours since Leila and the girls drove off without them. Kiko was sure Leila would turn around once she'd realized they weren't following. But she didn't. Riley suggested they waited for morning to come, and surprisingly Kiko agreed.

Kale sighed, "Might as well get some sleep I suppose."

Kiko glanced over at Mr. Robertson as he stood at his perpetual spot on the edge of the forest. He nodded at her, face unchanging. She stood and smiled at Riley, "See you in the morning."

"Night," Riley said, raising his finger in a wave.

He watched the two Imprints enter their tent and took a long breath. This was it. His next actions would determine everything. He pressed his fingers against his temples, doubt creeping in. Leila kept telling him he made mountains out of nothing. Is that what he was doing now?

He'd already slashed the tires. An impulsive decision. Shit. His knees bounced under his elbows as he stared at the ground, small sprouts of grass breaking through the soil. His nerves had frayed from the inside out. He truly had no plan. All he wanted was to prove it to himself that the incessant thoughts he was having were true—or even that they weren't, he'd settle for being delusional. He just needed to know if he was making it all up or not.

Kale's voice drifted from the tent. "Why did you let Sebastian go anyway?"

"He's rogue," Kiko replied. Her voice got softer, but Riley could still hear her. "They don't trust him. Without a clan, eventually he'll crack and his Fallen nature will prevail."

Then, she laughed.

Riley stood up. He didn't feel his phone slip from his pocket, but he felt the vibration of it landing by his feet and he saw the screen crack on impact. Everything became silent. Riley kept his eyes on the tent and his ears pricked, but he couldn't even hear a breath.

Out of the corner of his eye, two bright green dots shimmered in the darkness. He whipped his head to Mr. Robertson who was scanning the campsite, half-shifted. Mr. Robertson glanced to Riley's phone on the ground, sniffed once, and returned to human form.

Kiko peeked her head of the tent. "Everything okay?"

"I, uh, dropped my phone," Riley said. He grimaced, adding a nervous, "No cause for alarm."

She stared at him for moment, causing his heart to lodge into his throat. What had he gotten himself into? Samuel told him and Leila not to separate. Did he make a huge mistake? If his hunch was right, he was in a world of trouble.

As if sensing his unease, Kiko gave a warm smile. She tucked her long hair behind her ear and said, "Are you worried about Leila?" Before he could reply, she continued, "I'm sure she's fine. We'll make a plan in the morning on how to get out of here. Even if we have to walk until we get cell service. Just take some time to rest, okay?"

"Okay," Riley said. As she headed back into the tent, Riley sat down again.

He shook his head. It was almost laughable. She was good. Really good.

Quiet chatter began from the tent. Little whispers that

even with super hearing, Riley couldn't quite piece together. Words like "party" and "plan" and "Leila".

He needed to get closer. But he needed to get one thing out of the way first—the ever-present loom of Mr. Robertson.

Riley's history teacher-turned nonchalant servant of Kiko stayed at the edge of camp, back against tree, bored eyes blinking slowly.

Riley wandered over. "Hey."

Mr. Robertson squinted. He forced out an, "Mm?"

"You want to sleep? I can take over?"

Mr. Robertson ran his tongue along his front teeth. He glanced at his car and back. "So you can damage my car some more?"

"What?" Riley blew an out-of-character raspberry. "That wasn't me."

Mr. Robertson's eyes fluttered and he cleared his throat, pushing himself away from the tree. "Yes it was. Nice move sending Leila away, too. I respect that."

Riley froze. He studied Mr. Robertson's benign face. It wasn't so much the words he said, it was what he didn't say.

Tension growing in his chest, Riley asked, "Did I have good reason to send her away?"

A switch flicked, and the numbness on Mr. Robertson's face lifted. His eyed widened, and nostrils flaring, he whipped his arm forward and wrapped his fingers around Riley's neck. With force, he pushed Riley's head against the tree trunk. "You know the answer to that already, don't you?"

Riley gasped for breath, feeling the pinch of claws against his skin as Mr. Robertson half-shifted.

Eyes blazing green, Mr. Robertson snarled, fangs poking over his bottom lip. With his other hand he clasped Riley's face, squeezing tight under his cheekbones. He forced Riley's face to the side, claws digging into his cheeks. Mr Robertson pulled Riley's face back and slammed it against the tree so hard Riley's glasses cracked.

Riley half-shifted and scrambled to clutch Mr. Robertson's hands, prying them away from his neck. One finger at a time, he managed to loosen the hold. Inhaling sharply, Riley croaked, "Stop!"

Then, as fast as the emotion appeared, it vanished. Mr. Robertson's face dropped and he released Riley. And, as if nothing had even happened, Mr. Robertson dusted himself off and said, "I'll take you up on that offer."

Riley held his breath as Mr Robertson walked to the camp and entered his tent.

"I'm right," Riley muttered to himself, rubbing around his neck.

The realization didn't feel as relieving as he had hoped. Before, all his paranoid suspicions used to be merely possible. Now, it was fact.

Truth was, he had known it all along. He just didn't want to accept it. From the moment Leila said that Kiko was one of the first Guardians, he knew. She *was* the Fallen sibling.

Okay. Sure. That sounded absolutely ridiculous. But Ren had told him the first Fallen was female. Ren had told him there were three siblings, two boys and one girl in the middle.

Since he'd started questioning it, everything else began to make sense. When he lived in Seattle and was trying to find his sister… Kiko was there. She was desperate to turn him, but Ren demanded that he do it, even though he wasn't much into turning people. It didn't seem so important back then, but how different things could have worked out. Ren had saved him.

That was just the beginning, though. Out there, in the Washington forest, Kiko's plan became glaringly obvious to Riley. She was thinning the herd, picking them all off one-by-one. She sent Sebastian away… although, Riley couldn't tell if that was because she needed him to do her bidding elsewhere, or if he was actually a threat to her. And, then Gabby—he still held guilt over that. Riley had to beat them at their own game, pretending it was all for the good of the clan.

Somehow, amongst all of that, Riley kept thinking how Kiko was afraid of Tessa's Alpha. Because if she was Fallen and she was afraid of that clan… that meant they were True. Tessa was a True.

Riley shook his head. He was getting ahead of himself. He needed to do what he'd intended to — find out what they were planning.

His heart pounded as he tip-toed around the back of the camp toward Kiko and Kale's tent. He felt as if the whole world could hear him as he moved, could hear the blood as it pumped through his body. Beat. After beat. After beat.

He found a tree right by their tent and hid behind it, as if it alone could protect him.

"We'll be out of Cedar Falls by tomorrow night," Kiko whispered. "With our army."

"And what of Leila?" Kale asked.

Riley swallowed, willing his breath to remain silent. He squeezed his eyes shut and half-shifted, turning his ears toward the tent.

"Well, if your sister is smart, she'll stay away."

The taste of bile filled Riley's mouth. Hearing them talk of Leila made his wolf's instincts rise—it pushed forward, trying to take full shift. It took all Riley's willpower to remain.

"What do you need me to do?" Kale asked.

"Take those big bear arms of yours and break that boy's back."

That boy?

Kale chuckled. "And then you'll get what you've always wanted."

"Mm," Kiko mumbled. "We will be the only Imprints."

Riley's breath shortened; *that boy* was him. Kiko wanted him dead.

He pressed his palm against a tree for stability. Hunching

over, his heart speeding into overdrive. As he inhaled and exhaled on repeat, one thought circled his mind. He'd set himself up for slaughter.

There was movement in the tent and the shadow of Kale stood. Riley gasped for air, knuckles whitening as he forced himself to stand upright. Kale reached for the opening, bending down for the zip.

To most people, it would have sounded like a boy's girlfriend's brother unzipping a tent in the middle of the forest. But to Riley, it was more like the eternal judge Himself, hitting the gavel with His hammer and calling for the grim reaper.

Kale stepped out of the tent, bronze eyes shimmering in the night, searching for one thing only.

Riley.

TUESDAY

early morning

Sadie

Another dream. Another maze. Another hollow feeling in the pit of her stomach.

Sadie stood in a long, stretched out path with metal walls that reached to the night sky. Spikes protruded from them like silver leaves, their shadows creating ominous shapes along the path.

On the other side of a wall, somewhere unseen, a growl rumbled like a warning. A clattering of footsteps echoed around, seeming to come from every direction. They sounded like paws and hooves and wings flapping, like a mixture of beings standing off against each other. Sadie didn't know which way to run. Either way felt like doom.

A gazelle trilled—powerful and unnerving—and all Sadie could do was stand still, eyes widening. In front of her, a spike on the wall moved, falling to the ground without a sound. It left a hole in the wall, and a tiny bird, white and metallic blue, squeezed itself through. It flew upward, aiming for the sky. She wished it was her.

The gazelle trilled again as though demanding Sadie's attention. Through the hole in the wall, a flash of rose gold whizzed past. Sadie stepped closer, trying to see better.

Thump.

The wall moved as if something on the other side was trying to break through. Another thump and the sound of scraping metal gave her a chill. Two antlers pierced through the wall. Sadie stepped back in haste, but it wasn't enough; the antlers reached across the path and the tips dug into the wall beside her. She was trapped.

To the left, a tiger prowled toward her. Sadie looked up, the bird circling in storm clouds above them.

"Help!" she cried, her voice echoing five times over.

In the distance, faint yet clear, Sebastian called out her name. "Sadie?"

"Sebastian?" she yelled, tears streaming down her face. "I'm here!"

"Sadie?" he called again.

"I'm here!" she screamed, throat burning.

And then… there was nothing. No maze. No tiger. No antlers. No storm clouds. Just a blank space around her.

She felt soft fur push up beneath her fingers. In the darkness, the neon-blue aura of a wolf lit up the space around her. Next to the wolf, Sebastian smiled at her.

In the nothingness, it was only her and him. And, for the first time in a long time, she felt safe. To her, he wasn't a Guardian, or a Shape-shifter, or a Werewolf. He was her friend — her protector.

She sat down and crossed her legs, taking a calming breath. The wolf rested its chin on her lap, breath warming her bare feet.

"Let's get you out of here," Sebastian said. "You just have to wake up first."

Sadie peeled her eyes open. Sebastian leaned over her, his

hands looping under her neck and knees. Awake, the fog in her mind instantly appeared. She frowned and sat up, trying to take in her surroundings.

"Am I still dreaming?" She tried to recognize the room but all she could remember was falling asleep beside Summer. Her hands felt the bed in panic. "Where's my sister?"

Sebastian raised his hands in surrender, then moved a finger in front of his lips. "Shhh. She's with Immy in my car."

"I'm not tired anymore," Sadie blurted, staring at Sebastian. She felt like she'd been sleeping for years, but somehow still felt awful, as though death was lingering, waiting for one single drop of blood to claim her.

Closing her eyes, she inhaled through her nose. Memories sunk in. She was in Leila's guest bedroom. On a loud exhale, she opened her eyes and looked at Sebastian, wondering what the heck he was doing there... but also, glad that he was. He always seemed to be looking out for her, like when Damien flicked her feather out of her hair, and he kept it for her.

If only Sebastian was my first kiss instead, Sadie thought.

Her eyes widened at the revelation. Oh god. "I like him. I like the most popular guy at school."

Sebastian's lips twitched into a smirk. "Who's that?"

"Who's who?" Sadie asked frowning. Had she said things she didn't mean to? But what was she even thinking about anyway?

Oh yes. Kisses.

"My first kiss was lame. Those kinds of things should be exciting. Under the bleachers would have been better," Sadie huffed, shivering.

Sebastian gave a silent chuckle. He took his letterman jacket off and propped it on her shoulders. "You've already told me that."

"Blergh." Sadie felt like that time Gabby forced her to

drink tequila on a sleepover. "Just thinking about it makes me want to dry retch. You saw him in the restaurant, acting all macho."

Sebastian sat himself onto the edge of the bed. "Yeah I saw. He's wrong you know."

Sadie let her eyebrows fall, it felt like she had a million wrinkles on her forehead. "Wrong about what?"

"You gave him a tarot reading and he mocked you."

Sadie pointed to Sebastian, causing the jacket to slip from her shoulder.

"Then he goes—" Sadie scrunched her nose and put on a deep voice—"you're so cute when you're angry."

Sebastian chuckled out loud then. "Yeah. That's what he's wrong about. You're not cute when you're angry. You're gorgeous all the time."

Her insides swirled, as though they'd suddenly turned into goo. She was boneless. Muscle-less…. Brain-less.

"What are we talking about? Are you a figment of my imagination? Summer told me they kicked you out."

Sebastian lifted his jacket back onto her shoulders and pushed her hand through the sleeve. "I had to come back. To make sure you were okay. They're making dumb decisions, thinning their defenses. Half of me thinks it would be best to get you away from all of them. Would you want to?"

She touched his face, fingers slowly drifting around his jawline. "So handsome," she whispered, taking a long blink.

"No Sadie, wake up." Sebastian shook her. "I'm asking you a question. I need your permission."

Sadie opened her eyes. "Turn me."

"No way." Sebastian let her go. "You'll be a Fallen. Trust me, you don't want this torment."

"It's better than being a sitting target."

Sebastian sighed, threading her other arm through his jacket. "It's not a discussion we're having right now, Shorty. I'm asking you if you want to come with me. I'll take you somewhere safer than this."

"You're not a Fallen, though." Sadie pulled his jacket across her chest. She pinched the letter and brought it to her nose. "It smells good."

Sebastian looked dejected. He ran his hand through his hair, letting the tresses fall where they may. A strand landed on his eyelashes.

"You look like Riley when you do that," Sadie mused, half-forgetting everything they had talked about.

"Okay. One: that's insulting. And two: I *am* a Fallen. It's hard to explain but I think things. I get urges. It's not nice."

"But you never act on them!"

Sebastian's eyes hooded. "Sometimes I do."

Sadie's mouth felt dry. She touched her lips and asked, "Like what?"

"Doesn't matter." Sebastian stood. "Are you coming with me or not? I can't stay here forever, I'm not exactly your friends' favorite person here."

A wave of nausea washed over her. She grabbed her pillow and laid down. "You could stay with me forever. I don't mind."

Sadie waited a while for him to reply but he just stood over her, picking dirt out of his nails. So, she added, "I've only ever seen you do good things. You can turn me, and I can protect myself, and all will be well."

Sebastian glared at her, through gritted teeth he replied slowly, as if hoping this time it would sink in. "I am a Fallen. I'm not turning you."

"Leila doesn't believe that there's True and Fallen. There's good and bad in all of us."

"Yeah, but that's coming from someone who's inherited a True Guardian. Leila doesn't know how good she has it."

Sadie pushed herself upright, she let her pointed finger tap against his chest. "But you choose whether to kill or protect. I mean look at Gabby and yourself. You're both good people."

Sebastian looked down at Sadie's finger. He stepped

back, eyes to the floor. "I killed someone."

Sadie remembered. Leila said he killed Miss Carson. That Cap forced him to or he'd hurt Imogen. "And do you feel guilty?"

"Everyday."

"Then, you're not evil, Seb… does anyone ever call you that?" She sat up onto her knees and reached for his hands. Pulling him closer, she said decidedly, "Turn me."

Sebastian let out a puff of air and smiled. He pulled the collar away from her neck, eyes scanning her skin. "Your mark hasn't appeared. Besides, Leila would kill me, and if she doesn't, Riley would."

"I'll be killed!" Sadie collapsed off her knees and let herself sink into the quilt.

Sorrow clouded Sebastian's eyes. He sat on the bed and clutched her shoulders, thumbs caressing his own jacket. "I need to protect you, not turn you."

"What if turning me is protecting me. Being a Guardian will help me protect myself."

"Sadie!" Sebastian scolded, re-gripping her. "I'm done talking about this. Okay? If you want me to protect you, then you'll have to trust me. Can you do that?"

She gazed at Sebastian's blue eyes as they implored her to answer honestly. She softened under his hold. "Yes."

"Then, let's go." He swooped his arms under her back and knees and lifted her up.

Sadie let her head fall onto his chest as he carried her. She gazed up at him and muttered, "I trust you with my life… Seb."

TUESDAY

morning

Leila

Leila woke to the sound of Gabby screaming her name. The walls of her bedroom seemed to expand and retract as her eyes blinked open. She rolled her quilt off and sat on the edge of her bed, forcing herself to wake fully.

Her bedroom door burst open and Gabby stumbled in. "Sadie's gone! Summer, too. I stayed up the whole night keeping watch, and just as I let myself relax, I closed my eyes for one minute, I swear… And Odette isn't back yet. She said she'd be back!"

Riley's number went straight to voice mail. Leila threw her phone onto Gabby's lap and clutched the steering wheel with both hands. As she planted her foot on the gas, she said, "Keep calling him."

"He's not going to answer," Gabby said, locking Leila's phone. "There was no reception at that camp, remember?"

Three hours. The others were three whole hours away with no way to contact them. As they passed the Cedar Falls welcome sign, Leila felt panic rising.

"Try again," she demanded. "Don't stop until he answers."

Two hours and forty one minutes later, Leila pulled up to their previous camp. Mr. Robertson's car was gone but the tents were still up. Both Leila and Gabby bolted out of the car, leaving the engine to stall, as they ran in opposite directions around the site.

"Riley?" Leila called. "Kale?"

"Odette?" Gabby cried.

They met at the fire, smoke rising from the coals. Mugs were scattered on the ground. And by the edge of the forest, something glistened in the grass.

"What's that?" Leila asked, wandering over. She picked up Riley's phone, staring at the cracked screen.

Gabby snatched it off her and immediately dropped it on the ground, running into the forest and screaming, "Odette?"

Leila felt numb. She knew she'd made a mistake, but the emotions wouldn't meet with her thoughts. Something had gone wrong somewhere along the way. Was it when they lost Sadie? Or when they separated? Was it when they kicked Sebastian out? Or was it before then, when they removed Damien's Guardian? They'd gone from a clan of eight Guardians to two in a matter of days.

"What do we do?" Gabby asked, returning.

Leila stared at her blankly. She blinked once, all words lost within her.

"Leila?" Gabby scolded, grabbing her shoulders and shaking them. "What the hell do we do?"

Behind Gabby, movement caught Leila's eye. Three people weaved through the forest; one she hadn't seen before and two she definitely had. A man with long dreadlocks accompanied Tessa and her cat sidekick, and all three had half-shifted, eyes burning through Leila.

Gabby only had to look at Leila's face to know something

was up. She spun around and fully shifted, wasting no time to move toward the group. Leila stayed back and half-shifted, staring at them through the veil to see what she was dealing with. A cat, a wolf, and a stag. As the three approached and Gabby snarled a warning, Tessa held her hands up in surrender.

As Gabby slowed, Leila ran to stand beside her. "Wait! We need them alive. Tessa might have marked Sadie."

"We don't need them alive," Gabby replied, leaning on her hind legs ready to pounce. "We just need her blood."

Tessa left her two friends at the forest edge and stepped into the clearing. Hand still up, she said, "I don't want to fight."

"Where are they?" Leila hissed, claws retracted and ready for a fight.

Glancing around the campsite, Tessa frowned. "Where are who?"

Leila's fangs pierced her lips as she said, "All of them."

"Riley?" Tessa asked, fearful eyes meeting Leila's.

Her tone confused Leila. It was almost as though she cared…

Gabby howled into the air, digging her paws into dirt. Then she ran full steam at Tessa. A pink aura shimmied around Tessa, and she shifted into a light-brown wolf. Its size was much smaller than Gabby's. There was no doubt who'd win that fight.

Numbness washed over Leila again. She watched Gabby leap and swing her paw, connecting with Tessa's jaw. And as the small wolf tumbled to the side, rolling into a ball, she wasn't sure if she should feel sorrow or satisfaction.

Seeing Tessa fall, her dread-locked friend shifted into his stag. As he ran, he bent his head down, antlers pointing ahead like a jousting stick.

Gabby jerked her head back at Leila. "A little help?"

"Enough!" A voice called through the wind.

Out from behind a nearby tree, Ren stepped out. Leila

stared at him in disbelief. He looked as though he'd aged a few years. He'd lost his mohawk, too. And his clothes weren't exactly Ren-like, no leather in sight.

He positioned himself between Gabby and the stag. Holding his palms up to each of them, he growled, "This is not the answer."

Tessa rubbed the back of her head. "Sorry, Makoto. It was self defense."

"Mako who?" Gabby said, half-shifting and rolling onto her backside. "Ren, what the hell is going on?"

Leila stood back, confused. This man looked like Ren, he even spoke like Ren. But the Guardian that stood beside him was a golden wolf not an obsidian panther. He glanced at her, eyes flashing as bright as the sun.

Face softening, the man Tessa called Makoto asked, "Leila?"

"Who are you?" she replied, pulse rising.

"I am the first True Guardian." He reached his hand down to Gabby, offering to help her up. When she brushed his hand aside and stood on her own, he smiled and shook his head. "And you are just children flailing in the forest. None of you are True Guardians, watered down by the venom of those before you."

"Some of us are True, brother." The actual Ren stepped into the clearing, Mohawk intact. He nodded at Leila, giving a small smile.

She would have smiled back if she wasn't stuck on what Ren just called Makoto. Brother. Leila looked between them —the similarity was uncanny and it obviously made sense, but at the same time, it didn't add up. Kiko was the eldest, Ren was the youngest, and the middle sibling was the Fallen.

"Ha!" Tessa scoffed. "The Fallen are great at deception."

"Ha!" Gabby mocked Tessa. "That's something a Fallen would say."

Tessa raised her brows and pointed between herself and

her friends. "We are not Fallen. You are. Kiko turned Riley, and he turned all of you."

Leila frowned. *She* certainly wasn't fallen. What made Tessa think that Kiko was Fallen? She was about to open her mouth to say so, when Ren spoke up.

"Actually, I turned Riley. I am not Fallen, I am not my sister."

Leila's frown deepened. There it was again. The sister was the Fallen.

Tessa turned her gaze to Makoto. "Does that mean Riley isn't a Fallen?"

"Maybe," Makoto replied.

Ren rolled his eyes. "He's not."

"Of course he's not," Leila scoffed.

"But he destroyed our home, hurt our mother. He ran me out of town…" Tessa's voice hitched at the last part.

Gabby shuffled herself to stand beside Leila. Leila could feel her eyes on her as she clutched her hand. Piece-by-piece a new past emerged. Leila didn't like it.

She spat, "He told me *you* did that."

Tessa shook her head, and glanced over her shoulder. Leila noticed her then, the cat girl creeping up closer to them all. She had tears streaming down her face. She was pretty, too. And probably smart. Someone Riley would like.

Leila clenched her teeth and repeated, "He told me you did that. He told me you set him up with your friend and distracted him while you became a monster."

Tessa turned back with downcast eyes. "That's not the whole truth. It wasn't my clan that hurt Mom. It was Riley's, it was yours."

Leila shook her head. "No. You don't know him. He is True, he wouldn't do anything to hurt another soul."

Makoto shared a glance with Ren. "You have not been honest, brother."

Ren's jaw clenched. He turned to Leila. "Where is she? Where is my sister?"

“I don’t know.” Leila felt her stomach drop.

“You must have a vague idea,” Makoto said.

She stared at him. He spoke with authority, like a leader. She fought the realization but it settled anyway—Kiko wasn’t the eldest. He was.

Emotions swirled from her gut to her head. She fought back tears as she said, “She’s gone. Kale’s gone. Riley’s gone.”

“Sadie?” Tessa asked.

Leila could barely get the words out. “We don’t know.”

The look on Tessa’s face made Leila’s heart surge. She had known, always known, that something else was going on. Riley believed that Tessa was a Fallen, but Leila struggled with the idea that one truly existed. Except for maybe Cap. But that didn’t matter. Because right in front of her, was the truth. Riley’s sister was a True.

“I know,” Makoto huffed, pointing wildly at Ren. “I know exactly who has them. I can’t believe you let her get away with this.”

In an almost equally assertive tone, Ren said, “Hey! I’m not the one who abandoned her. I’ve kept her under control. I’m the one who’s made sure it hasn’t gone too far.”

“One life is too far.”

Leila’s eyes danced between the brothers. She wanted to cut in and ask them to clarify who they were talking about, but she knew.

Makoto pressed his fingers to the bridge of his nose. “She’s an Imprint again isn’t she?”

Ren just nodded.

Gabby balked. “Wait. Back up! What do you mean again?”

Ren ran his palms up the sides of his mohawk and looked away. He took a deep breath, then turned to Leila. “It’s time you know the full truth.”

TUESDAY

noon

Leila

They were the first Guardians ever.

Yes, she knew that, she'd said. Kiko told her. Kiko also told her that Makoto would try to make her look bad, make her look like the Fallen.

Kiko was the first Fallen.

She didn't know if she could believe that.

I tried to prepare you for the truth.

The revelation rang through Leila's mind like an alarm. Both Ren and the Elder of the Veil told them stories of the first Guardians. Three siblings, one of them Fallen. She always thought that his stories were meant as a warning for her and Riley, to not let their Imprint power go to their heads. She never realized they were to warn her about Kiko.

Ren sat beside her on a log by the fire pit. Gabby sat on the other side of Leila, clutching her elbow. She hadn't left her side since the others arrived. Makoto had walked off somewhere, while Tessa and her friends hovered back in the forest to give Leila some space.

"I don't understand," Leila said, sobbing. "How can she be the Fallen?"

Ren leaned over, resting his elbows to his knees. He glanced at Leila with mournful eyes. "A long time ago, she fell in love."

Leila recalled what the Elder of the Veil said. The middle child fell in love and when she turned her lover, they became the first ever Imprints. But somewhere along the way their power became too much for them and they veered away from the Veil's guidance. They killed people. Turned people against their will.

"Is that why you were scared of what Riley and I were?" Leila asked. "You thought we'd let the strength take us over?"

Ren shrugged and looked away. "Maybe. I was more concerned that she'd become an Imprint again."

"With my brother?" Leila's hands shook involuntarily.

"Leila, listen to me. She's done a lot of things. Coming to Cedar Falls to simply see how quick it would take a small town to fall apart is just a drop in her ocean of misdoings."

"Oh my god!" Gabby exclaimed. "She turned Cap didn't she?"

Ren nodded. "I stayed close then. I mean, she turns people often. I try to clean up her mess as she goes, but a few slip through the cracks."

Leila wondered what he meant by cleaning up the mess, imagining him slaughtering those she'd turned as they moved from town to town. Her heart sank. It all seemed so surreal.

Tears burned her eyes. "I can't believe it. I just... I can't..."

Gabby slipped her arm around Leila's elbow. But it wasn't enough to comfort her. Leila whipped her arm out and stood. She paced in front of Ren and Gabby, her mind waring against her heart.

"I mean, turning someone isn't a sin. Not really. Riley did it to Damien, to Gabby, to me. What else did she do that was so terrible?" Leila winced as she asked the question. Did she really want to know?

Ren gave a sympathetic smile as if he knew she was fighting to grasp it. He took a long breath. "There's too many to list. She's turned people on both sides of wars. Pearl Harbor? Yeah, that was her idea."

Leila stopped pacing. She opened her mouth to say something, but nothing came out. So she began pacing again.

"Once," Ren continued. "She convinced a boy that his sister who had just become a True, was actually a Fallen. She even tore his house apart and hurt his mother enough to convince him to become a Guardian. I turned him though… I had a feeling that he needed to be a True."

"Riley," Leila whispered.

"Why couldn't you do that with all of those people? Step in before she got her claws in them?" Gabby accused.

Ren shook his head. "You have no idea how tiring it is. She's the hurricane and I'm always one step behind, trying to find all the scattered debris she's caused."

Gabby chewed on the inside of her mouth. She kicked her foot against dirt, scattering dust toward the fire. "Let's all grab a freakin' broom then."

The look on Ren's face transformed from somber to amused. He jerked his face to Gabby and nodded in approval, as if relieved he didn't have to do it alone anymore. Turning back to Leila, he added, "Well, her most recent wrongdoing included kidnapping some girls from your school. I think they were sisters of your friends—"

"Summer and Imogen," Leila interrupted.

"Right," Ren took another breath. "She arranged it all so you would come out here for *safety*. It's all a game to her. She gets a kick out of seeing people afraid and vulnerable."

"Sicko," Gabby jeered.

"As soon as I heard about the missing girls, I went to Makoto for help. I knew what she was planning."

Did she plan to mark Sadie? Leila wondered. A small flicker of hope ignited. "But she didn't mark Sadie, she couldn't have."

Ren stared at her with a blank expression. "You're not getting it."

She was getting it. She just didn't want to. She splayed her fingers through her hair, clasping her skull as if trying to control the mass of thoughts swirling.

Kiko was kind and thoughtful. She'd comforted Leila on many occasions. She was her sister-in-law.

Hands knotted through her hair, Leila shook her head. "We all put blood in ointment, it didn't cure her."

"Sometimes..." Ren paused, as though choosing his words carefully. "She doesn't mix it properly. She leaves the vervain out so the cure isn't complete. She fakes it to throw you off her scent."

"She's a weasel not a fox," Gabby cried. "Think about it, Leila. She threw Sebastian out of the clan because he wanted to keep Sadie safe. She tied me up because she caught wind of me being a Fallen. What a great excuse to have one less person on the right side. She allowed us to separate, be sitting ducks."

The truth sat at the edge of Leila's mind. It taunted her. The sound of it was painful.

"I know, Gabby," Leila cried, letting the tears fall down her blushed cheeks.

The truth finally sunk in. It was Kiko all along. She caused the mess with Cap. She caused the mess with Riley and Tessa. She caused them to run out into the woods and, as Gabby put it, split them up and become easy targets. And Sadie.

"She marked Sadie," Leila stated.

"Oh, I doubt it," Ren said. "She gets her clan to do the

dirty work for her, so she has an alibi. She does love to turn people though."

"I'm gonna be sick." Leila dropped to all fours, her stomach retching. After nothing came up, she wiped her mouth and rolled up on her knees. Still crying, she started, "Kale... ?" But she couldn't finish the question. Did that mean he was a Fallen, too?

"I'm sorry," Ren said, knowing exactly what she meant. "But I'm assuming the answer is yes."

As Gabby reached for Leila, offering her a hand, she asked, "What happened to them. Kiko and her first Imprint?"

Ren shivered and crossed his arms across his chest. "Makoto separated them and killed him. At the time, I didn't agree with it, and I don't want to do that again, trust me. But Leila, you have to know, I swallowed my pride and went to my brother for help because of you."

Leila took Gabby's hand and stood. She felt weakened but the look on Ren's face sent her instincts wild, as though he'd just called her to arms. Her lion was close, she could sense it itching to align. "Me?"

"And Riley—" Ren's eye twitched as if debating whether to continue.

Leila straightened. "What about Riley?"

"She doesn't like other Imprints. She's killed every set I've ever heard of." He stopped for a moment, keeping his eyes on Leila as if making sure she was keeping up. "She's truly in love with Kale, so I doubt she'd want to hurt you, his sister... but she won't like the two of you bonded."

Leila gasped, her mind taking her to the worst place. Half-shifting and itching to run, she cried, "Do you think she's already killed him?"

"Show me your mark." Ren jumped up and reached for her arm.

He pushed her sleeve up and counted the spiral's rungs. Relaxing, he said, "There are still four. He's alive."

"Oh, thank god," Tessa said from behind them. Cheeks flushed pink, she lifted her phone and wiggled it. "I found reception out near the highway. Sadie texted. Kiko doesn't have her, she's with Sebastian."

Leila and Gabby sighed in unison.

"Have you ever had an assignment?" Tessa asked brows raised. Without waiting for an answer, she continued, "You might be relieved, but I still don't trust that Sebastian kid. I'm going to meet them."

As Tessa marched off to her waiting friends, Gabby half-shifted. She clenched her fists and said, "And we go find Kiko and the others, right?"

The sound of metal against metal echoed around the campsite. Makoto wandered over, carrying similar chains to the ones that Riley and Leila used to hold them while they went to the veil. As the chains bounced along the ground behind him, he smirked at Ren.

"I think it's time you revisited your roots."

Ren let out a muffled groan. "I haven't been in… years."

"I know. They'll be pleased to see you," Makoto said, opening the neck clamp. He glanced at Leila. "You too, golden girl."

For the first time since she woke, Leila felt a sense of peace. The thought of visiting the Veil calmed her. She watched Makoto gently secure the brace onto Ren's shoulders, giving him a comforting wink the moment the clasp clicked shut. Leila wondered if that was what a True leader looked like.

Confident, she brushed her hair back, ready for her turn. "Let's do this."

TUESDAY

noon

Sadie

Trees whirred past. Or was that her whirring past trees? Sadie couldn't quite grasp it. She was on the verge of everything aligning in her mind, senses not quite connecting to her brain. She gazed out the front passenger window of Sebastian's beat-up old Bluebird at nothing but blurs of emerald and teal and the darkest greens. Trees, trees, always trees.

"How did you know where we were?" Summer asked Imogen.

Sadie kept staring out the window as she heard Imogen reply, "We followed you."

A spark ignited inside Sadie. She rolled her head to Sebastian, "You did?"

"Yeah," Sebastian shrugged, eyes on the road. "Gabby took damn near forever to go to sleep."

The scent of Sebastian, more garden dirt than aftershave, made Sadie's nostrils twitch. Her eyes drifted down, noticing his letterman jacket around her. She pulled the material across her chest and mused, "You care about me."

Sebastian gave her a quick side eye. "Duh," he teased.

In the distance, a gas station came into view. The sight of it sent Sadie's empty stomach into chaos. The churning grumble resonated through the car.

"You hungry, Shorty?" Sebastian asked, taking his foot off the gas.

Sadie crossed her arms around her stomach, and giving an embarrassed grin, she replied, "I must be."

Sebastian pulled up in the parking lot. "Any requests?"

"A burger!" Summer yelled, enthusiastically clasping Sebastian's head rest.

"Yes, burgers," Imogen repeated, almost as excited.

Sebastian looked at Sadie and with his brow raised he pointed to her. "You want a burger?"

The gesture seemed to tip her over the edge, stomach rumbling again louder than before. She squeezed her arms tighter around her body. "Anything will be great. Thank you."

Sebastian headed toward the station with Imogen and Summer bouncing behind him. Like a switch, the fog that clouded Sadie's mind shifted. She blinked a few times, settling into her body, her surroundings, herself. Everything fell into place. Finally.

Sighing, she lifted her hand to her neck and caressed the curve, pulling the jacket off her shoulder. Her skin was rough, flakes peeling off at her touch. Wincing, she returned her top and jacket back in place.

Now that she was feeling better, it was only a matter of time. The spiral mark would come soon. And the signal of it would attract Guardians, True and Fallen.

A low buzz vibrated in the back seat followed by a three note trill. It sounded like her text message alert. She twisted in her seat and saw her phone sitting in the groove next to Summer's seat belt buckle. As she reached to retrieve it, she saw the notification light up the screen.

I'm on my way, where are you?

Confused, Sadie unlocked her phone. She ignored the countless texts and missed calls from both of her parents—lord knew she didn't want to lie to them over the phone about where she was and what she was doing—and scrolled through to the mysterious message. The number was saved under "Tessa". Sadie knew for a fact she never saved Tessa's number in her phone, she'd given Tessa's business card to Summer to keep safe. Above the new message, was one that seemed to come from her own cell.

I'm with Sebastian. We're heading somewhere away from all of this. Your help and protection would be welcome.

Okay, Sadie knew for sure she didn't write that. Her jumbled thinking wasn't exactly up to whole sentences lately. Summer must have sent it.

Sadie read over the texts again, wondering if she should reply. Everyone said that Tessa marked her, but she knew better. It was Mr. Robertson. Since her head became clearer, it was obvious.

As Sebastian and the girls exited the gas station with food in hand, Sadie made her decision and quickly typed in the name of the gas station and noted that they weren't far from Astoria. Within a second of hitting send, her phone buzzed and a message from Leila appeared.

Tessa isn't the Fallen, Kiko is. Stay safe. I love you.

Sadie nodded to herself. Relieved that she made the right call. She was half-delusional the last however many days, but she knew one thing, she wanted to be turned. Leila had refused her. Sebastian had refused her. Maybe Tessa would agree?

As soon as she locked her phone, another message from Tessa came through.

I'm an hour away.

Summer and Imogen clambered into the back seat as Sebastian opened his door and threw a burger onto Sadie's lap. She peered over her shoulder and held up her phone for Summer to see, eyebrows raised in a silent question. Summer gave a nod and a shrug, then glanced nervously at Sebastian as he sat down.

So, it seemed that Summer sent the text to Tessa in secret. Oblivious, Sebastian smiled at Sadie and put the keys into the ignition. Sadie considered telling him that he needed to wait for Tessa to arrive, but Summer was right to hide the text from him, he wouldn't have a bar of it.

"Can we sit here for a bit?" Sadie asked, unwrapping the paper from her burger. "I get car sick when I eat."

"You do not!" Summer said, mouth full of bread.

Sadie glared at her sister and mocked, "Well, really? What do you know about me?"

Summer thought for a moment, then shrugged. "Good point."

Pulling his keys out of the ignition and resting them on the dash, Sebastian settled back into his seat. "We can wait. Don't want you to vomit in my car."

Sadie took a bite and let the juicy meat patty zing over her tongue. Closing her eyes, she savored the taste. When she opened her eyes again she found Sebastian staring at her, smiling.

"This is going to take a while, isn't it?" he teased.

Sadie feigned a laugh. He was right, though. She continued to eat slow. Excruciatingly slow. It was almost torture, considering how hungry she was. As soon as she took the last bite, almost twenty minutes later, Sebastian shoved the keys into the ignition.

Dammit. Tessa was still at least half an hour away. Sadie swallowed and blurted, "I got a text from Leila."

Before starting the engine, Sebastian jerked his head. "What did she say?"

Sadie cleared her throat and eyed Summer. Putting on her best firm and direct yet sweet voice, she said, "Tessa isn't the Fallen."

"Knew it!" Summer exclaimed.

"Interesting," Sebastian said, facing the front. He started the car, giving the gas a few revs.

"Kiko is," Sadie added quickly.

"Really?" Sebastian seemed surprised. He nodded to himself. "That means I made the best choice. Kiko won't know where the hell you'll be."

"Ugh," Imogen huffed. "Do we really have to go to Dad's though?"

Sebastian stared ahead, hands gripping the unmoving car. "I've got no other ideas."

Sadie hadn't thought about where they might have been heading, she just thought he was going as far away as possible. She gazed at his face—scrunched and unpleased. He didn't want to see his dad, that was obvious. But he would regardless… he was doing it for her.

They were all silent as he pulled out of the parking lot and started down the highway, Tessa nowhere in sight.

Dammit. Dammit. Dammit.

"Pull over!" Sadie cried, clutching the dash. "I'm gonna be sick."

She didn't have to repeat herself. Sebastian slammed on the brakes and turned onto the side of the road. She yanked at the temperamental handle, kicking the door open, and ran across the gravel into a field. She kept running, even as the grass grew longer. When she was sure she was far enough out of view, she fell to her knees and made retching noises.

"Are you okay?" Sebastian called, stepping into the long grass.

Sadie flung her hand over her head. "Stay back! Don't want you to see this."

Sebastian muttered something and she heard his footsteps back on the gravel. She hunched over, staring at the pressed strands of dry grass under her hands.

How long does a person usually vomit for? she wondered.

After ten minutes, she heard someone walking through

the grass toward her. She jumped up, wiped her lips for added effect, and turned back to the road. Summer met her a few yards from the car.

"Are you all right?" she asked.

The care in her voice was something Sadie would have to get used to. She smiled and pulled her sister in close. "I'm faking it. I told Tessa where we were but it will take a while for her to get here."

"Good. But Sebastian is getting impatient. I think he's worried other Fallen will find us… find you."

"What do we do, though? Tessa isn't here yet."

As their shoes crunched along the gravel on the side of the highway, Summer stopped and looked down. "Get in the car. I have an idea."

Sadie plonked herself in the front seat, giving Sebastian a sheepish smile. "Sorry."

Sebastian stared at her, all color gone from his face. The only other time she'd seen that expression was when he was looking for Imogen at school. He said, "We should get you out of the open. It isn't far to my dad's."

The way he gazed at her, unassuming but completely petrified, burned a hole into her heart. She wanted him to look at her like that all the time. Swallowing, she nodded, resigning to the fact that she'd have to text Tessa the address when they got there.

The back door opened and Summer threw herself into the back seat. Surprised, Sebastian flung around. Summer's eyes grew as she innocently looked between Sadie and Sebastian as if she didn't just take an odd amount of time to get into the car.

Shaking his head, Sebastian turned the ignition on and veered back onto the highway. They'd barely driven a few seconds when a loud bang went off. The car jolted and the rear end dipped to one side.

"What the hell?" Sebastian mumbled, slowing the car. He peered into the side mirror, and cried, "The tire blew!"

A clacking noise repeated on the bitumen, until they came to a complete stop. Sebastian stepped out of the car, mumbling obscenities to himself as he walked around to the trunk.

Summer tutted. "Geez, rocks can be so sharp."

As Sebastian hauled the spare tire from the trunk, Sadie tried not to look back, holding in a smile. A rebellious sister was becoming quite useful.

When Sebastian had finished, he slammed the trunk and made his way back to the driver's seat. As he sat down, he huffed, "Is that it? Is anything else going to go wrong today?"

Something in front of them caught Sadie's eye. She turned, catching sight of red hair blazing in the midday sun. Tessa ran toward them.

"Yes!" Summer cried from the back.

Imogen unbuckled her seatbelt, leaned forward and pointed wildly. As Sebastian let his gaze follow her hand's direction, she said, "That's Tessa."

"You've got to be kidding me!" Sebastian huffed. He darted his eyes to Sadie, brows lowering.

Sadie didn't smile. She needed him to see this was serious. Tessa was needed. She pleaded, "Just talk to her."

Sighing, shaking his head, and frowning deeper, Sebastian wound down his window. As Tessa leaned over into the gap, he said, "What the hell do you want?"

Ignoring Sebastian, Tessa looked at Sadie. "You're still my assignment."

Sebastian began rolling his window back up, and said, "Thanks, but I've got her in my care."

As if on cue, a tingle danced across Sadie's neck. It felt as if ants were marching around in circles. She slapped her hand over shoulder, trying hard not to scratch.

Tessa winced and grabbed Sebastian's half-open window, holding it firmly in place. She finally let her eyes land on him. "She's been marked. So, forgive me if I don't think you've done a real great job of it."

"Sebby?" Imogen cooed from the backseat. "Let her in, she just wants to help."

Sebastian slammed the back of his head against his seat. Through clenched teeth, he said, "Fine. Get in."

They drove another half hour, the Pacific Ocean to their right. Every now and then, through a gap in the trees, Sadie caught a glimpse of the water. A feeling of freedom and excitement would wash over her, and in the back of her mind she wished she had chosen the sea over the mountains in her dream's choice.

"Uh, where are you going?" Tessa asked dubiously.

"Our dad's." Imogen replied, shoulders touching Tessa beside her. "He lives near Cannon Beach."

Tessa made a weird chortle.

Right before the town, Sebastian veered his car to the right. They traveled along the thin and winding road, climbing a slight incline. Close to the end of the road, Sebastian turned into a driveway with the number five on the letterbox.

Tessa unlatched her seat belt and leaned forward half-shifting. She held her sharp claws close to Sebastian's neck. "Why did you bring me here? Is this a joke? You're a Fallen working for Kiko, aren't you?"

"No," Sebastian replied, leaning his head out of harm's way. "I mean, yes, I'm Fallen. But I don't give a crap about Kiko. This is my dad's place."

As he pulled the car to a stop outside a log cabin, Tessa returned to human form. Her eyes widened as she stared ahead and said, "But this is *my* dad's cabin."

TUESDAY

Sadie

The five of them stood on the porch of the cabin, silent and uneasy. Sebastian hit his knuckles against the door mumbling to himself. Sadie could just make out the words "Riley" and "not my brother" and "bullshit".

Summer scooped her arm through Sadie's elbow, clutching tight like a shy child hiding behind a parent. Sadie led them to step back a little, letting Tessa, Imogen, and Sebastian process their discovery.

"So, this means you're my sister?" Imogen had barely finished saying the last word before she wrapped her arms around Tessa in a giant hug.

Arms pinned to her sides, Tessa shrugged Imogen off. "Let's just wait and see. It could all be a misunderstanding."

The door opened, and a man with Riley's eyes and Sebastian's jawline stepped out. Sadie gasped. How could she have not seen it before? Riley and Sebastian were half-brothers!

The man spotted Sebastian and his eyes twinkled with happy surprise. "Seb?" he smiled, letting his gaze move to Imogen. "Oh." He gasped, clutching his chest. "My sweet!"

Then he saw Tessa and all color left his face. He looked between the three of them. "Tess? What? H… how?"

"So, it's true?" Sebastian scowled. "Tessa and Riley are your *other* family?"

Sebastian's dad flung his hand to the door, using it to stabilize his weakening knees. He managed to say, "You know them?"

Tessa opened her mouth but only a squeak came out. She sniffed, wiped tears from her face, and brushed past her dad to go inside. Within a few moments she stormed back out again. "No, you know what? You don't get off that easy. Why do I have siblings I didn't know about?"

Sebastian ushered Imogen inside and signaled to Sadie and Summer to follow. As soon as they stepped in, Summer rushed for Imogen, who grabbed her hand and dragged her down the short hall, disappearing into a room. Sebastian paced the length of the living area.

The cabin was quaint and homely, walls lined with timber. Above a fireplace, Sadie noticed a mantle adorned with two pictures. One frame contained an image of Riley and Tessa cheek-to-cheek, before her hair was dyed red. And next to it, another frame held a photo of Sebastian, Imogen, and both their parents. Sadie wondered if Sebastian's dad hid one when certain kids visited. It would have been a challenge to remember who was who, and what was what. But going by what Sebastian and Imogen have said, they didn't see him much. Sadie guessed Riley and Tessa didn't either.

Sebastian kept pacing the room, stopping every now and then to shake his head or throw his arms in the air. As Sadie walked around him and made herself comfortable on the sofa, the sound of Tessa's voice wafted through the open door.

"I can't believe you have a whole other life. Kids. A wife. You left us for them?"

"No, I..." Sadie could hear the heartbreak in Sebastian's dad's voice as he answered, "I was married before I met your mum. It was only supposed to be a quick affair."

"Oh. My. God!" Tessa boomed. "But then she got pregnant with me and you kept dragging it on... until when? After Riley obviously?"

"I'm sorry. The lie got too big for me."

"Oh, I'm sorry." Tessa mocked. "Mum said you left when Riley was born because you met someone else. But you were already married! These were your choices, no one else's."

Sebastian stormed across the room and slammed the door, shutting out the conversation. He kicked the wooden floorboards as he turned around. "Why does Riley have to be my brother? Why him? I'd rather wimpy Damien."

"There are worse people to be related to," Sadie offered.

Sebastian whipped his eyes to her. "Worse than a self-righteous goodie-two-shoes? With his *perfect* grades and his *perfect* girlfriend, being the *perfect* Guardian."

Perfect girlfriend? "Are you jealous? Do you like Leila?"

"No. God, no. She's... not my type." Sebastian balked and began pacing again. "It's just—he's got it good, you know? And he takes it for granted."

Sadie stopped herself from laughing. "Says the most popular guy at school."

Sebastian stopped in his tracks and looked at her. He shook his head. "Good girls don't like me."

Now he was being ridiculous. Scoffing, she admonished him, "Of course they do."

Sebastian plonked himself onto an armchair by the window. His whole body slumped as he said, "C'mon Shorty, look at me. Look at my life. Look at what I am. I'm damaged goods."

"See, that's the problem." Sadie said, rushing over to crouch in front of him. "You go on about how Riley has it good and that he takes it for granted. But you've got it all in front of you, and you dismiss it because you don't think you're worthy."

Sebastian readjusted himself in the armchair, resting his elbows to his knees. With a smirk, he said, "You know, this crush you have on me is very endearing."

Sadie stood, crossing her arms. "I don't have a crush on you."

"I know you do." Sebastian stood, too. His head hovered inches above her as his amused eyes bored through her. She wasn't sure where to look, so she stared right back.

In a few moments, the twinkle in his sky-blue eyes disappeared. Sebastian sighed, his shoulders dropping. The look on his face broke her heart. "This whole thing is a mind fu—"

"I'm… umm…" Sadie interrupted. She felt the urge and ran with it. "I'm gonna give you a hug now."

Sadie moved in, wrapping her arms around his torso. Her heart pounded, feeling his chest rise and fall against her. He sighed and grasped her tight.

He whispered, "Thank you for being here."

The front door opened and Tessa stormed in; she caught a glimpse of Sadie and Sebastian, caught in each other's arms, and rolled her eyes. Sebastian's dad staggered in behind her, face blushed from crying.

"Dad!" Sebastian exclaimed, letting Sadie go. He threw a thumb in her direction. "This is Sadie."

Sebastian's dad lifted a hand in a lazy wave. Giving a sad smile, he replied, "Hi Sadie. I'm Reece."

"Nice to meet you," Sadie said, Not knowing what to do with her hands, she tucked them into Sebastian's jacket pockets. "You have a beautiful home."

"All right. Can you give us a minute, Dad?" Tessa huffed, cutting the pleasantries short.

Reece nodded. "Of course. I'll give you guys some space."

As soon as Reece left the room, Tessa stepped toward Sadie, eyebrows creasing. "How are you? You look better."

Sadie involuntarily lifted her hand to the rash and ran her nails over the bumps. "Itchy. I do feel better, though."

"The mark could appear anytime, it's probably not a terrible thing for us to be here," Tessa said, avoiding Sebastian's glare.

"Anytime?" Sadie gasped. "Leila said she had a rash for two days before her mark appeared."

"It's different for everyone. Once your fever lifts, the mark could appear in a few hours or a few days," Tessa explained.

Sadie kept her hand over the rash, pressing hard as if her own hand could bring forth the magic to turn her. For all the things in her life that she was indecisive about, this one was clear. She was going to become a Guardian. True or Fallen, it didn't matter anymore. Being a helpless human amongst the ever-growing clan wasn't an option.

As if knowing what she was thinking, Sebastian shuffled closer and picked up her fingers, gently prying them from her shoulder. He whispered, "Stop scratching."

Two sets of footsteps shuffled down the hallway. Imogen stopped at the doorway, Summer close behind. She gazed at Tessa with sorrowful eyes. "You didn't know about us, did you?"

Tessa glanced at Sebastian, before her eyes floated to the framed photos above the fireplace. Frowning, she turned to Imogen and shook her head in reply.

"It's okay," Imogen said, giving an understanding smile that seemed too old for her years. "I get how strange it feels to know you have other full-grown siblings out there. We found out about it a year and half ago."

"Great," Tessa said, sarcastically. She turned to the kitchen and called, "Just another way you've shown them more love than me and Riley."

As if he was standing right behind the archway, Reece

popped around the corner, shaking his head wildly. "No, I… that's not true, Tess. I love you all the same. All four of you, exactly the same."

Sebastian moaned. "Riley goes to my school, did you know that? He's a —"

Sadie nudged him with her elbow.

"He's something," Sebastian finished with a huff.

Reece's lips curved down at their edges. It reminded Sadie of the way Sebastian expressed deep concern, and a hint of Riley when he'd get annoyed. Flustered, he said, "I didn't know. I'm sorry. You have to believe me. I messed up. I thought it was best if I left, stayed out of all your lives."

A chortle flew out of Tessa's mouth. She crossed her arms; eyes searching the floor as she mumbled, "I guess it all makes sense now. Why you were never around for us."

Reece nodded slowly — painfully He seemed heartbroken but also resigned to the fact that he deserved all the animosity Tessa gave him. Sadie decided then that she liked him, mistakes or not.

"Tessa?" Imogen cooed. "I know it's a shock. I cried for weeks when I found out I had a brother and sister out there. But do you think, sometime, when you're ready, we could get to know each other?"

Tessa's eyes softened. Her breath hitched and fresh tears pooled in the corners of her eyes. Her bottom lip quivered as she gazed at her newfound sister.

Sadie's heart flipped. What a moment she was witnessing. She brought her arms around her own body, trying to contain herself.

Imogen continued, stepping toward Tessa, "I've always wondered what you were like. What you'd look like, who you'd be. If we were similar in any way."

Behind Tessa, Reece covered his hand over his mouth, eyes glistening over with tears. He back-stepped toward the kitchen. "I'm just… you all look hungry… I'm going to cook us some lunch."

Sadie didn't have the heart to tell him they'd already eaten.

"Ugh, I need some air." Sebastian peered at Sadie. "You wanna go for a walk?"

TUESDAY

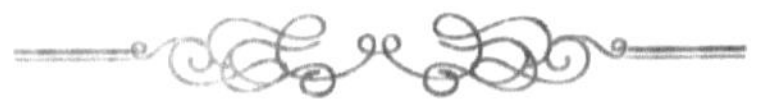

afternoon

Leila

Leila looked through the shimmering light that separated the Veil from the human world. On the other side, Makoto held her lion with both hands as Tessa's dread-locked friend struggled to keep a good grip on Ren's leopard. She hoped they were strong enough to hold them.

"They'll be okay," Ren said, as if reading her thoughts. "The worst my leopard will do is kill a few deer."

Leila didn't know what her lion would do, but she liked his confidence. "You've been at it a while, huh? You're leopard's not so wild?"

"Nah, he just doesn't like the taste of human flesh," Ren stated, walking ahead.

Leila chortled. Oh, the things she was learning about him. Slowly but surely, the enigma was fading and beneath all the pensive stoicism was someone she actually liked.

Sighing, Leila took one last look at the world they were

leaving behind. As Tessa's cat friend grabbed a chain in each hand to help hold onto the big cats, she pulled herself away and rushed to catch up with Ren. They headed toward the light that she and Riley had found only a few days earlier. How much had changed since then.

They entered the sanctum and headed straight for the temple doors. Before they'd reached the steps, the door clunked open, and an Elder in a hooded cloak stepped through. The heavy door closed behind the elder and they waited a moment before removing their hood.

It was Samuel again, and Leila was relieved it was someone she was familiar with—however familiar one could get with an Elder. Samuel stared at Ren, his top lip quivering into a smile. "Greetings, my children."

Ren grimaced and fixed the collar on his leather jacket, even though it was perfect before. He licked his lips and said, "I have strayed. I am sorry."

"Hush," Elder replied, tapping the side of Ren's shoulder. "All is well."

"Is it though?" Leila thought out loud. She tugged up her sleeve, to make sure there were still four rungs on her mark.

Elder let his eyes drift to her. He frowned. "We warned you of the Fallen. We warned you and Will... Riley, not to separate."

"I...I..." Leila stuttered, taken aback by his disapproval. "I was manipulated. Blindsided by her lies."

The words felt like poison in her mouth. She felt like such a fool. She cast her eyes back to her mark; one rung, two, three, four. If she just stayed with Riley, maybe he wouldn't be missing.

Samuel must have seen the guilt in her eyes. He reached for Leila's hand. "Don't blame yourself, child. The Fallen are great at deception and that one, in particular, has had a lot of practice."

Leila nodded. She knew his words were meant to soothe her but it didn't help. If only she had known about Kiko's past, she wouldn't have let Riley go it alone. She peered up at Samuel, and as a rush of resentment washed over her, she spoke before she had a chance to think, "Why didn't you just tell me it was her?"

Ren gawked at her as if appalled she would dare question an Elder. He hissed, "They do not speak her name."

She returned his glare. "*You* could have told me."

"I don't want her dead." Tears welled in Ren's eyes. He turned to Samuel. "I had hoped I could quell her instincts and control her urges. I helped her. Or so I thought."

Samuel nodded. "We know."

He helped her? Ren truly thought he helped Kiko? Leila felt rage well inside her. "How did that work with Cap? Or Sadie?"

Ren bowed his head. "I thought she'd healed her pain. But I guess she lied even to me. When she first came to Cedar Falls, I knew then that she hadn't changed. But I was a coward. By the time I realized how much she'd gone back to the way she was, she'd already found her Imprint. I wasn't strong enough to stop her. Not alone."

Seeing Ren so vulnerable and remorseful pinched at Leila. All anger whittled away. He wanted to stop Kiko but he was afraid, she could see that now.

Samuel cleared his throat. He spun around, cloak catching the wind like wings. "Let us walk."

As Samuel walked off, Leila hurried to follow, Ren right at her side. As they stormed up the hill, she grabbed Ren's elbow and pulled him close. "You said you killed her Imprint. How did you stop him?"

"We used their own power against them. That's why we're here, to see if we can replicate it." He stopped beside Samuel at the crest of the hill. "Do you think we can?"

Samuel lifted his fingers to his lips, running them across his mouth. Peering out to the ocean view, the skin at the side of his eyes wrinkled. He stated, "Your mom has a lovely garden at home."

Leila side-eyed Ren. "Okay then. But what about how we stop Kiko and save Riley?"

Samuel raised his brows, an amused smirk on his face. He glanced at Ren briefly before looking back to the waves as they crashed against the rocky shore.

"Oh!" Ren said. "Leila, what plants does she have?"

For a moment, Leila thought they'd both gone crazy. "I don't know. Vervain mostly."

"Does she have rosemary?" Ren asked. After a moment, he added, "It's pale green with blue flower buds."

Leila tried to visualize her mom's overgrown patch. "Does it grow up like spikes?"

"Yes," Ren replied, eyes bursting wide.

Leila had no idea what it meant or what it was for but going by Ren's relieved yet enthusiastic expression, it was a good thing. She nodded eagerly. "I'm certain she has that."

Ren turned to Samuel. "What do you need on this side?"

Samuel gazed out to the view before him. Smiling to no-one in particular, he said, "The same as last time."

"Will Leila and Riley's blood suffice?" Ren asked.

Leila balked. She opened her mouth to object, but then she remembered where she was—in a physical reality no human could see. The shock passed as quick as it came. Why not their blood? Of course their blood.

Samuel seemed to ignore Ren, turning back to the direction they came from. He took one step, and as he passed he gave one slight nod. Then, as if he was simply enjoying an afternoon stroll, he continued down the hill.

"I think that's a yes," Leila whispered.

"Oh, it's definitely a yes." Ren winked and started down the hill.

Leila sped to catch up. As they came to the temple entrance, and Samuel stood in the open doorway, Leila caught a glimpse inside. Or at least, she tried. Bright light streamed through the gap and Leila squinted, willing her eyes to adjust. A silhouette of a body rushed in behind Samuel, their purple eyes shining directly at Leila.

Samuel slammed the door and stared at Leila. She felt his dark eyes pulse through her, punishing her. She dropped her gaze to the ground.

"Okay. Thanks for your help," Ren said, quickly. He grabbed Leila's hand and dragged her down the steps to the path. "I really gotta teach you how to respect the Elders."

"Sorry," Leila whispered, cringing at herself.

"Oh son!" Samuel called out. "When this is all done, it's your time."

They both stopped in their tracks and gazed over their shoulders. Samuel flashed a smile before ducking into the temple.

Wondering what the hell that meant, Leila asked, "Was that a threat?"

"I don't know. I don't think so. Honestly, I've no clue with him," Ren replied, walking again.

"Do you ever speak to the others inside the temple?"

Ren groaned and gave her a pained expression. "No. And we're not allowed to ask."

"All right, all right," Leila said, raising her hands in surrender. As they followed the curve of the path, Leila asked, "I didn't really catch the gist of most of what happened. I'm assuming we have a plan?"

"Yes." Ren quickened his pace. "You asked me how we got rid of her last Imprint."

"Mmm?"

"We created a rift between the human world and the Veil. The only way we could create it was with vervain extract, the blood of the Imprints, and an Imprint surge."

Leila couldn't find any words. Instead, she nodded and tugged her sleeve up past her mark to check.

Ren peered across, eying her mark. Once he'd counted four, he continued, "And then, we pushed him through. He threw his arm toward the dark forest. "It was sent there to exile."

Leila remembered seeing Cap's cougar there. "Right."

"His human body wasn't supposed to die, though."

Shivers ran through Leila. "He wasn't?"

"I think it was because he was in his human form. We pushed him through, and Samuel managed to grab his Guardian into the Veil. The act killed his mortal body but kept his Guardian alive inside the Veil. I don't want to do that again. They'll have to be at least half-shifted to survive."

They'll? "You're sending Kiko through the rift, right? Not Kale?"

Ren winced. "The problem we had before was only sending one. Leaving Kiko behind allowed her to become set on revenge."

"Kale won't. I know him. He's kind and thoughtful and —"

Ren stopped walking. "So was Kiko. You've seen her, right? She knows how to be those things because she *was* those things. That didn't stop her from hurting others in the process."

A sharp pang squeezed inside Leila's chest. Tears streamed down her cheeks unchecked. The thought of Kale being something other than himself ripped her in two.

"Please Ren," she begged. "I'll help him."

Ren lifted his hand and dabbed at her chin, stopping a tear from falling. "You're hopeful... like I was. I followed her for years thinking that I could save her broken soul."

"He's not her. I promise."

Ren nodded but she knew it was to appease her. "We'll see," he said, pointing at the shimmering light in front of them. "But we'd better get back."

Leila stepped through the light and into the shadow world. Before her, the door between the worlds shimmered, and beyond it she could see Makoto, holding a chain with one hand. His head was turned away from her lion as it tore its teeth through the flesh of a deer.

"Eww," she gasped, wiping the last of her tears away.

At the sound of her voice, her lion lifted its head as though it could feel her near. She moved closer and stepping through the veil, she aligned with the lion. The tang of blood filled her throat. Coughing, she returned to human form.

"That's disgusting," she said, smacking her tongue to her mouth.

Makoto turned around. "It was getting restless, so we went for a walk. What did Samuel say?"

"A lot of nothing." Leila unlatched the neck brace. A few yards away, Leila saw Ren running toward them. "But I think *he* knows what to do."

Ren threw his chain on the ground and puffed. "Mak, do you have your gold chain?"

Makoto dipped his finger under his collar and pulled out a chain with an arrowhead. "Locater spell? We need rosemary."

"Ohh," Leila said, finally catching on. "My mom has it in her garden."

"Your mom? Is she a Guardian, too?" Makoto asked.

"Nah. She's been studying a few things, though."

Makoto's jaw clenched. "But she knows about you and your friends?"

Leila nodded slowly, staring at the veins popping on his neck.

Makoto thwacked Ren's shoulder with the back of his hand. "Do you follow any rules?" Without waiting for an answer, he walked off, muttering, "Civilians every-damn-where knowing every-damn-thing."

TUESDAY

Sadie

Sadie followed Sebastian along a steep forest track for what felt like hours. It was more like twenty minutes, but her body ached regardless. She slowed her pace, trying to catch her breath.

"Just a few more yards!" Sebastian called, still facing ahead.

Sadie forced her legs to move. She closed the gap between them and stood beside Sebastian, looking out. If she wasn't already gasping for breath, the view would have made the same effect.

They stood on the edge of a hill that overlooked Cannon beach and Haystack Rock. The Pacific Ocean swept before them as far as the eye could see. Even the gathering clouds couldn't make it any less beautiful.

"Wow," Sadie puffed.

Sebastian spun around. "Are you all right?"

Sadie waved her hand in dismissal. "All good. Hard walk."

Without taking his eyes off her, Sebastian weaved his arm around her elbow. "Use me to rest on."

She clasped his arm and leaned into him, gazing out at the view below. Spots of white scattered her vision as heat pulsed through her veins. Closing her eyes, she said, "I thought the fever had gone."

"My fever came and went until the mark appeared. It was stupid to think you were better. I shouldn't have brought you up here."

"No, it's fine." Sadie opened her eyes and tried to take in the scenery, but her swaying made it hard to focus. She rested her head on his shoulder to stabilize herself. "I'm glad you did. It's something nice to see on my last day as a human."

Sebastian tugged his arm from Sadie's grasp and threw it around her, holding her tight. "Dammit Sadie, don't say things like that."

She turned to face him. They were so close she was sure she could hear his heartbeat and Sadie made a note of how he wasn't quite as tall as Damien. Before she had a chance to brush the thought away, she was taken back to the moment with Damien by the lake, right before he kissed her.

Their proximity was where the similarities ended though. She felt different with Sebastian, held in his arms. When she was this close to Damien she was frustrated and annoyed. He wasn't being himself, he wasn't seeing the real her. But as Sebastian peered down at her, his caring eyes sent shivers down her spine. He saw her, the real her. And she saw him, too.

"I know it's weird," she said, stepping back. Sebastian held his hands out for her to hold. She took them and continued, "I'm glad that this has happened to me."

"Why?" Sebastian frowned.

Sadie shrugged. "Because it means you're here with me now."

Sebastian's expression changed. He smiled. Genuine and wide.

It was almost too much for her. Sadie moved her gaze back to the ocean. "Told you it was weird."

His hand brushed her cheek and her heart skipped a beat. She willed her eyes to remain on the waves as Sebastian moved himself back in front of her. Still touching her face, he stepped back and leaned down so their faces were level. With nowhere else to look, she dared to set her eyes on his.

As his eyes flitted between hers, he said, "Well, I don't want anything bad for you, but I'm glad you're here with me, too. It makes everything a little… easier."

Sebastian gazed at her like she was the rarest gem in the world. As much as her brain screamed at her to break away, she couldn't—his stare fed an unknown craving. She let her eyes drift to his mouth, and she watched them lift into a lopsided smirk.

"You know, tomorrow night will be the first time I've missed the Falls Party for the whole year," Sebastian said.

Sadie chortled, "Mr. Popular not able to socialize with his team. Whatever shall they do without you?"

"They'll manage," Sebastian's smile dropped. He moved in, a change in the air around them. "I'd rather be with you."

She knew then that he was about kiss her. There was no part of her that wanted to deny him. She closed her eyes as his hand smoothed over her neck, his soft skin soothing her itch. Almost as soon as his fingers reached the marked area, he jerked his hand away.

Sadie reached for him, clutching his wrist. Worried that he thought he'd hurt her, she said, "I'm okay."

Sebastian flinched at her touch. His eyes fixated on her shoulder and in an instant, they flashed neon-blue. As fangs grew between his lips, he took a few steps back.

Sadie's hand hovered in the space between them. "Are *you* okay?"

Darkness flooded his eyes, cobalt behind the neon. As though ashamed, Sebastian looked away. "You'd better go."

"Why?" Sadie asked, reaching for him.

He grabbed her wrist. His eyes darted to her lips and then fell down, lingering on her neck. He curled his top lip, showing the sharp tips of his fangs.

Sadie's stomach retched. The way he looked at her, hungrily and threatening, reminded her of Cap, right before he tried to kill her.

Sebastian dropped her hand. He stepped closer—his face inches away, downcast eyes blazing through her body. He growled, "Go, Sadie. Now. Before I hurt you."

A chill shuddered from her skull to her toes. She stumbled back. And as much as she wanted to escape the sight of him like this, she couldn't turn, she couldn't run, she could only stare back in silence.

"Get away from me!" He roared.

As if knowing she couldn't, or wouldn't go, Sebastian made the move. The dirt crunched under his feet as he turned a half-circle and ran. The last sight she had was him shifting into his wolf, leaping deeper into the forest.

Sadie hunched over, breaths coming in thick and fast. She clutched her knees for support, trying to make sense of what had just happened. Was this what he was talking about, a buried instinct? It was almost as though he couldn't control himself.

Is that what a Fallen was? Sadie thought. Someone who couldn't control themselves?

It didn't add up to her. Leila believed in redemption and so did Sadie. The whole time Sebastian had been trying to protect her and that moment, right then, he was doing the same.

In the depths of her heart, she believed he wouldn't hurt her. Just like he'd never hurt Imogen. It dawned on her then.

Sebastian wasn't a Fallen in the sense that most Fallens were. He'd told her that he'd felt a rush of darkness cover him when he turned, but the moment he saw his sister, it calmed him as though her innocence gave him his humanity back—or at least reminded him of it.

Sadie decided that being alone was the worst thing for him. If he lost himself now, after how hard he'd fought to keep his humanity…

She didn't want that. She couldn't have that. He was the first person who saw the real her. The first person to accept it, even like it.

No. She knew the real him, too. He wouldn't hurt her.

A rush of bravery filling her, Sadie stormed after him. She followed his paw prints into the pathless forest, past oaks and pines. She lasted three full minutes of running before her pumping heart urged her to rest. She held her hand against a tree, sweat pouring from her neck. White dots reappeared around the edges of her vision, and a hastening dizziness buzzed like bees in her head. She bent her knees and slid her back down the trunk until she was sitting on the mossy ground.

Around her, the forest morphed into itself, a blur of green budding leaves melting together. She blinked a few times, watching with fear as the green pulsated outward into a different shape. Tall hedges surrounded her. Not a maze this time, just her tiny body trapped in the middle of a square. In the distance, she heard the snarling growl of a large cat. Her breath quickened as the hedge rustled and a swallow flitting to the sky.

Not again, Sadie mumbled to herself.

Two antlers appeared through the thick hedge, tips aiming for her. She forced her eyes shut and declared, "It's just a dream." When she reopened them, the hedge had gone.

Sadie sighed and rested her head against the tree, feeling her hair stick to the sweat on her neck. As she blinked slowly, letting the fog of sleep shroud in around her, a howl echoed through the woodland. The sound sent her heart racing. A wolf was close. Closer than a normal person would care to be near. But as much as she wanted to, she couldn't rise let alone run. All her strength had faded.

The heaviness won and she drifted to sleep.

"Sadie? Sadie?"

The voice had a sense of urgency to it. Hands gripped her shoulders and shook her body.

She peeled her eyes open.

Sebastian was crouched beside her, clasping her tight. Notably human. He stared at her waking face and sighed. "Do you have a death wish?"

Sadie gave a lazy shrug and rasped with a new confidence, "You won't hurt me."

Frowning, Sebastian rolled back and collapsed his backside to soil. "How are you so sure?"

With hair catching in flaking bark, Sadie lifted her head from the tree. She smiled. "Because you have a crush on me, too."

She winced as soon as the words were out. Had she said that out loud?

"Is that so?" Sebastian raised an eyebrow. He reached for her hair, de-tangling it from the bark. "And what makes you think that?"

Sadie figured her admiration for him was out in the open now, there could be no turning back. "Because I've seen the real you. And Sebastian Weir, most popular boy at school, doesn't show anybody his true self."

Sebastian was silent, his head jerked back as if taken by surprise. Then his shoulders softened and a slight chuckle danced inside his closed mouth. He shook his head and weaved his hand around her waist. "C'mon, Shorty. Let's get you some rest. Tessa's gonna kill me."

They rose together, Sebastian holding all of Sadie's weight. As they walked, she dragged her feet, clutching the back of his shirt. She let out a quiet guffaw, and muttered, "Tessa can't kill you. She's your sister."

TUESDAY

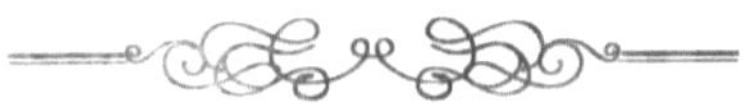

late afternoon

Leila

Leila stood on her back porch with Ren, Gabby, and dreadlock-haired boy, who she'd found out was named Jamal. She overlooked her mom as she enthusiastically led Makoto to her garden, pointing out the rosemary. Upon meeting Aileen, Makoto had crossed his muscled arms across his chest and squinted at her with doubtful eyes. At first, he seemed skeptical, and reluctantly followed her as she frolicked with excitement into the backyard turned herb sanctuary. Aileen pulled a bunch of rosemary branches from the ground and held them to her nose, smiling at Makoto.

When Makoto nodded, arms uncrossing, everyone sighed with relief.

The rising smell of frying kalua pork wafted through the kitchen window. Leila closed her eyes and let the familiar scent take her back to days gone by. Family evenings of love and laughter, back before she was a Guardian and when

Kale wasn't in love with a monster. When she opened her eyes again, a tear rolled down her cheek.

To make the moment a hundred times worse, *the cat* lingered in the corner of her vision. Luckily, she remained a few feet away, as if knowing what Leila thought of her. *She* had a name. Calice. But Leila preferred to think of her as a measly little stray.

It wasn't logical or helpful. She knew it. Jealousy sat within her like tar—unwanted and heavy. But that's how she felt. And as long as Riley was out there, in danger, *the cat* was wise to know her place.

As Makoto and Leila's mom, Aileen, collected rosemary, Ren squeezed himself between Leila and Gabby. He grabbed Leila's wrist and rolled up her sleeve. Leila ran her fingers over her mark, and together they silently counted four rungs.

"We need table space," he said, dropping her arm and heading inside.

Gabby shuffled into the space that Ren left and glanced at Leila's mark. "We'll find him."

Leila took a shaky breath. Every part of her wanted to believe that they would. But an overwhelming fear lingered. What if they couldn't?

She gave Gabby a sad smile and swiveled around, heading inside. She walked past her dad in the kitchen and when she entered the dining room, she found Ren lifting a leather bag onto the table. He pulled out a map and rolled it across the flat surface.

Without looking up, he said, "Do you have anything of Riley's or that was once his?"

"Even a photo would do," Makoto said, behind her. He threw a bunch of rosemary branches onto the map.

Not wasting a moment, Leila bounded upstairs and into her bedroom. She dove across her bed and opened the drawer on her side table. Shoving aside a box of tissues, and a fake diamond ring the size of a potato, she grabbed her collection of Polaroids. She shuffled through the photos until she came upon one of her favorites—a shot of Riley in the library, book in hand. She'd called his name and just as he looked over the rim of his glasses, smiling like a love-sick puppy, she pressed the shutter button.

Leila's heart lurched to her throat. She jumped off her bed, glanced at her mark, and ran downstairs. Everyone had gathered around the dining table and she squeezed between her mom and Ren, holding out the Polaroid for Makoto to take. He pinched the edge carefully and placed it on the table in front of him. Aileen made an excited peep when he broke the rosemary branches into little pieces up and dropped them into a small ceramic bowl. With all eyes on him, he half-shifted. As his golden eyes blazed, he lifted his hand, briefly glancing at Leila before digging his fangs into his skin. Blood trickled down the curve of his palm. He let the drops fall over the violet buds in the bowl and began crushing them together.

Aileen stepped back to the archway between the dining and kitchen, her eager eyes peering over Jamal's shoulder to see. Leila waved her back over. She ran her hands over her hair that led to her high bun, trying to flatten the frizzy parts that escaped the tie. Leila scooped her arm through her mom's and leaned her head on her shoulder. Aileen squeezed her arm in return, resting her head on top of Leila's. No matter what she'd been through, and how strong she'd become Leila was still grateful to have her mom.

Makoto kept blending the ingredients as he eyed Aileen. "You know, there aren't very many civilians who know about Guardians."

Aileen lifted her head, brushed hair from her eyes, and guffawed endearingly. "I hope that means you won't have to kill me."

Everyone who knew Aileen, knew she was joking. But Makoto didn't know her, and it seemed he didn't trust her either. He stared back, golden eyes shimmering without emotion.

"Right?" Aileen asked. A nervous laugh danced in the back of her throat, before her smile faded.

Makoto's mouth twitched, a fang popping through the gap in his lips, and Leila swore she could see a smile hit his twinkling eyes.

"Then you'd better not give me reason to," Makoto said, lip curling into a smirk.

"Ha!" Aileen blurted, waving her finger at him. "You had me there for a moment."

Makoto chuckled to himself as he lifted the bowl, checking on the concoction.

"Excuse me, Leila?" a demure voice said from the kitchen door. "Would you be able to tell me where the restroom is?"

Leila spun around. As soon as her eyes rested on Calice, a fire ignited in her belly. She growled, "What? Don't you already know where it is? Or is it just Riley's house you snoop in?"

Calice's shy stance buckled. She stood up straight, her chin rising, and bit back, "I was on assignment."

"In Riley's lap?"

Everyone froze. Makoto turned to Calice, brow deepening over his eyes. Gabby threw her palm across her mouth, smile behind her hand evident.

"Yes," Calice said, confidently. "I was gaining his trust."

"Ha!" Leila snickered. "Like before you mean... in his car."

The accusation hit Calice hard. Her eyes turned to saucers, and Leila could tell Calice didn't realize Riley had told her the truth. The way her face twitched under the scrutiny—made Leila feel good.

"Do you both know each other?" Makoto asked, unlatching his arrow necklace. "Because if there's bad blood, you need to let it go. At least until this is all over."

Leila swallowed. Makoto was a harder read than Ren. And that was saying something. She flung her arm to the stairs. "Up the top and to the left."

"Thank you," Calice said, shuffling past.

Gabby moved next to Leila, and leaning over she whispered, "You have to tell me what that was about."

"I need silence," Makoto demanded, dipping the end of his necklace into the rosemary and blood mix.

Makoto held the necklace at the clasp, letting the arrowhead dangle over the Washington state map. With his free hand, he slid the photo of Riley onto the edge of the map. He creaked his neck side-to-side and stared at his hand.

Leila half-shifted so she could see what was going on within the Veil. Makoto's golden aura shimmered around his whole body and right at the tips of his fingers the light extended into tiny lightning bolts. They weaved around themselves, following each link of the necklace, until the arrowhead became shrouded in an intense glow. The necklace began swaying widely in a circle. With every rotation the circles became smaller and smaller until it stopped moving altogether, remaining at an odd angle. The arrowhead pointed directly at Cedar Falls.

"We need a town map!" Ren commanded.

Aileen whipped through to the kitchen. The sound of a magnet hitting the floorboard echoed into the room, followed by an; "Ahh crap, hang on." She stormed back in, holding a pizza delivery brochure with a map of Cedar Falls on the back.

As soon as she placed it on the table over the previous map, the arrowhead began swirling in large circles again. It continued its motion until once more, the arrow held in a spot.

"Where is he?" Ren asked, peering closer.

Gabby leaned over the map. She looked up again, confused. "He's here."

The front door burst open and Leila jolted on the spot, arms splayed, ready for action. It only took Riley's voice calling her name to make her move. She ran into the living room, skidding along the floor as she turned toward the front door.

Riley stood in the doorway, hair falling over his eyes. He stared at Leila through cracked glasses.

Her heart leapt to her throat and back. She ran, bounding herself into his arms. He buried his face into her hair, holding her tight.

"It's Kiko," he muffled, pulling away. "She's the Fallen, she's the one who—"

"I know. We know," Leila said, leading him to the dining room.

Riley stopped in the archway. Noticing Makoto, he asked, "Who's this?"

Ren rushed over and clasped Riley's shoulder. "I'm glad you're okay. This is Makoto. He's my brother."

"Brother?" Riley repeated, glancing between Ren and Makoto.

Leila took his hand and added, "He's also your sister's Alpha… a *True* Guardian."

"Tessa's clan is True." Riley said it as a matter of fact. Then, realization hit. He jerked his head around, looking around the room. "Where is she?"

"She's with Sadie," Calice said, returning from upstairs.

Riley's mouth dropped open. He cleared his throat and let out an awkward, "Hi."

The cat smiled sweetly. "Hi. It's good to see you."

Leila kept her eyes on Riley, waiting for his next move. He winced and turned to Ren, "Kiko's still in the woods."

"Where's Odette?" Gabby asked.

"She's not with you?" Riley frowned.

Gabby made a noise that resembled a fish trying to breathe out of water… as if it took all her might to remain silent.

Avoiding Gabby's glare, Riley turned to Leila and continued, "I'm sorry if I scared you. I needed a way to get you all away from them. So I slashed their tires."

Leila clutched the edge of a dining chair. "And Kale? He's not Fallen, too, is he."

Before Riley could respond, Makoto let out a chuckle. He shook his head and leaned his back against the wall, crossing his ankles. "It doesn't truly matter. If they want you to think they are True, you'll believe they are. The Fallen are great at —"

"Deception," Leila snapped. "Yeah, we get it."

Riley ran his hand down Leila's arm and tugged at her wrist. She fell against his side as he took her in his hold. Leila didn't mean to, but her eyes drifted to Calice to make sure she was watching. She wasn't — her back was turned as she headed for the back door with Jamal.

Leila let her head snuggle into Riley's shoulder. The fear of losing him had made her forgive him for his god-awful past mistake with Calice. She whimpered, "Are you okay?"

"Mm," was Riley's answer as he wrapped her into both arms. He breathed in deeply, as if soaking in all her being. "I'm good now."

Stepping back, Leila asked, "What happened?"

Riley licked his lips and turned to face the others, Ren, Makoto, Gabby. "I had a hunch. A few signs here and there that she was lying. I haven't trusted her since Leila asked me to turn her. When she realized she wasn't the one who was going to turn Leila, I saw a flash of darkness in her." He glanced at Leila over his shoulder. "I didn't say anything because I was worried you wouldn't believe me. When you said that Kiko was the first Guardian, it was then I knew that it wasn't just a hunch and that I needed to prove it for sure."

It had been months since Riley turned her. Months of Riley not trusting Kiko and not saying anything. Months of questioning everything he was told, everything that Kiko had led them to do.

"And you proved it?" Leila asked, even though it wasn't really a question at all.

Riley didn't reply, he ran his fingers from his ear lobe to his chin, catching his nails along dried blood spots. He breathed out a puff of air that resembled the start of a laugh.

"Does she know that you know what she is?" Ren asked nervously.

"If Mr. Robertson told her..." Riley took his cracked glasses off and placed them on the dining table. "I'm assuming she knows."

"It helps that you're here, Riley. You made the right choice," Ren said. He promptly lifted his hand to his mouth and began chewing on his thumbnail. "We have to get this right. Now she knows you're onto her. There's no take two."

Riley squinted his eyes, scanning the faces around the room. "And what are we doing exactly?"

Leila said, "We're going to send her to the Veil. Kind of like what we did with Thomas and Crystal, but with an added boost because it's *her*."

Nodding slowly, Riley replied, "Sounds easier than what it probably is, right?"

"Like always," Leila said.

Makoto wandered over. He half-shifted and stood in front of Leila, claws out. Holding a small cup, he said, "For the Elders."

"Oh, right." Leila held her hand out. As Makoto dug his claw into her palm, she winced and looked at Riley. "They need our blood."

Riley raised his brow. "Of course they do."

He half-shifted and clenched his fist until a line of blood dripped down his wrist. He held his hand out for Makoto. "I heard Kiko mention something about a plan, and after that they'll leave Cedar Falls. It feels like she's already a whole day ahead of us."

"Everything we do is inconsequential." Gabby huffed, pulling out her phone. She headed for the living room and said, "I'm calling Odette."

"Making a plan?" Makoto repeated, taking the cup of

Leila and Riley's blood to the table. "It's the same as always, no doubt."

Leila and Riley exchanged glances.

Ren explained, "She's done this before. She wants to raise an army."

"An army?" Leila shivered. "For what?"

"To kill me and my sire-line," Makoto stated. He poured the blood from the bowl into a small vial and screwed the lid on. After placing it inside the leather bag, he stood up straight and threw the bag over his shoulder. "I'll take this to the Veil. Ren, chains are in my car. Will you do the honors?"

Ren smiled with his lips pressed tight. He nodded once at Riley and Leila, then once more to Makoto.

"We'll help," Calice offered, speed walking from the kitchen through the dining room. Jamal followed her. He raised his finger to his forehead in somewhat of a salute.

Before following after them, Ren turned to Riley and Leila. "We'll reconvene tomorrow. If she's going to making her move, she'll be heading back into town. We need to make sure we're ahead of her game."

"Here we go!" Leila's dad boomed, coming from the kitchen and carrying a large pot. Behind him, Aileen carried another, steam rising in front of her face.

Tate looked at Riley, then Leila, and finally Aileen. His face dropped. "Where's all our guests?"

"Just us, Dad," Leila said, folding up the maps to clear room for his pot. She smiled. "Looks like we get to enjoy kalua pork for a week."

TUESDAY

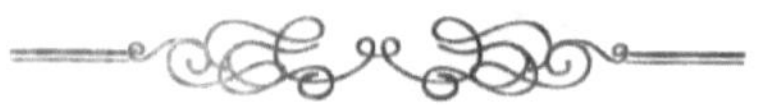

evening

Leila

Leila sat on the edge of her bed, staring at her wall filled with Polaroids. There were so many, they almost reached the ceiling. At the bottom, one in particular caught her eyes. A snap of Kale and Kiko that she'd taken the day before they left a few months ago. Tate had made Hawaiian malasada, and as it was cooking, the two lovebirds were snuggled on the outdoor daybed looking at each other with twinkling eyes. Leila had sneakily taken the shot without them knowing.

As she stared at her wall of pictures, it took Leila a moment to realize she was smiling at the memory. She inhaled sharply, coming back to the present moment. Turning to Riley she scoffed, "Siblings are stupid, hey?"

Instantly regretting her terrible timing and utterly pathetic excuse for a joke, she cringed. Riley didn't seem to hear her, though. He laid on her bed, gazing at the ceiling.

Shuffling closer, Leila asked, "How did you get here?"

Riley's eyes drifted to her. He gave a quick smile and sat up, crossing his legs. "I ran."

Eyebrows raising, she tilted her head like a confused puppy. "You ran the whole way?"

Riley chuckled. "I mean, I can run but I'm not you. About halfway, I managed to hitch a ride with a trucker."

Leila watched Riley's eyes glaze over as if he was reliving the moment. She wanted to know what happened before he ran… but she was afraid of the answer. Tentatively, she asked, "What are you thinking about?"

"Odie."

"She'll be okay. You know that, right?"

"Mmm." Riley bunched Leila's blanket into his fists. "I can't help thinking that my choice doomed her. He was coming after me, what if he found her instead?"

He. Riley meant Kale. Leila pushed the thought to the back of her mind, turning her attention to comforting Riley. "You can't think like that."

Riley gazed at her. "It's how I always think. Every choice I make seems to have dire consequences. We shouldn't have separated at camp. I should have trusted Gabby, too, and not listened to Kiko. I should have told you the truth about me when your mark first appeared. I should have listened to Tessa instead of forcing her away."

He was on a downward spiral. Leila was great at covering up her fear with jokes, but she couldn't do it this time… not with so much on the line. So, she did the next best thing, she straddled his lap and clutched his biceps, and looking deep into his eyes, she scolded. "It's not all on your shoulders. You need to stop blaming yourself for things beyond your control."

Riley cocked his head back and closed his eyes. "What if I could control it, though? What if the decisions I make change things? I should have known Odette would come back to me last night. If I didn't run, if I stayed and took their attention, maybe they wouldn't have caught her. But I left, and —"

"Stop!" Leila said a little too loudly. She took his face in her hands and forced him to look at her. Quieter, she repeated, "Stop. You don't know if they caught her."

Riley gave a half smile but the sadness remained in his eyes. "I'm really sorry."

"You've nothing to be sorry for," Leila said, climbing off Riley's lap. "Odette will show up."

Wincing, Riley said, "No, I'm sorry about something else, too. I heard them talking in their tent. They planned the whole thing. To get us out of town and vulnerable. To turn us against each other. They want Sebastian rogue. They want Gabby offside. They want you and me apart."

Leila took a deep breath, filling her lungs to capacity. Closing her eyes, she imagined Kale wanting all those horrible things. The concept seemed ludicrous.

Her eyes glazed over. She felt the urge to laugh, to find a joke, to say something sarcastic or off-handed. But merely a peep left her voice box.

"Leila?" Riley asked.

"Are you sure it's both of them?" she managed to squeak.

Riley's whole body slumped as if the way she looked broke his heart. "I'm sure. Kiko ordered him to take me out of the equation. And if I didn't run, he would have."

Leila had tried not to think about it. But there they were, definitive words. Her brother wanted to hurt Riley. Her brother was a Fallen.

As words escaped her, emotions began swirling. The swelling in her heart was too quick, too overwhelming. She felt as if she might explode. And that couldn't happen. She couldn't lose it. Not now, not when they were on the verge of stopping Kiko from hurting anyone else ever again. Sadie depended on her. All the innocents in the town depended on her. Riley, and all his anxiety-induced decisions, depended on her.

She swallowed hard and closed her eyes, forcing tears to remain unshed. She'd have to deal with those emotions later. One deep breath in. One deep breath out.

Think about the plan, she told herself.

"Are you okay?" Riley asked.

Opening her eyes, settled and centered, Leila nodded.

They were both quiet for a moment.

"Sure you're okay?" Riley asked, taking her hand in his.

Leila felt a lump form in her throat. Tears teasing her eyes, she pulled her hand from his. She needed a change of subject.

Rolling her eyes, she scoffed. "It's so obvious now, isn't it? Kiko turned Cap, you know? Started all that mess."

Riley blinked slowly. He kneaded his knuckles, pressing into his skin as if it were clay. "Right. Well, that makes sense, I guess."

Leila's phone dinged and a message from Ren lit the screen. *Makoto has sent two of his clan to spy on Kiko. They'll report back soon. If it even looks like Odette will be harmed they'll step in.* Leila read the text out loud, then said, "That's good, right?"

Riley collapsed back onto Leila's pillow. He was silent as he ran his palms down his face.

"Do you want to go home?" she asked.

"Probably best we don't separate again," Riley replied.

Shuffling closer, Leila laid down. "Ever?"

"Ever."

He leaned over, running his hand along her jawline. Leila met him halfway and they kissed. The way his lips moved slowly, as though every stroke meant the world, filled Leila's heart with sadness.

She'd hoped that their moment in the tent that morning would have made the day memorable in the best way. But then Sadie got marked. And they found out about Kiko. And, his ex showed up.

Leila rolled onto her back and looked up. "I hate Calice

by the way."

"Who?"

Leila frowned, then instantly remembered that he didn't even know *the cat's* name. "Your sister's friend. The feline stalker."

"Oh." Riley remained quiet for a few seconds, before adding, "I didn't think you hated anybody."

He was right. As always. She managed to find the good in just about anyone. But this time, she didn't even want to try. Admitting that wasn't something she was willing to do.

"Let's get some sleep," Leila said. She rolled to her side and pecked him on the cheek. "We need rest."

Riley rolled over to face her. Eyes twinkling, he whispered, "I love *you.*"

It was late. Maybe midnight. Riley slept peacefully while Leila couldn't bear to fall asleep.

Slipping out of bed, she tip-toed across her room and into the bathroom. She flicked the lights on and closed the door. For years she'd shared this bathroom with Kale, her showers forever cut short by his incessant knocking, urging her to hurry up.

As Leila turned the shower on, she noticed her hands were shaking. She stripped her clothes off, dropped them on the floor and stared at the streaming water, waiting for it to warm. Visions swirled through her mind—of Riley running through the forest to get away from her own brother. How could it have come to this?

She stared at her mark as steam filled the room. It reminded her of when she first got the mark and how frightened she was in that moment.

It was nothing compared to this.

Kiko's lies had sunken in. She was willing to accept that Kiko had manipulated them all. Justice for everything she'd done was coming.

But Kale? She feared for him.

If something went wrong with the plan. If he sacrificed himself for Kiko. If she did her Fallen thing and pushed him through the rift to save herself…

And then there was Riley, with the biggest target on his back. Literally. Kiko wanted him gone.

Leila stepped under the hot water. She rested her forehead on the tiled wall, letting droplets coat her back. She hoped against all hope that they could put an end to it all without losing her brother or her boyfriend.

Three loud bangs thumped against the door. Kale's voice boomed, "Are you gonna hog all the hot water?"

Leila turned the taps off, turning her ears to the door. As remaining droplets fell off her chin, she asked, "Kale?"

The house was silent. She stepped out of the shower and wrapped a towel around herself. Tentatively, she opened the door. Cool air from the hall wafted over her bare arms and legs.

There was no one there. Her wet feet dripped over the carpet as she shuffled from the bathroom to Kale's bedroom. She opened the door. No-one was there.

The smell of Kale's aftershave hit her nostrils. She quickly closed his door. Shaken, she rushed back to her room, slipped on her pajamas and climbed into bed.

Riley rustled beside her. "You okay?"

"Is anything ever okay?" Leila retorted, nestling her body as close to him as possible.

Riley scooped his arm around her, pulling her closer still. She closed her eyes. Finally. Maybe. She might get some sleep after all.

"Leila?" Kale's voice echoed through the whole house. "You're making me late for work."

Leila sat up, bedding falling to her waist. Riley's arm dropped onto the bed, out like a light. Leila frowned, wondering how much time had passed. Did she sleep? Was she still asleep?

Footsteps marched across the floorboards downstairs. Leila swallowed and made her way out of her room and to the stairwell. She peered over the banister. "Kale?"

The movement downstairs stopped suddenly. She crept down each step, calling her lion close. As she got to the ground floor, she peered at every corner, walking through the living room to the dining, and then into the kitchen.

"I must be hearing things," she muttered to herself.

While she was there, she figured she may as well have a glass of water. As she sipped, she looked out the kitchen window to her mother's garden lit by solar lights. Rain fell onto rosemary and vervain and other unknown herbs.

A shadow moved on the back porch. Leila jumped, spilling water down the front of her top. She placed the glass down and peered through the window to get a better look. It was hard to see anything in the dark and she thought for a moment her eyes were playing tricks on her until two glowing, bronze circles appeared on the other side of the glass.

She stared through the window heart lodged deep in her throat. "Kale?"

Leila didn't even think to half-shift to see with her Guardian's eyes until the bronze bulbs blinked into nothing. Body pulsing to life, Leila bolted for the back door. As she half-shifted, she flung the door wide open and stepped out onto the porch. But no-one was there. She ran out into the middle of the back yard, rain streaming around her. "Kale? Are you there?"

She stood out there for a good ten minutes, bare feet sinking into the cold, wet grass. Every now and then, she'd pace across the yard, peering over neighbors' fences. Eventually, she gave up, deciding she was probably over-tired and losing her mind.

When she got inside, she reached for her cup to finish the water, but it was gone. As she tried to remember if she'd spilled it all or not, a loud thud that seemed to come from upstairs shook the house.

Riley? she thought, realizing her mistake.

While she'd been outside, hoping against all hope that her brother had come to tell her he wasn't Fallen after all, he was actually just distracting her while Kiko came for Riley. Heart pounding, Leila sped up the stairs to her room.

Her bed was empty, the sheets crumpled at the end of her mattress. The patter of raindrops hitting the window caught her attention first, followed by the way her drapes moved as if they were breathing. The window was open.

Fearing she was too late, Leila fled to the window. She leaned through the gap and screamed into the night air. "Riley?"

Two strong hands clasped her shoulders and she was spun around on the spot like a ragdoll. Leila half-shifted, flexing her muscles, ready to attack whoever it was. Riley stared back at her with furrowed brows. His eyes drifted to her splayed claws.

"It's me," he said, voice as soft as silk. "Leila, I'm here."

Leila crumbled. Her body collapsed onto him as she returned to human form. She blubbered into his shoulder, "I thought they took you."

"I'm okay," he said, taking her face in his hands. "We're okay."

He took a step back, eyes exploring her body. "Where have you been? You're soaked!"

"Dancing in the rain," she said.

After she'd changed and wrung her hair semi-dry, they slid into bed. Leila pulled the bedding up over her shoulders and snuggled her back onto Riley's chest. She reached for his hand and placed it around her.

She couldn't sleep though. She lay there, eyes wide open, waiting for tomorrow.

WEDNESDAY

morning

Sadie

Sadie sat on the sofa in Reece's living room, blanket wrapped around her. Birds chirped outside, and sliver of sunlight streamed through a gap in the drapes. She stared at Sebastian asleep on the floor in front of fire, silently begging him to wake.

As footsteps scurried down the short hallway, Sadie instinctively covered her neck with her hand. Reece peered into the living room and gave a quick smile before ducking through into the kitchen. Sadie sighed and dropped her hand.

She cleared her throat, staring at Sebastian. He didn't look so tough when he slept. His mouth was parted and he gave a slight snore with every inhale. She cleared her throat again and his mouth smacked together a few times before he rolled over.

Sadie rolled her eyes and grabbed a cushion. She hauled it in his direction. It hit his shoulder and continued over his body.

Sebastian rustled, rolling back around. His eyes peeled open one-by-one and, as he caught sight of Sadie staring at him, he grinned. He croaked, "Can't keep your eyes off me."

Sadie glared at him and pointed her finger to her neck. He sprung to his feet, blanket dropping to his ankles. She'd never seen him move so fast. He stood in front of her in nothing but his cotton boxer shorts. He had abs. Because, of course. And his mark curved around the top of his left pec.

Sadie stared, imagining what his skin would feel like beneath her fingertips.

"Tessa!"

Sebastian's cry made Sadie jump. She blinked a few times, remembering what she wanted him awake for. It was definitely not to drool at his body.

Tessa burst into the room, her eyes immediately shining bright pink. Her gaze darted to Sadie and she winced. "Already? Mine took four damn days."

Tessa spun around and bounded off in the direction she came from. Sadie leaned her head against the couch and rolled her face to Sebastian. He was staring at her, half-shifted. The darkness behind his already neon-blue eyes returned.

"Seb?" Sadie asked, uneasy.

Sebastian made some unnatural moan as he forced his gaze to the ground. His jaw clenched and he dug his claws into his palms as he began pacing in front of her. He muttered to himself. "Don't look. Don't look. Don't look."

"Does it make you want to hurt me?" Sadie asked.

Tessa returned carrying a yellow and white polka dot scarf. She jumped next to Sadie on the couch and swirled the scarf around and around to cover the mark. To make sure it was hidden well enough, she half-shifted, scanning the area with her Guardian's eyes.

Satisfied, she pouted and nodded. "That'll have to do for now."

Sebastian relaxed, letting his claws retract from his palms. He let his eyes scan Sadie and he sighed. "That's rough," he said, running his blood-spotted hands down his cheeks.

"It's a call sign, isn't it?" Tessa said, patting Sadie on the shoulder. "The mark on an un-transitioned Guardian produces this kind of beacon. It's like a bright neon sign saying—turn me."

"It's different for a Fallen," Sebastian said, collapsing onto an armchair.

Tessa nodded. She leaned forward, resting her hands on her knees and pushing herself up. "You've impressed me. I've not met a Fallen who could control themselves like that before."

"What's it like for a Fallen?" Sadie asked, wrapping the scarf around one more time for good luck.

Sebastian squeezed his eyes shut and threw his head back onto the headrest. A few moments later, he opened his eyes. "I can taste the blood in my mouth." He let his gaze rest on Sadie. "*Your* blood in my mouth. Every cell in my body aches as though the only way to quench it is to bite you."

Sadie grabbed the ends of her blanket and raised it over her chest. "Oh. Is that all?" she tried to make a joke but fear laced every syllable.

"And that's just with normal people. When a marked one is waiting for transition, it's…" Sebastian's head dropped as he finished his sentence, "a hundred times worse."

Tessa dropped back onto the couch. "You live like this? I mean, I know about it in theory. But I always thought the Fallen liked it."

Sebastian whipped his head up, eyes pierced his half-sister. "You think I like to be tortured?"

"Will you turn me?" Sadie blurted, clutching Tessa's arm. "Now?"

"Oh? Really?" Tessa gasped. "No, I…"

"C'mon, Tessa," Sebastian said, whipping his arm in Sadie's direction. "She's a sitting duck."

Tessa winced. "I just don't like turning people who didn't choose to be marked. If we can cure her, that would be my first option."

"Mr Robertson," Sadie stated, still holding Tessa's arm.

"He's the one who marked me."

Tessa pried Sadie's fingers open. "You're my assignment. It's my first priority to make sure that the cure happens. But that also means I need to find him to get his blood."

Sebastian slammed his hands on the arm rests of his chair and stood. "I'll help you."

Two fifteen-year-olds clamored into the living room. Imogen beamed, eyes moving between Sebastian and Tessa. "Good morning brother. Good morning sister."

Tessa smiled and scratched the place between her eyebrows. "It's gonna take me a while to get used to that."

"Immy," Sebastian moaned. "Just take it chill, yeah?"

"Okay, yes. Sure." Imogen nodded emphatically. She pressed her lips together as she tried not to look at Tessa. Her cheeks puffed out like a chipmunk before she let out a blast of air. "But, there's one thing. When do I get to meet Riley? I've seen him at school but I'd like to *meet* meet him."

"Just stop!" Sebastian yelled. "He might not want to meet us."

Imogen rolled her shoulders back, glaring at Sebastian. Sadie saw her eyes shimmer with tears, but Imogen didn't let them fall. She returned fire. "No, it's just *you* he won't want to meet."

"Listen." Tessa held her hands up in surrender. "Riley's been through a lot. I think maybe we'll ease him into it. I'd like to be the one to tell him."

"Agreed." Sebastian said, heading for door. "I'm going to get the car ready."

"Whatever," Imogen huffed. She marched toward the kitchen. "Dad, do we have pancakes?"

Summer stayed behind. "Are we going already?"

"Actually," Sadie said, protective instincts kicking into gear. "Maybe it's a good idea if you girls stayed here. No-one will know where you are."

"Actually." Tessa repeated, facing Sadie. "Maybe it's a good idea if you stayed, too?"

Sadie balked. "What, and have no protection when the Fallen come for me? Hell to the no."

Tessa looked down her nose at Sadie, one eyebrow curved upward. "You yourself literally just said that no-one will know you're here. You'll be safe."

"They don't have a freaking lighthouse on their bodies." Sadie tugged on the end of the scarf, sliding it away from her neck. "I'd be putting them in danger if I stayed."

The front door opened and Sebastian walked in. He took one look at Sadie and growled, "Shorty, geez. Cover the thing!"

"Sorry," Sadie mumbled, wrapping the scarf snugly around neck. "But I'm coming with you."

"I assumed you would be anyway," Sebastian said. He looked at Tessa with confusion. "She stays close to us for protection, right?"

"Fine!" Tessa threw her arms in the air. "My opinion obviously doesn't matter at all anyway."

WEDNESDAY

morning

Leila

"Hurry up scatterbrain, you'll make me late for work."

"Kale?"

Leila sat up fully awake.

Riley rolled over, half of his face still mushed into the pillow. He muffled, "Are you all right?"

Leila blinked a few times, staring at her closed door. She must have been dreaming. Looking down at Riley, she said, "Yeah. Good morning."

Riley smiled and reached for a curl that sat on Leila's shoulder. He wrapped his fingers through the tendril and replied, "Good morni—"

The bedroom door swung open and Gabby barged in. "Hi lovers. Sorry to interrupt. Odette's fine... in case you were wondering."

"Oh, thank god," Riley said, sitting up.

Gabby raised her brows. "Oh, you *do* care?"

"Of course I care," Riley scoffed.

Gabby ran her tongue across her teeth. "Yes. Well. I couldn't sleep so I did that reckless thing that people in love do."

Riley leaned forward. "You love her?"

"What? No..." Gabby took a breath. "Well, maybe..." She wandered to Leila's dresser and fiddled with a chunky gold necklace.

"Back up," Leila said, swinging her legs over the side of the mattress. "What reckless thing did you do?"

Gabby tilted her head over her shoulder, a smirk lighting her face. "I went to save her."

"You did?" Riley asked, bounding out of bed. "Is she here?"

Gabby stared at him for a moment and let out a small huff. "No, I didn't save her. I wanted to but Calice and Jamal convinced me it was best to spy first before jumping right in with a rescue. We found Kiko and Kale on the edge of town. Odette was with them, tied up but alive. They're still out there now, keeping an eye on things."

Riley reached for the ground and dragged his jeans under the covers. He said, "We're going to get her out. I promise."

The bedsheets bounced over him as he wriggled into the jeans. Gabby watched him, bemused. Leila tried not to laugh, he had underwear on but was still obviously too embarrassed to let Gabby see him without proper clothes on.

"Anyway," Gabby said, shaking her head. "Makoto and Ren are downstairs. Ready with some plan to bring justice!" She pointed to Leila's closet. "Wear your leopard print cargos, Leila, they'll be great to kick some ass in."

As Gabby ran off, Leila opened her closet. She pulled her cargo pants off their hanger and slipped them on. Next, she grabbed two jackets off their hooks, a black one with bright yellow cuffs and a teal one that shimmered as the light hit it.

Turning around, she held them both up and asked, "Which one should I wear?

Riley smacked the side of his jeans and a puff of dirt wafted around his legs. He looked up. "Huh?"

"Maybe you could check Kale's room for something to wear?" Leila suggested, putting the teal jacket back in the closet.

Riley picked up his shirt and jacket from the floor. Scrunching his nose, he replied, "That might be a good idea. I've worn these for too many days."

As Riley ran off, Leila slid the jacket over a comfortable T-shirt and reached for her phone. A message lit the screen. "It's Sadie!" she called to Riley, heading out of her room. "They're on their way back."

"With Tessa?" Riley asked, buttoning up a pair of chinos.

"Sadie, Sebastian, and Tessa," Leila said.

Riley made a face that Leila couldn't quite decipher and turned back into Kale's room to find a top.

As she waited, she punched a reply. *Come to my house. We'll keep you safe, I promise.*

She hovered her finger over the send button. How many times had she made a promise in the last few days? Promises she couldn't truly know she was able keep. She hit send, adamant that she'd make sure she wouldn't break any.

When Riley was fully dressed, they clambered downstairs.

Ren was slumping in the armchair, making himself completely at home. Seeing Leila and Riley enter the room, he asked, "Have we heard from Sadie?"

Leila wiggled her phone in Ren's direction. "They're on their way."

"Thank God!" Gabby exclaimed standing in the arch between the dining and living rooms. She looked at Leila and motioned her head to the dining table.

Sitting at the table with herbs and vials and satchels in front of them, were Makoto and Aileen. Makoto glanced up and waved them over. He threw a satchel across the table.

"That's yours, Riley," Makoto said, tying up another.

Aileen took the next satchel and stood, she walked to Leila and pinched her chin between two fingers. Her auburn hair was in messy bun for the third day straight, and pieces of flyaway strands circled her forehead. Tears welled in her eyes as she said, "My baby is all grown up."

She opened Leila's jacket and tucked the satchel into an inside pocket. Leaning in, she whispered, "This is one thing we won't tell your dad about, okay. He wouldn't understand it."

The quiver in her mom's voice gave Leila chills. As if she knew that Leila might have to make the ultimate betrayal against their own flesh and blood.

Leila took her mom's hands. She darted her eyes quickly to Makoto to make sure he wasn't watching and leaned in close to whisper. "I won't let anything happen to Kale."

"Okay." Makoto placed his palms onto the table and stood, his commanding presence taking up the whole room. "It's time you both knew exactly what is in store. Take a seat."

Riley and Leila sat down. Leila's nerves caused her heart to flutter and her fingers to shake. She took a hold of her chair and shuffled closer to the table. The legs of her chair scraped along the tiles and she cringed at the awkward noise.

Makoto waited for her to settle then nodded to the satchel in Riley's hand. "They are mixed with vervain, moonstone and soaked in your combined blood… and my blood. Keep it on you at all times."

"Your blood?" Leila asked.

"The blood of a first Guardian, it won't work without it. I've given the Elders your blood, they have smeared it in the sanctuary. It will work as a door. We open from this side, they receive on that side. But it's really important that you get your timing right. Are you able to do the surge on command?"

"On command?" Riley said, turning the satchel around in his hands.

"Yes," Leila interjected. "We've got it sorted."

Makoto nodded. "Good. It's imperative you only use the surge when you are close to Kiko and no-one else. We don't want to risk sending an innocent through. The rift will open fast and once she realizes what we're doing, she'll retaliate."

"Okay," Leila said, understanding why her mom was so nervous. "How do we get Kiko away from Kale? So he doesn't go through?"

"She'll need to be physically pushed. Ren or I or probably both will have to do it. You two just need to focus on making sure you're together at all times, so when I say go... You go."

"We can do that," Leila enthused.

Riley clutched the satchel into his fist and shoved it into Kale's chinos. He gave Leila a side-eye, nerves written all over his face. He muttered, "It sounds dangerous."

"It is." Makoto exhaled. "Any questions?"

"When will this happen? Will we have time to practice?" Riley asked.

"Mmm. I've been told the timing and location will be made known soon. For now, we sit and wait." Makoto glanced between Leila and Riley, waiting for more questions. When they remained silent, he stood. "Excuse me. I've just gotta make a call and check on Calice and Jamal. They were taking turns keeping an eye on Kiko's movements."

Leila pulled her jacket closed, feeling the satchel in her pocket, and turned to Riley. "Are you feeling all right?"

"Do you think we can do it on command? We've only really tried once," Riley said, his eyes not quite meeting hers.

Shrugging, Leila said, "We have no choice, right?"

Creases formed between Riley's eyebrows. Leila felt her throat go dry. He was panicking, she could sense it. Both of them had to be committed to this, there was too much that could go wrong. If he wasn't in the right frame of mind, she didn't want to think about what might happen.

Wincing, Riley finally let his eyes land on her face.

"There's so much pressure on us to get it right. The timing has to be perfect. We need to make sure Kale is nowhere near the split when we create it. That's if we can even do the surge in the right moment. And I can't help but think—"

"Riley?" Leila interrupted, sliding her hand over his shoulder. "Do you love me?"

"Yes!" Riley replied without hesitation.

Leila felt her heart warm. She gave a small smile. "Then we can do this."

WEDNESDAY

noon

Tessa

Butterflies swarmed inside Tessa's chest. She sat in the back seat of Sebastian's car, cracking her knuckles over and over. They were headed to Cedar Falls — Leila's house to be precise. And wherever Leila was, so too was Will. Or Riley, as he now went by. Remembering his new name was going to be hard.

It had been a strange few days. The whole time since she'd found out Riley was a part of Kiko's clan, she'd thought he was Fallen. Damn that kid brother of hers. He'd taken her to hell and back. She mourned him for almost a year. To find out he was True lifted a heaviness from her soul. And then, to discover they had a brother and sister? It was a lot to process.

As the trees made way for houses and they passed a sign that said *"Welcome to Cedar Falls"*, Sebastian quickly peered over his shoulder. "You ready?"

Tessa could have sworn there was a hint of empathy in

his voice. She stared at the back of his head for a moment, wondering how on earth a Fallen could be so… so… not evil.

Sadie turned around. "Riley's going to flip when he sees you." Her eyes widened and she quickly added, "In a good way, I mean."

The butterflies in Tessa's chest made her nauseous. She felt the tears well. Double damn that kid brother of hers.

"I've missed him," she said.

"Was he a self-righteous knob before he turned?" Sebastian asked, catching Tessa's eyes in the rear-vision mirror.

A twinkle hit his sky-blue eyes. The way he smirked reminded her of Will… Riley. It was his mouth and jawline. Maybe the shape of his eyes, too. Sebastian had sharper cheekbones and bushier eyebrows than Riley. But the similarities were definitely there, now that she knew.

She smirked back. "Yeah, he kinda was."

Tessa shuffled along the seat to catch her own reflection in the mirror. Everyone always said she had her brother's eyes. She scanned her face, eyes landing on her nostrils as they flared with breath. Oh, there it was. Sebastian did that.

As they drove past Cedar Falls Academy, Sebastian glanced at the gates and scoffed. "I bet mom doesn't even care that I've missed three days."

Tessa's heart sank. They'd each led such different lives. Her and Riley grew up with a mostly absent father and very little money but a mother who would do anything for them. And Sebastian, from what she'd gathered, grew up with both parents until recently, all the riches they needed, but his mother was distant and selfish.

"I'm sorry," Tessa said, knowing that truly wasn't enough. "Tell me about her. Your mom."

Sebastian jerked his head, eyes not quite meeting hers before he faced the road again. He sniffed and with a straight face replied, "No."

"My mom cares," Sadie said, looking at her phone. "Too

much, I think. She's left me a billion messages."

Sebastian glared at her, eyebrows raised. "A parent can't care too much, Sadie. Geez."

"Sorry. You're right. I know it means she cares, but what more can I do? I spoke to her last night. I told her we found Summer and that we'd head home today. What else can I say? Yo! By the way, I'm being hunted by werewolves... werefoxes... whatever."

Tessa knew she was joking but just to be sure, she piped up, "Just don't say anything. We'll get the cure for you and you can go home without them suspecting a thing."

Turning her head to the window, Sadie muttered, "Always with the cure."

Tessa studied Sadie as she retreated within herself and wondered if she even wanted a cure. The more time she spent with Sadie, the more she was sure of her assignment — she was meant to save Sadie from herself. Because it was more than choosing between a cure and turning her. To Tessa, Sadie seemed... lost. Like she didn't know who she was. There was a brave front; the girl who seemed to be able to move mountains. And then there was the irresolute; the girl who hid behind a facade, her true self simmering just beyond the surface. Could someone like that make a good Guardian? Tessa doubted Makoto would choose to turn her.

Sebastian pulled the car to a halt along the curb and Tessa sat up straight. They had arrived. She peered through the car window in time to see Leila's front door swing open and Riley rush out onto the porch.

Tessa was out of the car before the ignition was even off. She bounded toward the house, butterflies turning to excitement.

She cried, "Will!"

Her feet couldn't seem to move fast enough. She watched her long-lost brother wait for her, tears already streaming from his eyes. As she reached the end of the path, he leapt the steps to greet her.

Her body slammed against his as she wrapped her arms around him. Had he grown in a year? She twisted her head around, to peer up at him. Yes, he had.

"It's Riley, now," he whispered as a tear fell from his chin and landed on her forehead.

"I know," she mumbled, squeezing him tighter. "I know."

WEDNESDAY

noon

Sadie

Sadie and Sebastian sat in the car for a moment, both sets of eyes glued to the reunion on Leila's porch.

Sebastian sighed and dropped his head to the steering wheel. "I have a half-sister."

"And brother," Sadie added.

Sebastian whipped his face around and glared at Sadie. A week ago, a look like that would have made her feel like the scum of the earth, but she knew better now. It was just a knee-jerk reaction, his defense mechanism.

A moment later, Sebastian sighed. He leaned across Sadie and wiggled the door latch, twisting it at an angle. A slight popping noise reverberated and he pushed the door open. As the cool breeze seeped in, Sebastian remained where he was, trapping Sadie on the spot.

He faced her, eyes turning to slits. "And if you tell him —"

"What?" Sadie said with a confidence she'd never had before. She slipped her body out from under him and stepped onto the curb. Flinging the end of the scarf over her shoulder, she quipped, "You're gonna kill me? Pretty sure we've established that you're not gonna do that."

She walked down the path, willing herself not to look back. Tessa and Riley had made their way inside and Leila was waiting at the door, hair pulled back. As Sadie approached, a fierce determination hit Leila's eyes.

Sadie grinned, "You look like whoever faces you is in trouble."

Leila replied by exuberantly bursting onto the porch and enveloping Sadie into an almighty hold. Sadie noted to herself it was one of the best hugs she'd ever received. Including the one her dad gave when he stubbed her toe for the first time when she was four years old.

Inside the house a few steps, Sadie could see Tessa with Riley. He was crying. She was crying.

Tessa blubbered, "I'm so sorry I put you through all this."

Riley's eyes drifted to Leila. "It's kind of all worked out for the better."

Leila pulled away and the zip on her jacket cuff managed to get caught on Sadie's scarf, pulling it loose. As Sadie stepped through the door, all eyes panned to her mark. She hurried to cover it, but the truth was out.

Tessa hurried over, readjusting the scarf back into place. Sadie felt her face blush. She wasn't used to that kind of attention. Not when she wasn't prepared with her fake and flirty personality.

"No!" Riley shouted as Sebastian stepped in behind them. "You're not welcome."

Tessa placed her hand onto his chest. "He's fine. It's fine." She turned to Sebastian, giving an apologetic frown.

"I just want to help," Sebastian said, his hand warming Sadie's lower back.

"We will take all the help we can get," Ren said much to Riley's disdain. He sat, body slumped, in an armchair by the window.

"Is that Sadie?" A voice cried from the kitchen. Gabby burst through the archway, running toward Sadie. "I'm so glad you're okay!"

As Gabby bundled Sadie up in her arms, Sadie returned with a tight squeeze, and said, "You, too. I heard they tied you up."

"We won't talk about that," Gabby said, waving her hand in dismissal. She clapped her hands together, beaming at Leila. "One down, one to go."

"Huh?" Riley asked.

Gabby's joy disappeared. With a twinge of spite, she retorted, "People to be safe. You still have a cousin out there, remember?"

"Yes," Riley hissed defensively, "I know."

A loud sigh resonated through the room. Ren pushed himself up as though he was lifting five ton weights. He sauntered up the stairs. "I'm gonna go have a nap—get this panther rested for what's to come."

Ren wandered into the living room from the dining room. Sadie did a double take. No, that wasn't Ren, he just went upstairs. And his mohawk was gone. And... he was taller, muscular, a little older.

The lookalike frowned and said, "Where's he going?"

Leila replied with a shrug, "He said he's taking a nap."

The man's body moved as though he laughed but no sound came out. "Sounds about right."

Sadie leaned toward Tessa, and whispered, "Who's that."

"Oh," Tessa shuffled closer. Pointing to the man, she replied, "That's Makoto, my Alpha. He's also Ren and Kiko's brother."

Sadie stared at her blankly.

"They're the first Guardians," Tessa added.

Sadie shared a glance with Sebastian, and at the same time they both said, "Riiiiight."

Tessa smiled. "I'll catch you up to everything soon. How

are you feeling?"

Sadie hadn't thought about it for a while. She felt pretty good, if she was honest. "I feel fine. Maybe a bit hungry."

"Oh, I'm so sorry, I should have offered!" Leila said, acting as though she had killed a kitten. "There's a whole heap of kalua pork in the fridge. Seriously, help yourself."

Turning her head to Sebastian, Sadie asked, "You coming?"

"Don't have to ask me twice," Sebastian said, grabbing her hand and hauling her out of the room.

She almost had to run to keep up. It would have been funny, but she didn't dare glance back to her friends. She knew what faces they'd be pulling. Especially Riley. Disgust.

As they entered the kitchen, she relaxed into a fit of giggles. In between spurts of laughter, she teased, "You couldn't get out of there fast enough."

"Self-righteous kooks make me want to hurl," he said, opening the fridge and pulling out a massive dish.

Sadie settled herself and shook her head. "They're nice people."

"To you," he muttered, peeling the lid off.

A smoky and salty scent wafted into the air around them. Sebastian dashed to the cutlery drawer and sifted through the silverware. He leapt back to the dish and as he passed a fork to Sadie, he sent his own into the mix.

"You don't want to heat it up?" Sadie asked watching him shoveling strips of meat into mouth. "Or put some in a bowl?"

He looked up at her and shook his head. "Too good to wait."

Sadie squinted at him and sent her own fork in. She scraped a tiny bit of pork for taste testing and lifted it to her lips. As the seasoned meat hit her tongue, she quickly dug in for more. Within a few minutes she'd devoured at least ten mouthfuls. Sebastian looked on with amusement, as he did —his eyes twinkling every time she dug her fork in.

Full and a little bit embarrassed, Sadie wiped her mouth. "You coming back in to the jury?"

Sebastian curled his lip. He carefully placed the lid back onto the dish and returned it to the fridge. He sighed dramatically for effect, and said, "If I must."

He was such a brat. Sadie smile and whacked his bicep. "Come on, tough guy."

As they made their way through the dining area, Sadie heard her name and stopped. She lifted her finger to her lips and crept to the archway, hanging back out of sight.

"Sadie can't come with us, what if Kiko turns her!" Gabby exclaimed.

"We need Mr. Robertson's blood," Leila said.

"I'll get it, while we're out there," Riley said. "Gabby can stay with Sadie."

"I'd like to stay," Tessa offered.

Sadie glanced at Sebastian and rolled her eyes. She whispered, "This Sadie chick sounds like such a burden."

"Screw this," Sebastian said, barging into the living room. "I'll stay with her."

"Are our choices really between two Fallen?" Tessa moaned, adding a quick, "No offense."

Rare courage rising, Sadie stepped into the living room. "Do I get a choice?"

Tessa smiled. "Of course you do. What's your choice? Remember you're *my* assignment."

Everyone looked at her in anticipation. She swallowed and scanned the room. There was no way Gabby would want to stay, not with Odette out there still. Riley and Leila would need to be out there using their Imprint strength. She had no idea who this Makoto dude was. And Tessa was nice, but...

"I choose Seb... because he's kept me safe so far."

"Damn straight," Sebastian said, puffing his chest up.

The truth was, she didn't want anyone staying back because of her and her frailty. She was sick of being the one who needed saving. Before they headed out, before anyone left, she was going to be turned.

"Leila?" Sadie asked, pinching the sleeve of her shirt. "Can I borrow some clothes?"

"Yes, sure."

Together, they climbed the stairs, Gabby rushing to join them. Leila led them into her room. Sadie made a point to close the door behind them.

"So, you're on nickname terms now?" Gabby asked, eyebrow lifting.

"What?" Sadie said, innocently.

"Seb? Really?" Gabby sat on the edge of Leila's bed and glared at Sadie in a way that only she could. A glare that said, *girl, you're a mess.*

Sadie tried to think of what to say to divert Gabby's attention from Sebastian. But every time she thought about him, she couldn't help but smile. She glanced at Leila, who looked on expectantly, a twinkle in her eyes. Turning back to Gabby, Sadie lifted her chin and said proudly, "Yes. Sebastian Weir and I are friends. Maybe more. What are ya gonna do about it?"

Leila guffawed. She spun around to her closet, and failing to hold back laughter, her shoulders bounced up and down. Gabby slapped her hand to her mouth, eyes widening with shock. Behind her palm, a few chuckles escaped.

"Nothing," Gabby muttered through pursed lips. "I won't do anything."

The sight of her friends' laughter, broke Sadie. Grinning so hard her cheeks hurt, she blurted, "He's different, you guys. He's shown me a side to him that I… that I like."

"What about Damien?" Leila asked over her shoulder. Sadie's glare must have answered that question real quick, because Leila averted her eyes and added, "Never mind." She sifted through her shirts. "I'm trying to find one that you won't get lost in."

"It's just…" Gabby started. She grimaced, "I don't want

to say what I think of him. I don't want to upset you."

There it was. Sadie knew it would take Gabby time to warm to Sebastian. She didn't have that kind of time.

"None of that matters. Not right now. We can talk about it another time, in depth and detail and you can list all the ways in which he's a terrible person. But right now —" Sadie plonked herself in the middle of Leila's bed and unraveled her scarf. "Turn me."

"What?" Leila balked, swinging around. As she did, her hand got caught on a hanger and she brought half the contents of her closet down.

Clothes sprinkled the floor around Leila's feet but she didn't dare take her eyes off Sadie. "You don't want the cure?"

"Cover it up!" Gabby snapped. She leapt off Leila's bed and turned to face the wall. "Hurry up and cover that mark right now."

Remembering what Sebastian said about the mark being a torture call for the Fallen, Sadie wrapped the scarf around her neck again. "It's covered. Sorry."

Gabby glanced over her shoulder and noticing the scarf back in place, she sighed and turned back around.

Leila sat down next to Sadie on her bed. She placed her hand on Sadie's knee. "Do you really want this?"

"I want to not be scared," Sadie said, telling the truth. "I don't want to be a target."

"Yes, but do you want *this*?" Leila asked again.

"Who would be our human?" Gabby said, bottom lip rolling into a frown.

"Damien?" Sadie suggested, cringing.

"Oy!" Gabby said, throwing herself onto the mattress. "That won't work at all."

Sadie sighed. She knew then and there that they weren't going to agree.

"Listen," Leila said, standing up. "We'll get through tonight. Sebastian said he'll stay here and protect you. Riley will get Mr. Robertson's blood for the cure. We don't need to turn you."

Sadie was sick of everyone making choices on her behalf. As if they all knew what was right for her. They were supposed to be her closest friends but they barely knew her. Not the real her. Not like Sebastian knew her.

She leaned across the bed and opened Leila's top drawer. Grabbing a pile of Polaroids, she sat back up and flipped through them. Photos from back when they were all human, before they even knew Shadow Guardians existed, before she was a target.

"Okay." Sadie gave her best smile while on the inside she was screaming. "Human sounds good."

Leila smiled satisfied and shuffled through her clothes on the floor. She threw Sadie a black top with sunflowers down the sleeves. "Sorry, I know it's not your style but it's the smallest one I have."

Then, she sifted through her drawers and pulled out some black sweatpants. Pulling at the waist she said, "Just roll them over a few times."

"Thanks," Sadie said, holding the top up to her chest. "Can I have a few minutes? I'll be down soon."

As Leila headed for the door, Gabby hung back and gazed at Sadie with saddened eyes. "You've got this, Sades. We'll be back to normal in no time."

Sadie nodded, not believing it for one second. Not for her, not for Gabby either.

"Love you!" Leila sang, waving over her shoulder.

As soon as the door clicked shut, Sadie whipped out her cell phone and tapped a message.

I need you. Leila's room. Don't let anyone see you come.

WEDNESDAY

early afternoon

Sadie

Sadie had rolled the waistband of Leila's sweatpants for the second time when the door creaked open. Sebastian peered in. "What's up?"

"Did they see you come up here?" Sadie whispered.

Sebastian's brows raised. He gave a tilted smirk and stepped into the room. "What's going on, Shorty?"

Jumping up from her spot on the bed, Sadie closed the door. Spinning around, she demanded, "Turn me."

"Ugh." Sebastian sat on the very edge of the bed. "Not this again."

"It will stop them worrying about me like I'm porcelain."

Sebastian chortled. "You're not porcelain, Sadie Sloan."

Sadie took a long inhale and on the rushed exhale she climbed onto Leila's bed and leaned against the bedhead. Sebastian watching her every move, he was right where she wanted him. Sadie pinched the end of the scarf and in one sweeping movement, she ripped it away and threw it across the room.

Sebastian half-shifted on impulse, glowing eyes finding the ceiling. "Ugh, stop. Why do you do this to me?"

"Just bite me, like you want to." For good measure, she added, "On my mark."

Eyes like a magnet to her mark, Sebastian returned his gaze to her. "Are you sure?"

He was all fangs and blazing irises and claws digging into his palms. Her heart ran what felt like a million miles a second, but there was nothing more she was sure of. She nodded in reply.

Licking his lips, Sebastian shuffled closer. Wincing, he said, "It hurts."

"I know," Sadie said, moving across to make room for him on the bed. "I can handle it."

As he sat right beside her, he dragged his eyes from the mark, forced them to hers. He swallowed and said, "You'll feel out of it for a while, caught between the Veil and our world. But I'll walk you through it, I'll be here the whole time."

"Spoken like a True Guardian."

Sebastian closed his eyes and made a muffled groan. He whispered, "Are you truly sure?"

Sadie took his hand and pressed his fingers against the mark. "Do it."

His eyes darted open. So did his mouth. Venom dripped from his fangs and he held himself as still as a mountain. For a while, his gaze lingered on her eyes, as if waiting for any sign that she might change her mind.

"Do it," she said again.

Sebastian's cheeks twitched. He swallowed, as if controlling himself in that moment was the hardest thing he'd ever done. Slowly, purposefully, he ran his thumb around the mark and moved in. He pressed his lips to her neck, kissing her gently.

Sadie felt the heat of his breath as he opened his mouth.

A quiet rumble crept from his voice box. Sadie's heart flipped at how animalistic he sounded. She took a shaky breath, hesitation creeping in. Then, before she could change her mind, he clamped his mouth around her mark.

It hurt more than she expected. The sting of his fangs piercing her flesh, digging deep into her body. It felt as though he might tear her in two.

She cried out in pain. *Wait!* She wanted to say, *I've changed my mind,* but words escaped her. Sebastian covered her mouth with his palm, biting harder around the mark.

Tears rolled down her cheeks as his venom ripped through her veins. Darkness filled her body from her mark to the depths of her soul. Splotches of black clouded her vision.

Sebastian let her go. He clutched her face with both hands. She could just make out his face through her tears. Red stained his lips, her blood fell to his chin, dropping onto Leila's bedspread.

His mouth moved but she couldn't hear a word. Her heart dropped to her stomach but never returned to her chest. It felt like it left her body and connected with the earth —as though she was sinking into mud. Heaviness fell over her as the taste of bile rose to her throat. She wanted to vomit but her muscles wouldn't do what her brain wanted them to. She was choking, stuck in a body that couldn't move.

Her eyes rolled back and she could faintly hear the sounds of someone calling her name. Was it Sebastian? Maybe Leila? Or even herself.

"What do you choose?" The voice said. It started off as a whisper, growing with urgency until all she heard was a chanting into her ear. "Fallen or True?"

But she couldn't answer.

She was paralyzed.

She was drowning.

She was dying.

WEDNESDAY

afternoon

Sebastian

Sebastian Weir knew he made a mistake the moment he looked into Sadie's eyes. Even through her tears, the fear hit him like an anvil. As her vibrant life seemed to fade, he stayed half-shifted, straining to hear the sounds of her heartbeat. It was faint, but constant. Blood was pumping, that was the main thing.

He licked his lips without thinking. The taste of her rolled over his tongue and he closed his eyes, savoring every drop. He'd forgotten how good human blood tasted. The fact that it was hers made it all the more sweet.

Sadie whimpered and Sebastian shot his eyes open. Her head rolled from side-to-side on Leila's bedhead, wincing in pain. Sebastian remembered what that felt like, transition. Like darkness itself had found solid form and filled his body from toes to head. He wouldn't wish that upon anybody, and yet, he'd given her that pain.

Guilt ripped at his heart. He knew he shouldn't have

turned her, he knew it with all the good that remained in him. But her doe-like eyes had begged and he couldn't say no. He should've just said no.

Sadie gasped. She sat up straight and her eyes sprung open. She wasn't awake, her Guardian was simply making itself known. It was stepping into her body, completing their merge.

A tiger. Sebastian smiled. She had a rose gold aura and he thought that was perfect.

"Hello, Shorty," he said.

Sadie's eyes shut and she collapsed back onto the bedhead. Sebastian sighed, gearing himself up to tell the others what he'd done. Maybe he'd just say she was sleeping and worry about it after the night was over. He ran his knuckle down her tear-stained cheek, warmth pooling in his chest.

She was right. He had a crush on her. Major, too. Like he'd do anything to keep her safe. He kinda already did.

Sadie sat up again and Sebastian scuttled back. That didn't seem normal. He gawked at her as her eyes opened again.

This time they shone blue. Not neon, like his, more turquoise, with hints of green in the swirl. Sebastian glanced around her, noticing a swallow beside her head.

Definitely not normal.

Sadie blinked, eyes re-opening to pure black. Sebastian stood, staring at the gazelle beside her. He looked further into the Veil behind her, seeing the tiger and swallow from before. They bumped against each other, urging themselves one in front of the other.

Sadie blinked and the tiger pushed itself forward. The gazelle bowed its head, stomping its foot in protest. Another blink, and the gazelle fought its way back.

Sebastian was a Fallen, but he knew that something wasn't right. He stumbled to the door, flinging it open. Wiping his mouth and chin from Sadie's sweet blood, he called, "Leila!"

Ren wandered out of another room, rubbing his eyes. "What's going on?"

"Nothing!" Sebastian snapped. "Go back to sleep."

Ren raised an eyebrow. As he stepped into the hallway, Leila ran up the stairs, Riley close behind him. Sebastian rolled his eyes and returned to Sadie.

She was sitting up straight, arms and legs stiff—her human body unable to move as the Guardians fought to be her companion. Sebastian cringed. The last thing he wanted was to talk to Riley, and he didn't even know Ren, but if he was honest Sadie needed help, so he'd have to suck it up.

"What's happening?" Leila asked.

Without looking back, Sebastian replied, "Look at her with your Guardian eyes."

He stared at Sadie, wincing every time she blinked. Rose gold, turquoise, and black in a loop.

"Oh my god, what's happening?" Leila gasped at the same time Riley spat, "What the hell did you do to her?"

"I didn't do anything… well…" Sebastian finally turned around to face them. "She wanted me to turn her. That's all I did. It's like they are all fighting to be her Guardian."

Leila ran to Sadie's side, leaning in front of her face. She waved her hand, but Sadie stayed immobile paralyzed within the fight. She spun around. "Ren, what do we do?"

"I've seen this before," Ren said, moving around Sebastian. "We need to make one Guardian stay, long enough to attach."

He grabbed Sadie's shoulders, and as she opened her rose-gold eyes, he commanded, "Stay!"

Everyone was silent as they watched Sadie's eyes. They stayed open for a while, the tiger happy to remain with her. Her eyelids dropped. And when they opened again, turquoise shone out.

Sadie screamed. High pitched and piercing. If death were a noise, that's what it would sound like. Her body began writhing, face contorting as though every bone in her body was breaking. As though her soul was on fire.

Sebastian tightened his fists. "Why is this happening?"

Leila looked at Ren. "Is it because she was marked and turned by different Guardians?"

"Is it a Fallen thing?" Riley suggested.

Through gritted teeth, Sebastian said, "But Cap marked all the cheerleaders and the boys turned them, they didn't struggle like this."

Riley snapped, "So, you watched them turn others, but you were so against turning Morgan a few months ago? And now you've turned Sadie. You're a hypocrite."

Sebastian faced Riley and he stared at his pompous, arrogant face. For a fleeting moment, he saw his father's eyes staring back at him through Riley. Retreating from the argument, he turned back to Sadie. "What was I supposed to do?"

"Stay!" Ren commanded.

Sadie settled. Black remained for a few seconds. She blinked. Rose gold. Blinked again. Turquoise. Her eyes fluttered, blinking at rapid pace. Colors flashed as she writhed.

"They're killing her," Ren stated.

"*You* killed her," Riley muttered to Sebastian.

Fear rose within Sebastian. It overtook the anger he felt at Riley's hatred against him. He walked to the edge of Leila's bed and dropped to his knees. He cried, "Stay."

But the Guardians continued to war over Sadie's innocent body.

"Maybe she'll listen to me," Leila suggested, urging Ren aside and taking his place. "Which one do I tell to stay?"

"Whichever."

As Sadie eyes burned rose gold, Leila demanded the tiger to stay. Sadie blinked, pupils focusing on Leila. She blinked again. The color remained.

Large fangs grew and Sadie snapped her mouth at Leila.

"Sadie, it's me, Leila."

Sadie growled, "Get off me."

Leila moved back, fearful eyes darting to Riley and back.

"Wow," Sadie said, rolling her shoulders. "Talk about squashing my bladder."

Relief fell over Sebastian in the form of laughter. His whole being felt like it had been set free from the pits of hell itself. He beamed at Sadie. "Are you okay?"

Sadie lifted her gaze, finding him. She smiled and the sight sent fireworks in Sebastian's chest. Letting her head rest back, she closed her eyes and muttered, "I'm tired."

Her body went lax, sinking into the bed.

Ren exhaled and faced Leila. "She wasn't ready to be a Guardian."

"What does that mean?" Leila asked.

"Time will tell." Ren brushed past Sebastian, leaving the room.

Sebastian looked at Sadie. Her breathing was back to normal. The tiger sat at her side. Close behind it, the gazelle and sparrow remained. Sebastian didn't know what that meant but it sounded like more trouble. Being a Fallen was enough. He cursed himself for acting so hastily. If only he'd waited for the cure.

"We could blast the Guardian out of her?" Riley said to Leila. "Once she wakes."

"Maybe," Leila said, sharing a glance with Riley. "She won't have killed anyone, so I'd say it's a high possibility."

Riley nodded. As he went to leave the room, he glared at Sebastian. "Something is definitely wrong with her."

Sebastian agreed. But he'd never let Riley know. He said, "What would you know. At least I did something about it. She would have been play meat. Now she can stand up for herself."

"You didn't think. Now she's Fallen. Just like you."

A new feeling emerged. It was a mix of offense and a desire for approval. Sebastian didn't like it. He retorted, "I'm not that bad."

"How many people have you killed?" There was a teasing tone in Riley's voice.

Sebastian lifted his chin. "How many have you?"

A winning smile appeared on Riley's face. Without saying anymore, he huffed out of the room.

Turning to Leila, Sebastian said, "I've actually only killed one."

"I know," said Leila, giving a sad smile. She made a quick glance to Sadie, then followed Riley.

"Well, two actually," Sebastian muttered, remembering Cap — if he counted. "I've killed two."

"Most people kill zero, Sebastian," Riley called. As he descended the stairs, he lifted his hand over his head, flipping the bird.

Leila and Riley were already half-way downstairs, but the niggle for approval had well and truly latched on. He yelled, "But Cap deserved it."

Turning to a sleeping Sadie, he moaned, "My brother hates me."

WEDNESDAY

late afternoon

Leila

Leila had tried her best to convince Sadie to wait for the cure. But somewhere in the last five minutes, she'd made the unthinkable decision to turn. Sebastian wasn't all that bad, Leila had always known there was good in him, but this? He'd made Sadie a Fallen.

As soon as they entered the living room, Riley unraveled. He grasped the back of a chair, breath rushing in and out through his mouth. Squeezing tighter for balance, his eyes darted around the room.

"Where's my sister? Where's Tessa."

"Right there," Leila said, pointing toward the front window.

Tessa leaned against the banister on the porch, talking wildly on the phone. Leila wondered if she knew about Sadie. Maybe she was telling Calice all about their failure to keep Sadie safe.

Riley gasped, bending over. "I can't take this."

Leila pressed her palm onto his back. Trying to soothe him, she said, "Sadie will be okay. We'll deal with it."

"Uh-uh." Riley shook his head violently. He sucked air into his lungs and exhaled.

"You okay, bud?" Ren asked, wandering closer.

Riley whipped his head up, glaring at Ren through half-shifted eyes. Leila noticed his claws piercing her mother's prized cushion. He snapped, "Did you not just witness that?"

Ren shrugged. "Just another day in the life of a Guardian. What are you worried about?"

"What am I worried about?" Riley stood up, shrugging Leila's hand off him. "How about the fact that you lied to me. Huh? When we first met. You said you were True Guardians—"

"I am." Ren's brows dropped. "I never said *she* was."

Riley huffed. "Well, that's a cop out. What about the fact that I thought my sister was a lost cause? I lived with the pain of losing her for months. And Kiko came to town, turned Cap. Messed up so many lives. How about the fact that she dragged us out into the woods to pick us apart one-by-one? And now she has Odette. And I'm supposed to sit here and not do anything?"

"That's it, brother, get worked up." An amused voice wafted from the bottom of the stairwell.

Riley's eyes turned to slits, piercing blue shining in a direct line to Sebastian. Through gritted teeth he hissed, "Don't call me brother, we're not even friends."

Makoto stepped under the archway, glancing around the room. "What's going on?"

Sebastian chuckled. "Poster boy is losing his mind."

Two fangs popped through Riley's curled lips. Leila reached for him, but it was too late. He launched for Sebastian.

"Oh." Sebastian's jovial expression dropped. He cracked

his neck as his half-shifted, fists at the ready.

"All right." Makoto hurried between them. "Let's save the fighting for later."

Riley side-stepped, trying to get around him but Makoto blocked his move. Riley groaned. "Just let me have him. One less Fallen the better."

Sebastian returned to human form — he was neither amused nor angry. Leila saw pure hurt in his eyes. He swiveled around and bounded back up the stairs.

Riley went to follow, but Makoto raised his hands. He peered behind him, looking at Ren. "Have you not taught your clan how to control their instincts?"

Ren avoided his brother's eye contact and rubbed the nape of his neck. "Well, I, uhh... I don't really have a clan..."

"Oh, for goodness sake, Ren," Makoto scolded. "You turn someone, they're your clan. At least until they make a clan of their own. But you're still there, guiding them."

"It's not really been my thing."

Leila almost choked. He could say that again. Those last few days were the most she'd ever seen of him.

"Okay." Makoto clapped his hands together, then pointed a finger to the middle of the room. "Riley, Leila, Gabby. Sit."

Gabby? Leila thought, looking around the room.

A head of brown hair with green streaks popped up from the sofa. Gabby rubbed her sleepy eyes. "Huh?"

The three of them did as they were told. Makoto was different to Ren, authoritative and calm. Much like Kiko. Leila frowned at the thought as she sat on the floor.

Makoto positioned himself on the edge of Ren's favorite armchair. He leaned forward, resting his elbows to his knees. "Your instincts are two-fold. Human and animal. Do you all notice that when you are shifted you feel more in line with the world? You can sense when things aren't quite right?"

Leila nodded. She knew that feeling well. She sat

forward, leaning toward Makoto as though he was the missing piece. As if he could teach them everything a True Guardian should be.

"Like what?" Riley asked. His eyebrows met.

"What do you mean, like what?" Leila replied. "Like everything is multiplied. There's a noise from behind and you know it's someone swinging their arm. So, you know to duck."

Riley stared at Leila blankly. "That happens?"

Makoto cleared his throat. "I see what the problem is. Your human has over-ridden your wolf."

Riley opened his mouth to speak but shut it again. His bottom lip rolled out.

"What that means," Makoto continued. "Is you trust your human side more than your animal side. Which can cause a few human-only problems. Like anxiety, stress, self-doubt, fear."

Lightning fired across Leila's brain. That was it. Riley had been ruled by fear. It consumed him.

She nodded and asked, "How does he fix it?"

"You think I need fixing?" Riley rolled his shoulders back.

Gabby peered around Leila. "Dude, you're firing on about a hundred cylinders. Yes, you need fixing."

Riley's eyes dropped along with his shoulders.

"It's a common thing. And possibly an easy solve." Makoto slipped off the sofa and sat in front of Riley. He crossed his legs and nodded at Riley to do the same. He rolled his wrists palm up and placed them on his thighs.

Leila settled herself into the position and nudged Gabby with her elbow to join in.

"Close your eyes," Makoto's voice was smooth and low. "Take a long breath in through your nose. Hold it. Hold it. Okay, now exhale. Longer. That's it, nice and slow. Repeat. Breathe in…. Hold… And out."

Leila peeled one eye open, checking on Riley to make

sure he was doing it. He looked a bit stiff but he was breathing slower. Satisfied, she returned to position, letting herself be calmed by Makoto's lead.

"Let yourself relax. You have nowhere to be. You are exactly where you need to be. Sink into your breath. Focus only on it and my voice. Now, align with your Guardian. See them in your mind's eye. Take some time to listen to them, sense what they are sensing, feel what they are feeling. You are not all human. You are not all animal. You are both, at once."

Leila imagined her lion standing before her, its golden aura shining like the magnificent beast it was. She saw herself running her fingers through its fur. It nestled into her hand, enjoying the touch.

"What do you feel?" she asked it.

The lion roared, sending a shock wave through her body.

It will take a sacrifice.

The words rattled her bones. With her heart pounding hard against her rib cage, she asked, "What kind of sacrifice?"

But the connection was lost. Her breathing had escalated. She slowed herself, one long breath in, one long breath out.

Her lion's face reappeared, its eyes a few inches from hers. It said, *"You're ready."*

A sense of calm rushed over her, as if she knew exactly what the lion knew, without knowing anything at all. And that was okay. She knew if she kept the connection, in time it would become clear.

Leila peeled her eyes open. The first thing she saw was Makoto staring at her and smiling. He nodded, and wagging a finger in her direction, he whispered, "I knew I liked you."

Gabby's eyes shot open. She looked between Leila and Makoto, on edge. In a few beats, she relaxed. She turned to Leila, "What did yours say?"

"That I'm ready." Leila left out the sacrifice part, whatever that meant. "Yours?"

Gabby shrugged. "I didn't hear words. I felt..." she clutched her throat. "Weird."

"Mmm," Makoto said. "Sometimes we see things, sometimes we feel things, sometimes we just sense things. What matters is that we are calm when it happens. That's how you know the difference between irrational fear and instinct. If you are calm and still sense danger, it's most likely right."

"We have to go to the Falls Party," Riley said in monotone. "That's where Kiko and Kale plan to recruit."

"How can you be sure?" Leila asked, dubious that he was being led by instinct or fear.

Tessa entered the living room. Waving her cell, she said, "I've just heard from Calice and Jamal. They've followed Kiko and Kale to the edge of the woods, right near the falls. Odette is still with them."

Riley inhaled slowly, taking his time to meet Leila's eyes. Exhaling, he said, "That's how."

WEDNESDAY

early evening

Leila

They'd spent the last few hours preparing as well as they could. Riley was decidedly calmer, his shoulders not so tense. They'd eaten. They'd run through scenarios. Now, they were just waiting for the party to begin.

Makoto paced the dining room as he chatted over the phone to his clan, making sure they understood the plan. He tucked his phone into his pocket and said, "Tessa is at the hardware store, grabbing a few more chains. Just in case. And Calice and Jamal are still following Kiko."

There was a moment of silence, a heaviness falling around them, the gravity of the situation feeling way too real.

Makoto sighed and leaned onto the table. He asked, "You still got the satchels?"

"Sure do," Leila said, patting the pocket on her jacket. Riley stood next to her, staring into space. She answered for him, "He's got his in his pant pocket."

Makoto frowned. Trying to gain Riley's eye contact, he asked, "Are you sure you're up to this?"

Leila turned to Riley. She pinched his sleeve, giving it a slight tug. "Riley?"

"Mm?" He blinked a few times, turning his attention to her. "What was that?"

"Are you up for this?"

Instinctively, Riley placed his hand over the satchel in his back pocket. "Oh, yeah. This madness ends tonight."

Makoto gazed at the clock. It was seven fifty-two. His left eye twitched before he blurted, "What time does this thing start again?"

Gabby leaned against the archway. She shrugged and said, "Eight. Round-abouts."

Nodding, Makoto said, "Timing is everything. If we're too early, they'll divert. I'm guessing they've marked a ton of students like they did Sadie. We need to make sure they're all there before we barge through. We can't risk any of them slipping through the cracks."

Riley rubbed his thumbs over his eyes. "Can we go over the plan once more?"

"Mm," Makoto grumbled, glancing at the clock again. He wandered into the living room, saying, "Leila, Riley, and Gabby, you're to head straight to the falls party, act like you're there for a good time. The rest of us will create a perimeter, and ambush. We need to make sure we have eyes on Kiko the whole time. Leila, at eight thirty, lead Kiko to the place where the road turns to gravel. "

"Got it." Leila tried to sound confident, but she'd unconsciously bunched the hem of her jacket into her fists. Apparently not so self-assured.

But that's because of what was left unsaid. Makoto hadn't mentioned it but there was an extra part of Leila's task. Kale. They said his presence would strengthen Kiko, and there was no way she'd risk having him near them when it all went down. She'd get Kiko away from him first and then lead her to the meeting point.

Makoto plonked himself onto the sofa, sharing a knowing glance with Ren. They'd been through it before. They knew what it was like to lose a sibling to the Fallen.

She crept across the room, conscious of not making a noise amid the tense air. Taking a seat next to Makoto, she looked between the brothers, and said, "How do you manage it? To love and hurt her at the same time?"

The question seemed to affect Ren the most. He leaned forward, elbows to knees, hands sweeping up over his mohawk. Shaking his head, he said, "The only thing I clung to was that somewhere deep down she could be saved."

"It's different for me," Makoto said, rolling his shoulders back. "It's not her. Not the real her. The Kiko I loved was lost a long time ago."

Leila licked her lips. The thought terrified her. Kale wasn't lost already. Surely, there was hope yet. She preferred Ren's outlook.

The door burst open. Leila bounced up to her knees and spun her head so fast her neck made a cracking noise. Jamal tumbled in.

"Mak!" he cried. "Kids are showing up for the party. Almost all of them are marked."

Riley parked his car half a mile from the falls parking lot. He'd veered into an overgrown track, leaving the car hidden by dense foliage. They crept through the woodland toward the entrance of the waterfall track.

For as long as any of them could remember, every first Wednesday of the month, a bunch of misled and misunderstood teens went to the Falls. They called it the *Falls Party*, and until she'd been marked, Leila had never been interested.

"Oh my god!" Gabby said, pointing to the tree tops.

Leila half-shifted and glanced up. Beams of light shot to the sky. Countless numbers of them. An army of them. This was so much worse than what she'd thought.

The three of them began running. As they jogged up the track, and they returned to human form, the beams of light vanished. Leila shuddered. It was still unnerving to her—seeing things in the Veil that a normal human eye couldn't see.

Leila grabbed Riley's hand and squeezed tight. It was happening. This was going down whether she was ready or not—she thought she was, but a sudden fear to face Kiko washed over her. She hadn't seen the real Kiko—the Fallen Kiko—she'd seen the version that Kiko had wanted her to see.

Leila said, "What are you going to say if they asked why you ran? What if they know we're lying? What if they know we're working with Makoto?"

Riley glanced at her, watching as her bottom lip rolled out. "Now who's panicking?"

He was right. She couldn't lose nerve now. Wiggling her brows in faux confidence, she jibed, "And now who's got all of the answers?"

The sounds of laughter and teen debauchery rose louder through the forest. Riley frowned, a shadow of fear creeping back to his eyes.

"Not me," he said.

They took the few steps into the clearing cautiously. Their fellow students danced and drank around a small fire as if they didn't have a care in the world. By the drink station, pouring liquid into a red cup, was a familiar face.

Damien spotted them at the same time they saw him. He stared at them through strands of black hair, blinking slowly as if trying to decide whether they were real or not. He must have decided they were, because he jogged over, holding his cup high.

"Ah, my friends! Where the hell have you been? Half the

damn school has been absent this week."

"They have?" Leila asked, sharing a glance with Riley. "Would've been good to know earlier."

Damien shrugged and gulped his drink. "Check it out," he said, pulling his shirt up on one side. A dark spiral curved high on his chest. "It showed up this afternoon. Thought I'd celebrate."

"Who gave you that?" Riley asked.

"You did," Damien said, swaying on the spot.

Riley eyed Leila, he leaned down, and whispered, "I tried to mark his shoulder, like before. Not his chest. Someone else has marked him."

Damien swept his hair from his eyes and glared at Riley dubiously, as if he had heard what Riley had said. He lifted his cup and pointed at the three of them. After a hiccup, he asked, "Want a drink?"

"You're a mess," Gabby said.

"Thanks Gabs, always count on you to be honest."

Gabby rolled her eyes. "Are you gonna ask how Sadie is? Or?"

Damien sculled the rest of his drink, and threw the cup toward the fire, missing it by a yard. He sniffed and said, "Shacked up with *Sebastian Weir* last I heard."

Gabby rolled her eyes harder, slumping her shoulders in defeat. "Because that's all that matters."

A flash of bright red darted at the edge of Leila's vision, followed by a scream ripping through the crowd. Most people ignored it, the noise passing as a joyful expression. But not Leila. She moved toward where she saw the flash, Damien, Gabby, and Riley following her. When they got to the edge of the clearing, Leila stepped behind a tree and half-shifted, letting her Guardian eyes search the area.

A beam of light shone a little deeper into the forest, and then, it stopped. Riley ran first. Leila quickly catching up. They found a boy no older than Summer. He was unconscious, arm turned up and resting on the forest floor.

His mark was on his forearm right above his wrist, and as Leila crouched down to examine, teeth marks healed around the spiral, leaving wet blood dripping down his fingers.

"It's happening," she said, peering back through the trees. The sight almost blinded her. Beacons charged up to the sky from almost everyone as they danced, oblivious and innocent and marked.

"What's happening?" Damien asked hesitantly, as if he didn't really know if he wanted the answer.

Leila gazed down at the sleeping sophomore. A wildebeest stood beside him, waiting for him to wake. She whipped her head to Riley. "We need to expel the Guardian before he wakes."

Riley nodded. "Will it work if he's unconscious?"

"Only one way to try," Leila said, reaching for his hand.

He wasted no time to take her hand. Leila gazed at him, feeling the warmth of his returned stare. She re-gripped his hand so tight she could feel his pulse under her fingertips. Hearts pounding in sync, Leila let their love wash over her, and together they surged, expelling a combined light around them. The surge grew like an uncontrolled fire, expanding through the newly marked body and pushing the wildebeest back. The wildebeest dug its hooves into the soil, but it was no match for the Imprint's power, its body dissipated, twinkling like dust particles until it was completely gone.

Out of the corner of her eye, Leila saw the red flash again, followed by a green stream of light. She knew it was Kiko and Mr. Robertson. They flew through the crowd, taking one more innocent victim each. A bronze bear leapt from the shadows and dragged another student by the feet back into the forest.

Everything happened so fast, but it felt like it was going in slow motion. Leila squeezed her eyes to stop tears from falling. *Not Kale. Please not Kale.*

"It will take too long doing it this way," Riley said, already running for the clearing. "We have to stop them first. Then, we'll save those who've been turned."

"Go home," Leila said to Damien, pushing his chest. He stumbled backward, long legs wobbling under him. "We've lost enough already to lose you, too."

Gabby ran for the clearing. And as she ran past Damien, she bumped him with her shoulder and hissed, "Now!"

Leila chased Gabby to the clearing, both of them meeting Riley near the drink station. He scanned the crowd, letting himself half-shift split seconds at a time.

A scream resonated through the crowd, and this time most people stopped to look around.

Leila overheard a nearby freshman crying; "Some Japanese lady just took Dee. Snatched her right in front of me."

Their friend replied, "I can't find Harry, have you seen him?"

"They're picking them out one-by-one," Riley said.

They're.

Leila's heart lurched to a shuddering stop. She'd tried so hard not to believe it, not to entertain the thought. But Kale was there, doing things that Fallen do.

"It's not just us who are stronger together." Riley grabbed her shoulders, shaking a little to bring her back to earth. "Leila? Do you hear me?"

She blinked a few times, staring into his fearful eyes. He frowned and ran to the portable speaker. Turning the volume down, he yelled, "Everyone! There's no need to be alarmed but there's been a bear sighting."

Another scream echoed into the forest and that's when it sunk in. Everyone around began to panic—screaming and running in circles, calling for their friends, one even began packing up the fairy lights that hung in the trees, as if it were normal pack-up time.

"Hey!" Riley cried. He seemed to grow an extra inch as he said, "We are safer together. Everyone gather at the very edge of the waterhole."

They heeded Riley's command, huddling together near

the edge of the water. Leila joined Riley in front of them. They turned around to face outward, half the school at their backs. Riley reached across to grab Leila's hand, and Gabby took the other.

There they were, a three-person barricade.

The wait was eerie. Quickening breaths, shuffling feet, anxious chatter. In front of them, the bonfire blazed unaware. Beyond it, darkened forest.

"Leilani Bel-bottoms!" a familiar voice said from within the crowd behind them.

Leila peered over her shoulder and spotted Taj standing in the center. She released Riley and Gabby's hands, pushing through bodies to him. "Taj? What are you doing here? You never come to these."

Taj let his gaze drift. Frowning, he said, "I don't know really, some kind of inkling. Like a tug."

A tug? Leila's heart sank.

"Anyway—" Taj shook his head—"You missed the game. Seriously Leila, I'm going to have to hire a new photographer. Did you have the same sickness as me?"

"Wolf!" Someone screamed.

Tiny groups of people dispersed in panic, breaking the protective huddle apart. Leila heard Riley shout at them to return, that they were safer together, but only a handful listened, the rest running in hysterics back to the parking lot.

Riley appeared through the crowd and told the remaining few to go to their cars and leave. Taj jerked his head toward Riley's voice and a big black spiral on his neck stared Leila in the face.

"Not you, too," she whimpered.

Taj would have made a great Guardian. He was an activist and seeker of the truth. But not like this. Not as a pawn in Kiko's game.

He turned back, raising his brow. "What?"

"The mark on your neck."

Taj cupped his palm around the side of his neck. "Oh

yeah, I've had a weird rash. Super glad the itchiness has stopped."

"Leila!" Gabby's voice was a warning. "Things are getting out of hand."

Leila glanced around, noticing a trio of sophomores running for the path to the parking lot. A wolf—Mr Robertson's wolf—chased them. Down by the fire, Kiko held a cheerleader down, fangs out ready.

"I'll be back," Leila said to Gabby. She spun around, grabbed Taj by his jacket, and dragged him down the track to the fall lookout. When she was sure no-one was around, she threw him into the shrubbery.

"What the hell, Bel-monster!" Taj immediately checked his blazer, dusting dirt from the sleeves.

Leila crouched over him, fixing his collar so it covered his mark. "Stay here until everyone is gone. Promise me."

"I always thought you were a little odd, girl," Taj peered into Leila's eyes. "But this is beyond—"

"Promise me!' Leila commanded, half-shifting, blazing her golden eyes in his direction.

Taj scrambled back and Leila's grip loosened. She could see his chest convulsing as he gasped for air. "I… I promise."

Leila nodded and as she marched back to the path, she heard Taj call, "But tomorrow you're telling me everything. Leila Bel-montage."

She winced. It was a risk showing him her true self. But he needed to stay safe. *She* needed him to stay safe. Her trust in Kiko had put everyone in danger, there was no chance she'd let another friend be hurt.

WEDNESDAY

evening

Leila

Leila dusted herself off and returned to human form. Bursting back into the clearing, she was shocked to find it empty. A few students lay asleep, their bodies moving through transition. It was only a matter of time before they woke and became Fallen.

"Riley?" she called, scanning the area. They needed to do the surge. Like, now! She tried again, "Riley?"

Out of the corner of her eye she saw a bear run toward the path to the parking lot.

"Kale?" she said to herself. Then louder, she cried, "Kale! Stop!"

The bear halted in its tracks. It half-shifted in broad moonlight, peering over its muscled shoulder. Kale stared at Leila with bronze eyes. "Leilani?"

His earnest expression made all sense drift away. She couldn't help herself—she began running toward him. He met her halfway and wrapped his arms around her.

"I'm so glad you're safe," he muttered, wrapping her tightly.

The hug was strong and comforting, like the ones he'd give her at home. A hint of hope washed through her. Maybe he wasn't a Fallen. Maybe he wasn't turning those kids. Maybe he was there, trying to save them from Kiko.

"Leila!" Kiko appeared from nowhere. She leaned over to catch her breath. "Thank God we found you."

Leila stared, mouth agape. Kiko was wearing the blue dress, the one she bought for her and Kale's reception party. Her hair was smooth and her eyes were lined with kohl. She looked stunning.

Kiko noticed Leila staring, she brushed the front of her dress and smiled embarrassed. Leila caught sight of Kiko's hand, a streak of dried blood lined her fingers. "I couldn't help myself."

"You." Leila said, voice shaking. "You're... you're..."

The word wouldn't come out. *Fallen! Just say it*, Leila scolded herself. *She's a Fallen.*

But the hope that Kale started, grew within her. She turned back to her brother. Were they both innocent? Had everyone gotten it all wrong about them?

As Kale smiled at her, he bared his teeth, and a canine coated in blood popped over his bottom lip.

Leila swallowed, reality hitting her at full force. She'd never been more terrified than in that moment — hopeful one moment, broken the next. She knew then that neither of them were innocent. They'd both deceived her.

Kiko ran a gentle hand over Leila's shoulder. "We've got a problem," she said, taking a worried glance over her shoulder. "Jay has turned Fallen. He's marked so many kids here tonight, I just don't know what went wrong. I trained him. I taught him everything I knew and still — "

As Kiko sobbed, Kale was quick to comfort her. They seemed so honest and afraid, but Leila knew better. The truth was: no-one had been marked that night. It took days for marks to appear.

She felt her insides weaken. Kiko was the real deal. The deceiving bitch had fooled her for a very long time. She could see that now.

The thought of innocent lives being discarded as though their lives were meaningless, was enough to make her want to launch Kiko. But to win this war, she'd have to beat them at their own game. Even though she felt like vomiting, Leila bit her lip hard. She needed to react as though she didn't know the truth.

"Are you serious?" she gasped. "Although, Mr. Robertson has been acting weird lately." Then, she pointed wildly to the trail that led to the parking lot. "I saw him head that way!"

Kiko reached for Leila's hand and it took everything within her not to balk at the touch. "Don't worry Leila, we'll save your friends. You and Riley should take care of these marked ones."

"Where is Riley?" Kale asked, glancing around. "Last we saw, he ran from the camp like he'd seen a ghost."

How easily he told a lie within the truth. Leila's head felt light. Should she say she hadn't seen him? Should she say he wasn't anywhere near the forest? Should she say she didn't know? Playing their game wasn't so easy.

"Anyway, find him and clean up Jay's mess," Kiko said, walking. She gave Kale a look and a head flick toward the parking lot.

He nodded and followed her. Leila watched the two of them pick up speed, until they turned around the bend and out of sight. She scowled and glanced around the clearing. What was Kiko up to? She'd already turned half the damn school and the rest were ripe for turning.

Leila began sneaking down the pathway, slow enough that they didn't know she was following but quick enough to catch up if she needed. As she crept along, she whipped out her phone and tapped on Riley's name. He didn't answer. Of course not, his phone was broken.

"Where the hell are you, Riley?" she muttered to herself as she scurried toward the parking lot.

When the path ended, she scoured the lot for Kiko and Kale but there was no sight of them. Most cars had gone. All but one black Pontiac.

Mr. Robertson sat in the driver's seat, and in the passenger seat beside him was Riley. Her heart soared as their eyes locked. Riley lifted his hands, showing her chains wrapped around them. He shook his head wildly, mouthing at her to help.

As Mr. Robertson started the ignition, Riley slammed his tied hands to the window, screaming her name. Leila ran. But she wasn't fast enough. She felt like she'd never be fast enough. As her feet hit the gravel, the car clunked into gear and drove off.

She knew what was about to happen. They both did. The Imprint threat would be eliminated. Riley would be eliminated.

Leila's head felt fuzzy. Her feet led her, storming through the woodland toward the lights of the town. There was no logic, just instincts. She felt out of control, as though she was floating above her own body unable to make sense of things.

It was raining. The droplets rolled off her as she ran, leaving a streaming trail in her wake. She barely noticed—it didn't matter. Only one thing mattered. She needed to find Riley. Screw Kiko. Screw Makoto. Screw the plan. Riley was all that drove her.

Leila had gotten used to this part of the forest. She knew it's dips and crests and clearings. Almost every week, she'd found herself shifting and running, giving her lion the freedom it craved. But under the eerie moonlight, knowing Riley's safety was under threat, she felt anything but free.

She burst through her front door, and cried, "Mom?"

Tate ran from the kitchen. "She's in the shower. What's happened?"

"I need some rosemary." She brushed past her dad and into the kitchen. She ripped the pizza delivery map of the town off the fridge and unfolded it onto the bench, pinning the edges down with salt and pepper shakers.

"Rosemary?" Her dad asked, heading for the back door.

She nodded, and as he wandered outside, she stared at the map, trying to remember how Makoto did the location spell before. He used rosemary, his blood, what else? Oh, his arrow necklace.

"Shit." Leila jerked her head up and clutched the sides of her face. "Shit! How am I going to find him?"

Sebastian peered through the kitchen doorway. Grimacing, he asked, "Not going well?"

"They have Riley!" Leila exclaimed, curling her fingers until her knuckles turned white. "They're gonna kill him."

Sebastian's face dropped as if, for once, he actually cared about Riley. He strode toward Leila. "How can I help?"

"Here," Tate said, waving a collection of rosemary stems. Droplets of raindrops painted his face, he wiped his brow, and held the plant out for Leila.

"I can't use it." Leila felt her heart-rate rise. She took her phone out and stared at the locked screen. "What's Makoto's number? What's Ren's? Oh my God." She spun around. "Sebastian. I don't know what to do."

Sebastian, suddenly the coward, turned and ran up the stairs.

Tate placed the rosemary onto the bench and held his palms up and out as if in surrender. "Breathe, Leila." He lifted his hand up and pushed it back down. "In and out."

Leila didn't feel like breathing slow. She didn't feel like taking a moment. She needed to find Riley already.

"I saw her. Kiko. She's something else, Dad. She knows what she's doing. Pure evil. Once you know the truth and look into her eyes, you'll see it." Leila knees buckled. She stumbled toward Tate, leaning on him for support.

Tate put his comforting hands on her back. He asked, "What are you saying about Kiko? Being evil?"

The sound of her dad's low voice sent her reeling. She pushed his chest. "You gotta get out of here. Take Mom, go hide for, I don't know, five years."

Tate inhaled sharply. "You're scaring me, honey."

"You should be scared. We could all die tonight!" Leila exclaimed.

Tate took a few steps back, shocked at his daughter's outburst. Then, he rolled his shoulders and stood up straight. He grabbed Leila's shoulders, and with a steady yet commanding voice, he said, "Leilani Isidora Belmonte, you used to be my baby. I used to worry about you all day at school. I used to fear leaving you alone just going to the store. I used to watch you sleep, making sure your chest rose and fell with breath." His cheeks lifted into a wince. "Not anymore. I don't worry about you anymore because you're the strongest person I know. You've dealt with huge change, like a pro I might add. You're kind and thoughtful and you've not got a bad word to say about anybody. You're incredible Leila, I don't think there's anything you can't handle." His hand squeezed hers as he said the last part. "I'm so proud of who you've become."

Word by word, Leila's breath evened out. Held by her father, she closed her eyes. Long inhale, long exhale.

Breath in.

Hold.

Breath out.

For a moment, she believed him. Maybe she could handle it. One moment of surrender was all it took for clarity to arrive.

Just as Makoto taught her, she let herself relax and half-shifted, calling her Guardian to her. Her lion appeared in her mind's eye, its regal fur shimmering with gold.

"Where is he?" she asked.

Her lion shook its head, sending flecks of light over its body. One word rang through her mind.

School.

And then another.

Hurry.

Leila burst her eyes open and flung her arms around her dad's neck. "Thank you, daddy. Wait here with Mom. I'll be back soon."

She kissed his forehead and bolted for the front door.

"Leila!" Sebastian called, running down the stairs. He held out Sadie's phone. "Tessa's number's in here."

Delirium may have played a part, but Leila felt like laughing. Of course Sebastian wasn't a coward, of course he was helping. She took the phone and squeezed his chin. "Thank you, you delightful piece of goodness wrapped in bad."

WEDNESDAY

late evening

Gabby

Gabby wandered through the forest, scanning the area for any remaining students. She didn't know where Leila had gone, or Riley either for that matter, but she was glad she couldn't find any humans. Gabby headed back to the clearing alone. Well, technically she wasn't alone, a few bodies were scattered around, teeth impressions healing around their spiral marks. Most others had run to their cars, afraid of bears and wolves and foxes.

She was glad they were gone because being around all those innocents was unbearable. Their scent. Their heartbeats. Their blood.

She'd tried to tell Leila about the incessant darkness that grew within her, but that sweet face was forever trying to believe that Gabby wasn't capable of bad things. Truth was, Riley was right to doubt her. He was right to question her. His dubious eyes were constantly watching her. Most of the time, he'd try to hide the fact he was following her every move, but she saw him. She always saw him.

It made her feel grateful and resentful all at once.

Gabby sighed, taking in a long breath. The tang of open flesh hit her nostrils, and her mouth watered as she remembered what human blood tasted like. The clan would disown her if they knew exactly what she did sometimes.

When they did the meditation with Makoto she'd lied about what happened. She'd said she felt weird, but the honest truth was, her wolf had spoken to her. It whispered an order, a desire. *"Set us free."* She didn't want to know what would happen if she let that happen. So, she kept herself reeled in, a tight string to contain both her and her Guardian. She swore she wouldn't succumb to the darkness, but she knew part of it had already taken hold. Little things she knew she shouldn't enjoy but did. Like seeing someone in pain or manipulating someone to make a bad decision or pretending to help someone who'd cut themselves.

Pushing the line never truly hurt anything, right? Licking her lips, she wandered to the path where Leila had taken Taj. She pushed past leaves that tried to cling to her shirt, as though nature itself knew what she wanted.

Just a little bit, she said to herself. *I won't hurt him.*

She found him cradled inside a shrub, holding his collar up over his neck and rocking back and forth. He glanced up, and spotting Gabby, he threw his arms in the air. "Oh thank God, can I go home now?"

Gabby crouched down beside him and smiled. "Not just yet."

She turned his collar down and his mark stared back at her, taunting her. The pulsating urge to rip his throat out scared her. Turning her head, she let her hand drop.

"Are you hurt anywhere?" she asked.

Taj rolled up his sleeve, and bent his elbow, showing a line of blood that dripped to his wrist. "Just this gash from when Leila threw me in here."

Gabby half-shifted before she even looked at him, the

smell of his fresh cut energizing her. She blinked a few times, pushing her wolf away. It took patience.

She faced him and clutched the groove of his arm. Smiling, she hauled him up, "Here, let me help you."

Taj stood beside her and dusted himself off. "Thanks." He pressed his lips together and gave a thin smile. "I should bounce."

Gabby nodded. And as he ran off, her body collapsed. Controlling herself was getting more difficult every time she did this.

When he was out of sight, Gabby lifted her hand, coated in his blood. She half-shifted again, wolf begging for a taste. Moaning out of hunger, she lifted a finger to her mouth and gently touched the tip of her tongue and bottom lip. She closed her eyes and swallowed, letting the tang reach her throat. In a short moment, a zing soared through her, as though the blood was laced with caffeine. She held her whole hand up, licking her palm and each finger feverishly until not a drop remained.

It didn't satisfy the incessant craving. It never did. She wondered how much she'd need to drink for that to happen.

Sitting alone in the dark on the damp forest floor, guilt settled over her. She was a monster. Becoming darker and more rotten with every day that passed.

She allowed her body to roll to the ground, and she laid there, face to the sky, hoping that the ground would swallow her whole for what she'd just done. It took a moment for her to remember what she was there for in the first place—to stop Kiko. Guilt layered upon guilt. Lord knows, what trouble Leila and Riley were in.

She sat up and took a deep breath, one last smell of lingering human blood for the road. As she inhaled, she sensed a different type of blood—not fully human, not fully animal, either.

Springing her eyes open, she realized. It was a Guardian's blood. It was Odette's blood.

Wiping her mouth, she began running. Gabby sniffed at the air, letting her wolf's instincts guide her. She followed the scent west, crying, "Odette?"

She tore through the forest, her wolf's body surrounded by pines that reached for the sky. Above them, the half-moon teased its presence behind ghostly clouds. She used her heightened senses to listen. She strained to hear something, anything to indicate where Odette might be. At this point, she'd settle for the crunch of a foot against a twig.

The sound she heard was much more intense. A scream that encompassed everything grief would sound like. It drowned out every other sense. There was no touch, no taste, no sight, no smell. Only sound.

Swinging around a red cedar, Gabby ran into a small clearing, where smoke billowed from a forgotten fire. To the left, under a wide fir, Calice hovered over a body.

Odette's body.

The girl that Gabby loved laid on the damp ground, her long legs curled under her. It almost looked like she was sleeping, if it weren't for the pool of blood circling her head.

The world around Gabby seemed to vanish. As if she were floating in a broken moment between time and space. She even felt her heart stop.

Calice's knees buckled and she dropped to the ground with a thud. She pressed her fingers against Odette's pulse point, and soon after, she cried, "I'm too late."

Gabby didn't know where to look. Not that it mattered, her tears concealed most of her vision.

Calice stood—tears rolling down her cheeks. Her shirt had rips in three places, and through the holes Gabby could see the slashes in her stomach healing. Gabby let her eyes drift to the ground, to Odette, and she slowly walked over.

Calice pulled her jacket across her torso, and said, "I'm so sorry. I tried to fight them off... I tried..."

Peering down at Odette's breathless body, Gabby felt her emotions tumble together, not knowing whether she was sad or angry or ashamed. As she crouched down, more tears came.

"Odette?" she asked, wiping her eyes. She checked Odette's wrist, too, just in case.

No pulse. No heartbeat. No life.

She felt it then, an overwhelming sense of loss. Her heart felt like it had cracked in two and each broken part had exploded inside of her. She hunched over, unable to contain herself. A guttural moan vibrated from her chest and spilled through her lips.

She was already broken. Now she was torn apart. She let the feeling sit within her, a black hole spinning and growing.

"I deserved this," she stated, sobbing. And then she darted her head up, blazing her eyes through Calice. She screamed, "But she didn't!"

WEDNESDAY

late evening

Sadie

Sadie woke.

Her eyes took a while to adjust, blurry silhouettes taking the shape of Leila's room and belongings. She sat up slowly, muscles aching. As blood rushed to her head, she could feel her pulse as it thumped in her ears.

"What happened?" she muttered to herself.

The last thing she remembered was Sebastian screaming in her face, right after…

Her neck. Sadie clawed at her collar, tilting her head trying to see the mark. The edges of it hovered at the bottom of her eye-line.

"Hey, hey!" a sweet voice cooed. Sebastian ran across Leila's room, throwing himself onto the bed. "How do you feel?"

Sadie wasn't sure. Confused. Tired. Her mouth felt dry. She said, "Hungry."

Yes, she was starving. But she couldn't quite tell what for.

"Mm." Sebastian's brows deepened over his eyes. He reached for her face, running a thumb across her cheek. "It's the worst part. But you'll get used to it. I'll help you."

Sadie clutched his hand, holding it against her face. "Thank you, Sebastian Weir. You saved my life, again."

WEDNESDAY

almost midnight

Leila

Mr. Robertson held all three of his classes in the same room. His teaching methods of late were a little less than ideal. It didn't matter if the schedule said history, it wouldn't be unexpected for Leila to wander in and find an earth science textbook on her desk. There was no arguing. He'd sit at his desk, peeling apples with his swiss knife, and stare blankly out the window.

For a long time, Leila had thought that something was up with him. But he was always so guarded, like a rusted lock on sunken treasure, she could never get close enough to figure out why. Now she knew why.

Leila ran down the school's corridors, skidding along the linoleum as she turned each corner. She slowed down as she approached the classroom. Voices wafted from the open doorway, her heart pounded as she heard Kale and Kiko discussing how horribly Kiko had been treated by her brothers. Holding her breath, she poked her head ever so slightly around the frame. She spotted Mr. Robertson sitting in his chair with his ankles crossed on his desk. He rolled his swiss knife over his knuckles, a bored expression on his face. Behind the chair, hunched in the corner, was Damien. He held his long legs against his chest as his black hair hung over his face.

Damien straightened as he saw Leila, hope flashing across his face. "I wanted to help," he said. "But I'm no match without my eagle."

Mr. Robertson glanced up, head jerking to the doorway. Noticing Leila, he grabbed the knife's handle and plunged the tip into his desk. As he stood, he clenched his fists, eyes on Leila.

She wanted to be mad at Damien for giving her away, but he just seemed so helpless. So, she swallowed, and stepped into the room, ready to fight Mr. Robertson.

"Jay, wait!" Kale commanded.

At the back of the room, Kale stood near the window, he held his hand out in surrender, staring at Leila. Kiko stood a few rows of desks away, she wore her flowing sapphire gown and wild eyes. In front of her, tied to a chair—blood oozing from a gash above his eye—was Riley. Out cold.

Leila's insides wound into a knot. Her gaze darted back to Kale as she cried, "Why?"

"Leila!" Kiko exclaimed, her body's tension dropping like melted butter. "Thank God you're here. We just found him like this."

The switch in Kiko's disposition caught Leila off guard. It was obvious that her caring demeanor was nothing but an act. Still, the fact she still kept trying to play the good guy, played havoc in Leila's chest.

Kale waved his hands in her direction as he emphatically said, "We're not going to hurt him Leila. Trust me."

"Trust you?" Leila felt the knot inside her tighten. "How can I?"

Kiko blinked a few times, and as if she knew the jig was

up, she laughed to herself. As easily as the laugh flew out of her mouth, so did the venomous words. "Oh shoosh. I'm not going to hurt him. Well," — she dug her nail into the already healing cut on his forehead—"not much. It's just a little ritual, to remove the Imprint curse."

Leila stepped around the first desk. "What are you talking about?"

"Leila, listen," Kale said, rushing to her. "It's to keep you both safe. Get you out of the line of the Fallen."

"Ha!" Gabby blurted behind them.

Turning around, Leila stared at a version of Gabby she'd never seen before. Her eyes were sunken, like she'd cried every tear she'd ever had. Her hands were soaked in blood and her hair had matted to her forehead with the rain. And yet, she spoke with strength. "You're right Leila, this is a mind-twist. Look at the both of you, still trying to convince us you're True."

"Who let her out of her restraints?" Kiko snarled.

"I did." Leila spun back around and took a hold of Kale's wrist. "I think it's time you listen to me. She's been fooling us… she's been fooling you. You need to let Riley go."

Kale tensed, his eyes twitching. "We can't do that."

The way he hesitated made her feel sick. She'd held out hope for him. Hope that he didn't know what Kiko was and the things she'd done. But of course he knew.

"Why not?" Her voice sounded foreign to her own ears. Meek and soft and spectacularly petrified of the answer.

"Because," Kiko declared, bashing her fist onto a desk. "I am the first Guardian. I am the first Imprint. There can only be one Imprint couple."

Kale gazed down at Leila, eyes that were once filled with love, now hollow. "And that's us. Not you."

There it was, undeniable proof that her brother was a Fallen. Leila let him go, her whole body weakening. She whimpered, "No."

"Finish it. I can't pretend to care any more," Kale said,

turning his back to Leila and moving to the window.

Denial was no longer an option. Makoto was right, her brother was already gone. There was only one thing left to do.

She moved to the second row of desks. Eyes falling on Riley, unconscious and bleeding, she demanded, "Let him go."

"Nah," Kiko said. She knocked a desk over and ripped the leg from it. As she faced Riley, she twisted her wrist and re-gripped the leg, holding it like a javelin.

Mr. Robertson cleared his throat and plucked the knife from his desk. "I'm outta here."

Leila watched him leave and she glanced at Gabby. They needed his blood for the cures. As if reading her thoughts, Gabby nodded, said "I'm on it," and fled after him.

Damien peered over the top of Mr. Robertson's desk. Leila glared at him, making "get down" motions with her hand. He crouched back down out of sight.

"We've got company," Kale said, tapping on the window.

"Who is it?" Kiko said, annoyed. "Sebastian? Tessa? Odette. Oh wait, it can't be Odette..." Her eyes twinkled at Leila. "Because I killed her."

Ren stepped into the room. His gaze fell directly to Riley and his brows wrinkled as though he himself was in pain. He whipped his head to Kiko, a black shimmer coating his eyes.

"Brother!" Kiko threw her arms above her head and the desk leg hit the wall behind her. "Here's the angel on my shoulder."

"Come on, Kiko. It's over. Let Riley go." Ren moved next to Leila.

Kiko chuckled. "Yes, it's over. You tried to purify me, but you failed. I must disappoint you."

"Immensely," a deep voice boomed from the corridor.

Before Makoto even entered the room, Kiko lost all color

from her face. The desk leg rolled out of her hand and crashed to the floor. She gasped, "No, not him."

Makoto's presence filled the room. He held the space as though he ruled over everything. And by the way Kiko cowered at the sight of him, she believed it, too.

"Time to start again, sister."

Kale frowned, side-stepping toward Kiko. He pointed at Makoto, "Is this him, Kiko? Is this the one who ruined your life?"

"Yes!" Kiko cried, running to Kale. She stood in front of him, arms splayed out in protection. "Don't you take him away from me."

"I'm not," Makoto replied.

Leila used the distraction and took another step toward Riley. She was three rows in. Only one to go.

"Not again," Kiko pleaded.

"I'm not going to kill him Kiko, he is not like Ryuu."

"Don't you dare say his name. You have no right!" Kiko screamed.

Leila tiptoed to the fourth row, just arms reach from Riley.

Kiko spun to Leila and noticing her move closer to Riley, she leapt to stand between them. She half-shifted, red eyes staring deep into Leila's soul. "You think you can be the True Guardians? You cannot be, you are not pure blood. I am pure blood. I am a True."

She gave a maniacal laugh that pulsated around the room. Snapping her mouth shut, she swung her head to Kale and said, voice as smooth as silk, "And now I've found my love again, I can have my rightful place as the only Imprint. There cannot be another."

Kiko sighed dramatically, raising her shoulders up and dropping them down again. She bent down and collected the desk leg, and without waiting another second, she plunged it through Riley's chest.

"No!" Leila cried.

Riley's eyes sprung open and he gasped for air. Drops of red hit the corners of his mouth and fear filled his eyes as he searched the room, as if trying to figure out what was happening.

With a twisted smile, Kiko pulled at the chair leg impaled through Riley's chest, and raised his body up with it. She slammed the end of the leg into the cork wall, trapping him there. Seeing Riley like that gave Leila both heartache and rage.

"Kiko stop!" Ren bellowed.

Sacrifice. The word rang through Leila's mind.

Not his sacrifice. She said to herself. *It's mine.*

Riley clasped at the metal leg sticking out of him, blood pouring from the wound. He looked up at Leila, tears rolling down his cheeks. As if knowing what she was thinking, he shook his head and mouthed the word, "No."

"Yes." Leila lurched forward, grabbing Kiko by the shoulders. She threw her aside, sending her crashing into chairs and desks. She stood before Riley as he hung against the wall, neck twitching, eyes pleading her to stop.

But there was no other way. If she removed the leg, he'd bleed to death. Even Guardians couldn't heal from a gaping hole in their chests.

Leila inhaled. *Sacrifice.* She was ready.

"Don't—" Riley rasped.

There was nothing anyone could say to stop her. She'd lost him once, there was no way she'd lost him again. The risk was too high.

And so, she leapt, aiming her body parallel to Riley's. The end of the leg hit her sternum and, as the momentum of her body propelled forward, it sank into her skin. She cried out in pain as it slid further, deeper, until she had Riley in her hold—arms around his neck, legs around his hips.

"What have you done?" Riley gurgled, blood pouring from his mouth.

Her breath fell short, like she couldn't get air into her

lungs. It was now or never. Straining, she said, "Let's finish this."

The surge expelled from the both of them, entwined and holding on for dear life. Leila kept her eyes on Riley as they shared their auras, each of them with one gold eye and one blue. Lighted bloomed, moving around them in waves. The satchel in her jacket pocket warmed, heating against her ribs. Another color sparked between them—purple, like a vervain's bloom. It shimmered between them, reaching for the ceiling like an upside-down lightning strike.

When the ripples of their combined auras faded and the surge was complete, Leila felt her lungs expand. She glanced down; the desk leg was gone, wisps of its remnants falling to the floor. She didn't hurt, either. And no wounds remained.

Riley clutched at her back, nuzzling his face into her neck. "Thank you."

As they tore away from each other, Leila noticed it. The rift. A blazing purple light, tearing at the Veil, creating a door between their world and the Sanctuary.

Kiko clambered to her feet. Her eyes darted between Kale and an approaching Makoto. She grabbed a chair, placing it in front of her like a shield. "We're stronger than all of them, baby. We are Imprints, we can take them down."

Leila looked at Kale, hoping to see his Guardian had been ripped from his side from the surge. Hoping, because that meant he hadn't killed anyone yet. But no-one in that room had been stripped from their Guardian. Everyone except her and Riley had killed an innocent human being.

As Kale and his bear aligned, angry and ready for a fight, Ren looped around the room. Quiet as a ninja, he sneaked around Kiko and leapt for Kale. Ren was svelte and fast and accurate, pinning Kale against a wall, but Kale was big and strong, especially with Kiko nearby. He pushed Ren off with ease, throwing him across the room.

Ren landed in front of Mr. Robertson's desk. He flipped to his feet, wagging a teasing finger to Kale.

"Don't,' Kiko warned. "It's a trick."

But Kale didn't like to be taunted, even before he became a Fallen. He fully shifted, slamming his paws to the floor. As he bounded for Ren, Makoto made his move on Kiko.

"Brother!" she cried, scratching at his face. "Don't do this. You'll regret it."

Makoto struggled against her, trying to drag her to the split between worlds. Leila knew he wouldn't be able to hold her alone. Riley moved first, sweeping behind Kiko and wrapping his arms around her waist. Leila soon followed, pulling Kiko's wrist from Makoto's face.

"To the rift," Makoto commanded.

Together, the three of them dragged her over. She resisted and screamed and dug her heels, but she had no hope against two Imprints and her brother. As they held her in front of the rift, Makoto pushed.

Leila and Riley both let go. As Kiko toppled backward, Makoto held on for a moment. His fingers curled around the collar of her dress, his eyes filling with sadness.

And, as he released his grip, he said, "I loved you, sister."

Losing the battle against gravity, Kiko fell backward into the rift. Kale let out an almighty roar. He ran for his wife, but he wasn't quick enough. Kiko passed through, leaving the human world behind. Kale slammed his fist against the wall beside the rift. Panting, he stared in, as though wondering if he should go after her.

Inside the Sanctuary, Kiko tried to climb through the rift, but Samuel appeared. He wrapped his arms around her in a tight hold and dragged her toward the exiled forest. He whispered something to her and threw her inside. Kiko swung around and lurched for him, immediately slamming into an invisible barricade, unable to reach him. And there she would stay, trapped forever.

Kale ripped his bereaved eyes away, letting them land on Leila. His face changed, sorrow turning to anger. Scowling, he stepped right up to her and just inches away, he slowly curled his lips, showing his blood-stained teeth. He roared, the vibration rattling her soul, and saliva strings flew out and stuck to her hair. For a moment, Leila thought he might kill her — rip her throat with just a simple flick of his bear claw. But instead, he tore himself away. He barged across the room, pushing desks aside as he went.

And, with that, her brother was gone.

THURSDAY

early morning

Leila

Leila slammed her front door shut and stormed down the path from her house to the sidewalk. As she ran, she felt the weight of her backpack thump against her back. She needed to be quick. Today of all days, she really needed to be quick.

The wind whipped against her face and it took everything within her not to half-shift. Despite everything that had happened, she felt exhilarated and excited. She kicked up her heels, speeding toward Riley's house.

They'd won. Kiko wouldn't be able to create her team of Fallen. No more lives would be lost because of her. Of course, those she'd turned in the past were still out there, but that was a matter for another time. Now was the time of celebration.

But after all that, only part of Leila wanted to celebrate. Because while they'd won, she'd also lost. Kiko. Odette. Her brother. Her trust in people.

Makoto had said he'd give Kale a chance for Leila's sake,

but any sign of him causing trouble, he'd have to step in. Leila agreed with that, but she couldn't help but think of all the ways in which Kale could cause trouble. And then, all the ways in which Makoto could step in.

Stop it. Leila scolded herself, clutching the straps of her bag. Today was not the day for misery.

There was more to celebrate. Gabby had gotten the cure from Mr. Robertson. Not with a struggle either. He'd just given his blood to her without debate.

That meant that there was a little bit of good in him, just like Sebastian. The thought of Sebastian's growth let a glimmer of hope for Kale remain, too. Somehow, sometime, he may forgive her for what she did.

And today? Today was the day Riley got his sister back.

Leila leapt over Riley's broken fence and ran across his front yard. Before she had a chance to knock, Riley flung the door open, and Leila fell into his arms. The force pushed them both inside.

As she pulled away, she whispered, "Is she here, yet?"

"Not yet," Riley said, glancing over Leila's shoulder. "Soon, I hope."

"Leila!" Riley's mom, beamed, leaning over the kitchen bench. "I feel like I haven't seen you in forever." She waved her wooden spoon at the table. "Sit, sit, sit. Breakfast will be ready soon."

Leila clutched Riley's arm and pulled him to her. She whispered, "Does she know?"

Riley shook his head and closed the front door. "I want it to be a surprise."

Leila took her seat at the dining table and stared at the door. Her knees bounced with anticipation. For so long Gail had thought her daughter destroyed her life. That she'd turned evil, never to be saved or seen again. Any moment from now, Tessa would walk in and cure Gail's silent but aching heart.

Every bone in her body ached for the same with Kale.

Maybe one day.

"You know," Riley said, taking a seat. "You didn't have to hurt yourself to do the surge. You could have just held my hand."

Still gazing at the door, Leila shrugged. Wistfully, she said, "If you die, I die."

Leila felt Riley's fingertips grazing behind her ear. "Really?"

She snapped her eyes to him, realizing what she'd just said. Clearing her throat, Leila gave a sheepish smile. "Riley. We may have had our disagreements over the last few days, but I love you. I *would* die for you."

Riley closed the gap between them, pressing his lips to hers. He murmured, "I love you, too."

A knock at the door made them both jump back. Riley jogged across the room, peering through the small window beside the front door. He glanced back and grinned. "She's here!"

"Who's here?" Gail asked, holding a plate of pancakes.

Leila smiled, looking at Gail's confused expression. "You'll see."

"Is that Mom?"

Tessa's voice was tender. She brushed her hair behind her ears nervously, staying a step behind Riley.

The plate slipped out of Gail's hands, crashing on the tiles and sending pancakes flying across the floor. Her eyes widened, tears welling. She quivered, "Tess?"

"It's okay, Mom," Riley assured her, pushing Tessa out in front of him. "Tessa's a True Guardian. Always has been. It was a wild misunderstanding."

Tessa seemed so young in that moment. All her twenty years of life, all the experience of being a Guardian, everything she'd been through diminished. Here she was, a little girl, begging for her mother to love her.

"Oh my baby girl!" Gail sprinted around the table. She wrapped her arms around Tessa and they both exploded into sobs.

Riley hiccuped, watery eyes glancing quickly at Leila before taking his family into his embrace. They stayed there, all three crying tears of joy.

Leila silently got out of her chair and wandered past them. She squeezed Riley's shoulder and whispered, "I'll just be outside."

She wanted to see the moment, feel comfort from Riley and his mother being reunited with Tessa, but there was a time for privacy, and that was it.

Leila wandered outside and sat on the front porch. Makoto's car was parked in Riley's driveway, Jamal sitting at the wheel. In the back, hiding behind him, Calice stretched her neck to see through the middle. Noticing Leila, she snapped her eyes away, then slowly, hesitantly returned them. Calice smiled then, a kind of hopeful smile. Leila didn't like the jealousy that remained inside her. She lifted her hand, gave a quick wave, then looked away.

Her eyes fell on Makoto and Ren as they leaned against the hood of the car, chatting.

Another family moment. It both warmed and chilled her heart. Everyone had gained someone… except her.

"I need a nap," Ren muttered, sliding his palms up his mohawk.

Makoto chuckled. "You know what you need, brother? A vacation. Take a break, be normal. Travel."

"Samuel said something to me. He said when it's all over, it's my turn. What do you think that means?"

"It means that you've been her shadow too long. Now it's your turn to live." Makoto noticed Leila and gave a friendly nod.

"Ha." Ren scoffed. "Live? What's that?"

Leila smiled to herself. She was almost starting to understand Ren. He'd been so preoccupied trying to keep his sister out of trouble that he'd forgotten how to live his own life.

Makoto threw a thumb to the car. "You can join a clan for starters. I'm already in the middle of a school year with my recruits, but maybe you could join the next one?"

Ren raised his brows. "And be taught by you?"

Makoto glowered. "I'm not so bad."

"I think..." Ren crossed his arms and pushed himself off the hood. "I think I need to be my own self. Without running after any sibling."

"I can respect that."

Leila caught Ren's attention. As he spotted her, his mouth tilted into a lopsided smile. "I've always wanted to go to school, though. Maybe here in Cedar Falls?"

"Leila?" Riley poked his head through the doorway.

Leila jumped up. "Is everything okay?"

"Yeah. They're just making up for lost time." He reached for her hand, clutched it tight and pulled her inside. "Come on."

He led her past the dining table, where Tessa sat next to her mom, head resting on her shoulders, and headed to his room. As he closed the door behind him, Leila sat on his bed.

Riley rarely closed his door the whole way. It was a rule of the house. Leila wondered if Gail would relax that rule now that she knew Tessa wasn't Fallen—that it wasn't Riley's fault for being too distracted by Calice to notice something was up with Tessa. Regardless, it must have been serious for Riley to close the door.

Riley grabbed the chair from his desk and spun it around. He swung his leg over and leaned forward, resting his elbows to his knees. Gazing at her, he said, "There are some things I want to talk to you about, but it's hard to say."

"What are they?" Leila shuffled to the edge of the bed and folded her legs up underneath her.

He gave sad smile. "When we separated at camp—" he sighed—"I'm so sorry. We should have stayed together. Samuel warned us but I didn't listen. I had this stupid idea to do it all alone and—"

"Stop, Riley. It's not your fault. I did a pretty good job of pushing you away, too."

He held his hand up for her to stop. "You had every right to be upset with me. I was such a jerk to Gabby."

And because of Calice. Leila thought. She bit her tongue, then said, "Okay, then. We're both sorry. Done."

Riley looked over the rim of his glasses and she knew what the look was. It was not done. "There's something else. Something Tsukiko told me. Back before I realized she was… Fallen."

Leila waved a dismissive hand. "Well, anything she has said can be forgotten except for the truth that the Fallen are great at deception."

"I know. I know. But maybe she was right about this one. She said that we are dangerous. As Imprints."

"Yeah, of course," Leila scoffed, rolling her eyes. "Dangerous for her."

"I know." Riley winced, sitting back. "It's just I think she was talking from experience. She said that being an Imprint makes you powerful, and the stronger we become the more likely we are to let it go to our heads and do things."

"Fallen things?" Leila asked.

Riley nodded, shifting his eyes to the ceiling.

Leila burst out laughing. "Oh my God, Riley. No. You are the truest, right? You and me. We are True. That won't happen."

A hint of a smile danced at the edges of his mouth. He returned his gaze to her and reached for her face, letting his thumb caress her cheek. "I love your certainty. But it's not just that."

"Oh Lordy, there's more?" Leila flailed her arms, landing her palms onto the bed with a thud. "You're like one of those magicians with a never-ending handkerchief."

Chuckling, Riley said, "Just let me get it off my chest!"

Leila cleared her throat and sat up straight. "Sorry. Carry

on."

Riley inhaled through his nose and rubbed his palms down his thighs. He rushed an exhale and said, "Everything is different now. In my head. Finding Tessa like this, it made me realize how much I built a lot of the story up in my own head, you know. When I found her standing above mom with blood all over her and our house a mess, I didn't give her a chance to explain. I just assumed she was bad."

"Does it change your opinion on Gabby or Sebastian?"

"Gabby, yes. Sebastian…" Riley paused. "I'll work on it. I've just realized I've been seeing things as either black or white. And, maybe, I'm a little colorblind. You see things in color and shades and tones, so maybe I shouldn't try and carry the burden alone, maybe I should let you fill in the blanks for me."

Guilt burned through Leila. She'd tried to help him, tried to make him see things differently, to lighten up, but she didn't want him to lose faith in himself and his abilities. "But you were right about not trusting Kiko. Don't discount your instincts because I'm not very good at taking things seriously."

Riley shook his head vehemently. "I wasn't using my instincts, though. I was thinking too much about what could go wrong. Leila, you've been amazing. You know when things matter, and you know how to kick me into gear when I'm wrong. Like yesterday morning—" A twinkle hit his eyes as they dropped to her mouth, and further down.

Leila's heart fluttered. She smiled. "I'm proud of you. For admitting that… do you wanna…?" She patted the bed beside her.

Riley threw his head back and laughed. "No. Not with these paper thin walls."

Leila shrugged. "Thought I'd ask."

"I'll be a work in progress for a while." Riley turned his attention back to her, hair falling onto his brows. "Will you be patient with me?"

What a question. Leila shook her head in disbelief and rose to her knees. She climbed between the bed and Riley, settling herself onto his lap. Squeezing his cheeks in her hands, she kissed him. As she pulled back, she said, "I'll be here every step of the way. I'll be here when you fall, and I'll be here when you fly."

THURSDAY

morning

Sadie

Sadie knew she was a Fallen. She knew it when Sebastian turned her and all she felt was the sludge of darkness as it settled within her soul. She knew it when Summer gave her a hug that morning and she wondered what her blood would taste like. She knew it when she entered the school and the halls just seemed to be filled with the constant stench of human.

Leila and Riley could do the surge at any moment she wanted. Rid her of this burden. Cure her.

But if she was honest with herself, she didn't want to be cured. She didn't want to be the victim anymore. She was no longer the weak and innocent human in the clan.

If Gabby and Sebastian could do it and live with the darkness, then maybe so could she.

Sadie opened her locker and threw her bag inside. The overpowering scent of aftershave hit her nostrils and she knew what she was in for. She swallowed and pulled out her math textbook, chanting to herself, "You got this Sadie, be strong."

"Hi," Damien said, leaning against the locker beside hers. He'd rolled his shirt sleeves up and unbuttoned his collar, showing his muscled shoulder and the very top of his spiral mark.

"Riley turned you again?" she asked politely.

He gave a cocky grin and jerked his chin as if to say yes. "Want another date?"

Sadie cleared her throat and closed her locker. "Actually, I think we need to talk."

Damien's face dropped with his arm, his hair falling over his face. He looked down at her. "I just told you I'm a Guardian, though."

Sadie tried not to roll her eyes. How shallow did he think she was? "That's not it."

"Then, why?" He crossed his arms, trying to make his already built-up muscles seem bigger.

Most girls wouldn't protest so much. But Sadie wanted more than biceps and popularity and confidence. Her eyes drifted down the hall, falling on Sebastian as he spoke to his jock friends.

He caught her staring, lips curling into a smirk. She swallowed. Sebastian had biceps and popularity and confidence, but he had something else, too. He saw her. The real her.

Damien jerked his head over his shoulder and within a second whipped it back again. "Him? That jerk will tear you into a million pieces."

He already has, she wanted to say. "It is what it is."

Damien's eyes glistened, tracing the shape of her body and resting at her neck where her mark was. His chastised expression turned fearful. "Are you Fallen?"

"No." Sadie rushed the lie. "Of course not. I'm fine."

"Damn fine," Sebastian said, joining them.

Damien rolled his eyes. "Don't you have cheerleaders to

terrorize?"

Sebastian raised a brow and chuckled. He took a step, leaned into Sadie, and whispered, "Meet me at the bleachers." He turned and walked backwards toward the entrance. "Catch ya later, Damo!"

"Ugh." Damien scowled. "This is a mistake Sadie. But just—" he sighed, giving up. "Just know that I'll be here for you, when everything falls apart."

Sadie watched Damien walk away. His words sat with her for a moment. *When it all falls apart.* He said it as though it was inevitable, as thought it was a risk to trust Sebastian. But as he saw her, she saw him, too. And the real Sebastian was worth the risk.

She opened her locker, threw the textbook inside, and hightailed it outside. As she walked down the path between the school and the field her heart pounded at what felt like a hundred beats a second. The anticipation almost drowned out the Fallen-induced thoughts that taunted her.

Under the bleachers, with its peeling blue paint, stood a good-looking senior in his letterman jacket. Sebastian Weir —the captain of the varsity team—was waiting for her, mousy little Sadie Sloan, who had no idea who she was. His hand clutched a seat above him as he watched her. His face remained expressionless but his eyes gave him away. As she ducked and weaved through the bearings to him, Sadie worried he could hear her heart pounding through her chest.

"Hi," he said softly.

"The bleachers?" she asked, trying not to smile.

Sebastian let his arm drop and he stepped toward her. He took her fingers and as he lifted her hand, he threaded his own fingers between the gaps in hers. "It was something you said, remember? You'd rather kiss under the bleachers than have had your first kiss with Damien."

"I was being sarcastic."

A wry smile made its way to his lips. "I know." Then, he swallowed, and his smile disappeared as quickly as it came.

"Sadie, I care about you."

Sadie winced. She liked him. In a heart-melting, life-changing kind of way. The way he looked at her made her feel everything she never knew she wanted.

"I'm Fallen," she blurted.

Sebastian dropped her hand. "What?"

"I can feel it." Tears escaped her eyes. "It's a hunger, a yearning. I see people walk past me and my first instinct is to grab them... to hurt them. I wouldn't, I don't think. But it's there, this nagging voice, like a bad dream I can't wake up from."

Sebastian hunched over as though she'd punched him in the gut. He whimpered, "I'm so sorry."

"For saving me?" Sadie almost scolded him. "Sebastian Weir, you're the best thing that's ever happened to me. Don't you dare say sorry."

Sebastian straightened, face suddenly blooming to sweet life. He swept her hair behind her ear. "The best thing?" He tsk-ed and shook his head. "What am I going to do with you?"

"There's more," she said.

His expression faded. "More?"

Sadie closed her eyes and called her Guardian forward, just like Sebastian had taught her the night before. As her teeth lengthened into fangs, she grimaced. It was a pinch, painful but bearable. The claws hurt a little more. She opened her eyes, feeling the rose-gold glow of her tiger surround her.

She could see Sebastian's wolf beside him, and a neon-blue glow shimmered around them both. He opened his mouth to say something, but Sadie held her finger up to stop him. "As I said, there's more."

She closed her eyes again, and feeling another Guardian near, she called it forward to align. Her fangs and claws retracted, the tiger stepping away. Pressure formed in two spots on her forehead right in front of her hair line. They hurt even more than the claws. It felt unnatural, like two spears had cut her skull from the inside out. Once the antlers stopped growing, she relaxed and opened her eyes. Black shimmered around her, like onyx being lit by the sun.

Sebastian gawked at her in sheer amazement. Or was it terror? She waited for him to tell her she looked like the devil. But he didn't.

"One more," she said, closing her eyes again.

The antlers retracted, and she decided in that moment never to half-shift as the gazelle again. The stabbing pain wasn't worth it. She called the last Guardian forward, bracing herself for agony.

The space on the insides of her shoulder blades tingled and she held onto Sebastian's forearms to keep her balance as what felt like a hundred knives stabbed her back. She made sure she lifted her fingers away from Sebastian's skin as her fingernails curled into talons.

She opened her eyes, wiping tears with her knuckles, and met Sebastian's gaze. Out of the corners of her eyes, she caught a glimpse of feathers. Two wings sprouted on either side of her body, a mix of white and black and blue. Her aura was aqua, her favorite color.

"I always thought you were an angel," Sebastian mused.

Sadie took a hold of him again, returning to human form. She winced as the wings retracted, trying to bear the pain.

"It sucks doesn't it," Sebastian said, grasping her shoulders to hold her weight.

Sadie looked up and gave him a glare that reeked of sarcasm. "You think so?"

Sebastian chortled. "You kinda get used to it. I've learned to embrace the pain. In a way, it reminds me of what I am capable of. It's a physical reminder to keep myself in check."

He really was the strongest person she'd ever met. To deal with his dad's secret; to deal with being a Fallen all on his own; for promising to support her through it all. Everyone misjudged him.

Her eyes darted to his lips, and not wanting to wait a moment longer, she moved in.

Sebastian grasped her forearms, holding her back. "I was just teasing about kissing under the bleachers, we don't have to rush this."

Sadie shook her head. "I don't want to waste time."

Sebastian's eyes found the ground. He muttered, "And, I don't want to ruin you. I feel like maybe I already have."

"No, you haven't." Sadie pinched his chin, forcing him to look at her. "You saved me, remember?"

He hesitated to let his sad eyes meet hers. "I've killed people, in case you haven't heard? You're too good for me."

"Yeah yeah, bad boy Seb." Sadie clutched his collar. "That's my point. If this doesn't last, I want to make the most of it while I have your attention."

Sebastian's brows fell. His eyes opened wide. "You misunderstand me, Sades. You've had my attention for a long time. And, you'll have it for a long time still."

For a moment, Sadie lost herself in his blue eyes. She felt herself soften and warm, her heart turning into a pool of lava. The way he looked at her sent her to the moon and back. Time seemed to disappear—one moment she was gazing at him, wondering how on earth she could be so lucky, and the next, he was kissing her.

It was soft, so gentle and tentative they barely touched. Then, he shuffled closer, taking her face in his hands and letting the flesh of their lips press together. His movements were slow, as though savoring every second. Sadie's heart soared. There she was, under the bleachers, kissing the boy she'd fallen for… kissing the boy she'd become a Fallen for.

She wondered if he felt the same.

The bell rang out, signaling the start of class. Sebastian released her in silence, letting his dreamy grin tell her everything he was thinking.

"Should we get to class?" she asked.

Sebastian bit his bottom lip, eyes tracing her mouth. He

ran his thumb along her jawline, and said, "You know, I have a feeling everything is going to change."

"For the better?"

"Yes!" He squeezed her cheeks between his palms. "Of course, for the better. Because of you, Shorty." He smacked his lips onto her forehead, then muttered into her ear, "You've saved my life, too."

THURSDAY

very early morning

Seven hours earlier

The Beast

At the back of Mr. Robertson's classroom, against the bare cork wall, a tiny sliver of purple light glistened. It started out small and grew into a tear, creating a gap between the human world and the Veil. Through the rift, a shadow loomed. Its eyes shone silver, like daggers glistening off the moonlight.

The shadow belonged to a Fallen Guardian that once roamed the earth—one of the first. It was larger than a bear, with nine-inch claws and oval bumps rising from its spine. Some used to call it the devil, others thought it was a mythical dragon. But titles didn't matter, it was there for this only:

Hunger.
Blood-lust.

Revenge.

It pierced its claws between the worlds and dug them into the classroom wall. The creature, black as a new moon night, wedged through the gap and stepped out of the Veil. As its feet touched the linoleum floor, the purple sliver zipped shut.

The creature sniffed the human world air and flexed its rippling muscles. Catching a scent, its eyes brightened. It tore through the empty school halls. For revenge? Yes. But first it needed a human counterpart.

ACKNOWLEDGEMENTS

This book has been a long time coming. My utmost appreciation is for my readers, who have been so kind and patient while they've waited two whole years for this sequel. It's finally here!!

There was a point a little while ago where I lost the joy in writing and publishing. I took some time to make sure I returned back to the joy of creating. My mindset shifted and I stormed through the final part of this book. There's something in doing something for yourself and then seeing how that affects others positively. I hope that means my work will only get better.

I need to thank my beta readers: Liss—for your companionship and understanding and being the best cheerleader; Kalli and Debbie—for always willing to jump on board and being super quick with your feedback; and Jasmine—for always saying "yes, of course, send it through."

A massive shout-out to my ARC team, who fill my soul up with your enthusiasm and support. You make this publishing journey that much sweeter.

To my kids and husband and mum, who see me sitting in my spot and know that I'm in writing mode. I found a great rhythm this year and I'm grateful that you're happy to work around it with me.

I have big plans for book 3 and 4. And I cannot wait for you to read them. It won't take two more years, I promise.

Until the next book …
Elle xxx